HOWDY, STRANGERS

Steeling herself, Blaine crept in above the strangers' camp. Those few who were up were crouching over faded fires, stirring them into new flame. Hunkered in above the slight scoop in the terrain that held the camp, Blaine became very still as she focused on the flurry of movement just below her. She wasn't expecting what she found; it took a moment to realize that the lump on the ground between four of the strangers was a man, that the funny noise was his choked cry of pain.

That the man was Dacey.

She gasped; she couldn't help it. Tied at the wrists and ankles and perched haphazardly against a rotted-out sycamore, Dacey answered their murmured questions with a single shake of his head, sending his untrimmed bangs into his eyes. Blaine winced as one of the men backhanded him. The trickle of blood dripping down his chin followed a path already forged, and his face held a storybook of bruises.

The strangers weren't just passing through. . . .

BAEN BOOKS by DORANNA DURGIN

Dun Lady's Jess
Changespell
Barrenlands

Touched By Magic
Wolf Justice

Wolverine's Daughter

Seer's Blood

Forthcoming:
The Bounding Dark

SEER'S BLOOD

DORRANA DURGIN

SEER'S BLOOD

This is a work of fiction. All the characters and events portrayed in this book are fictional, and any resemblance to real people or incidents is purely coincidental.

A Baen Books Original

Baen Publishing Enterprises
P.O. Box 1403
Riverdale, NY 10471
www.baen.com

ISBN: 0-671-57877-4

Cover art by Larry Elmore

First printing, July 2000

Distributed by Simon & Schuster
1230 Avenue of the Americas
New York, NY 10020

Typeset by Brilliant Press
Printed in the United States of America

For Darlene, Albin, Gloria and John, who taught me much and gave me much

For Strider, who gave me everything

and of course to Boomer, Esther, Goofy & Fred— for the ten o'clock howl!

For the Curious

(For the alarmed, be reassured that aside from a few oft-used terms that become self-evident in the text, you don't really have to know this. It's here for the Curious and for the author.)

Annekteh Terms:

anne-nekfehr	the experience of vicarious emotions through humans
Annekteh	the Taker's name for self
annektehr	A unit within a *nekfehr* (taken vessel)
nekfehr	taken being, also called a Vessel
nekfehr death	the death of an *annektehr* when trapped within a vessel when it dies
nekferhta	linking box
nekteh	A unit within the Annekteh whole
suktah	sassafras wood

Shadow Hollers terms:

Takers	the Annekteh. Most do not distinguish between the Annekteh whole and the units, or *nekteh*.
Taken	possessed by the Annekteh, *nekfehr*.

The world spread out before the *nek-fehr*, the slight curve of the horizon partially obscured by hazy clouds. Unlike the flat plains directly before the possessed vessel—a raven, black, sleek, and intelligent—*this* horizon rose in a nubbled, broken line.

South.

They would go south.

It hadn't worked out well, last time; so many years, spent just in recovery. The hill folk had been waiting and ready, forewarned by their seers . . . seers once grown thickly in that nurturing land.

The Annekteh had lost that fight—but they had made sure the next generations of the hills had no such guidance. They had burned the seers' painstaking records—generations of wisdom, lore, and observations—every one. They'd ransacked houses, stripping all charms,

1

all the protections that could be copied and used even without a seer's understanding.

Every one.

And the seers themselves . . . dead. Or fled.

The raven's wings caught a thermal; the bird adjusted—a shift of feather, a tilt of wing—and the *annektehr* within barely noticed. That was what the *nekfehr*, the vessels, were for; to do the things the Annekteh could not. To see, to fly . . . to feel. The *annektehr*—one of many, so consumed by the Annekteh whole it didn't even understand the concept of individuality—stared at that bare hint of the mountains, letting the bird mind control their flight. *Yes.* It shared the image among the whole, among the Annekteh, even as it maintained awareness of each of its fellow *annektehr* at work in other vessels. Human bodies, mostly, supervising the insignificant, unTaken individuals that served the Annekteh.

Yes.

South. Where the lumber was not only abundant, but was imbued with the natural magic of the mountains—the same subtle magic of the plains, distilled and amplified and then submerged to run deep along the ridges. Magic that would protect the Annekteh, so deep that the humans barely knew it was there.

But the Annekteh knew.

And the Annekteh intended to have that magic, and that land, for their own.

→ 2 ←

Blaine tugged on her soft leather boots in quick succession, her mind already in the mountains and on the newly arrived traders, the ones no one else had seen yet. Moving quietly in the near darkness of the morning, she divided her hair into sections, fingers flying to braid the insipid brown plaits, damp rawhide laces waiting on the bed to fasten them.

Usually the hills provided her escape from her cousins' taunts. *Skin-to-bone! Head-tetched! You been beat with an ugly stick?*

But yesterday they had given her mystery as well. *Strangers.*

Only her older brother Rand knew of Blaine's frequent trips into the mountains that cradled their hollow; if anyone else ever found out, she'd be denied them. Years ago, her flight from teasing kin had turned into a true appreciation of the woods, even of the steep climbs and often treacherously slippery slopes of damp, humus-covered soil. The ribbon of level ground that wound along the ridges lured her, for there the air was free of wood smoke and the view

3

revealed something besides the opposite hillside of
Owlhoot Holler.

And there, she could ponder the remnants of the
book. There, she could sit on her favorite rock and
gaze at the unfathomable patterns of rock and tree
in the well-worn, close-set ridges of the Shadow
Hollers community. A deep hollow dropped between
each ridge; along with the inevitable silver ripple of
a creek, the bottoms held small patches of flat land.
Dotted along the creek, crammed onto the flat places
and even up against the slopes, sat homesteads like
her own—sparse populations that blossomed at the
broadened hollow's mouth where each creek met the
Dewey River.

Yesterday, drawn down into Fiddlehead Holler by
the conversations below—conversations held by men
who must not know the mountains funneled noise
uphill—she'd found that the bottom of unsettled
Fiddlehead Holler held more than a creek.

Strangers. Here to trade? Must be, with the number of wagons they had along—small ones, for easier
travel through the hills. Maybe they'd have books, or
fine riding horses, or pretty ribbons. Maybe there'd
even be a family, with a girl her own age. She hadn't
had the nerve to find out, not the day before. Not
to close in on them, for even her blinder—made of
sassafras, soaked in a new moon fog and painted with
the slick sap of slippery elm, just of the size to fit
in her pocket—wouldn't keep their eyes from her if
she left the cover of the spring rhododendron patch
she had found upslope of them.

Hanging onto her braids, Blaine patted the bed
quilt, in search of the rawhide strips—hidden in the
dim, early morning light of the rough-hewn log house.
There. Jerking them into tight knots around the ends
of her braids—knots she'd no doubt regret when it
came time to turn her hair loose again—and pretending not to hear Lenie's sleepy question, Blaine pulled

on her jacket and hurried out onto the porch, her footfalls ringing hollow on the old planks—

—Where she stopped short in dismay. How had her daddy gotten out here before her? And gotten old Prince harnessed, to boot?

But there he was. Cadell. Short and wiry, already topped by Rand's sturdy height, and blessed with a pair of blue eyes sharp enough to spot a child in mischief through a barn wall.

There would be no sneaking off into the mountains today.

Their stout-limbed horse stood by the post at the edge of the chicken-scratched yard, and she knew Cadell had decided to break spring ground today. It was her particular job to hold the lines while he steadied the plow, mostly because she had the patience to deal with the horse, who occasionally played like he was stupid and had forgotten what plowing was all about.

Blaine looked at the white clouds scudding across the crisp blue sky. A perfect day for plowing; there'd be no talking him out of it. And the wind picking up the edges of her ragged bangs would do a fine job of drying the overturned earth so disking it the next day would be less of a chore.

No, no mountains today, nor the morrow. By the time she worked through all the phases of plowing, those visitors would have passed by and been long gone—or if they had trading, their goods would be picked clean through. She sighed, suddenly feeling the chill of the frost that rimed the porch rail. Cadell jerked his chin at the horse, never of a mind to tolerate her fits of melancholy or her dream frights or even her sighs. Work to be done.

She sighed again anyway.

Dacey shifted his shoulders beneath his pack, hesitating below the modest log house. He'd followed its chimney smoke down out of the mountain and walked the creek to approach it from the bottom, but now that he was here, he wasn't so sure of his course. So far, none of the Shadow Hollers locals knew of his presence. It was probably wiser to keep it that way . . . nor was he ever inclined to socialize on his own.

But the dogs needed food.

Dacey's hand fell to Mage's head, rubbed the dog behind his long, soft ears; he smiled when the hound leaned against his leg. There was no denying a hound his dinner.

On the nearly level ground to the side of the house, two figures worked a plow. Too soon to plant anything but early lettuce and peas, but a smart man got those into the ground as soon as he could. In the yard, two little ones hung on the porch, and Dacey caught the brown swish of a skirt disappearing into the house. Then the youngest, his steps still unsteady, scooted out to the rough-logged barn. A moment later, a young man—almost old enough to have his own family, but still some years younger than Dacey—came out carrying the child.

Dacey had no illusions about the meaning of that little tableau. The older boy was heading for the house, and would probably have a bow at the ready.

He glanced back at the two in the garden, close enough to see that the slighter figure was not a boy, but a girl, a young woman. Her woven straw hat tipped down against the sun, and two hip-length braids wrapped into one halfway down her back. Her legs were too long for the skirts she wore—he saw a flash of calf above her boots. *Scrawny*, he thought, and then tried to chase the unfortunate word away. It wasn't kindly.

He stopped and watched father and daughter for a moment, seeing in their economic movements the evidence of a long partnership. They reached the end

of the row, where the girl hesitated just long enough
for her daddy to flip the trace chain over so it
wouldn't twist, and then directed the horse in a tight
turn that brought Dacey right into her field of view.
She stopped, startled, and it was enough to bring her
daddy's attention Dacey's way. They both glanced at
the house, then—looking to see if the others had
noticed.

It was his cue.

He walked up to the edge of the garden, meeting the man's slightly challenging look but distracted
by the girl's open curiosity, and by the bemusement
on her face as she considered Mage. *Crippled hound.*
White, spattered with brown freckles, big handsome
blocky head, long, angular legs. Good breeding, fine
dog—except for the stiff hind leg, and the peculiar
gait it forced upon him. A wry smile crooked Dacey's
mouth; he couldn't help it. *Mage.* Bred from a line
long owned by his family, ever loyal, always by his
side.

The girl looked away, like she knew she'd been
caught staring, and then couldn't seem to help herself; she looked back from beneath lowered lids,
watching them both with poorly disguised interest on
her lean features.

"Hey," Dacey said, a mild greeting the man returned
with a nod—likely all he would get, in these hills
where few strangers walked. "My name's Dacey
Childers. I was wonderin' if you'd be in the mind for
a little tradin'."

"All depends on what's to be traded," the man said
after a moment's studied deliberation of Dacey and
his pack, his gaze piercing and unapologetic. Aside
from the stubborn-looking chin, his square features
held nothing of his daughter's. "And who's doin' the
tradin'."

Who had nothing to do with the name he'd already
been given. *Who* meant Dacey's people, his place.

"My daddy's folks took us south from here after the Annekteh Ridge fight."

The girl's head lifted, a quick, direct stare with surprise behind it; she caught herself and looked away again. Dacey added, "Not many people there now. I been huntin' something and it's took me to your hills." He shrugged. "Once I get what I'm after, I'll be heading home."

"Cadell Kendricks," the man said, a friendlier tone in his voice. He gave a nod at the empty porch, a mere lift of the chin that Dacey might have missed if he'd blinked wrong, then looked at the girl. "My daughter Blaine. What're you needin'?"

A shadow at the window rose; Dacey pretended he hadn't seen. "We've been moving so fast we've had no time to store up on food, especially meat for the dogs." Dacey garnered another sharp, cryptic look from the girl. "I've got some skins here, though, and we could do without them."

"We?" she asked, stepping on whatever her daddy had been about to say and earning herself a frown.

"Me an' the dogs, of course," he said. It didn't seem to be the answer she expected, although her father showed no such awareness of other strangers in the area. His response elicited a quiet sort of smile from her—the smile of someone who is keeping some thoughts to herself, and intends to continue doing so.

Cadell nodded toward the house. "Lottie'll be putting the noon meal on. We might do some tradin', but only iff'n you'll join us."

"I'm glad to." Dacey dropped his hand to Mage's head and said, "My dog won't be causin' any fights, should you have your own around."

"Mine's tied. Don't have much patience for a dog hanging around the yard," Cadell said, though he quickly added, "I didn't mean nothing by that. I never had the time to fool with a critter so's it'd behave as well as your'n."

Dacey nodded at the horse and plow. "Why don't you let me take those lines. It'll make me feel better about eatin' at your table."

Blaine looked to her daddy for guidance, and he gestured to Dacey. "Give 'im the lines, Blaine, and go help your mommy with the meal."

Blaine's expression did not indicate she thought this was any great trade. But she handed over the lines with a warning that the horse liked a light touch, and walked the furrow to the edge of the garden. Mage followed, knowing enough to get out of the way, and sat at the corner of the garden, patience in his very posture. Dacey gave him a half grin—affection for the dog, an acknowledgment to the watching girl that he did indeed set such store by the animal—and turned to the work at hand.

He knows there're strangers here. Other strangers. *He calls it Annekteh Ridge.* Not Anneka Ridge, as everyone in Shadow Hollers named it, even though the long-abandoned ridge lay just north of them and they should know better. But then, they didn't have her book to read from . . . not even the incomplete remnants of her book.

Blaine hesitated on the porch and watched the man plow with her daddy, handling the tight turns on the sloped ground almost as well as she did. And my, did he care for that dog. And that last smile he'd given her . . .

Five-year-old Sarie eyed Dacey shyly from the house, then came out onto the porch and tugged Blaine's skirt. "Mommy says t' get taters from the springhouse."

Blaine made the exaggerated face that always gave Sarie the giggles. "That nasty old place." But she quickly disentangled her skirt from Sarie's clinging fingers, leaving the child on the porch while she hastened to do her mother's bidding. Lottie would be harried enough, what with another mouth to feed and them at the end of their winter rations, and no new crops save the greens.

She selected the least wrinkled of the potatoes, even if they *were* going to be cut up and fried, and ran them back to the house where she was set to work peeling and slicing them. Three women—Lottie, Lenie, and Blaine herself—worked in the too-small kitchen alcove while Sarie ran in and out with table things, imagining herself important as she set and reset the table.

Though the heat of the cookstove warmed Blaine after the cold yard, she quickly found the house oppressive, and didn't waste any time finishing her task. Unlike Lenie, she hated being shut indoors; she found the fuss with stove dampers and cook surface hot-spots tedious instead of challenging. Setting the potato fry pan on the cookstove where Lottie could keep an eye on it, she escaped to the porch, where she lowered herself into the swing. She pushed herself back and forth on her toes and watched Dacey handling the workhorse. Prince had gone to playing dumb, and she smiled—half amusement, half sympathy.

Soon after, wiping her face with her apron and pushing stray wisps of hair back into the knot at the back of her head, Lenie joined her. Hers wasn't a severe bun like her mother's, but a loose imitation that—as she had explained to Blaine—gave her maturity while at the same time didn't look too old. "Grow out of those braids and try it," she told Blaine, far more often than Blaine cared to hear it. If Blaine wanted she could make plenty of comments about Lenie's age and single status, but it wasn't Lenie's fault her intended had been killed in a logging accident, and it certainly wasn't seemly to tease her about it. Besides, Lenie, with her rounded curves and eye-catching blonde hair, was a pretty sight and there was no arguing that.

Lenie sat next to her, uninvited. "Never thought I'd see the day you were makin' eyes at someone."

Blaine's smile disappeared. "Not hardly. I'm watching he doesn't hurt ole Prince's mouth. And you mought not primp. He's from the south and he aims to get back as soon as he can." *South.* The seers had gone south after the Takers were killed. Everyone knew that.

"There ain't no harm to it. You could use the practice. Get your hair out of those silly braids and put it up like a woman, or you'll be Daddy's despair when it comes to matchin' you." Lenie plucked at the wrap that kept Blaine's braids together for the plow work.

Blaine snorted, easily drawn into the same argument she'd argued uncountable times before. "I ain't in no hurry to have a brood like ours. Mommy's not hardly got the time to sit an' draw a breath for herself. Don't seem right a body should *have* to live that way, if you ask me." *Besides,* she didn't say, *my face is too thin to wear my hair your way.* Two braids, weak brown in the winter and sun-kissed in summer, did best by her.

Lenie frowned. "Daddy keeps us safe here. It's only right he should have us carin' for him."

"That's not what I meant. Don't you ever—" she broke off and looked at her sister, then shook her head. "No, I don't guess you do. Get a man to keep you home, and you'll be happy enough."

"I should say so. And you'll be sayin' the same, ten year from now, an' you still a maid."

"I can take care of myself," Blaine mumbled, knowing that wasn't a complete truth, knowing that at seventeen, she alone among her peers was unspoken for—a prospect that horrified her but did not yet worry her. Lenie had to be paired again, and she would go first. Besides, no man was wont to cast a longing eye on her—she'd been told *that* often enough. The men of these hills liked some substance to their women—visible proof of ability to withstand the rigors of mountain life.

Lenie snorted, unaware of Blaine's musings. "Wise up, Blaine. This one's family may be too far off for Daddy's likin', but it wouldn't hurt none to practice giving a man a kindly eye."

For once Lenie's advice was meant to be helpful, but Blaine was having none of it—even if her gaze did wander to Dacey again, to the way he'd shed his jacket to take up the plow, and to remember how his eyes, intense blue and green and brown mixed up into a bright kind of hazel, had been so thoughtful. Not dismissive or pitying of her. And his hair, a dark mix of ashy blonds, reminded her of the heartwood of white oak. He wore it longer than the short, bristly cuts of her family's men; she liked that.

But he was going back home, far from here, and something made her glad of it.

"Blaine, Lenie!" Her mother's call, with a pleased note in her voice telling that the meal had turned out well. "Come help put the food out. And give those men a holler to wash up for dinner."

Blaine pushed out of the swing with vigor, setting Lenie to swinging harder than she liked, and leaving her to speak to the men. Let Lenie *practice*.

And practice, Lenie did. Over fried potatoes, bacon and greens, she braved Cadell's scowls as she smiled and chattered, and Blaine was free to let her thoughts wander. Not, as they generally did, to whatever strange dream she might have had recently, or to what she'd seen in the mountains or along the creek that day, but to the south, and the seers that had moved there.

And to her book, the badly damaged partial pages of which she nearly had memorized—and from which she had learned to make her blinder. The smooth-worn chunk of wood kept her hidden from the casual eye, as long as she carried it against her skin; it fit perfectly into her palm. She hadn't tried anything else from the book—the healing teas and poultices, the protective charms, the warnings . . . she'd had little opportunity, and counted herself glad that no one else knew she had found the book at all, jammed in the cellar corner of a burnt-out house in Fiddlehead Holler that she shouldn't even have been near.

Cadell would no doubt throw it out as trash. She'd heard his opinion of seers and seer things. *The Takers are dead*, he'd say when someone got him started on the subject. *The Takers are dead, and the seers done left us. We don't need none of theirs, not any more.*

Blaine did. Blaine wanted to know the things the book couldn't tell her, with its thick, hand-inked pages and faded drawings. Mouse-nibbled, stained by dampness, bound in charred and cracking leather . . . she kept it well hid in the barn. Dacey came from the south, where the seers' kin had gone; maybe one of his people had made that book.

Her gaze wandered to him, found him making some polite smile at Lenie's words. She had first thought that he was closer to her daddy's age than to her own, just from his manner, the confident way he'd walked up to their yard and introduced himself. Now, as the waning light from the open door slid off the angles of his cheeks and the high-bridged, barely curved line of his nose to be lost in the shadows beneath dark brows, she realized that age had not yet left any great mark on his features. Six or seven years older than she, perhaps . . . the light spilled into his eyes as he turned his head and caught her staring.

She blushed, but realized soon enough that his gaze held appraisal rather than reproach, and that he showed none of the faint pity she often saw in people's faces when she sat next to Lenie. "Do you know much of the seer lore?" she blurted, stopping all conversation and raising her daddy's brow. Well, the deed was done. Likely she'd not have another chance. "Like the northern sky yesterday, did you see the color?"

"An odd one," Dacey agreed, a hint of surprise on his face at the question.

"Blaine," Cadell said sharply, "that ain't table talk."

"Sky was just sky-colored yesterday," Rand said.

"I heard," Blaine said—ignoring the darkening expression on her daddy's face, the somewhat startled look on Dacey's—"that seers put some meaning to that color sky." Strange, hazy . . . and a hint of purple, quickly swallowed by a normal dusk. She knew Rand hadn't noted it, even though he'd been looking straight at it. She hadn't puzzled that out yet.

Dacey watched her, the light still splashing across half his face, hiding one eye in shadow but showing the shine of interest in the other. "Seers used to call it a Taker's sky."

"What's Takers?" Willum demanded, as only a three-year-old can.

"Somethin' long dead," Cadell said, plenty of meaning in his voice, and in the look he pinned on Blaine.

"Smelly dead?"

Cadell snapped, "Past smelly. And I've said it ain't table talk."

"He's going to hear it sooner or later," Lottie said. Solidly built on a small frame, her blue eyes the exact same shade as Blaine's, tonight she looked less tired than usual, engaged by their company. "Tell him some, Dacey. Save me from havin' to tell it before he'll put down for the night."

Dacey's silence held while Cadell's gaze went from Blaine's studied innocence to Willum's pleading face and Lenie's disinterest. Rand shrugged without taking

time out from his eating to consider the matter, and
Cadell finally gave a short nod. "Give 'em some on
it," he said. "Keep in mind the age of their ears."

As if the children were the ones who really cared.
Blaine perched on the edge of the bench seat and
stuck her elbows on the table, absently toying with
the end of a braid and the loosening tie there.

Dacey obliged. "Some say the Takers ain't tidy with
their powers, and it clouds up the sky. They come
from the north plains . . . they control things there.
They call themselves Annekteh. We've always thought
Takers fit them better."

"Why?" Willum said, and his eyes narrowed. "They
ain't gonna take *my* things!"

"They're dead," Lottie murmured. "This is tales,
Willum, not for real. Not no more."

Dacey gave a wry smile, one he didn't explain.
"They call 'em Takers because they take people over.
Slide inside 'em, control 'em, like."

Willum scowled. "No one can c'ntrol me!"

"Ain't that the truth," Lenie muttered.

"Well, maybe not you," Dacey allowed, grinning.
"But other people. It's like ole Prince with a bit in
his mouth, and me with the reins, if I was a Taker."

"Are you?" Sarie asked, not looking particularly
alarmed.

Blaine slid her plate and its leftovers in front of
Rand, who winked a thanks. "No, 'course he ain't.
Takers don't have no form, Sarie. No bodies. No fat
little tummies." She reached over to poke Sarie's
belly.

Willum looked at her, already well-infected with
his daddy's dismissiveness of Blaine's thoughts and
dreams. "How do *you* know?"

"We all know some, son," Lottie said. "We're lettin'
Dacey tell it, tonight, is all; he knows more of it, I
reckon, from bein' around seer folk."

"She's right enough," Dacey said. "When they

need a body, they up and borrow one. I heard it's like seein' things in a dream. If they want something done, you just watch yourself doin' it, and don't have no say. Or sometimes they Take you just to learn somethin'—say you had a secret, and they wanted to know it. One of 'em might Take you just long enough to learn it—there ain't no keepin' anything from 'em when you're Took—an' then let you go again. All they got to do is touch you flesh to flesh, and they got you."

Lenie wound a loose strand of hair around her finger, pretty, bright hair even in the failing light. "How can they tell of which 'em has Taken who? Spirits, how can they even keep their own selves straight about who'd got who?"

Blaine flipped her mousy brown braid back over her shoulder, out of sight. Away from where it could be compared to Lenie's hair. But in truth it suited her just fine to have Lenie asking questions—to have any of them asking questions—except Rand, who always put his mind to eating his fill. Maybe her daddy would forget that *she* had been the one to start this conversation, when he hadn't wanted it.

Dacey hesitated. "It ain't that simple. They always know. . . . The Takers ain't single beings, like I'm me and you're Lenie. They all know what the others're thinking . . . they all think *together*. When one is in a body, it acts like a . . . well, like a stream channel, for others. Say I'm Took and they want more of 'em here. So I grab aholt of you—it's got to be skin on skin—-and channel for another Taker, and that one Takes you. *Annektehr*, they call the ones inside people, and they're powerful strong. You ain't got a chance oncet they grab on to you."

Silence followed his remark, and suddenly the house seemed too dim, the warmth from the stove not nearly enough. Blaine simply stared at Dacey, never expecting to find so many answers in one person—never expecting to find anyone who knew so much about a menace from the distant past.

Then Cadell cleared his throat. "You've heard some," he allowed. "More'n us in these parts. But these days, the sky tells us no more'n the weather, and that's plenty."

Dacey shrugged. "My kin's fond of a good story."

"Stories is right," Lenie scoffed. "We got so many, old men's tales. Magic in these hills—I'd like to see that."

He gave her a little half grin, one that won him an instant smile in response, while Blaine wondered if she couldn't see the wryness of his expression, that he wasn't agreeing with her at all when he said, "So would I."

"It's a dumb story," Willum declared. "Not a prop'r story."

"*I'll* tell you a proper one," Sarie said. She slid off the bench seat and ran over to tug Willum off his folded quilt riser next to Lottie. "Come to the porch, Willum, I got one about bug ghoulies."

Bugs and ghoulies together. Blaine hid a smile. As far as Willum was concerned, a body couldn't ask for anything more. She watched out the door to see that the two stopped on the porch, and gave Lottie a nod when they hunkered down to whisper together. "I'll watch," she said, and Lottie nodded, nudging the taters closer to Dacey.

As the conversation between Dacey and Cadell turned to hounds and the best breeding lines, Blaine thought of the strangers she'd seen, and thought again that Dacey might know of them. Not that it mattered. She couldn't ask while her family was there to hear she'd been in the hills, and soon enough the strangers would announce themselves and their trading goods and their needs. Blaine sighed, and swung her gawky leg over the bench. She lit a coal-oil lamp and set it in the center of the table, and headed outside to sit on the swing and attend the lisping syllables of the little ones and their whispered secrets about bug ghoulies.

Dacey stood at the edge of the garden and listened to the pig grunt as Cadell's middle daughter made her way to the barn-side pen with supper scraps; Mage lifted his nose to take in the smell of the scraps, and dismissed them, nudging Dacey's hand for a quick lick. The house door hung open yet, and the smell of supper still hung in the air—along with the sporadic noises of cleanup for both the kitchen and the young 'uns.

Family life in the mountains. He'd been a long time from it.

He heard a man's hard-heeled steps behind him, and cast just enough of a look over his shoulder to be taken as greeting.

"We ain't got no extra room in the house," Cadell said, "but you're welcome to use the barn."

"Clear night," Dacey said. No need for shelter.

"Clear as they come," Cadell agreed amiably.

Dacey hesitated, knowing what he had to say, and knowing it was not likely to be harkened. "Said I come here on a hunt," he started, as Blaine's bucket clattered against the pigpen in her efforts to shake loose the bottom scraps.

"That you did." Cadell moved up beside him, offering him an open pouch of chewing tobacco.

Dacey shook his head. "I reckon you need to know what I'm hunting." It was a cautious game, handing over such news. "No easy way to say it. I've seen signs the Takers are comin' back."

Cadell stuffed a wad of tobacco in his cheek and spent a moment jockeying it into place. "Up till now, you seemed a right sensible fellow."

"It's hard to find a way to go at this so's it *does* make sense, after all these years," Dacey admitted.

"But those that remember best know the Takers weren't kilt at Annekteh Ridge. They were drove off, that's all. Hurt bad, but drove off, not kilt. Ain't nothin' to keep 'em from comin' back."

Cadell spat. "Then we'll drive 'em off again."

Dacey said nothing. If it was that easy, he'd not have bothered to come up here at all, seein's or no. *As if he could ignore them.* Not this time.

It was Cadell who spoke again, and his voice had taken on an accusing note. "You think you know quite some bit about the Takers, then, don't you?"

"More'n I'd tell over a supper table with children present," Dacey said promptly. "I've told how they Take folks for the use of their hands. But it's more'n that. They like what they can do in a body—the pleasures it gives 'em, and the pains." Especially the pains, it seemed. "And they don't take no care about keepin' the *nekfehr*—the Taken—whole, neither—just use 'em up and move on." No, that wasn't the sort of thing to say in front of babies like Willum and Sarie. He wished he could have told it to the middle girl, though. She seemed to have an interest, as much as she tried to hide it.

Unlike her father. Cadell's silence in the dark did plenty to tell Dacey of his expression, his opinion. Nothing more than Dacey had expected, from the man's reaction at supper.

But Dacey wasn't ready to give up. Not yet. Not with the stakes what they were. "Last time they come, we almost kilt 'em . . . but we *didn't*. And now they've done come back to Shadow Hollers."

Cadell snorted, all his polite apparently used up. "I ain't no Willum, to suck that one up," he said. "We ain't seen no sign of 'em."

"They're here," Dacey said with quiet conviction. "Or they're coming. And you'd best be thinkin' how you'll handle 'em."

Another dull splat of tobacco juice against the

overturned garden earth. "What makes you think so?"

No real curiosity in that voice, but Dacey answered anyway. "Seein's," he said. "From those still of the seer's blood, down my way."

There was a long silence in the darkness. "Don't reckon I can put any stake in what some South-runnin' folk calls seein's."

"Maybe not," Dacey said. "But I've come a certain sure long way because of 'em."

>+<   >+<   >+<

The vessel's single successful act of defiance had been to deny the *annektehr* his true name, and so the Annekteh called him Nekfehr. The Taken. In the end, the name turned into a title, and only served to further intimidate those under Nekfehr's unwilling command.

They did their best for him, those unTaken soldiers did. They were afraid to do elsewise.

And now, far from home and uneasy with the mountains that filled their sky and denied them the horizon, they had found for Nekfehr signs of a clandestine visitor. Smudges against the hillside, a few damp undersides of last year's leaves exposed to the air. Two days ago it had been, and no more sign; no cry of discovery, no spirited but futile attacks.

The humans, it seemed, had not learned all that these mountains had to offer, and how much the land had recovered from the last conflict waged here.

The magic was here, waiting. Could they but find the *suktah* they needed, the Annekteh could begin this invasion in full.

Nekfehr's intention—driven by the

vessel's quick wit, the answers and thoughtfulness he provided the *annektehr* in spite of himself—had been to find a substantial growth of *suktah* before revealing Annekteh presence in the hills. But he was no longer so sure that he could accomplish this task, despite the intensive search along this hollow and others—uninhabited hollows that, generations earlier, had held seer families and stands of *suktah*. But his plains-born men didn't know where to look.

Their clandestine visitor was another matter—an incident Nekfehr might have been willing to assign to raccoon as much as to human. *Might have been.* Had it not been for the feel in the air, a grating sensation of antipathy and intent.

Would that the Annekteh had serious magic to command, magic other than their own innate abilities and a few insignificant tricks. For then Nekfehr might have been able to pinpoint the origin of such deliberate antipathy.

No matter. He'd find it, sooner or later. And he knew, well enough, what it was.

A seer.

Somewhere, in these hollows full of people who had blinded themselves to magic, there was a seer at work.

The first target.

→ 3 ←

A bruised sky lowered its clouds on Owlhoot Holler and let loose torrential rains, rains that filled the creek to overflowing with foul water and spilled up into the garden. The plants turned to slimy blackened fronds; an ominous rumble filled the air. Blaine turned her eyes up to the mountain slope, barely able to see through the rain pounding her face, searching for the cause of it—and recoiling when she found it. The trees were sliding right off the hill! They built momentum, crashing to the ground, tangling, rolling—

—rushing down toward the Kendricks homestead.

"Blaine!"

Willum, on the porch, his chubby face contorted in fear. "Blaine!" he shrieked again, terror distorting his voice.

"Willum!" she cried, and ran for him, reaching out to scoop him up as each step forward took her further and further away. Despair grabbed her ankles, tripping her, slowing her. "Willum!"

And the trees came crashing down.

❖　　　　❖　　　　❖

23

Blaine startled awake, scared by the intensity of the dream—and found her ears full of sound, an extraordinary howl cutting through the night. She lay in the bed she shared with Lenie and shivered, spooked, and still stuck in the twilight between asleep and awake.

As if she'd never heard a critter howl. It wasn't nothing but a dog or a rare wolf, lonely in the night. Nothing to raise her hackles over.

The uneasiness clung to her; she suddenly realized that she'd heard this very noise four days earlier—on the ridge, right before she found the visitors; the day before Dacey Childers had walked into their yard. Visitors, she suddenly realized, who hadn't yet shown up to trade anything. All travelers needed supplies.

And here it came again. Spirits of Those Before! She felt it vibrate through her body before she actually heard it, a low noise that lifted to a howl, clear and mournful and somehow menacing all at once. The sound shivered across her neck, this time joined by a brief chorus that quickly died and did not repeat.

Blaine slid out of bed and into the chill of a woodstove nearly gone out, leaving her heavily sleeping sister undisturbed. Pulling the door open a crack, she sniffed the cold night air—as if the air would bring her any answers. After a moment, she heard Rand rustling in his loft bed.

She turned to find him watching her, and whispered, "Wolves?"

"No." Rand shook his head and left it at an angle that told her he was as puzzled as she. "Dogs," he concluded. "But no one went a-huntin' our hills last night. Leastways, no one that checked with Daddy."

His whispered answer gave her no peace, for it would have been more like Rand to grunt "dogs" and roll over for a few more moments of sleep.

Blaine returned to the bed and patted the footboard in search of her clothes. She quickly donned them, feeding a few logs into the stove before quietly slipping through the door. Rand would assume she was visiting the privy, but . . .

She had a sudden hankering to know if those strangers were still there.

She drew water and set kindling on the porch, then fed the chickens and left the pail out so Cadell would know that she had done it. If she had some semblance of her chores done, things would go easier when she returned, even if she did delay the disking he had planned for the day.

It was breaking light when she finally did stop at the outhouse, on her way to the springhouse trail and the strangers. The ridge trail was easy to follow despite the shadow the opposite mountain threw, and Blaine climbed up into the sunlight even as it crept down the hill toward her. Clouds bloomed in the sky, hazy and red and proclaiming rain. Worse news for her; if Cadell couldn't get the garden disked before it rained, breaking up the great clods of plowed earth, she'd be in certain big trouble.

But not enough to make her turn back, not with the thought of the strangers in her head and the echo of the howl still in her ears. She put the rain from her mind and paid attention to her feet; the mountaintop was almost half a morning from home if she slacked her pace, and she didn't have that much time to waste.

When she reached the ridge Blaine turned north, toward the mouth of the hollow, aiming for her favorite rock—a jutting, rough boulder that pushed aside the trees in its lone stance at the top of the world. It was twice Blaine's height but she knew the handholds, and she knew that no one would ever think to look for her there. That alone had been enough to make it a favorite perch, never mind that it was a place to study the maze of mountains that wove and undulated around her own hollow. It was from there that she'd learned the subtle flavors of the seasons, and learned to know from a glance just what kind of mood the mountains were in.

Today she gave the rock only a wistful glance, and used it as a marker to cross over to the downslope on the other side of the ridge, down into Fiddlehead Holler and the side of the hill still blanketed in frost and shadow.

As sudden and eerie as the first time, the early morning howl repeated itself—a crystal-clear noise cutting through the peace of the mountain, and through Blaine's peace of mind. The fine hair on her arms stood up.

Quit your foolishness. It was just from going out of sun into shadow, that was all. *Plain old goosebumps from cold.* She continued down off the mountain, her progress somewhat more cautious than before, and the blinder already clutched in her hand. She heard the men before she saw them—muted morning noises that meant they probably weren't all awake—and grew more cautious yet.

In all her seventeen years, Blaine had never heard of the arrival of so many travelers—at least, not travelers who hadn't brought plenty of trade with them. Hesitating just within sight of the men, when they were still only fractions of people moving behind bare-branched trees, she realized all at once that she *should* have simply told her daddy what she'd seen, and borne the consequences.

But she hadn't. She moved on.

Steeling herself, she crept in above their camp, heading for the clump of rhododendrons with last year's limp, dead-looking leaves hanging down, looking like wept tears. Moving with painful slowness, glad for her dull brown clothes and the perpetual dampness of late-spring leaf cover on the ground, she finally got close enough to take a good look. *Oh, my. So many of them!*

Three times as many as the last time she had been here. And not one of them had come to talk to her daddy, head of the closest homestead to their camp.

Most of the men were just waking. Only a few were up, crouching to stir faded fires into flame. Hunkered in above the slight scoop in the terrain that held the camp, Blaine made herself very still while her gaze skipped over the normal camp activities and settled in on the flurry of movement just below her. She wasn't expecting what she found; it took a moment to sort out the details, to realize what she saw—that the lump on the ground between four of the strangers was a man, that the funny noise was his choked cry of pain.

That the man was Dacey.

She gasped; she couldn't help it. Almost immediately she realized the danger she had put herself in with that faint sound—but the strangers were too busy with Dacey to note it. Tied at the wrists and ankles and perched haphazardly against a rotted-out sycamore, he answered their murmured questions with a single shake of his head, sending his untrimmed bangs into his eyes. Blaine winced as one of the men backhanded him, though it clearly wasn't the first time. The trickle of blood dripping down his chin followed a path already forged, and his face held a storybook of bruises.

Not passing through. Not here for trade. Oh, no.

And definitely not from the mountains, not even distant ones, not with the odd, clipped speech patterns that came to her ears in the fits and starts of their demands to him, not with those clothes. Dacey wore what she expected to see on a man: rough homespun and leather, and a thick short-waisted wool jacket that gave him reach to his belt knife—now merely a conspicuously empty sheath. The strangers, on the other hand, wore thick, hard leather strapped over their arms and chests, and over padded, finely

woven shirts and trousers. Their boots were padded
along the shins, almost like a good pair of snake
guards—but it was far too early in the season to worry
about snakebite.

And they wore long blades, blades of which she'd
never before seen the like. Sheathed, heavy-hilted
blades far too big ever to be called hunting knives.
The kind of blades not meant for anything but killing people. Swords.

The man who had hit Dacey stood apart from the
others. He alone was not covered with the hard
leather, but wore soft and comfortable-looking
clothes topped by a warm cloak. In the hills, only
womenfolk wore cloaks, and only on the fanciest
outings—but Blaine wasn't tempted to think of this
man as anything but masculine and dangerous. He
stood back from Dacey now, the cloak spread wide
by his elbows as he adopted a posture of finality,
hands on hips.

"We're going to get our answers," he said, no
longer speaking in the confidential murmurs of his
questioning. "By now I hoped you'd realize that. I'm
not particularly interested in torturing it out of you."
His dark eyes were hard. "But I will."

Funny. His voice was smooth, and not at all in
keeping with his attitude or actions. And even though
his speech had those unfamiliar clipped patterns, there
was still a kind of rhythm to what he was saying, one
that made his voice pleasant to listen to and totally
at odds with the words themselves. The man gestured
without turning around, and one of the strangers
stopped warming his hands by the main campfire and
scooped up a pouch, which he presented with a stiff
salute.

Dacey tensed; Blaine could see it from her perch,
no further away than from the Kendricks' porch to
the barn. Tense, and . . . *Scared. Oh, he was scared.*
"There ain't no point in this," he said, his voice

intense . . . though his face held no hope. "I ain't got nothing you need to know. I'm here on my own, and nary anyone else knows aught about you."

"So you've said," the man replied, dark amusement in his eye. "But we'd like to know other things. How did you find us? Why can't you be made *nekfehr?*"

Blaine frowned, losing the word in the man's accent. Hard enough just to think, finding herself so close to such pure meanness, so close to where a man sat hurting—and about to take more of it, she had no doubt of that.

The man hefted the pouch. "And of course I don't believe that you've come after us all by yourself. Not to worry, Dacey Childers. I've got a way to show you more fear than you thought a man could handle. Then, I think you'll do anything—*anything*—to avoid that fear again. Even if that means telling us your precious secrets." He fumbled in the pouch, extracting something small, something dark and ugly and—from the way he handled it—sticky.

Blaine loathed the sight of it.

Two of the men knelt to take Dacey's arms. A third, donning gloves, took the small blot of darkness and grabbed Dacey's jaw. Blaine watched in shock. *They're going to make him swallow it like a dog, like some kind of worming mix.*

Only this was no wormer; she knew it and Dacey knew it. He fought them with every wile he had, tearing cloth and flesh. His mouth clamped shut, his eyes grim and hopeless, he kicked—connecting solidly, and sending the gloved man down the hill on his back. Blaine gave a silent cheer, inner hope cut abruptly short as a hulk of a man joined the fray and simply sat on their prisoner, dealing him a resounding pair of slaps that left him dazed and panting. The gloved man scrambled forward and poked darkness into Dacey's mouth.

The conflict began anew; Dacey flung his head to

first one side and then the other, evading their hands as he sought to spit out the vile lump—and although all three of the others were larger than he, Blaine found herself leaning forward, her hands clenched into fists and her heart crying out for him, hoping, hoping hard—

The leader stepped calmly into the fray and covered Dacey's nose and mouth with his ample hand.

Dacey fought for air; his back arched, his body bucking, eyes widening . . . and finally, as Blaine's lungs ached in sympathy, rolling back in his head.

The man released him. Blaine groaned quietly as the strange pill went down with Dacey's first whooping gasp for air—though not easily, not to judge by the gagging and choking.

With quick, rough efficiency, ignoring his struggle to draw a clean breath, the men tied Dacey's hands to his belt and left him. The leader stood before him another moment, waiting, until Dacey regained the wits to look up, bleary-eyed and conquered. The man shook his head, a gesture of false pity. "You should have cooperated," he said. "We'll leave you alone, now, and when we come back, I think you'll be more than willing to talk to us."

Not wormer. And not poison, not when they still wanted something from him.

Then what?

Dacey sat alone, propped against the sycamore stump, eyes closed and defeat on his face.

She should leave. Now. The strangers were distracted, breaking fast around the campfire. She couldn't imagine how any of them had the stomach for food after what they'd just done, but they acted like nothing out of sorts had happened. Blaine shuddered, thoroughly chilled in both body and soul.

But . . . somehow she felt she had witnessed too much of this man's drama to leave now.

She crept a few feet sideways, a few feet closer

to him; a slick patch of leaves skidded out from the heel of the hand that held the blinder, and in clutching for solid ground, she lost hold of it. Dacey's head swivelled around; he looked straight at her. She stared back, aghast, exposed, and hating that he knew she had witnessed his futile struggles. He had too much privacy about his ways to take that well. He met her gaze with eyes that had recently held courage and confidence, and now only revealed bleak hopelessness. It was only a moment of silent communication—though she wasn't at all sure of the meaning of it—and then Dacey looked the other way. So his gaze might not give her away, she realized suddenly, and briefly closed her eyes in a sudden wash of helplessness. Helpless to help.

She took up the blinder again.

Beads of sweat broke out on his face, a face that had suddenly gone grey. Blaine watched, appalled, as he began to tremble, as his breathing turned quick and panting, turning into jerky gasps. As his eyes glazed, the pupils huge, he pulled against his bonds, then fought them outright—mindless and random resistance, opposing no one but himself.

Blaine had never heard a man moan in fear before. She found it a terrible sound.

And then the low howl, now almost familiar, tingled through her body, rising slowly to audible sound. Dacey cried out in response, a sudden and harsh noise that sent Blaine tumbling backwards in surprise. She could only watch for a few more horrified seconds, long enough to see the leader lift his head from his meal and give a satisfied nod. Then, as the man looked away again, Blaine ran.

Under the cover of Dacey's screams, she ran.

She flung herself up the mountain, on all fours more than she was upright, and then slid down the other side with just as much careless haste, a journey that seemed to take forever and left her legs trembling from effort, too tired to catch her when she stumbled at the bottom of the slope behind their farm.

Rand, who had watched her noisy progress with evident surprise, stuck his pitchfork in a wheelbarrow of compost and just looked at her a moment, his dark brows lowered.

"Rand!" Blaine gasped, climbing to her feet again and making it to his side where she clutched his arm for support, unable to spare the breath to tell of her discovery.

"And what were you doin' up there anyway?" he inquired as she tried to gather herself together. She waved the question away—today might be the first time she had come down in his sight but he knew well enough how much time she spent in the hills.

"Rand," she said, barely able to voice words through her panting, "there's men—over the ridge—in Fiddlehead. They got Dacey. Tied him up and—" she gulped, unable to come near to explaining what she'd seen. "They got *swords*—"

"Swords!" Rand snorted. "Didja fall asleep chewin' on some strange weed? You been dreamin' again, Blaine." He shook his head and muttered again, "Swords!"

Chewing a weed? Blaine straightened herself and smacked her hands on her hips, putting all she had into her indignation. "Rand Kendricks, do I look that dumb? A *weed*! An' do I look like I've been sleepin' up over the rise or do I look like I've just run back from the other side of this hill?"

"Well," Rand admitted, jerking his pitchfork from the manure and gently bouncing the tines off the ground at his feet, "you kinda look like you run a ways." He hesitated, squinting down at her, his square-jawed face uncertain.

Blaine braced herself—Rand's squint was a signpost of his reluctance. "I seen this, Rand! Men, across the ridge, and they ain't up to any good! I seen 'em days ago, and they're still there!"

The squint stayed in place. "You tell this to Daddy, you'll hit *real* trouble. Use sense, Blaine. You *know* you always think those dreams are real right at first."

"But—" Blaine started, as the rest of her protest died unspoken. It wasn't like he didn't have plenty of reason to say such a thing. She did have dreams, and sometimes she did wake from them—*trees, rushing down the hill*—even at seventeen years old, and needed her mommy's comfort, reassurance that the things she'd seen so vividly were not real. "But this ain't right at first, Rand, not any more! I'm tellin' you certain truth!"

"All that aside, it's a far fetch to think a whole mess of men wouldn't notice you snuck up on 'em, and then you just walked away from 'em, pretty as you please. An' you know if *I'm* sayin' that, Daddy's just pure gonna laugh out loud. You done a pretty fair job over the years of convincin' him you don't even care to go face the spiders in the springhouse."

"He'd believe me iff'n you back me," Blaine said, hurt blooming in a small place inside her, knowing she could never explain about the blinder. *Never.* "You know he would."

"You've just got that Dacey feller on your mind," Rand said kindly. Infuriatingly. "Him an' all his tales. Blaine, you run to Daddy with this dream and he won't believe nary a word, no matter what I speak for you. He'll tell you never to go in them hills again, and right off start lookin' for a husband who'll settle you down."

Cadell didn't understand her to begin with—not her nor her dreams nor her unhidden reluctance to start her own family. He would likely do just as Rand said—and that wouldn't help Dacey, it wouldn't help him one bit. It wouldn't warn her family about those men, with their swords and their fearsome ways.

"Come with me, Rand," she begged. "You'll see what I seen, and Daddy'll listen to *you*."

Rand grinned, a rueful expression. "Can't, little sister. Got plenty to do around here—Daddy's got through pitchin' his fit 'cause you was nowhere to be found, and he's got me spreadin' the old manure pile out in the garden. He wants it done timely, and he ain't in no mood for another one of us to slack off, iff'n you follow my meaning." He pulled her long braid, a gentle tug to jog her out of her scowl.

She glared at him. "All *right* then!" Tired and afraid, and grieved by the lack of support she'd counted on, Blaine lost her temper but good. "I'll go back there myself, and after it's been long enough, you'll come and find me!" She turned her back on him and marched out of the barnyard and back up the hill, ignoring the cry of protest from her tired legs.

"Blaine!" Rand called, sounding uncertain. "Spirits, Blaine, don't cause yourself trouble over a dream!"

Blaine only straightened her back and continued to climb, boldly, the blinder stuck safe in her pocket. This time she didn't care if her daddy *did* see her, not if it meant he *followed* her, too.

But once she was out of sight of the Kendricks farm, her shoulders slumped and she leaned over, hands braced on her knees, to relieve the ache in her legs. It was then she felt the first cold ping of rain against the back of her neck.

She almost laughed out loud, deciding, as she straightened and tugged her woven wool jacket back into place, that she wasn't at all surprised that the rain was trying to discourage her, too.

She resumed her climb, more slowly now; the rain drizzled steadily onto her head, dripping down her ragged bangs to trip off her eyelashes. The sweat she had built up turned cold and clammy inside her clothes, and she ducked her head and clambered on—

fervently hoping she'd scared Rand into following her, although he was as stubborn as she and could just as well wait out the day before his assurance gave way to worry.

The rain, never enthusiastic, faded off as Blaine reached the ridge—but a low rumble of thunder warned that it was not yet over, despite the sudden bright slash of sun. She reached her rock and climbed it, glad to rest, and to spread her skirts out in the sunshine. Sprawled on her back, exhausted and lulled almost to dozing by the lazy thunk of a wood hen driving at a dead tree and despite the startling events of the morning, she nonetheless immediately stiffened at the sound of scuffing feet and grumbling voices. Rand, so soon? And with someone else along?

She rolled over on her stomach and peeked over the edge of the rock. Instead of Rand, she saw two men in fine cloth and hard leather coming from the other direction, and she turtled her head right back out of sight.

"I still say it's a deer trail—maybe fox," one of them said, sounding irritated. Blaine didn't have to take a second look to know they were talking about her own tracks.

"Do deer run the hills like they do the flatlands?" his partner asked uncertainly. "I don't see any clear hoofprints."

"How do I know? The sooner we get a few of these families helping us, the better. Then instead of all this sneaking around and trying not to get lost, we can watch *them* do the work."

The voice grew loud enough that they must be right next to the rock, and Blaine shrank against it, even though she knew they couldn't possibly see her. When their unfamiliar accents didn't fade, she realized they were resting right there below her, their backs to her rock. She groaned inwardly—but her breathing stopped altogether when she heard them speaking of how useful these mountain-grown trees would be. About searching out the sassafras groves.

Her book said something about sassafras. And it used sassafras in almost all the recipes that she could see. But the way he said it, the way he spoke of *the* groves, like there was a specific grove, something special, and not just the occasional tree along a ridgeline.

The meeting hall was made of sassafras, she suddenly remembered; the building was so old, the wood so faded from its normal burnt-orange bark lining, that hardly anyone mentioned it anymore. But the logs were smaller than most building logs, and if you scratched one, you could still smell the spicy scent of the living tree.

It had taken quite a few trees to build the hall, there was no escaping that fact. And quite a few trees meant . . . once, at least, there had been a grove of them. A grove these strangers seemed to know about. No, *groves*.

Up on her rock, hidden, the blinder once more in her hand as well, Blaine grew bold enough to scowl. Rand just *had* to follow her, *had* to help reveal them and their strange plans, before all of Shadow Hollers was taken by surprise, and facing those swords.

Then she had another sudden thought, one that sent her heart to racing. *They were following her trail.* They could trail her right back to the homestead!

No. She took a deep breath. *No.* She'd been over two sections of bare, gritty rock. Surely they would lose her trail there. Surely they would give up when they got that far, considering that they still weren't sure if they were following deer, fox, or human. Blaine's light step in the woods might just do well by her this day.

At last the men had moved on; she strained to follow their conversation as it faded, but they had

turned to recounting lewd stories, anyway. She waited
a good long piece after their voices dwindled, and
then climbed down the rock, blinder clutched securely
in her teeth.

This time her descent from the ridge was careful,
as stealthy as she could make it. At least she didn't
have to make any effort to cover her trail—the two
men and their big careless feet had blazed a path in
last fall's flattened leaves, and she easily kept within
their marks. Her final approach was one step at a
time, with plenty of opportunity to remember to
breathe in between, to be thankful again for her bland
clothes, to remind herself of the blinder. As long as
she stayed silent and slow, it would keep her hidden;
she'd had enough close calls with her cousins in the
barn to know that much for sure.

Most of the men were gathered in the middle of
the camp, where they sat on the ground with slicker
capes over their heads to keep off the fitful drizzle
that had started again. From the tone of his voice,
the leader instructed them on something, though she
could hear none of the individual words. Blaine
blinked a raindrop out of her eye and crept closer,
worming through the rhododendrons, looking to see
if Dacey was where she'd left him.

She'd been gone several hours. There was no
telling what else they might have done with him. Or
to him.

But, no, he was there. Motionless. Asleep? *Not
dead, please not dead.* With an eye on the camp,
Blaine crept back to her old position above Dacey
and then some closer. Enough to see the rise and
fall of his chest beneath the gape of his coat, where
his struggles had pulled it open and no one had
bothered to close it. Enough to see that after a few
short hours, his face suddenly looked like it belonged
to an entirely different man. Haggard, drawn . . .
haunted. Drained of the quiet spirit she'd seen in

him, facing Cadell over the supper table. And battered by more than human hand.

He stirred then—she thought it was the rain dropping off his nose that roused him. After a hard look at the camp, Blaine set the blinder aside and made a quiet rustle in the leaves. He shifted, barely enough to see her, brief surprise on his face. Maybe he thought she had been there all along.

At least he seemed to be in his right mind again. With a glance down at the camp and a moment to convince herself that they could not hear her over the distance and above the sound of trees shedding old rain, Blaine inched even closer and murmured, "Rand is coming to help," even though she was sure of no such thing.

Dacey nodded and closed his eyes, looking infinitely weary, and not very hopeful. She couldn't blame him; she'd promised Rand, but all he *had* was her. She hugged her jacket closed, tired and cold and uncertain, jamming the blinder into her pocket along with her hand.

The gust of wind warned her, would have warned anyone who knew these mountains, though the plainsmen below ignored it. Blaine hunched inside her partial shelter as the drizzly rain, driven by the suddenly frenzied wind, lashed around in a dozen directions. Another instant, and the sky abruptly opened up in a wild deluge of rain and thunder and lightning.

Even halfway down the mountain, the sky was never far away; the storm enveloped them, wrapping the camp in chaos. Simultaneous lightning and thunder terrified the mules while the wind wrapped the men in their slickers, fighting them at every turn, strobing the camp with brilliant flashes of light against the storm-dark air. Rain stung Blaine's face, tripping her eyelids closed more than they were open—but she saw enough to recognize the tumult below.

She didn't even think about it. Suddenly she found

herself sliding down to Dacey, fumbling her pocket-
knife from her skirt to cut at the ropes that bound
him. They were thick and many but she didn't pause
to answer the fearful prickling at her neck, the sure
inner voice crying, *They've seen us!* or to check the
cuts she inflicted on herself. Then she had him free,
and he stumbled to his feet on awkward legs that
didn't seem ready to carry him.

He grabbed her arm—or maybe she grabbed *his*
arm—and they ran, both of them slipping on rain-slick
leaves and stumbling over root and rock hidden by rain
in their eyes. With terror on their heels they ran south
along the side of the slope, clawing their way upward
with the instinctive desire of the hunted—*go to high
ground.* When the storm slackened—almost as suddenly
as it had started—they were still holding on to each
other, and by tacit agreement, they sank to the ground.

"I can't believe you did that." Panting, Dacey shoved
the wet hair from his eyes, still looking plenty dazed
but eyeing her with some incredulity nonetheless.

"Daddy always said I didn't have no sense," Blaine
gasped back. They listened to each other breathe for
a while, until the sound faded enough to hear the
drip of water from the trees and the occasional rustle
of small indignant animals. In the face of her own
audacity, Blaine retreated to practical matters. She
wrung the water out of her skirt and said, "They're
lowlanders. I heard 'em say so. They sure don't know
nothing of our spring storms. Pure luck, that was."

"Not all luck," Dacey said, giving her a look she
couldn't read. He got to his feet with some effort,
hesitating halfway up; she stood, wanting to offer her
hand and not sure of it—he was so private, this one
was—and then he was standing beside her. He gave
her a wry little grin and struck out along the ridge.

Blaine just stood there, entirely befuddled. Was he
walking off, just like that?

But he turned and looked at her, then gave a little

jerk of his head, an indication that she should come along.

She didn't. "Reckon I'll head home now." Home to warn Cadell—to *convince* him.

"There ain't nothin' but trouble that way," Dacey said shortly. "Trouble for your family, if those men find us on your farm. This ain't no easy matter you've got yourself into, girl."

"Blaine," she said, polite but pointed. "And what did they want from you? What do they want from *us*?"

"Blaine." He looked at her a moment, and then straightened his back some. "Blaine, you can't go home. Not now. You know they saw you, even just a glimpse. How long do you think it'll take to find you there? You seen what they can do. You want your family facing that?"

Fear gripped her, made her rigid. "Then I gotta *warn* 'em, Dacey, how can I not *warn* 'em?"

He took a few quick, sudden strides, startling her, coming right up to her. "Because it'll do 'em more harm than good right now, that's how!" He took a deep breath, closed his eyes—eyes surrounded by bruises, by puffy flesh and split skin, though the rain had washed away all but traces of blood. Exhausted, haunted eyes that drove home his every word. "I done warned your daddy already, Blaine, that night I was there. Right now we got to go back to my last camp, and then we've gotta leave your hills for a piece." He startled her again then, resting a gentle hand on her arm, giving it the slightest of squeezes. "I'm obliged and owin' you, Blaine. I hope you don't come to regret what you just done . . . but I reckon you will."

As she blinked in surprise, he turned and moved off again. Still, she hesitated, weighing his words against what she'd seen, and what she knew. He'd warned Cadell already. *And I warned Rand.* Had either of them listened? Would they actually be prepared for those sword-bearing strangers?

Not likely.

Briefly, she considered making her way home despite Dacey's convictions, but couldn't bring herself to deny what he'd said. Bad enough if those men found her at the farm . . . what would they do to the rest of her family, for harboring her?

He stopped again, turned his head just the slightest bit to say back at her, his voice gentle and understanding, "Blaine. It's best."

Numbly, Blaine found herself following him.

⇥ 4 ⇤

Rand stood on the porch, listening to the rain drip into the gutter barrel and looking out at the new-washed hill.

No sign of Blaine.

He'd been so sure the storm would drive her home. But maybe she knew these hills even better than he thought, maybe she had some hidey-hole to keep her warm and dry, and no need at all to return home for such things. Maybe she was safe somewhere, rightly satisfied to know that at this very moment, he was worrying about her.

No. That would be too easy on him—too easy a way to salve his conscience.

Dammit, Blaine, I'm trying *to protect you!* Trying to protect the solitude she found so important, and the escape he didn't blame her for hunting out. No one deserved to listen to such teasing all the time, to have their daddy's disapproval heaped on her just for what she was. And there wasn't any point in losing it over a damn dream!

Not that any of that would matter, soon. If she

wasn't back by nightfall, he'd have to tell, and tell it all.

Blaine struggled to keep up with Dacey, fighting all the exertions of the day. How many times had she gone over that mountain? And how fast?

Her legs, gawky as they were, were strong and sturdy and never failed her. Until now.

She tripped again, hissing an almost-curse as she caught herself on a tree; Dacey didn't look back. But soon enough, their pace slacked, and after that it wasn't long before he stopped, just standing there, one hand against a tree. Blaine gave the area a befuddled inspection, and after a moment realized that there was a small pile of undisturbed belongings shoved up against a long-fallen tree, and a couple of sacks double-hung high off to the side. Spread out on the other side of the fallen tree was a jacket, and on the jacket lay the crippled white hound that had accompanied Dacey to Blaine's yard, his chin resting on the tree trunk to regard Dacey with much affection while his tail thumped the wet ground. As Dacey went to him, the dog struggled to rise, revealing a dry spot where he had waited out the rain.

Dacey reached down to take the dog's head between his hands. "Ah, Mage, I bet you got hungry waitin' for me. You're a good ole fellow." Stiffly, he hooked one of the hanging sacks with a stick and pulled it down where he could reach it. Blaine sank to the fallen tree, sitting on its soft damp seat of moss, while Dacey came up with a roughly wrapped mess of bones and meat—a package Blaine remembered her mother exchanging for furs.

She watched amazed as Mage carefully—delicately, even—took a bone from Dacey, and absently felt of the scar on her hand where she hadn't been quick enough in feeding the Kendricks' hound. She was even more bewildered when Dacey lifted his head to emit a fair approximation of dogs on fox scent. He paused to listen, then repeated the cry.

Far below them, Blaine heard a rustle in the wet woods. Dacey smiled faintly and divided the rest of the meat stuff into four piles, finishing just before four dogs arrived, descending upon Dacey with eager, whimpering cries as they licked his hands and leaped for his face. Overwhelmed, Blaine made herself small on the log as Dacey slapped their wet, hollow-sounding doggy sides and pulled their long ears. At last they calmed enough to notice the food and, with apologetic glances, they left him to wolf it down.

"I never seen any dog act like that," Blaine said, purely taken aback.

"Gotta give 'em the chance," Dacey replied, a reproof except for his mild tone. He looked down at the dogs—three reddish-brown and white spotted dogs and a bigger one so dark with rain he just appeared mottled grey-black. "I'll show you to 'em when they're through eating. You hungry yourself?"

She didn't answer immediately, still in the realization that he planned to show *her* to the dogs, and not the dogs to Blaine. "I could eat," she finally admitted, surprised all over again to realize that he intended to do the cooking himself, as stiff and awkward as he was; he'd already gone to his pack tarp for dry wood. She'd never seen her daddy cook when her mommy was present.

Not that she questioned her luck. No, she drew her feet up and clasped her arms around them, resting her cheek against her knees and hugging in all the warmth she could. Above her, a white-eyed cheerbird sang about spring, filling the air with his broken, repetitive phrases.

Not quite enough to drown out the worry, thoughts of Willum and Sarie and Rand and even Lenie, the notion of them facing what she'd seen today.

Not quite enough to drown out Dacey's noise of

effort as the wood tumbled from his grasp; Blaine's eyes flew open quick enough to catch him in the stumble, and to see how poorly he recovered from it, how jerky his movement was. Not like the Dacey who had walked up the Kendricks garden, so casual and confident, not at all. "What's wrong?" she asked, sliding her feet to the ground—*oh, that air was cold!*—and eyeing him as uncertainly as he eyed his own empty hands. Trembling hands, like a palsy had set in.

"Must be leftover from . . . from what it was they gave me," he said finally.

She opened her mouth to ask would it go away, and then thought better of it. He obviously didn't know—but he had to be wondering the same. "I'll make the fire," she said. "I got to get moving about anyway—too cold to sit still."

Carefully, looking as though he thought his body might betray him at any moment, Dacey sat on the fallen tree. Mage wasted no time in sidling up next to him, resting his chin on Dacey's thigh, his brow wrinkled and his eyes worried. "It's got damp even under the tarp," he said of the wood, reaching to stroke Mage and then withdrawing his hand when it no longer looked steady enough even for that. "There's a candle in the pack."

She found it, and a tin of finer looking matches than she'd ever seen in her own home—where it was her chore to make sure that there was always flame going, somewhere, be it in the stove or a candle or one of their new coal-oil lanterns. She set the wood up and shaved off some tinder, then lit the candle and let wax dribble over it. Between the candle and the waxed tinder, she coaxed the larger pieces into burning, and soon enough sat back on her heels to regard the fire, her face red from leaning over to work close to the flame. "Let it build," she said, and then glanced at him. "Unless you're feared those men will find us."

Dacey glanced at Mage, then at the fire, watching the smoke drift away. "We're too wet, and facin' a night too cold, not to have it built up."

She heard the decision with relief; already the chill crept back into her cheeks. At least her jacket was good sturdy wool, and her skirts the same. Now if only she had a scarf, or a blanket to huddle under. She glanced at Dacey's pack. Surely he had at least one, traveling in the hills like he was, this time of year.

And he should be under it, looking like he did.

That was when something in her suddenly took over, and she went to the pack as if she owned it, pulling out the blanket and draping it around him. While the dogs lolled around in vast contentment over their bones and making horrible cracking and crunching noises, she found the greens he'd picked the day before—young jewelweed and some marsh beauties; he must have been near water. She found the corn meal and a small sack of flour, and the small stoppered jar of syrup, and set it all out to wait for cooking heat in the fire. And then she marched her tired legs out onto the ridge, wishing for cohosh roots or tickweed for tea and knowing that she was in the wrong place, wrong season; she settled for scraping a generous handful of black cherry bark to ease his muscles, and was on her way back when she spotted a handful of stripling sassafras.

If only she had the book . . .

But she *knew* the book. She knew it well, with all its incomplete pages and half truths. Well enough to go to the largest of the trees—barely taller than her head, it was—and carve off a section of bark. "Sorry," she whispered to the tree, for it was hardly large enough to offer such insult. But black cherry tea wouldn't be enough, not for the muscle jerks that Dacey had.

Her blinder had worked, hadn't it? Maybe this recipe, incomplete as it was, would work as well.

She returned to their rude camp, commandeered the fire and a little pot from the pack, and then wrangled his shirt from him, tying the bark in the sleeve—tying the concoction to him. "It might not come out the same color, but it'll stay whole enough," she told him, making sure he wrapped back up in the blanket. But the sassafras needed that, to make it work with the cherry bark—needed steeping in something related to what she was trying to cure.

By the time darkness fell, she was warm from exertion, and Dacey had forced down the strange tea, as well as the inexpert pone and syrup Blaine had mixed up. And about the time his shakes eased, as his expression turned to surprised relief and he stared at his steady hands as though to convince himself, she realized she'd taken her mommy's role after all . . . and that she hadn't minded it one little bit.

Not when there was someone who needed caring.

Not when she did it from need, and not because she was *supposed* to. Or told to.

That was shock enough that it didn't bear thinking about, not on this day with too many shocks already. She finished scouring the cook pan and set it aside to sit beside Dacey and take up half the blanket, nibbling on one last, cold pone cake. Within moments, the four hounds sat ringed before her, drooling slightly and licking hopeful lips. The crippled dog curled comfortably beside Dacey, and although he did not stoop to begging, he definitely had his eye on her.

"You *can't* be hungry!" Blaine held the food well away from them, though they'd not come any closer. "Look at your bellies—y'all are about to burst!"

"Brains ain't caught up with their stomachs yet," Dacey said, though it had been some time since they'd eaten. He gave her a little grin. "Point of fact, their brains never catch up with their stomachs."

Now *that* sounded like her family's hound.

Dacey nodded at the dogs in turn. "That one's Chase—he's a young dog, but he's steady and he's got as clear a voice as you could ever want. That's his sister Whimsy," he said, indicating a long-nosed but sweet-eyed dog next to the brown-faced Chase. "She's a bit touched, but put her behind Chase and she'll unravel the trail he misses. That there," he pointed at a slightly smaller, mostly white dog with a gold patch over one eye, a bitch who had just given up on her begging to lie down with a grunt and a sour look, "that's Maidie, the mommy of the last two. She's the boss."

He paused to look at the last dog, which had wiggled forward on his bottom until his big-joweled, ticked, tan, and black face nearly hung over Blaine's knees—despite the fact that she'd just tucked the last of the pone in her mouth. She tried to inch away without being noticed, but for every move she made, the dog had one to mirror it.

He was by far the largest of the lot, with long, lanky legs and a broad, deep chest; he'd dried enough so she could see that he was not really black, but had black spots over a heavily ticked base coat. Suddenly she saw he wasn't at all interested in food; his intent gaze riveted on her braids, which had fallen over her shoulder. Slowly, drawing his lips up just enough to expose his teeth, he stretched his neck and opened his mouth—

"That's *Blue*," Dacey said, and the name was put in such tones that the dog backed guiltily away. "He hunts when we're treeing for meat. The others don't care for nothin' but the foxes." His attention turned to Mage; he scrubbed the dog behind the ears. "An' you know Mage."

"Mage. That's a fanciful one," Blaine said, smothering a rude snort.

"Reckon it is. People around here used to believe in the magic of these hills, and that's where his line comes from. His grandaddy was Mage, too."

Blaine regarded the dogs, now slumbering, and cast a quizzical eye at Dacey. "Why, you treat these dogs like they was *people*."

"They're more respectable than a sight of the people I've met. If you don't care to, you don't have to talk to them none." Dacey dropped his hand and his last morsel of food down to Mage, but there was no malice in his words. " 'Course," he added, and a glint of hardness came into his voice, "don't be rough with 'em, either. They might not be people, but they got feelings."

"I don't talk rough to nothin'," Blaine said, but was forced, in honesty, to amend her statement. " 'Ceptin' Lenie sometimes, but I swear, she does deserve it!"

"Lenie?" Dacey repeated blankly. "Oh, your sister. The one who's looking for a man."

A laugh slipped out of her, though she'd never expected to do any such thing on this evening. "It shows, don't it."

"Sure it does. But there's plenty of men appreciate that."

"That's what she tells me," Blaine said sourly, and was hit with a sudden surge of grief that she might not ever hear it again. How had she gotten herself into this? *Dacey*. How had *he*—

"Dacey," she said, slowly, "how do you come to be here?"

He looked at her; she wasn't sure he was seeing her. "Fear, I reckon," he said finally. "Of not being here. Of not listening."

She had the feeling he'd just said something profoundly reflective of himself . . . and she hadn't understood a word. "Try sayin' that so it makes sense," she told him, not a little cranky.

Dacey looked away. "We need to be movin' early tomorrow," he said, as if they'd not exchanged those words at all. He reached to his pack, drawing out what made up the bulk of it—two wool blankets and a quilt, none too generous in size but looking mighty good to Blaine. "Find yourself a good spot, see if you can't sleep some. I'm gonna be at your back—we need the warm. And . . . don't worry, tonight. You'll be safe with the dogs here."

Blaine wasn't sure if he was reassuring her that the dogs *were* safe or that they would *keep* her safe. She gave Blue a look—he had never moved very far from her—and slowly inched off the fallen tree to curl up against it, pulling her lined skirts tightly around her chilled legs and accepting the blankets, wondering how they'd be big enough for two. She didn't think she'd get warm enough to sleep even if her skirts *were* wool, and her jacket finally dry. When Blue and his massive bulk wandered over and settled down beside her, her first impulse was to push him away—but only until she felt his warmth seep through her clothes.

As long as he stayed warm, she decided, he could lie as close as he wanted.

→ 5 ←

Blaine stood at the top of an unfamiliar ridge and inhaled the fresh, crisp air, breathing in the pure joy of living, so full of it she just had to share it with—

But when she turned, smiling, there was no one there. Who had she been expecting?

Suddenly she didn't know.

A howl sliced the air, and Blaine whirled to catch a glimpse of something white, moving fast and awkward but evading her gaze just the same.

"Blaine!" From behind her again, and again she whirled, finding Dacey clinging to a thick tree, his eyes blank.

"Don't worry, Sissy. I'll help."

She spun to the voice, feeling dizzy. Rand stood before her—Rand who never called her Sissy as he did Lenie and Sarie—his hand outstretched. "I'll help," he said, and smiled. She reached for him—

Another howl smacked her ears from behind, made her lose her balance, step back and away. Danger, it whispered, trickling into her conscious thoughts and turning into fear. When she looked back, Rand was

*no longer there, and the outstretched hand belonged
to the smiling leader; in it was a black, sticky bolus—
a horror.*

"Blaine!"

First Dacey—then the howl, shouting, Blaine!—*and
then the leader, laughing. Laughing. Laughing,*
"Blaine . . . Blaine . . . ."

Before supper, Rand went to his daddy and did
his best to accomplish it all—protecting Blaine's
solitude, and finding a way to tell of her predicament.

It didn't include mentioning men with swords. He
still couldn't believe that one, himself.

He found Cadell in the barn, sharpening the plow
blade. "Daddy," he said, "I ought to have told this
before, but . . . Blaine and I had a little fuss, an' she
lost her head and ran up the hill."

Cadell lifted his head from the plow, brows raised.

"I wanted to give her time to come back on her
own—I figured she'd be back quick enough," Rand
said, and that much had certainly been the truth. "I'm
about to get worried, though." *No, I'm long past
worried.* What if she *had* been caught in the storm,
and slipped in a bad spot? Plenty of those, in these
hills.

"Well," Cadell said, and left it at that a moment.
"That girl is a certain-sure one for making trouble.
I ought to have drawed the line with her a lot sooner
than this."

Not the reaction Rand expected, and he couldn't
find a response, nothing but, "It'll be dark soon."

"She's got to be ready for marryin'," Cadell said,
slowly applying the whetstone to the plow blade. "And
she ain't noways near it. She's got too many notions
in her head." He frowned, and looked up at Rand
again. "Could be this is a good thing, son. Maybe a
night in the open will calm her down some, so she'll
act as befittin'."

"She could be hurt—"

"Can't imagine so. She gets along better off the farm than she lets on, Rand. I seen her sneakin' around, now and then. And some of those berries she brings back, they ain't from along the creek where we send her. No, son, I think she's took a real hissy fit, and thought to hare off to some life other than the one she's got. If she ain't back first thing of the mornin', we'll go lookin' for her. I'll get Jason's dogs on the trail—he likes to brag about how they found Bayard the Younger's boy last year."

"If she ain't back by then, I'll take to lookin' for her while you get Jason," Rand said.

"You always were the one to spoil her," Cadell said, a smile in the corners of his mouth. He turned back to the plow. "I'm surprised you didn't come to me before this."

"I was trying to save her some trouble," Rand said. "Now I wish I hadn't." That was the certain rueful truth, and it rang in his voice. He hoped Cadell heard it, hadn't been put off by what of the fibs might have shown on his face. In looks he was closer to Lenie, with the same, squared-off sort of features they'd both gotten from Cadell. Blaine had the lean features that went with her lean body, and aside from a faint resemblance to her mother, looked like no one else in the family. But Rand had always felt closer in spirit to Blaine, who listened to his thoughts instead of scoffing them off like Lenie did. Like he'd done to her. *Could have gone with her, even if it* was *a dream.*

"Don't worry yourself," Cadell said. "She's upset, sure, but beneath it all, the girl's got a good head on her shoulders."

Rand was glad his daddy had turned away, and was unable to see the surprise on his face. *Why don't you ever tell* her *that?* Out loud, he simply said, "Yes, sir," and went to wash up for supper.

Morning came with no sign of Blaine, leaving

Cadell puzzled but Rand unsurprised—and glad to be out in the yard when Lottie cornered Cadell on the porch, showing a temper the children rarely saw.

"Only a crazy man would leave his girl out there all night. There's no tellin' what she could have run into and you know it!" Her eyes sparked anger, showing the inner fire Blaine never seemed to know to bank.

"Now, Lottie . . ." Cadell shifted back against the porch rail, looking just as cornered as he was.

"Now *nothin'!*" One hand on her hip, the other aiming an index finger at him, she said, "You ought to have gone out last night when Rand told you of this! Just because Blaine's the only one of our children to show a little gumption, to have some idea of what she wants for herself, you've got the notion it's your job to pound it out of her. Well, you can just let her be when she comes back! *If* she comes back." Lottie's voice broke, and she turned suddenly away. "You ought to at least have *tried* last night."

"Ahh . . . ." Cadell ducked his head. "All right, honey. Don't take on so. I'm on my way to Jason's, and Rand's goin' out to look for her right now—ain't you, son?"

Rand eased back a step, not happy to have been pointed out. "I'm leavin' now, Mommy."

Lottie had her back to them, a good, sturdy back that suddenly seemed too slight for this worry, and she stared off the porch to the seeded garden patch past the front yard. Abruptly, she turned to the house, her face hidden, but her voice as revealing as ever—this time, determined that things would turn out well.

"You just wait a minute, Rand. You'll need a lunch, and a little extra for when you find her." All practicality and back to the Lottie they knew, but Rand wondered at the little bit of Blaine he thought he'd seen in that moment of confrontation with Cadell.

❖   ❖   ❖

Blaine woke with an immediate feeling of trepidation, unsure which parts of the previous day had been real and which were merely memories of the night's intense dreams. She lay with her eyes closed and determined that she was numb and almost too stiff to move, and that, yes, she really must have had the adventures she remembered. Dacey had already risen, leaving her with the luxury of all the blankets to herself—though she'd slept hard, and didn't remember him coming to rest at her back, or even that he'd been there at all.

Finally, she ventured a look around. Although the weather had faired and the sky was clear, the sun hadn't yet breached the opposite mountain, and everything was damp, including Blaine. To her relief, the big ticked hound was nowhere in sight. His warmth at night was one thing—confronting his big face during the day was another. She sat and stretched painfully, straightening her skirts from where they had rucked up around her knees—not that they were much longer than that any more anyway. She thought of the new set she'd been working on, folded neatly in the trunk at the end of her and Lenie's bed, and wondered if she'd ever finish them.

She'd thought she was alone, but then she heard Dacey's low chuckle. It was a warning—for Blue was trotting into the rough camp, an offensive vision of bloody, drooly hound. A giant lump of smeary brown fur hung from his big jaws, and Blue, minus a small chunk of nose, had blood dripping from both his ears, tinting his chest pink. He stopped in front of her and gave the furry blob a proud little shake; the offering swung heavily in his jaws.

"He ain't goin' to hurt you," Dacey assured her, not moving from his spot somewhere behind her.

That was a matter of opinion. Blaine drew her feet in close.

Blue dropped the fur at those feet; it struck the

ground with a dull thump and rolled limply over to reveal itself as a groundhog, a large fellow already fat with early spring greens. Blue plumped his bottom to the ground and watched her expectantly.

"I believe he's got a crush on you," Dacey said, amusement in his voice.

"That's silly." Blaine was *not* amused. "I ain't that fond of dogs."

"Maybe not, but a dog's got a way of looking into a person's heart, and ole Blue must've liked what he seen. Now tell him he's a good fellow or he'll sulk all day, and I don't have time for that."

Uncertainly, Blaine regarded the dog. Too much encouragement and he might come closer, smearing her with that gory face. She offered, "Good boy, Blue. Nice dog."

How that tremulous praise could have meant anything, she didn't know, but the ticked hound thumped his tail on the ground, and his jaws fell open in a happy pant.

Dacey gave a grunt of satisfaction and interrupted the scene by scooping up the groundhog. He looked much better today, his face healed up more than she ever would have thought possible, his movements easy. *It worked. The tea worked, just like the blinder.*

"Atta boy, Blue," he said with satisfaction, and quickly field-dressed the groundhog. He fed the liver and heart to the dogs, the rest of whom had wandered in after Blue, wrapped the carcass, and stowed it in his bulky pack. "Ready to go?" he asked.

"Go?" she replied blankly.

"They're gonna be lookin' for us today. And even if they can't track worth nothin', they've got enough men they could stumble on us by chance."

Blaine staggered to her stiff legs and excused herself into the brush. On the way back she shook some wet rhododendron leaves off on her hands and scrubbed her face, a crude washing up that nonetheless made

her feel better—and gave her time to think. Dacey
and the five hounds were waiting, more or less
patiently, when she returned to the camp. Waiting to
leave.

"I ain't so sure I want to go a-traipsin' off with
you," she said, trying to look him in the eye and
ending up with her gaze on Mage instead. "It's one
thing to avoid my daddy's farm. It's a big 'nother one
to go further off than we already are."

"Blaine . . . we done gone over this."

She fidgeted with the end of her braid, and burst
out with, "I don't *know* you, Dacey Childers! I don't
know *nothin'* about you. I only helped you 'cause no
man deserves what those strangers did. I don't even
know *why* they were doin' it! But . . . my daddy's got
to be warned of 'em."

"I've done warned your daddy—I told you that."
Dacey shifted the pack against his back. "You *do*
know somethin' of me, Blaine. You know I come
from the seers' line. You know I ain't mean to these
dogs, and that I never come near you last night."
His voice made a subtle leap from its sensible tone
to intensity. "And you know you was seen when you
got me loose—mebbe all they seen was skirts and
braids, but that'd be plenty. Those men'll be looking for us, and it won't go easy for neither of us,
should we be found." He gave her a moment to
think about it. Then he said, "Best you come with
me, Blaine. I can't stay, and I can't have your harm
sitting on my shoulders."

"I guess . . ." she said faintly, and then tried again
in a stronger voice, "I guess maybe I will."

Rand didn't even try to find the signs from Blaine's
flight behind the barn; yesterday's storm would have
washed them clean away. Instead, he picked up the
trail behind the springhouse. Blaine was in the habit
of taking that dog path, and he didn't need to follow

exactly how she'd gone the day before, as long as he ended up at the same place.

A quarter way up the slope, the trail hit a fork along the hillside. Both paths, he knew, got a body to the other side of the mountain, where she said she'd been—but at vastly different endpoints. He was betting she made a habit of taking the easiest.

He struck out on his own, glancing only occasionally at the signs of her previous passages. Once he reached the rock she had sometimes mentioned—it couldn't be anything else, not that brute—he saw a new trail, one left by bigger, clumsier feet than Blaine's, a new trail that had survived even the storm. Full of sudden foreboding—*Rand, there's men, over the ridge*—he slowed his pace, stopping often to take note of the forest. A few jays screamed above his head in occasional alarm, but he heard and saw nothing else that seemed disturbed.

The new path led him straight to a camp.

She'd been telling the truth.

Men. Men with swords.

But there was no sign of them now; no sign of Blaine. Cautiously, he moved closer.

Within the camp area, last fall's leaves were shuffled and cleared in spots for fires. Rand started in the center of the camp and spiraled outward, moving slowly, carefully. He made a slow inspection of the area and found signs of horse or mule, temporary latrine areas, and game-cleaning spots. One fire pit still held considerable heat. Startled, he instantly crouched to scan the trees.

No, he was alone. He must be. But where had so many men gone, unnoticed? Cautiously, he continued his spiral, gradually passing to the edge of camp. Recent sign there indicated that the whole group had retraced the path they'd come in on, toward the creek at the bottom of the hollow. Travel was easier on the ridges; only men who didn't know the hills would travel the creek, which they could follow to the river branch and thereby not go astray.

And after then, where? And why?

He wondered if Blaine knew. He wondered if she was with them. And much as he hated the thought, he almost hoped that she was, because otherwise . . .

It took him a moment, then, to uncurl his fingers from clenched fists, and continue his search. He walked a few circles past the camp perimeter until he happened on a tangle of threads the color of Blaine's winter wool, snared in greenbriar.

There was no other sign of her.

He stopped, wiped his hands over his face, and thought. Daddy and Jason would be trailing Blaine soon enough, and the dogs would find sign that Rand walked right over. But he was the only one who knew of the strangers.

So rather than walk the ridge hollering for his sister, Rand took a deep breath and made his way to the creek—and then stood there frowning at the still-muddy water. The strangers were heading for the river branch all right, and from there they could easily find their way to the river and the settled creek mouths. Those families needed to be warned.

He didn't hesitate, not any more. He headed for home. It was time to come clean about Blaine's wanderings and his part in covering for her . . . and what she'd said about Dacey and the strangers.

He half expected to hear Jason's dogs sounding before he made it back, but the hills remained silent; he made it back to the final slope above the spring-house without sighting any other searchers. Strange.

The farm looked quiet; the children were nowhere to be seen, not even Willum—who, at this time of day, was usually the color of grime and possessed of a collection of insects, dead and alive. Then he remembered that today was a quilt party at the meeting house. All his family was there, except for his daddy; even Lottie had decided to go, hoping to spread the word about the search for Blaine.

Good. It would be easier if he could talk to Cadell alone first.

But his relief was short-lived. As soon as he rounded the house, Rand discovered the men grouped about his porch. Neighbors all, and some he hadn't seen since winter set in. Why, there was old man Bayard, who had declared years ago that anyone with something to say could just walk down to his little shack and say it—and iff'n they didn't see fit to visit an old man, Bayard didn't see as they'd be good company anyway.

But now he was on Rand's porch, commanding the cushion on the swing. Rand mounted the steps to the porch and went unremarked as the loud buzz of talk continued.

"I don't see how you could have heard the same dogs, seein's how you're two hollers away from us," Wade was saying to Cadell, who answered with a shrug.

"I didn't ride that mule all the way over here to talk about who heard dogs and who didn't," Bayard said, his voice as overloud as usual. "Things don't seem quite right around here, and it's *that* we've got to talk about. Don't reckon I'm the only one to note the northern sky some days back!"

Only Jason nodded—sandy-haired Jason, standing at the outside corner of the porch with two of his big brindle hounds on lead; the others looked baffled.

"Bayard, you put too much on them old eyes," Wade said. "Sky's been the same as always."

"I seen it." Jason lifted his head, a challenge to Wade. "Funny kind of haze over the northern ridges, a downright sickly, dark thing."

Cadell surprised Rand by adding, "My middle girl—the one that's gone missing—she said the same."

"Any of you have any sense, you're thinking of the

Takers." Bayard tamped his walking stick on the porch in emphasis, looking right justified in it.

Cadell gave him a startled look; Rand saw uneasiness mixed in, as well. No one else seemed to note it.

"The Takers are dead," Wade said. "And the sky is fine."

"Don't try to tutor me on the Takers, young man. You should reckon well enough that I'm the only one in these parts to know my granpappy and hear of his time on Anneka Ridge. I've certainly told you all enough times!"

At this unintentional confession there were low snickers all around, and Bayard let them pass. "Let me tell you, I heard often enough myself about that battle. Sure those men thought they'd cleaned up the Takers for good. But for all the times you've heard about the battle, how many times have you heard about the only sure sign that came before? *The purple-like sky in the north.* Comes off o' their magic, I was told, and it ain't no wonder can't all of us see it—how many boast a seer's blood, these days?"

Silence—an admission of sorts—greeted his remarks. Finally Cadell spoke, and his voice was tired. "All right. Supposin' we're dealing with more Takers. Just supposin'. What then? We ain't got a seer to point out which of 'em, and maybe which of our neighbors, are Took. And if it *is* like the tales we've heard, they'll come here with a passel o' men—too many for us to fight without the Takers gettin' to us. Our only chance is to tell who's Took, according to what I've heard, an' kill those men first."

"Or those women," Bayard said grimly, adding a dimension to the history they'd never heard before.

"Not women!" Jason, wed within the year and already waiting for his first child, stiffened.

"Or children," Bayard said firmly. "You know all it takes is a touch on flesh for a Taker to put some of its power in you. Then you might as well be dead, an' better off, too, because you can't stop from hurting your neighbors and kin. What better way for them Takers to get close to us? Be a woman, and the menfolk don't think to be wary of you. Or a child, cryin' in the dirt. Go to pick it up and comfort it, and you're one of *them*."

"So what do we do about it?" Cadell repeated— slowly, distracted. Thinking of something he hadn't owned up to yet.

"Find us a seer?" Jason said hopefully.

"Quit scarin' each other like little ole women," Wade scoffed. "Start payin' attention to raisin' crops an' children and not our hair."

"Might be best." But Jason sounded tentative, even if most of the men nodded at his words.

Cadell's jaw set, a thinking look. Rand knew it. Knew his father wasn't happy about what he was about to say.

Knew he'd be even more unhappy about what Rand had to say.

"Daddy," he said, stepping the rest of the way up to the porch.

Cadell didn't let him get anything else out, showing an anxiety he hadn't revealed that morning. "Rand! Did you find your sister?"

"No. But I found something else, and I think these men'll care to hear it." He hesitated, and Cadell nodded him to continue. "Yesterday at noon, Blaine came down from the hills and told me she'd seen some men in that wild hollow over the ridge."

"Fiddlehead Holler? No one lives there, not since that seer family was burned out in the Taker fighting," Bayard said.

"Blaine don't go that far into the hills," Cadell said, but he'd turned to wariness, one that spoke of his own lack of conviction. He believed it already—he just didn't want to.

"Meanin' no disrespect, but she does. She always walks the hills, to get away from—" Rand glanced at his uncle, sitting there beside Cadell, and changed his wording to "—Lenie's teasing." Cadell knew well enough what he'd really meant. "She's never been in the barn like you all figured, an' I—well, I didn't figure it was my business to tell hers. By the time I found out about it, she already knew the hills well enough to take care of herself."

"So what's the point?" Wade said.

"Yesterday she came and told me about these men, all ruffled up about it. She wanted me to come see, but . . . well, you know how she gets these things in her head sometimes." He shrugged, unable to meet anyone's gaze. "I figured she'd just dreamt something. So she headed back up the hill—she was trying to get me to follow. And . . . this morning when I followed her trail, I found signs of a big camp. Horse sign, too. Fresh, from earlier today. They'd left out towards the creek, headed downstream." He looked at Cadell. "I couldn't find any trail on Blaine. Just enough to know she'd been there. But listenin' to your talk, I thought this was something that concerned more'n just us."

There was silence then, as the men considered the significance of the Takers sky and the presence of armed strangers; even Wade had sombered.

Rand sat on the porch rail to face his father. "Y'know, she said something about that Dacey fellow. Said they had him tied, and she was afraid for him. She said they had swords." He gave his daddy an apologetic look. "That's why I thought she'd been dreamin'. Who's even heard of them being used around here?"

"Dacey?" Bayard said sharply. "Ain't no one by the name of Dacey hereabouts."

"From the family of Childers, down south of us. Old seer family. Came to my place a few nights back with trade for a meal and dog scraps." Cadell hesitated. "I wasn't sure how to bring this up before, but . . . he done gave me a warning before he left. I didn't take no stock in it at the time . . . ."

Rand gave his father a sharp look, suddenly afraid of what he was going to hear—more afraid, even, than of what he'd already found.

"Spit it out, Cadell!" Bayard demanded.

Hard and sudden, Cadell did. "Said he'd had seein's. That he was here because them seein's told him the Takers were coming back."

There was silence. They were on Cadell's homeplace; no one wanted to offend. And as they took that moment's hesitation, their skepticism turned to the same mixture of half-believing wariness that still rode Cadell's features.

Jason was the first to break the silence, his brows bunched up over his strong forehead. "Say it's so. What're we gonna do about it? A stranger touches you and quick as that you're his? We're needin' a seer to tell who's safe? It's so, an' we're all in a mighty bad place."

"Sit in our homes and make damn sure no stranger sets foot on our land," Wade snorted, looking pointedly at Cadell.

"Quit yer bullin' at Cadell, Wade. We'd had no talk of the Takers when he made this Childers fellow welcome, an' he's the only one with a daughter missing." Bayard stuck his chin out at Wade, who subsided. "Now that we've had some talk about the situation, I expect we'll all be more careful . . . an' the first thing we got to do is track down those men." He trailed off to squint down at the end of the yard. "Cadell, ain't that your oldest girl a-runnin' up the lane?"

Cadell turned to spot Lenie as the girl's run turned into an exhausted stagger. Once she stumbled to her knees. "Rand!" he snapped, but Rand was already sprinting to meet her.

"Oh, Rand," she sobbed, barely coherent. She must have run all the way from the meeting hall. Her hair straggled from its usual neat bun and the sweat on her face marked a long run made in panic. Rand scooped her up and jogged back to the porch with her, where she slid out of his grasp to reach for Cadell. Unused to embracing this daughter who had outgrown him, Cadell nonetheless put his arms around her in an awkward, protective hold.

"Hush, Lenie," he said after a moment of her hysterical crying. "Try to calm a bit, girl. What's the problem? Has one of the children took sick or been snakebit?"

"Men, Daddy," Lenie gulped. "Men."

Rand straightened his back and looked Cadell square in the eye. It seemed, then, that they were in for some trouble.

>< >< ><

An entire communal house made from *suktah*, and the humans didn't even seem to comprehend its value. Why, if they'd had warding of even the weakest kind, inside that building they'd have been untouchable.

But they didn't, and now they were in the hands of the Annekteh, to serve their new masters as the Annekteh chose. Perhaps even to tear down this structure to use the old *suktah* for the *nekfehrta* the *annektehr* needed before they could truly establish themselves here.

Nekfehr surveyed the site, and the terrified women and children held within their own place of safety. A beautiful setup for Breeders . . . The *annektehr* contemplated it at length, simply to torment his vessel, and to experience the results of the man's emotional memories. *Nekfehr being Taken, chosen, torn from his family*—from within a Breeder camp, where such things were never supposed to happen. But Nekfehr had caught their attention with his thoughtfulness, his quick intelligence—even his devotion.

All of these things served the annektehr well—at first, by the intensity of anne-nekfehr the man provided, separated from his family and community. And later, when his natural quickness and drive provided answers and incentive for the Annekteh . . . solutions the Annekteh applied toward the management of his own kind.

Human betraying human despite himself.

So the *annektehr* within Nekfehr now drove his thoughts to Breeders and children and family, and greedily lapped the frisson of the vessel's anguish. And, after a regretfully short moment of that sweetness, released him from those thoughts; Breeders were not what they needed here—not yet—and they could not afford to waste time and concentration on irrelevant matters.

What they needed was cooperative labor . . . and Feeders, from which to taste the senses, for some of the *nekteh* among them craved the perception of human pain and fear—strong, intoxicating experiences—called *anne-nekfehr*—that the Annekteh could not encounter without the use of a vessel.

Nekfehr suspected there would be opportunities for such. People like these,

long out of touch with the Annekteh,
thought themselves defiant, and willing to
fight for their freedom. For their families.
They never thought such for long.

＞＜   ＞＜   ＞＜

As a group the Shadow Hollers men walked down
to the creek, following its well-worn path to the river
at its mouth—where the flat if narrow flood plain
made the walk to the meeting hall, several hollows
south, an easy one. Old Bayard, the only one mounted,
had to check his mule frequently, and often muttered
that he should just go on ahead. Cadell finally put
Lenie on the mule behind him, and that slowed the
animal enough for the men to keep up.

Lenie hadn't told them much—she hadn't known
it to tell. A score of men arrived suddenly, spent a
few moments terrorizing the women and children in
the hall, and then sent her and other youth out to
gather the men from their houses.

"They *sent* for us?" Rand puzzled as they paused,
the meeting hall in sight. "Don't make sense."

"Makes sense if they figured they've already got us
beat," Bayard said ominously. He was not perturbed
when the others rounded on him with words and
glares. "Hellfire, men! What were we just talkin' of?
Takers! And they don't have any call to be scairt of
us! Prob'ly just makin' sure we all know they've moved
in on us!" He gave his mule an unkind kick in the
ribs and guided it boldly into the hall yard, stopping
just before the row of unfamiliar pack and riding animals, and next to several other Shadow Hollers men.

Cadell and Rand exchanged a quick look—not
wanting to expose themselves by leaving the creek
brush, unwilling to have Lenie and Bayard out there
without them. Cadell nodded, grim and unhappy, and
they stepped forward, leading the others out into the
yard.

"Excellent." A voice spoke with confidence, drawing

their attention to the hall, and the voice alone was enough to tell the men that this was a stranger, without the drawling speech of their own. He spoke over his shoulder into the hall. "This should be just about all of them."

Rand found the tall man in the hall doorway, quickly taking in the high, shin-padded boots and the peek of mail from beneath a shiny leather shirt and rough cloth pants. At the man's side was a long sheath, a foreign shape to Rand's eye. No wonder Blaine had been alarmed. *And I called it a dream, wouldn't even follow her.*

The open door allowed some view of the hall within, where the day's quilt lay scattered in limp shreds and the women and children crowded into the far corner by the fireplace. The two men watching them stood well back, relaxed—one sharpening a dagger, the other leering now and then at whoever happened to catch his eye. There was another man there, ignoring the women as he spoke quietly to several others. He was shrouded in a dark cloak, and when he came out and stood in front of the hall, Rand could see the cloth was a fine, expensive weave. Not a man used to rough living.

A voice echoing from the nearby barn told Rand where the rest of the strangers were, but the cloaked man—the leader, Rand had no doubt—paid them no mind. Instead, he watched as inside, someone spoke sharply to the quiet huddle of women and children.

Frightened and unsure, the women just stood there, and men moved forward to haul them out of the safety of the crowd and shove them at the door. Rand stiffened as little Sarie stumbled and fell, and he caught Cadell's arm in restraint, though he wanted just as badly to rush forward. Jenna, one of Blaine's least favorite cousins, caught the child and swung her up into the safety of adolescent arms as she herself hurried for the door.

"It will be more comfortable out here," the leader said. His hair and eyes were dark, like black ice, and his voice made Rand shiver inside, especially when the man smiled as though he was offering them the hospitality of a neighborly porch. "I'm afraid you'd find it quite crowded in there, and I very much want you to be able to pay attention. No distractions."

He gave them time for families to unite and waited until they had settled, little nuclei of defiance and fear. Then he left his spot beside the door to stride out before them, the casual set of his body telling them more of their situation than anything else they'd seen. Mystified and intimidated, the same mountain men who would growl back at a wildcat merely stood and waited.

"I'm impressed," the leader said. "I'd been told it was harder than this to quell you people, but I think this is going to be easy on both of us. My name is Nekfehr; I command here. Please listen closely as I explain how things will be from now on."

Lenie's hand crept into Rand's; he took it gladly.

"We're from the plains to the north of you, although I think most of you know that already. We run things there, and we're very good at it." Nekfehr smiled—a slow, chilling smile. "Originally, we came from north of the plains, but we find the living more entertaining in the flat lands. More people there. More for us to do. And now we have needs that your mountains can fulfil. Conveniently for us, you're here to help us meet our goals, and to satisfy our needs."

Rand glanced at his father, and then at the others, seeing narrowed eyes and tensed jaws—hearing the same message he did. *You people are our playthings. Our slaves.*

With his next words, Nekfehr as much as told them so. "You're nothing but tools to us. Work for us, and we'll treat you well enough. Fail to serve us, and . . .

well. One throws a hopelessly broken tool away, does one not?" He adjusted his fine black gloves, pulling them more snugly over his fingers, apparently unconcerned about his audience—but Rand saw him watching them, a surreptitious gaze. The eyes of a man—a creature—who enjoyed the power he held over them. "For the moment, you will serve our purposes by providing labor. It's certainly too bad for you that you're so isolated in these mountains. Some of you might have gotten away, had you been forewarned." He affected another smile. "But oh, yes—you've lost all your seers, haven't you? No warning at all. Now it's too late, I'm afraid."

Rand's back stiffened in denial and defiance; the minute gesture echoed throughout the gathering, a collective of stubborn-looking faces. Rough faces, some of the men freshly shaved of winter beards, some of them still fuzzy and untrimmed, everyone in work clothes—unlike the women, who had put some effort into their appearance for the quilting party. Mountain faces . . . determined to keep the mountains their own.

Nekfehr seemed not to notice—but suddenly Rand was sure he had, that he'd deliberately evoked the response, and was now enjoying it. Playing them, like trout on the line. "To start with," the man said, crisp and uncompromising, "we have a need for *suktah*—that is, sassafras wood. We'll be searching for your groves. We'll also be starting extensive logging of other trees—your trees have properties you don't seem interested in exploiting, but we have no such weaknesses."

He waved a hand at them, his gesture encompassing them all. "The women will work the farms, aside from a select few who will watch the children—here, at this building. My men will be here at the hall also—you may consider your children hostages for your honest efforts.

"The men will be logging. We will assign you to crews and areas, and you will work at a reasonable pace or we will come to terms about it. Negotiations will not be pleasant." The man smiled emotionlessly, and at once Rand hated him.

"The younger boys," the man concluded, "will provide fresh meat and other forageables. I assure you the whole system is simple and workable, and I expect to have no trouble."

Rand shifted back on his heels and caught Cadell's eye—and could see his father's thoughts favored his own. The invaders were outnumbered; they were underarmed. What weapons they did have seemed to be for close-distance fighting—there was nary a bow to be seen. And maybe these mountains *were* isolated by the very nature of their structure, but that could be an advantage, too. There were always places to slip away to, plans to make . . . these heavily armored and bulky-weaponed men could never keep up in a pursuit, and hostages could always be freed. For a moment, lulled by the leader's calm attitude, the community thought of rebellion. As a whole, their faces were hard, hateful and defiant.

"What about my girl?" Lottie said, her voice sudden and low. "Blaine, my middle child. What have you done with her?"

Rand gave her a startled glance, surprised she had put it together so fast. But when the man seemed unlikely to respond, despite the raised eyebrow he bestowed upon Lottie, Rand backed her up. "She went to help Dacey Childers. We know you had him."

His statement started a stir of surprise and murmuring, people leaning over to hiss questions at Cadell.

The leader shrugged, uncaring. "She's dead. So's the man."

"*No*," Lottie whispered.

Rand did more. He'd been to that campsite; he'd seen no bodies. "Prove it!"

"Prove it?" That dark gaze held sudden danger. "Prove it? Never would you say such a thing, had you any memories of our history here. *Prove it?* I can see we need to remind you of those days. Perhaps we did ourselves a disservice, last time, by destroying your seers' records so thoroughly. But," he said, giving them a suddenly calculating gaze, "we can rectify that error." Nekfehr gestured to his men and pointed toward the gathered families, jabbing his finger once at each end of the crowd. Charlane Prater was yanked away from her family—while Willum, who'd been squatting in research on a bug, gave one surprised squall and found himself in front of the crowd. He offered the insect to the man who held his arm.

The man slapped it away.

Willum understood then; this was more than just some odd game. He tore loose and Charlane, rather than risk the ire of the leader, snatched him and gathered him close before her, her arms crossed over his chest to offer what protection she could. Willum watched fearfully as Nekfehr approached and laid his hand on Charlane's shoulder. Then his eyes widened, for Charlane's grip tightened visibly. He wiggled in protest, whimpering, casting questioning eyes on his mother.

"Hold still," Lottie whispered, her command strained, thinking, it seemed, the same as Rand . . . if he didn't fuss . . . if he was cooperative—

Too much of a chance. "I'm the one done said it," he said, stepping out—only to be brought up short by one of the men, one he dared not let touch him. "You got something to do, you do it to *me*."

Another man stepped forward, drawing his knife. He smiled at Charlane—and Charlane smiled back, genuine as anything.

"I'm afraid this is more effective," Nekfehr said, and nodded at Willum.

The plainsman drew his blade across Willum's throat.

It happened so fast Rand wasn't at first sure of what he'd seen—and then they all knew, frozen in horror as blood sprayed high in great heart-driven spurts, as Willum's astonished little face gathered itself for one last cry that he never had the opportunity to voice. As his eyes drained of life and his body sagged, as Charlane held him tightly without a hint of regret, as Lottie whimpered and fell against her husband, Rand's chest clutched with a fury and grief he knew he didn't dare express. Could only vow to avenge . . . while at the same time realizing there was very little chance he'd ever get the opportunity.

Nekfehr smiled his terrible, dead smile. "Take note. I could have made any one of you do that. His mother, his father, another child his age. And if you give me cause, I will."

His touch on Charlane's shoulder released her. She looked, aghast, at the body in her arms and the blood on her sleeves, and began to scream.

Nekfehr turned away, his face filled with cold, alien satisfaction.

→ 6 ←

Much to Blaine's relief, Dacey kept their course
on the ridges. Despite the occasional detour downslope to avoid rock outcrops, or abrupt climbs to
another level of the ridge, most of the path was flat.
Much easier than walking on two different levels of
ground with the same length legs . . . It was where
anyone doing serious travel in the mountains would
go—and the first place anyone looking for them would
go.

No, she told herself, *the first place* anyone used
to the mountains *would go*.

Poplar and maple, oaks and hemlock, ridgelines
that swooped from one chain of hills to another, subtly
veering east or west without notice—soon the land-
marks became a blur in Blaine's mind. A thoroughly
disorienting blur. She realized suddenly that it was
one thing to know the few ridges behind your homeplace, and quite another to know the pattern of the
hills well enough to guide yourself through them.

Without Dacey, she doubted she could even find
her way home; she marveled that he'd found his way

to Shadow Hollers in the first place. There seemed
to be no settled land in between.

And she badly wanted to find her way home. She
wanted to *be* home. She wondered constantly if she'd
done the right thing by going with Dacey, and she
wondered how things had gone with her family, if they
were safe . . . if Rand had ever come to look for
her . . . if Lottie was crazy with worry, adding more
lines in her early-aged face. And she wondered just
how far they would walk.

The dogs didn't make it any easier. Excepting
Mage, who traveled right at Dacey's heel, the dogs
ranged back and forth over the slopes, arriving and
departing in great frenzies of excitement that never
failed to scatter her thoughts and make her own
weariness seem greater simply by contrast.

"Don't they ever get tired?" Blaine asked, finally,
during an afternoon that seemed especially long, on
a day that seemed even longer—and only a day after
Dacey's escape.

"Never seem to." Dacey's hand dropped, as it often
did, to rest on the crippled hound's head. Then, as
if he sensed the reason she'd said anything, he
stopped, eyeing the trees around them. "Good place
to take a breather, you think?"

"If you like." Blaine tried to sound indifferent. She
dropped to the ground while he was still shrugging
off his pack, and watched with concealed surprise
when he threw together a quick pile of easily found
wood, started a fire, and spitted Blue's latest catch—
a rabbit, though Blaine didn't know how the big dog
had ever gotten his jaws on one—over it. Like magic,
the hounds quit quartering the ridge and came to sit
in an attentive circle. Blue, Blaine noticed, sat beside
her, dividing his attention between the cooking meat
and making sidelong glances toward her.

She pretended not to see him.

"Dacey," she said, absently catching the end of a

braid to fiddle with, "who *are* those men? What did they want with you? I mean, why *you* instead of— well, Rand, maybe. After all, Rand lives right there. You were a stranger."

He glanced at her, and then returned his attention to the rabbit. "I reckon that's why it bothered them that I was there—I didn't belong. They figured it meant I'd come there lookin' for 'em . . . and they were right. I warned your daddy of 'em the very eve I took supper with you."

"But what did they *want*? That they kept askin' and you wouldn't answer?"

"I reckon I did answer, and they didn't believe." His knuckles went white around the spit he turned; it took him a moment too long to let go of it. "They wanted to know what magic it was I had that could track them down."

"And?"

"And?" Dacey repeated, amused—which, she thought, was better than what he'd been a moment before. Haunted. "I told them the truth. Ain't got no magic of my own—least, not aside from some spare seein's now and then—and I'm beginnin' to think you might have some of *them* for your own. No, I trap and hunt and trade for a living. But that wasn't what they wanted to hear."

"An' that . . . that dark thing?"

There was a subtle tension in his face, a tightening at the corners of his eyes. "Jimsonweed."

"Jimson?" Blaine said doubtfully. "I've seen men on jimson before. Boys, more likely, trying to show off, for all it makes 'em look stupid." She couldn't think of a single reference in her seer's book—long left behind in the barn—to using jimson, never mind in such a manner as she'd seen with Dacey. It was touchy stuff, and one time it might trigger visions and silliness; another it might just plain make you sick.

"Jimson and other things."

She wasn't sure she liked to see his features draw on that cold look, the one that made his jaw seem harder and his eyes more shadowed. And she realized he hadn't at all answered her first question. *Who are those men?* She nibbled the end of her braid and frowned faintly at him.

He appeared not to notice, though his expression lightened some. "And now I'll ask you something, Blaine Kendricks. I'll bet anythin' you knew of those strangers before you come on me there. You knew of 'em the very day I come to your farm. I seen it on your face."

"I run into 'em the day before." She felt herself go stubborn, ready for censure, ready to not-care like she'd had to not-care about all the other disapproval in her life, in order to bear it.

"An' while I was at your table, you said nary a thing about 'em—nor did your daddy, an' he would've, if he'd knowed of 'em. Would have been natural, me bein' strange, too. Blaine . . . why didn't you tell him what you seen?"

Blaine drew her knees up, pulling her skirts down over them as far as they would go. A sullen, defensive posture. "You wouldn't understand."

"But I'm askin'."

She searched for a way to explain, until her frustration welled up and finally came out in a rush of words. " 'Cause he don't know I go to the hills, that's why! 'Cause it's a waste of time for a girl to learn the wilds, when she might be learning proper women things, and 'cause he'd forbid 'em to me if he knowed. And I got to have the hills, Dacey, I just *got* to— they're the only thing that makes me feel better when someone compares me to Lenie, or tells me I got to marry some man who won't much like my sharp bones pokin' him in bed. How're *you* gonna understand that? You're a *man*—you don't get wore out with babies. You're on your own, you don't got someone makin' all *your* decisions for you. There warn't *no way* I was gonna tell Daddy about those men, not till I *knowed* they were trouble enough to be worth the losin' I'd do over it. Anyways, up till I found you with 'em, I just thought they was here to trade. I never got a close enough look at 'em to tell me otherwise."

Dacey raised his eyebrows. "Huh," he said, as Blue sidled closer to her, gazing from one to the other of them in concerned perplexity. "Who'd've guessed that was in there. 'Course, I shoulda knowed, after what you done for me."

She realized, rather dazed, that he wasn't judging her for what she'd done. He'd just wanted to know.

And she didn't quite know how to react to that— but Blue saved her the trouble of figuring it out. Some decision had finally occurred in his doggy mind, and he was at last close enough to act on it. Slowly, as he had the day before, he reached for the braid she'd been twisting, his mouth open in anticipation, his lips drawn gently back—

"Shoo!" she exclaimed, and Dacey laughed, and that was that. She had the distinct impression that he'd sidetracked her with that question, that there were things he knew that she ought. Things she ought to be afraid of. But for now, dinner was all that mattered.

Rand was supposed to be grateful that Nekfehr had given him this time off to plant Willum's grave. But he felt far from grateful. *Hostile* was closer to the mark, rife with mutiny and half-formed plots to kill the Taken man. And he wasn't the only one. Despite the warnings, there was talk, and the planning had already begun.

He tossed another shovelful of dirt down on the almost-covered casket—the diminutive, Willum-sized casket—and wiped the sweat of his upper lip, pausing to stare down at the homestead from the little

flat that held their family graveyard. Lenie, her hair
in an uncharacteristic braid and her skirts soiled and
torn, planted in the garden. His mommy struggled
with the steps to the porch, one of which had given
way under the weight of the many friends who had
come to pay condolences on Willum.

He should be down there, wielding that hammer.
And Willum and Sarie should be playing in the yard.
And Blaine—

He still didn't believe she, too, was dead. He
couldn't. He'd have found her, surely—

That didn't bear thinking about. Rand turned back
to his shoveling; he had only half a day for this chore.
Willum's casket disappeared under the steady rain of
dirt, and soon enough he was tamping down the small
mound of extra soil it had displaced. Unlike the early
stages of this task, his mind no longer churned with
defiance and hatred—instead, he gave it over to the
repetitive nature of the shoveling, going blank and
dull, closed to the world around him.

Which was why he didn't notice when the leader
and two of his fighters climbed the path to the graveyard, not until he was flanked. He started around to
find Nekfehr regarding him with an unnerving false
geniality.

"We'd like to ask you a few questions," the man
said.

"You come all the way up here to ask *me*?" Rand
frowned, and tried not to. Tried not to show what
he'd been thinking moments before, or the trickles
of unseemly fear that made him clench his hands
around the shovel. "Ole Bayard's the one that knows
the most about things, not me."

"He doesn't know your sister."

Rand narrowed his eyes. "What about her? She's
dead, didn't you say so?"

The man ignored the question. "Not many people
seem to know much about her, other than the fact

that she's skinny, somewhat impractical, and hasn't garnered any suitors. But they all seemed to think that you know her better than anyone."

"I reckon I do," Rand said, sounding stubborn even to his own ears. "I guess that means I'll have the best memories of her."

"Two days ago you didn't believe she was dead."

Two days of time to decide that for Blaine, being considered dead was better than being looked for. He muttered, "I've had time to wrestle with the notion some."

"Where would she go, if she was looking for a place to hide?"

Rand shook his head. "She don't know the hills." It was an easy lie, after all this time.

The man considered him, his dark eyes cold, but without hostility. "She knew them well enough to elude my men when she came for Dacey Childers."

Realization bloomed within Rand, double-headed realization. *She'd eluded them. She was alive.* And— "It's Dacey you want, ain't it? They're together somewheres, and you're looking for them." He jammed the shovel into the dirt and let it stand up on its own. "Why say she's dead? Why make us think we've lost two?"

"Because it suited my purpose," the man said. "And because it's only a matter of time. Your sister is a symbol of defiance, and we will not tolerate defiance. Dacey will live until my questions are satisfied. Blaine will not."

"And you think *I'm* gonna tell you where I think they are?"

"Yes. I do."

That was all the warning he got. A physical threat he would have reacted to, he would have ducked or blocked. But the man simply reached out and touched him, and—

Rand's body stood, stiff in shock, while the force

that plundered his mind ignored it. His awareness, his *soul*, ran in frantic circles, trying to evade the tendrils of oppression closing in on him.

Suddenly there was nowhere else to run. His body grunted, a reflection of his inner scream of terror, and *purple haze over sifted jumbling memories, Blaine heading into the hills, Blaine talking wild dreams, needing soothing in the night, Blaine's well-hidden interest in Dacey's words at supper, words about seers—*

The oppressive force stopped there, hesitating long enough to come to some decision, and reached for another line of memories from much earlier days. *The seers moved south after their victory, south to some place Rand had never been, but that he'd occasionally heard about. South, a week's travel through the mountains, over the huge obstacle of Sky Mountain and into its valleys—unless you risked the much shorter trip along the swift, rocky river—dangerous travel that got you to the same place much faster.*

Rand staggered, not ready to catch his body when it suddenly became his to control again, too dazed to do anything but blink and throw himself to the side, retching in reaction.

He was only vaguely cognizant of the two plainsmen stepping away from his side and out of the graveyard. But he was painfully, distinctly aware of the satisfaction in the leader's voice.

"Thank you, Rand. That will do just fine."

➤＜　　　➤＜　　　➤＜

The *annektehr* within Nekfehr reeled with the delightful intensity of Rand's fear and revulsion—*anne-nekfehr*—and in the reverberating feedback from Nekfehr himself, the very same feelings generated from within the *annektehr's* permanent vessel. With the plainsmen at Nekfehr's heels, the *annektehr* let his information flow to the Annekteh whole, sharing with all the linked, those who were embodied *annektehr* and those who were not—the *nekteh*, whose incorporeal existence lent the *annektehr* strength.

None of the *nekteh* would have been able to say which brought the whole of them more satisfaction: the information gained—*a means to find Dacey Childers, to find the fled seers*—or the feelings stolen from the Rand vessel. The *anne-nekfehr*.

Survival, the Annekteh demanded.

The *anne-nekfehr*, the Annekteh craved. Needed.

Would do anything to get.

>+<   >+<   >+<

After five days of walking and climbing—with one fully devoted to simply crossing Sky Mountain, even though Dacey knew where the gap was—Blaine found it almost impossible to get moving in the morning. Short rations, long days, constant worries. They didn't talk much; she never had the breath nor energy to voice the questions with which his habitual silence left her. By now she at least knew that they were headed for his homeplace, that she was going to visit the hills to which the seers had fled. And that they wouldn't stay long—just enough for Dacey to visit some folks, tend to some business, and give them each time to take a breath.

For he hardly looked any better than she felt.

The strain around his eyes didn't disappear with the bruises her potion had helped to heal so quickly, and she had the feeling he hardly slept at night. Still, she knew he stopped for more rests than he'd have given himself, and at evening, when she collapsed, he set up the night's camp with efficient moves that Blaine only slowly grew used to seeing in a man. She watched him with his dogs, and lived with his silent companionship, and wondered what it would be like to have such a life. Confident. Independent. Making his own decisions, not minding what people like Cadell said about them.

It ain't seemly to covet. And that's what she was doing—coveting not his possessions, but his very life.

But when Dacey finally led her to a small clearing and ushered her into the tiny but well-built cabin that occupied it, Blaine's only thoughts were grateful ones. She didn't protest when he gave her a gentle push toward the bed in the corner; she fell on top of it and just as quickly fell asleep.

When she woke, sunlight poured through the open cabin door and the thickly glazed window. She found herself alone, and covered with a brightly patterned quilt which hadn't been there when she'd fallen asleep. The next day? Had to be, to judge from the stiffness in her bones and the pang in her bladder. Slowly, she hitched herself up in the bed to look around.

Dacey's was an orderly little home, one room with an alcove of stored food goods and a small door in the floor that Dacey had made no attempt to hide with a rug. She decided, since she hadn't seen many outbuildings on the way in, that it must be his dairy— cool, stone and underground. Everything he owned seemed to be neatly tucked away on shelves or in the cedar chest at the foot of the bed, except some herbs that hung high off the ceiling. Despite its size, the cabin lacked the perpetually cluttered look of Blaine's home—the result of a busy family with five children merely going about life.

She wasn't sure whether she liked it more, or less— but it was certainly *different*.

Dacey's recent absence showed in the dust and cobwebs—mostly occupied—decorating the corners and floor. She pushed off the quilt, grateful to see that the cookstove was going and had warmed the cabin despite the half-open door. Dacey was nowhere in sight, but Blue lay across the threshold, and he greeted her with a couple of hearty tail slaps. She ignored him, stepping over him to run to the outhouse and back, suddenly aware that she was starving. With some relief, she found tea simmering on the stove, and some precious sugar to put in it. A handful of dried turkey strips sat on the windowsill beside the stove, and she gnawed off a bite to soften in her mouth. And then, unable just to sit there and eat, not interested in wandering around to look for Dacey, she found a broom behind the door and put herself to work.

Blue watched her with great interest and an oft-thumping tail, making her sweep around him—for she couldn't bring herself to broom him when he aimed mournful eyes at her. When she finished with the broom she usurped a rag to clean the lamp chimney—and spent some time examining the lamp itself, a coal-oil lamp with a strange, perforated deflector under the wick sleeve, like none she'd ever seen before. Finally, she found a pan and cloth and went outside to draw water so she could clean the two thick-glassed windows.

She was admiring those windows when he came back, staring at the distortion in the glass and wondering how he got such a treasure up into the hills. She knew two families that had paid for glass windows, but her family did with open shutters in the summer and well-greased rawhides in the winter—which weren't clear but at least let in some light.

Dacey cleared his throat to let her know he was standing in the door and she backed away from the window to look at him. He was a sight she had grown used to, although the fading bruises were still changing the landscape of his face.

"I thank you for cleanin' the place up," he said. "It's been neglected some lately, I guess."

"It was plenty neat," Blaine told him. "I just didn't want to be sittin' around." *I want to be back home.* But she didn't say so; she'd said it often enough on the journey, and he well knew it. Instead she asked the questions their flight and breathless climbing had not left time for, fiddling with her skirts a moment to work up the nerve. "Dacey, you ain't once really told me what's happenin'. I been real patient, but I gotta know who those folks were, and what they want with us—us and some sassafras groves they consider we know about."

"Ah, you heard that, did you?" Dacey responded, setting a string of traps down inside the door. Blue gave them a perfunctory sniff and wandered outside into the sunshine, greeting Mage as he went by. Dacey left the door ajar—for the dogs, Blaine figured—and took the only chair in the cabin as Blaine backed up to the bed and sat down.

"Yes, I heard that," she said. "You know what's goin' on, Dacey—you have, right from the start. Whatever it is, brought you all the way up to Shadow Hollers. I think it's 'bout time you just spit it out."

"Ain't you full of questions." He gave her a crooked little smile, full of his wry nature.

"Always have been. Since you've done took me from my home, you might as well get used to it."

"What if you don't get no answers?"

"I reckon you'll get tired of hearing the questions after a while."

He studied her a moment, the smile gone. "And what iff'n you don't like what I got to tell you?"

She shrugged, feeling herself on the edge of victory. "I don't guess I can hold it agin you, can I?"

His gaze went inward then, and his foot twitched a couple times—a tense motion Blaine was certain he hadn't meant to do. "There's some I know about this, an' there's some I don't. Those men come from the north, and they want what they've always wanted:

more. Territory. Slaves. Things of magic, like these hills got. They're looking for the sassafras special, for the way it soaks up the hill magic."

She blinked at him.

"You knew that, didn't you? You and your sassafras potions?"

Numbly, she shook her head. "I guess things more'n I *know* 'em. I got this book . . . but it's just bits and pieces." Numb, because she wasn't thinking about sassafras, or lumber of any sort, or even potions. *They come from the north, and they want—*

"What hill magic?" she blurted—anything to keep from thinking—

"It's there," Dacey said gently, as though not to scare her thoughts from the path they were taking. "It's coming back. They know that. They needed to act before folks learn how to use it again. Before they learn to fight back."

"What makes you think we ain't no good at lookin' out for ourselves *now*?"

He raised an eyebrow into the shaggy bangs of his dark ash-blond hair. "You know the tales, Blaine. You'll know all the answers, if you'll only think on it."

No, she didn't. She didn't *want* to, even though she suddenly realized she had known for days, had hidden it in exhaustion and worry and annoyance at the hounds. Men from the north, men who knew magic. Men who intended to enslave her people. *Like before.* Dacey, seer's blood come north. And the sky she'd seen that one day, the one he'd so easily called a Taker's sky when he sat down to sup with them. "Spirits," she whispered. "It's them, come back."

Brief satisfaction flashed in his eye. "Last time, they came a-blazin' down from the north, figuring nothing could stand 'em off—but when we're prepared in these mountains, there ain't nothing can get in. This time they're sneakin' in quiet as they can, and they'll win iff'n we don't get to fighting."

Blaine sat back a little and let the air run out of her body. Five generations earlier, at Annekteh Ridge, they'd had seers to point out the dangers—the Taken.

There were no seers in Shadow Hollers, now.

"Everyone thinks they were killed at Annekteh Ridge," she said, her voice still hardly more than a whisper.

"Killin' the Taken don't do nothin' but kill parts of the Annekteh," Dacey said. "Not even that, if the *annektehr* can leave out of the Taken before the Taken dies, and return to bein' with the Annekteh whole." He ran a hand across the back of his neck, and that weary look was back. "But not many believed that. They wanted to think the Annekteh were kilt, and it was fussin' over that that drove my family south. That's why you've no seers up your way."

"No," she said, in borderline belligerence, "we've no seers. We haven't, for a long time. We've been gettin' along, though."

"For some time." Dacey tipped his chair back so the front legs lifted off the ground. "But I seen the signs so I come on back, hopin' I could help."

"I thought you said you didn't have any magic!"

"I did," Dacey said, deceptively mild. "Which means I don't. No one here does. The magic's not strong like in your parts. My grandmother had the eye, but it weren't common no more even then. Any longer, there ain't anyone to do real seer things, like callin' up visions a-purpose, readin' things in the hills and the sky, having the knack and the learnin' to work potions and charms and protections. I wish I *were* a seer, and could tell which of those men at the camp had been Taken, but all my grandmother left me was her hounds, and that were a long time ago. I got seein's now and then, like I told you before."

Something in Blaine didn't want to know, and she was surprised when she asked it anyway. "Seein's?"

"Dreamlike things," he said. "Come night and day, don't matter which."

"I got dreams," she whispered.

"Thought you might." His smile held sympathy. "The magic's coming back to Shadow Hollers, like Gran said it would. That's what drew the Takers. You hearken that your brother didn't see the Taker's sky like you did? It comes to some people different than others. That's why only some of our folks was seers in the first place." He tipped the chair upright, ending what was for him an abnormally long conversation. "If you've got seein's, you'll learn to sort 'em out from plain old dreams soon enough."

But Blaine wasn't ready to end this discussion, not yet. Not while she had him actually *talking*. She scooted forward on the bed, and Blue took it for invitation, sticking his heavy-boned head in her lap.

"Then what're we gonna do?" She gave the dog a halfhearted shove and twitched her braid back behind her shoulder, out of his reach.

"We-ell," Dacey said, rubbing his stubbly whiskered chin, "I'm goin' to have me a shave, handle a few chores around here. Then I've got to take a trip into town. My kin don't have no more magic, but they still got lore. Might be I can learn something of use. Got to warn them, in any case, though the Annekteh ain't got no call to come this way, not yet. Then we'll circle back up to your home and get you back to your folks. And I 'spect soon after that, you all will have another Annekteh Ridge for your winter stories."

Blaine shuddered. One Annekteh Ridge, kept far in the past, had definitely been enough for her.

Willum's soft crying—
Blaine jerked up straight, cocking her head to the breeze.

Nothing. Since her talk with Dacey the day before, she'd been hearing—

Nothing.

One of the dogs, likely, making some soft protest about its perpetually hungry belly.

Blaine sighed and settled back into place on the moss and lichen-covered rock above Dacey's covered spring, where she watched him soften the hides he'd had tanning while he was away. She'd seen fox, wildcat, beaver and wolf in the pile of pelts before him, and she'd already noticed, in the little shed behind the house, a stack of folded deerhide.

It seemed that Dacey and his dogs were very good at making a living for each other.

She hoped he was as good at dealing with the Annekteh.

Blaine sighed again and shifted her bony bottom against the rock, knowing she ought to offer her help . . . but pulling and stretching the dampened hides didn't much appeal to her. Besides, to judge from the sweat standing out on Dacey's upper lip, she wouldn't have the strength to do much good. Not the strength she saw in his shoulders, bare of his shirt in the sunshine. She recalled their run together, the dash from the Takers, and suddenly remembered the feel of clutching his arms, when they'd only been trying to keep one another going.

Spirits. That was a thought worthy of Lenie. She blushed good and hard, and concentrated on other thoughts. More familiar ones . . . the way she felt out of place and useless. The worry that plagued her every thought, the wondering about—

Willum's faint cry . . .

Dacey paused in his work, looking down at Mage, grinning a little at the dog's sprawl-legged position.

How could he look so calm? So normal? How *dare* he?

Hot breath gusted down her neck.

Blaine squeaked, wrenching around so fast she almost lost her balance and fell off the rock.

Blue. Grinning, drooly Blue.

She scowled at him and pointedly turned around, refusing him a greeting. As if she wanted to encourage him! The other hounds surged down the hill behind her and split to flow around the blue ticked dog, yapping breathless little greetings to Dacey. They quickly settled—if only after Whimsy stepped on Mage and provoked his quick snap of ire—flopping to the ground, happy and panting, their tongues looking twice as long as their heads.

Blue lay down and slowly inched up beside Blaine, ignoring the fact that half his substantial body wouldn't fit on the rock; he ended up draped over the side of the rock with two legs standing and two couchant. Blaine snorted at him and crossed her arms.

"One thing about a hound," Dacey said, grinning at Blue, "they don't spend too much time dotin' on you—but when they decide it's time for a little lovin', there ain't nothing you can say about it."

"I've noticed," Blaine said dryly. To keep the dog from pushing his big slobbery mouth into her lap, she patted him. He lowered his head with a contented *whfff*, and was soon slumbering in his improbable position.

Impatience stirred anew. It was too homey, this little scene of Dacey working on furs and his dogs watching him. Too *normal*. Here she was, sitting on a rock in the cool spring sunshine, and her family was . . . what? Facing down Annekteh?

She needed to be doing something, *anything*. "Got any greens planted around here, or ought I to find your creek and pick 'em wild?"

Dacey held a raccoon pelt up for inspection. "Creek's your best bet, but I got a patch. If it warn't more weeds than mustards this year, you'd near be able to see it from there. Blue, go check the garden."

"Don't tell me you've got him trained to pick your supper," Blaine said, unable to keep the smart tone from her voice as the dog gave a rumbly groan and rose. "An' do the other dogs plant it?"

Dacey laughed outright, a noise which took Blaine by surprise. Somehow she'd assumed that this taciturn man just . . . didn't.

"That makes a pretty picture in my mind," Dacey said. "But no, I done the planting, and do the picking, too. But I do have him check for rabbits and groundhogs of the evening—he likes that. Follow him an' you'll find the garden."

Blue seemed pleased to find Blaine behind him, and waited, his tail slowly wagging, while she ducked inside to get a bucket. Then he led her down a faint path through last year's tall, dried sweet goldstalks, until they came to a small square garden patch filled with overgrown greens and weeds. Blaine stared skeptically at it.

It took some scrutiny, but she finally spotted some lamb's quarters and pokeweed along the outer edges of the garden, both still young and tender, the poke not yet purple with its poison. She could mix them along with the mustard greens and some early leeks, and then bread-fry the poke for poke sallet. She drifted down to the creek—Dacey's mountains were enough like hers that she found it where she expected it—and found both jewelweed shoots and cowslip— enough greens to do them for a day of meals, and she'd be careful to cook that cowslip through. The hound, she noticed, had moved on to his own business and was searching the garden rows for the scent of furry interlopers.

The work didn't last half long enough to keep her busy, or take near enough concentration to keep her from fretting. But at least when she returned to the cabin she had the chore of washing and cutting the greens—and it *was* nice finally to add some effort of her own to this venture. She poked around the cabin and found some lard, corn and wheat flour, and an

egg beside the sink basin. Now where had he found
an egg? Were there chickens around here somewhere,
too?

Well, the hounds probably laid the eggs. They did
everything else.

Blaine put the pone together and set it aside to
wait on cooking until Dacey came in. It was late
afternoon, and they'd not had a midday meal, so
surely he'd look for something to eat soon. And it was
time to get the woodstove going anyway, to keep off
the chill of the early spring night.

When the fire was started and steady enough not
to need constant adjustment of the draft, Blaine
retired to the bed, curling up around herself to stare
out the window. A reminder she wasn't at home, that
window was.

Well, she'd be back home soon enough. Dacey had
said they were going into town, and then the next day
they would start back. She didn't know what they'd
find when they got there, but he had so much quiet
purpose about the whole thing that, for now, she was
inclined to trust his unspoken plans. For now. And
tomorrow—well, seeing a new place, a new town—
her first real *town*—was a lure to which she couldn't
help but respond.

The thick, wavy glass showed her Dacey's distorted
figure, and she uncurled from the bed. Maybe he'd
tell her a little about the town over their meal. Maybe
he'd even tell her a little about his family. Anything
to keep her mind busy.

Anything.

>←   >←   >←

Nekfehr's *annektehr* could feel the man
tremble inside, wrenching himself, if only
momentarily, far enough apart from the
Taker to do so. These hill folk might not
know what was coming next, but Nekfehr
did.

They thought to rebel. Of course they did. Just as Nekfehr's home village—an insignificant, failing little Breeder village—had once thought to rebel, shortly after Nekfehr himself was taken from them.

If the Annekteh had realized that the woman belonged to one of their most useful vessels, they might not have used her as an example for the others.

But oh, his anguish had tasted fine, when he'd come across her body. And his despair, the torment when the *annektehr* had released him just enough to hold her, but not enough to take his own life as he so badly desired—for anything, *anything*, was preferable to serving the bastard Annekteh.

So thought Nekfehr, the Annekteh's finest.

>← >← >←

Rand stared warily at the men inside the hall, standing out in the meeting hall yard in the early evening drizzle, along with everyone else from the Hollers. So much for their suppers. Most of the children sat together, trading bits of their hastily wrapped meals. In front of the barn, two small, sturdy, hollow-bred horses snatched at wet grass, their flanks and shoulders steaming; they'd run from the head of one hollow to another, spreading the news of this meeting and then galloping on to let the word skip down the hollow from homestead to homestead.

The meeting hall itself was filled with the plainsmen; most of them were at their own evening meal, and the others were simply keeping dry. Only the leader and two other men, Annekteh-Took both, were actually out in the yard with the locals. Rand had had no personal contact with these Taken, but he'd learned to identify them after a few moments of careful study. They often acted just as anyone else, but inevitably there came an odd moment when their expressions went vague, or their movements were awkward. For the most part, the Annekteh stayed with the same small group of men. Rand knew who they were, and so did everyone else.

But he had no idea what the gathering was about. He hadn't heard of any incidents besides the one the day before, when a pair of Shadow Hollers men had managed not only to fell a tree at just the right wrong angle, but then to yell their warnings just a tad too late to save one of their overseers from a broken arm and who knows how many broken ribs. As far as Rand knew, their red-faced apologies and proclamations of distress had convinced the guards it had been an accident. At least, there had been no interrogations, not like the one he'd been through by Willum's grave.

Rand realized that he was smiling—and that he was being watched. The chill that washed over him might have been the combination of rain on top of a long sweaty day . . . or maybe not. In any case, he was not smiling any longer.

Someone drifted up behind him; Rand barely turned his head to identify Nathan, a young man from the western edge of the Shadow Hollers territory. Lenie had turned his eye at one of the first of their enforced gatherings, and now Nathan had managed to partner himself with Rand in the timbering.

"Heard something today," Nathan said, in the quiet but natural tones they'd all taken to using when they didn't want to be either overheard or suspected.

Rand merely grunted in reply, his gaze on the one called Nekfehr; the man seemed distracted by something within the hall, and was naturally unconcerned by either the growing darkness or the continuing rain in which his slave labor stood.

"He ain't like the others," Nathan said; of course he was talking about the leader. "They say he's mad."

Rand glanced quickly back at Nathan, then at the leader, and another hard look at Nathan. *Mad Annekteh? Or mad beneath the annektehr within?* But he fought to keep his curiosity from his face.

"Our guards was talkin' about it today. When I was gettin' water, 'member—they was all takin' a break. The fellow even gives *them* the creeps, from the sound of it."

"Why would he be madder'n any of the rest of 'em?" Or a better question—*why weren't they* all *mad* . . . Rand shuddered, thinking again of the moments by Willum's grave.

Nathan's voice lowered even further. "He weren't ever supposed to be Took. They got Breeder villages—they sounded right scornful of 'em, though. Them inside are used for Breedin', left alone otherwise. But Nekfehr, they Took anyway, once they found him. And when the village rose up agin it, the Takers done *had him kill his family.*" He let the words settle, heavier than the rain, not as easily shed.

"*Spirits*," Rand said, eyeing the man, who had just made an imperious gesture to someone inside the hall. "Ain't no little wonder he comes across so spooky."

"Even the other Taken are some scairt of him, I think," Nathan said, then abruptly shut up as Nekfehr's attention turned on the group.

"We have something to discuss," the man said. He moved out of the doorway with little regard for the rain that fell on his fine white linen shirt. From behind him, one of his two attendants discreetly settled a black cloak on his shoulders. That, too, seemed to go unnoticed. "I'm surprised this conversation is necessary, after the little demonstration I gave when we first arrived."

Rand stiffened; he couldn't help it. When the leader looked his way, he aimed his glare at the ground, but he didn't try to school his face into bland respect. Willum, a *little demonstration.*

"My men seem to be having more accidents than usual. A sprain here, a stumble there, wayward falling trees . . . it adds up to something I don't like. For instance, there seem to be an unusual number of incidents with large animal snares."

They'd almost lost a man the day before, to a bear trap. Pity; it had been so close. Pity, too, it had come on top of the tree-felling, for that pointed to plotting amongst them.

But the Annekteh would find no collusion in the hollows. There was none. They knew better—it only took catching one, *Taking* one, to get the lot of them in trouble. So there was merely an unspoken, gritty determination to undermine these invaders. So far they'd done a surprising amount of damage. Minor damage, of course, but even the little things began to add up.

"Do you really want us to start random checks on you people?" the leader asked, inserting true surprise into his voice. Sometimes, Rand reflected, he sounded almost human.

On the other side of the gathering, a thin, under-sized youth with full-sized ears flashed a look of panic. He was flanked by two others of about the same age, Blaine's age. One was a strapping boy, larger in height and girth than Rand himself; the other was unremarkable, aside from a certain expression of adult determination, and had some of the awkwardness of a boy not yet come into full growth. They exchanged scowls; the larger boy nudged their skittish companion, an understated but urgent gesture.

"Ah, I see someone has something to say." There was that odd moment of hesitation, while the leader seemed to be listening to something none of the others could hear. "Estus, is it?"

The smaller boy seemed to steel himself. His voice was thin. "Yessir."

"Do you know something about the snares and

traps? Perhaps why they seem to be in such annoying locations? Perhaps, even, who is doing it?"

"I—" the boy said, and then quickly shook his head, his face reddening.

The leader said nothing, but crooked his finger in a distinct command for the boy to approach. It was the kind of gesture meant to shame, and in the damp twilight, the blush of the boy's face crept down his neck, deepening.

"It was mine." The middle-sized boy grabbed Estus' upper arm to keep him in place, though Estus had shown no sign of stepping away from his friends. "Can't help it none if your men done picked animal trails to patrol on. You sent us out to hunt, and by the spirits, huntin's what we're doin'." He tried to hold the leader's gaze, but couldn't. In the end, he joined his smaller friend in staring at the ground. But his expression was still more defiance than fear.

"I see," the leader said.

"Reckon you all done stumbled into some of my snares, too," the big youth said. "We got an unlikely number of big critters comin' around this spring. Got to keep 'em cleared out or they'll eat up all our game."

From the back of the crowd, another young voice piped up. "I been settin' some 'long my ridge, too—had some few sprung and nothin' but boot prints around." The anonymous confession prompted a number of murmured declarations; Rand hid a smile. No doubt they were all true, for the boys knew there was nothing to gain, and everything to lose, by lying. No doubt they'd talked amongst themselves of the large number of big predators in the area, and then carefully, individually, laid their traps along the obvious human trails. Any one of them might get caught, but it could never be traced to organized mutiny.

The leader seemed to realize as much. His features

were mostly shadowed by the darkness, but enough light from the hall washed over his face to show the tight set of his mouth. "Your . . . *carelessness* has wasted much time. There will be no more timbering accidents. There will be no more trapping accidents." He looked at Estus' friend, the boy who'd confessed to setting the bear trap; with sudden, smooth strides he was in front of the boy, and had taken his chin with gloved fingers. The boy had very little time for the fear that flashed across his face; his eyes rolled up, and his body trembled with little jerks that Rand thought were pain-induced. Some kind of Taker pain. Nekfehr smiled, pleasuring in the boy's reaction, and Rand was sure of it.

After a long, breathless moment, the leader removed his grip with the kind of disdain that Rand's daddy used to toss dead rats out of the barn. The boy would have fallen had not his strapping friend caught and easily held him.

With that same disdain in his eyes, the leader looked around the assembly with quiet menace. "Do I make myself clear?"

He did. There was nodding; there were murmurs of assent; there were shuffled feet. In the arms of his comrade, the dazed boy blinked and stood on his own, pale in the waning light.

The men and women of Shadow Hollers, enslaved to the Annekteh, dispersed without conversation, apparently cowed. But Rand knew they were not. They had made the enemy blink and take notice.

It was a start.

→ 7 ←

*The cold earth shoved against her from below,
bruising her hips and knees and elbows; hard wood,
edged and splintered, jammed down on her from
above. Crushing her, pressing against her spine, com-
pressing her chest . . . while something came for her.
Something looked for her, saw her, reached out to
her—*

*She squirmed, unable to break free, unable to
breathe . . . she sobbed in fear, tearing at the earth
with her fingers, not heeding the pain of bleeding
fingers, knowing only that it saw her—*

*And then strong arms gathered her up and held
and soothed her. Strong arms and a gentle touch. Safe
arms.*

Dacey watched Whimsy snuffling mouse scent
among last year's dried grasses at the side of the cabin,
and smiled at her enthusiasm. She snorted loudly to
clear her nose and the noise brought her brother
Chase to join the investigation.

He enjoyed the way they delighted in such small

103

things. Watching them had passed many a quiet afternoon.

But not today, even though the morning had dawned quiet and clear, still too cold for anything but a few spring peepers and some early birds. Dacey bent to pull on his soft-soled boot, pushing his back against the door frame. There was no time for such things today, if he was going to make it to town and back before nightfall, and he didn't want to leave Blaine alone after dark—especially after the fuss she'd raised when he made it clear she wasn't coming with him.

Besides, he'd been wakened by her nightmares enough to know how regularly they happened. Nothing too dramatic, just small whimpers of distress that brought Blue to her side—until last night, when he himself had taken her up and soothed her back to normal sleep.

Seein's or plain old nightmares, Dacey was unwilling to have her face them alone.

He straightened, wiggling his toes to settle the boot, but his attention was on Blaine. To the side of his cabin, right above the plank-sheltered spring, there was a big old rock, and she had taken to it immediately. She sat there now, her knees drawn up to her chin, coltishly long legs protruding from the bottom of her skirts and her dangling braids brushing the rock behind her. She had fire, Blaine did—maybe too much of it. She'd been scared some by their conversation about the Annekteh, but not scared enough. Not half scared enough.

Maybe he should tell her the rest of it, the things he knew through his seeings—the moments that possessed him, awake or asleep—although not, he suddenly realized, so often as before, now that he had finally acted on them. Seeings that he no longer dared to doubt—*never again*—had told him what history had lost—or perhaps never known. The extent of Annekteh

delight in the things a body could do—both *for* and
to one another. Annekteh disregard for how easy it
was to use up a body, how they tended simply to use
folks up and toss them aside to commandeer another.
Annekteh preoccupation with exploring the extremes
of human emotions.

A haunting flash of ice-crystal fear hit him then,
unbidden memory of just what the Annekteh could
do to a man. What they had done to him. How they
had come back to him in his fear and clustered
around him, touching him, watching him, envious of
his feelings . . . His hand tightened to white knuckles at the door frame; he closed his eyes and set his
jaw. *No. They're just memories.* If he let the Annekteh
have such power over him here and now, then they
had already won, and he couldn't allow that.

But neither could he help the shudder that passed
through his body, the violence of revulsion and
reaction washing through him. When he opened his
eyes to the morning, it seemed to have lost some of
its clean-edged purity.

His gaze fell on Blaine again, staring down the
hollow and blithely unaware of his inner torment.
Blue sat up the hill a piece from her, loyally joining her vigil even if he didn't understand what it was
all about. Even as he watched, the hound deliberately leaned forward, his mouth barely open, reaching for the braid that hung down Blaine's back. Dacey
shifted, deliberately; the hound's gaze slid back to him
and he froze, reconsidering, finally settling back into
place with resignation.

Blaine turned and saw Dacey then, and stood in
a motion that took him by surprise with its grace. For
an instant he saw what she was growing into, something of elusive elegance that these hills seldom
nourished. And then she was all legs and bony arms
again, staring awkwardly down at him.

"Can't see the harm in letting me come along," she

said, more frustration in her voice than challenge. "It'll be a far piece along in my life before I ever come this way again. Or come *any* way again, I reckon."

That was probably true. And it would be hurtful to tell her the truth, that he had a lot to do and little time to do it in. She was safe here, and in a few days, she'd be back to pushing herself, trying to keep up with him as they returned to Shadow Hollers. The rest would do her good.

"There's plenty of fixin's in the cabin," he said by way of answer, "and a goodly slab of ham hangin' in the dairy. Make sure you don't go hungry." For she was as apt to pick at her meals as eat them right down, and he thought she'd already lost weight, pounds she couldn't afford to do without.

She sat again, cross-legged, resting her chin on her fist. There was a stubborn, unhappy look to her light blue eyes, but she seemed resigned enough. Blue looked from one to the other of them and settled back on his haunches, trying to decide whether Blaine was staying on the rock or not.

"Blaine," Dacey said, riding the edge of exasperation, "I got things to do." He stopped short of saying she'd only be in the way, and so ended up saying nothing more at all. Nothing except, "I'll be back before dark."

She looked away and he thought maybe she'd understood those unspoken words after all. She reached out to pet Blue—not something she'd do if she was thinking about it—and shrugged, her expression full of sulk and hurt.

She was all up front with what she felt, anyway—there was no mistaking her feelings, nor her tenacity. Not like him at her age—everything hidden, if felt just as strongly—or now, for that matter. Although she *was* about at the age when people stopped taking his quiet nature for lack of fire, back when he'd lost his mother to a chance encounter with a drunken riverman. Back when he'd done something about it.

Dacey had the troubling certainty that Blaine was about to have her coming of age, too.

He leaned down to snag his backpack. Whimsy and her brother stopped their snuffling long enough to give him an inquisitive look, and he murmured, "Stay home," at them. They immediately dismissed him, absorbed by their important task of hunting those dangerous mice. Dacey smiled and started off, Mage at his heels. A last glance at Blaine showed her staring back down the hollow. Ignoring him. He felt a smile on his lips for that, too, though not one she'd ever see.

He took the long way into town. It was Trade Day, unless he'd misreckoned, and by noon he had a good chance of finding his uncles along the river front. On Trade Day, clunky steamers from deeper south came and offered their goods, but mostly it was trade between locals. A fresh spring morning like this one would bring out anyone who could make it.

Dacey would be there, if later than most. The long way would take him to his Aunt Pippy, who was too wracked with joint ills to make it as far as the market. She was his oldest living relative, a woman who still remembered the last of the Annekteh Ridge seers. If any of his kin had help to give him, she'd be the one. His trip on into town would be as much to warn the others as to gather information from them.

Pippy's house perched on a rocky little point just above the creek, a spot with sparse foliage over thin soil. She sat on the porch, bundled against the cool air and painstakingly darning a sock with her mis-shapen hands. It was easy for her to see him coming.

"Where have you been, child?" she asked, laying the sock aside. "Your cousin Rosabel went to see about getting some deer leather from you, and you weren't nowhere to be found."

"Been up north." Dacey climbed the stairs to the high-set porch, spotting one he'd like to fix. Aunt Pippy couldn't take chances for a fall, not with her bones.

Astonishment wrinkled her papery brow. "Whatever for? Hasn't been none of us found a need to go that way since we left it!"

"*I* had a need," he said simply. He sat in the rocker on the other side of the porch from her, and stared out over the creek a moment.

Pippy gave a dry little laugh. "You always did say more with those quiet spells than anyone else with a sack full of words. You done got something big on your mind, Dacey, and now come to me with it—so you might as well spit it out."

He couldn't quite do that. Such a big thing, and the words to say it seemed so small. He finally settled on, "I need your Annekteh lore."

She narrowed her eyes at him until they almost disappeared in the surrounding wrinkles. "You got a passel of *needs*, it seems to me. And I don't like the sound of none of them."

"Ain't nothing to like." Reluctantly, he came to it. "I been north, and I found the Annekteh there. I got to go back and do something about it."

"My, my, my," she said, and set her chair to rocking. After a moment, and with some effort, she pushed herself out of it and hobbled into her house. When she came out again, it was with a small pouch of thin, finely tanned leather. She pressed it into his palm. "I ain't got much for you, son. Our folk may not have believed the Annekteh was dead, but they never wanted to deal with them again, neither, and they'd lost most of their writings just like everyone else. So they came down here and tried to forget what they knowed. Your granny was the last of them that had any power a-tall. This was hers."

Dacey loosened the pouch tie and tipped the bag

so light would spill into it, but was not quite able to identify the dim, lumpy objects within.

"With those you can make a warding," Pippy told him.

Suddenly he knew what they were, remembered hearing his granny talk of them, her words never anything but grim. His voice was the same. "I know how to use them."

"Nothing else I can tell you, 'cept they die like any creature, iff'n you put an arrow or blade in the right place. Not that killin' the Taken is easy. Sometimes I think that's half the reason our folk came this way— so's they wouldn't have to look in the eyes of the survivors, the ones the seers made to kill their own." Pippy lowered herself back into her chair and looked at him, her gaze more piercing than it had been before. "What sent you north, Dacey?"

Not many would understand. But not many understood *him* as well as Pippy did. "Followed my dreams, Auntie."

"Figured. That seer's blood do find a way to get out, even if it ain't proper magic. Son, you got to learn—you can't fix all the ailments of the world. Better a few sleepless nights than gettin' yourself hurt again, or even killed."

The skin around his eyes got tight, the way it always did at the thought of his seeings, and of the first time he'd had them. The first time he'd ignored them. "I put the seein's aside once, and my mommy died for it. I ain't never going to live with that again."

She shook her head, looked away, sighed. "No, son. I know you ain't. But . . . keep yourself safe, d'ye hear? It'd break an old woman's heart to hear somethin'd happened to you."

He tucked the pouch in an inside jacket pocket and stood, leaning over to kiss her soft, wrinkled cheek. "Wouldn't do no good for my day, either," he said. "I'll let you know when I get back."

He left her yard with long strides, running away from the hint of tear he'd seen in her eyes. Running, because they both knew there was little assurance that he would return from chasing down *this* set of seeings.

Blaine used half the morning sulking, and then got tired of it. She spent some time in Dacey's garden, and when noontime came, she suddenly realized she was good and hungry. The thought of Dacey's ham was enough to set her mouth to watering, and she abandoned the hoe—she'd been trying to loosen the soil enough for at least a small patch of peas—and headed uphill for the cabin, carrying the small bucket of lamb's quarters she'd picked. Blue trailed along beside her, of course. Maidie sunned herself on the big rock, and Chase and Whimsy were nowhere to be seen.

Good. She wouldn't have to contend with their begging.

She washed her hands in the tin basin set outside the door and spent a few minutes tending the braids she'd ignored that morning, replaiting them, pulling the cloth strip from her pocket that she often used to bind them together at her back and keep them from flopping into her work. "All right, then," she said to Blue. "Time to see about that ham. And I ain't promising you none, so you mought as well not roll them eyes at me when I bring it up."

The dairy entrance was set to the side of the cabin opposite the stove, toward the front and almost at the foot of the bed. She hauled the heavy door up and peered down into the darkness. Hmm. She definitely needed a candle—she wasn't going to mess with his fancy lamp, not and chance breaking it. Dacey kept candles on a ledge over the window, hidden away from the mice in a tin box. The stove still had enough coal from the night's fire to light it and, clutching the

thick, cool column of wax, Blaine backed down the
ladder into the dairy while Blue hung around the
entrance and whined questions at her.

When she turned away from the ladder to face the
dairy, she couldn't help but be amazed at its size.
Nearly a third of the house, dug out and shored up,
it was lined with shelves on three sides. And the
shelves were full, with heavily wrapped cheeses and
straw-covered piles of last year's produce and rows
of canned goods. Dacey was nothing, she decided,
if not thorough. Or . . . perhaps *prepared* was a better
word.

Prepared definitely fit him, the way nothing seemed
to take him aback for long. If she'd been given that
Annekteh pill of fear, she'd have taken a week to stop
trembling, but not Dacey. Sure, he'd had that strange
reaction, and he'd been extra quiet the first few days
they'd walked, but it soon gave way to what she now
recognized as his regular kind of quiet.

A hot spatter of wax on her hand made her jump,
more startled than hurt. Spirits, but a dark, spider-
full dairy wasn't the place to get lost in thought! She
reached for the ham—hanging right out in the open
where Dacey had said—but hesitated when she heard
Maidie's angry bark. Above her, Blue's head swung
away from the dairy opening; he growled.

What? she thought, and then realization crowded
in on top of it—those were not *what* noises, they were
who noises. *Too soon for Dacey to be back*, not that
the dogs would bark at him anyway. She climbed the
ladder, quick and unmindful of the further spatter of
wax on her skin. At the top, she found Blue standing in the doorway, growling in an uncertain manner. Not yet sure if it was something to be upset
about, she decided.

But how many strangers came to this cabin? How
many people would the dogs classify as out-and-out
intruders? She was careful as she peered out the door,

for it seemed to her that they must be as rare to Dacey as they were to the Kendricks.

And then she saw him, and dropped the candle. Black leather pants, boots with padded shins—*How'd they find us?* Her heart beating a runaway course, Blaine clutched at the rough log wall and slid to her knees anyway. She was cornered here. There was no way to get out without being seen. She was quick and agile, but . . .

The open dairy beckoned her, and frightened her. To be trapped down there while he moved in . . . a sob escaped her throat, an echo of the very noise she'd made last night during the nightmare that now came flooding back to her. *Caught in the dark, cowering from the hand that reached for her—*

She broke, scrambling for the dairy, snagging her skirts on the ladder and ignoring the rip of sturdy material. Except—*the candle!* Halfway down she reversed course and reemerged, stretching for the warm-wicked object that would surely give her away. This time she remembered the dairy door, too.

It was barely closed when she heard Blue whine above her.

"Blue, no!" she hissed, but knew it was no good. *Something came for her*—but she'd been alone in that nightmare. *Not this time.* Out she popped again, to take hold of Blue's collar and jerk him forward with such sudden determination that he tumbled into the dairy with time for little more than a muffled yelp. Then down came the door and darkness closed in on them.

Blue whined again while Blaine huddled at the bottom of the ladder and stared anxiously at a door she could no longer see. In the darkness, he bumped up against her and sought out her hand. "Shhh," she said, her voice squeaking slightly, "hush yourself or you'll have us *kilt.*"

He reached the door, not bothering to knock, just

opening it slowly and walking right in. Boot heels hit the floor above her and stopped. He was looking around. Seeing no one. Looking, she knew, at the hinged door in the floor. Did they have dairies in the plains? Would he think to look down here?

Suddenly she knew she couldn't take the chance. She'd gone to ground like a muskrat to water, and she'd have to keep going. She had to find the deepest, darkest corner of this place.

The unshelved wall. It wasn't quite perpendicular—in her memory, it looked like Dacey hadn't completely finished digging there. Blaine groped along the shelf beside the ladder, cringing at the noise from the potato she knocked down. *He* was by the stove now, on the opposite side of the cabin from her.

There. Her fingers hit dirt, scrabbled against it in her distress. She suddenly realized she was shaking, shaking hard. *Stop it*, said a harsh inner voice, fighting the rising flood of hysteria in her throat. *You just stop it, Blaine Kendricks.*

At the top of the wall, she found what she thought she remembered—a narrow crawl space between the floor beam of the cabin and the undisturbed ground. Not a space her sister would have fit into. Maybe, just maybe, she could squeeze herself that flat. Something thudded to the floor above her head and shattered. Footsteps moved toward the dairy.

If it broke every rib in her body, she *would* squeeze herself that flat.

Another ripping noise, her shirt this time, and the gouge of chunky splintered wood against her skin. For an instant she was stuck at the hips, with her legs hanging down the wall and her elbows digging futilely against the damp and slimy ground. Then her fingertips found and wrapped around an old root, and she *pulled*—and was through. To her immense relief, once she scraped herself past the floor beam at the crawl space opening, the area opened up a little; she could do more than take a deep breath, she could get up on her elbows as she wriggled to face the door, and even hitch up on her knees a little.

And then Blue whined. He was standing on his hind legs, his nose poking in at her. Above them, footsteps made a thoughtful sort of circle around the dairy door.

"C'mon, Blue," Blaine whispered. "Come up here with me, then. Hurry up!"

She could only imagine the doubtful expression on his face, but knew it was there, a big wrinkle above his brow and forward-cocked ears. He made a half-hearted effort and slid back to the ground again.

The man fumbled at the leather strap that served as a door pull.

"C'mon, Blue, *c'mon*—" first panic, then inspiration, struck. "Blue—come and get it. Get it, Blue, get it! It's back here!"

Potent words for a hound. His doubts forgotten, Blue lunged upward, making it halfway through the narrow spot in one good squeeze. No time for pained curses; she snared his collar and pulled. Forced sideways, he popped through into the crawl space, inhaling scent and determined to get whatever Blaine had holed up in here for him.

Dim light created greys and shadows as the door opened. Lying as flat as she could, as far back as she could get—which meant to the next floor beam—Blaine watched the backs of high, dark boots descend the ladder. Blue, confused and determined to get *some*thing, scrabbled around to face the dairy, rumbling in his chest.

Blaine surprised him into temporary silence by clamping her hand around his muzzle as the man reached the floor and turned around to face her. He scanned the contents of the shelves as his hands rose to his hips, irritation on his face. Blaine eased all the breath out of her body and imagined herself as thin as a skim of ice on a frosty morning.

Something looked for her, saw her, reached out to her—Blaine shook, hiding the paleness of her face against Blue's short, slick coat, even if it did mean losing sight of the one who hunted her.

After a moment she heard the man grumble something in disgust; she heard his foot hit the bottom rung of the ladder. He was going to leave, and she would be safe. Dreams were just dreams, and she'd be safe . . . she clenched her hand, unmindful that it held the dog's muzzle, wishing hard for those safe arms she suddenly remembered, the ones that took her up and ended the nightmare—

Blue whined and pawed at her hand, his tail thumping once in apology for whatever he had done to make her grip his face.

Blue, no! She tightened her fingers and shook the dog's muzzle a few quick, fierce times, daring to peek out at the dairy.

He had heard. He had turned back, his head cocked but not certain . . . .

But a sweep of the room must have confirmed his earlier conclusion—nothing bigger than a rat could hide here. Blaine jumped as the man abruptly jerked a shelf over, a violent move that spilled its contents across the floor and completely concealed the growl Blue could not contain. As the shelf creaked, settling unevenly, the man climbed the ladder and slammed the door down.

Darkness again. Footsteps, brisk and decisive, leaving the cabin. Maidie barked, sounding peevish, but after a moment her complaints grew intermittent and then died to a few final grumbles.

Blaine cautiously released Blue's muzzle, and then had to dodge his tongue. "Quit!" she muttered, as loud as she dared, ducking her head between her arms. Then she had to move quick to grab him again;

he was ready to bolt out into the dairy. "Oh, *no*. We're staying right here." Right here, until she felt safe enough to move again.

For now, all she could do was shake. She held the dog tightly, just glad to have something to hold at all.

Despite Dacey's quick pace, it was after noon when he reached town. But the way he'd take home was much more direct; he'd beat nightfall easy enough.

Town was little more than the river front and a few buildings—one to hold the river merchants' goods, one for gatherings and social occasions, a few to hold the blacksmith's forge and the animals he stabled. There was Annie's small boarding house and its diner, and a smattering of homesteads that were built close in to town.

As he'd expected, the street was full of people for Trade Day. There was a boat in dock, one of the odd new steamships that weren't of any use further upstream. There were lots of odd things from downstream, things that were one step beyond the needs of living, wanted but not always afforded, and other things from which the community turned away. Dacey's windows had made that trip. So had a number of pistols, loud and awkward weapons that hardly ever aimed true, and that meant a lot of fumbling with powder and ball when it came to taking a second shot.

So far, the hunters of the area had chosen to stay with their bows, snares, and knives. Now, looking at the steamship with narrowed eyes, Dacey found himself wondering if pistols were used on the plains, and trying to remember if the Annekteh camp had had any. Just one more thing Blaine's endangered community wouldn't be prepared for . . . though the Annekteh eschewed projectile weapons as a rule, and with luck they'd extended that ban to pistols.

Dacey raised his hand in return to a friendly hail, but didn't pause. He was looking for his kin, and as he walked the half-dried mud of the lane in front of the river, he didn't really register anyone else.

Until he saw the high-booted men close to the dock. Dacey stopped in mid-stride, unmindful of the folks who were forced to take a sudden detour around him and Mage. For a moment his breath caught in his chest, his sight narrowed to tunnel vision . . . his body remembered fear, in an instant of reaction he couldn't suppress. Then he started to breathe again, to think. They were *here*! How had they—

They'd come down the treacherous river, obviously. He forced a deep breath, dropped a hand to Mage's head as the dog tensed and growled deep in his chest. "With me," he reminded the dog softly. *Down the river.* They'd probably simply Taken a few of Blaine's kin and neighbors to figure out how to get to the seers' new territory—*and to Dacey*—

He wondered if they'd lost any men on the way— and how many were here now. The two he saw moved from wagons with local trade goods to tables that held river merchandise, ducking into buildings along the way. The plainsmen remained casual and natural; they even appeared to be polite.

But what were they up to? They worked independently of one another, nodding to this man, brushing up against that one, smiling and ducking their heads at the women. At first baffled, Dacey suddenly saw the pattern of it. Touch, Take, and release. *They were not just plainsmen. They were Annekteh Taken. Vessels.* Touch, Take, and release, so quick the victims weren't even sure what had happened. *Take and release.* Learn about the area. Learn about the seers' kin. Learn that they had nothing to fear from most of the people here—except, of course, for the one for whom they were looking.

Him.

He started walking again, slowly—watching—Mage matching his pace. One of the men drifted closer to him, one further away. Carefully, he fell in behind the closer one. He shadowed the man, ignoring the greeting from his cousin Jimsy, playing a fine line between being noticed by everyone else for his odd behavior and being noticed by the Annekteh, period. Eventually he was behind his quarry, close enough to hear the man's meaningless remarks and salutations.

He hadn't really understood his own intent until that point, when he discovered his hand was tight around the handle of his knife. *Spirits, there had to be another way.* There had to be. From behind, like an unsuspecting animal? The man before him was Taken, was just an innocent *tool*.

But warning meant the *annektehr* inside him could escape. Back to the fold in the North—or into someone else here, most likely, someone he'd know . . . maybe someone he loved.

No, it had to be nekfehr death . . . that which the Annekteh dreaded above all, the death of the annektehr along with the vessel. Hating himself, hating that he was the kind of man who could even consider such action, Dacey targeted the man's heart from the back as though he were a deer walking into arrow range. Three swift, bold strides, and his arm was around the man's neck, pulling him into the rapid thrust of the knife at his back, through the ribs, driving up—

Dacey held the vessel close while the man gave a spastic jerk, and another, and—with a sudden sobbing exhalation, deflated. It wasn't until he hit the ground and quivered at Dacey's feet that the handful of people around them realized there was a problem, and even then they couldn't quite fathom it.

"Dacey, *what*—"

"*Spirits*, Dacey, what have you—"

Dacey ignored their gasps—Jimsy's protests, the hand that reached for him—and aimed himself at the other Annekteh. The man—*no, the vessel, the enemy*—must realize that something had happened to his *annektehr* partner, but wasn't ready to give himself away. Instead, he was closing in on Dacey's Uncle Sy. *Touch*—Dacey was running—*Take*—Dacey yelled a warning—

No, there was no *Take*!

The vessel's eyes widened at his failure, and as Sy jerked away and scowled at what he thought was simple overfamiliarity, the man dipped his hand into his side pouch and slapped Sy on the arm.

Dacey plowed into them both, ending up on top of them; someone running up hard on Dacey's heels overshot them all. There was too much shouting for Dacey to hear what the vessel cursed at him, and he ignored all the hands that plucked at him. He clenched his hands together and drew back to bring their combined strength against the side of the vessel's face.

Then Dacey was outnumbered, and virtually lifted off his enemy. He struggled to find his feet while being tugged at from half a dozen directions, and flabbergasted exclamations hammered him. *You done broke his jaw, Dacey! Are you crazy, man? Dacey! Stop!*

"Sy!" It was the clearest voice, and it held shock and distress that cut through the clamor. "Sy, what's wrong?"

Sudden silence, and the various grips on Dacey's clothes and arms slowly eased. The vessel lay unconscious before him; just to the side, his cousin Jimsy bent over Uncle Sy. Sy's lips were blueish; his face grey.

"What ails him, Jim?" It was Dalkin Fleming's demanding voice, nearly in Dacey's ear. He should have known it was Dalkin when he got lifted right off that vessel; few could match the blacksmith's casual strength.

"I—he's dead! I think he's dead!"

Not fast enough. *I wasn't fast enough.* Not quick

enough with his warning. Dacey stared at his uncle's body. *I didn't have no seein's for you, Sy.*

Jimsy had something in his hands, turning it over for examination and holding it far from his face to accommodate his notoriously blurry close-vision. "A dart," he said. "D'ye suppose—that fella—" He looked at the vessel, and then down at his uncle, and his face twitched in a battle between grief and fury.

"What's going on, Dacey?" Dalkin growled. He grabbed Dacey's shirt at the shoulder and yanked him around so they were face to face, then shouted, "What's goin' on here?"

Dacey looked back at him, eyes narrowed, face quiet. At the edge of the crowded confrontation, Mage growled. After a moment, the blacksmith released him and stepped back.

"Dacey," Jimsy said, a single word of intense demand. He got up from their uncle's side and joined Dalkin, the two closest faces in a crowd of distressed kinfolk and friends. For the most part they were still too shocked to react, but the tears were beginning.

Dacey took a deep breath. "Annekteh," he said simply.

Dalkin spat. "Kilt 'em all, Dacey!"

"I ain't goin' over that old argument with you— nor anyone. There's Annekteh up north, and I found 'em. I come here today to get the word out."

"You found *them*? Looks more like they found *you*." Dalkin glared. "And in findin' you, *us*. You want to go off on your little adventures, you better be sure to keep 'em to your*self*."

"Leave off, Dalk," Jimsy snapped, fairly bursting with the need to lash out at someone. "If they was kilt, this 'un'd never have got to Sy."

"Dacey's plumb on the mark about this kind o' thing," Annie said, her elderly voice quivering but clear enough over the noise of the crowd. "It ain't his fault we been runnin' away from this day."

"But what're we gonna do?" That was Susannah, fifteen and easy to rile. "Granny, they'll Take us all!"

"They're dead, now—or will be," Dacey said grimly. He looked at the second man, the vessel, with the *annekt ehr* trapped inside—only as long as the vessel was unconscious. He'd have to be killed before he woke. *Gran, I think you done told me too much.* A heavy weight, Gran's knowledge, when so few shared it with him. "And now you know to watch. They ain't much interested in here, not yet—likely won't be, as we don't have what they want. They're settlin' in at the hollers up north. That's where the fightin' is. Where the magic's comin' back."

"That's where you been," Jimsy said, understanding coming across his plain, stubble-jawed face as the pitch of his emotions cooled. "Rosabel said you were gone, an' I counted you as off huntin'. But you was a lot further than that, wasn't you?"

Dacey nodded. "But I was huntin', all right." He looked down at the vessel. "Don't none of you touch him, less'n you're direct of my granny's line. An' . . . you got to kill him afore he wakes." The man groaned, as if he'd heard and understood; all Dacey wanted was to be away before it was done.

"There was three of 'em," Dalkin said, his voice holding sudden alarm. "I seen three of 'em come past my place to Annie's last night."

Dacey discovered his hand was bloody, wiped it off on his pants. "He'll know what's happened." They all knew, all through the *annektehr* and the unbodied Annekteh. "I don't reckon he'll be easy to find, now. The *annektehr* may even abandon him. If he's been Took a long time, there won't be much left of him." He gave Dalkin a sharp look. "It ain't safe to have him around in any case."

Dalkin nodded slowly. "What of you, Dacey?"

"Goin' back north," Dacey said. He looked down at his uncle, a long look that held all the good-bye he would have the chance to give. "Goin' to try to make sure they don't get comfortable there."

His words didn't seem to surprise anyone. They moved aside for him as he walked away from the spot, and didn't bother him as he retrieved his knife from the first man's body and wiped it clean against the shin of the black padded boot.

Blaine was waiting.

→ 8 ←

Blaine stayed in the dark crawl space as long as she could, until even hugging Blue's warmth wasn't enough to stop her shivering. If only she hadn't taken off her jacket while she was working in the garden. And if only she'd used the outhouse *before* she'd come down to get the ham—

But she had, and she hadn't, and now she just couldn't stay here any longer. Surely the man had long since given up and gone away. She hadn't heard a peep from any of the dogs since Maidie's barking had died away. *Oh, please be gone*, she thought fervently as she crawled toward the opening on her elbows. Blue, once released, quickly scrabbled his way out. Blaine wished for his speed, but not the ungainly landing she heard.

Not that she had much choice. She had to go headfirst, and even though her arms were stretched out to break her fall, she landed with a pained grunt. It took some moments to sort out her skirts, a task that the darkness made no easier. Blue urged her on with his whining, and when she finally stood and

123

stretched out the kinks, she followed that noise to the ladder.

"Me first," she told him, pushing him aside. "Unless you can figure out how to open that door."

But once she reached it, she discovered she was none too eager to poke her head out. She needed a long moment to gather her courage. Finally she took a breath deep enough to do the job, and slowly pushed up on the door.

Nothing. There was no circle of Annekteh warriors waiting to snatch her, no padded leather boots standing in front of her as her head rose above the level of the floor. The light was surprisingly dim, dim enough to indicate that the sun had gone below the crest of the mountain behind Dacey's cabin, and Blaine had a sudden moment of panic when she realized how close to dark it was. *He said he'd be back before dark.* At the time he'd said it, she hadn't cared. But now . . .

She nearly jumped out of her skin when Blue bumped her from beneath, his front legs up on the ladder. "I sure hope you can climb," she said crossly, taking the last few rungs and stepping out onto the cabin floor, "because after that, there ain't no way I'm pulling you up. You're on your own."

In two lunges, and without actually touching his feet to the ladder that Blaine could see, the dog was up and out, running out of the cabin to see if the yard had changed significantly since the last time he'd been there.

Blaine was more cautious. She walked slowly to the open door, stepping over the bedding the man had strewn across the floor. The dogs were in the yard, carefree and busy checking out Blue—except for Maidie, who was still up on the rock, even though the sunshine had moved on.

Blaine didn't want to leave the house. She didn't want to expose herself to someone who might still be watching from the woods—after all, if they'd come all this way to find her and Dacey, they weren't going to give up that easily. She sure didn't want to take any chances.

But the privy was fifty feet down the hill.

Blaine tried to look casual as she walked the endless distance, and once inside, she hardly felt safe. Still, by the time she poked her head out of the small structure, she realized that if the cabin was being watched, she'd have seen some sign of it by now.

Which didn't mean they wouldn't come back. She ran down the hill to the garden and her jacket—dammit, her *blinder* had been in that jacket!—snatching it up and reversing course. Up past the cabin and into the long twilight of the mountain evening, heading for a grove of rhododendrons that would offer her cover. There she intended to stay, at least until Dacey was back. And maybe a good piece longer, if she didn't think it was yet safe.

The dogs had run into the woods on their own private mission, and weren't around to bother—or warm—her. Blaine curled up, hugging herself for warmth. She'd gotten so chilled in that dairy, she should have brought a blanket with her.

But she wasn't about to go back now.

There she waited, a miserable, angular huddle of girl with a growling stomach, red runny nose, and an anxious gaze darting around the abandoned-looking area below her. As it grew too dark to see, she alternately worried and seethed over Dacey's continued absence. Even the dogs would have been welcome, but they, too, remained truant. Finally, cold and alone, she curled around herself and dozed.

⊁⊰   ⊁⊰   ⊁⊰

They hadn't learned.

Not that Nekfehr was entirely displeased. The vessel's experience had

told him that indulging in the *anne-nekfehr* would demoralize these people, remove their incentive to work. And so, despite the numbers of fresh potential vessels here for that purpose, none of the *annektehr* had yet done so.

The *annektehr*, one and all—as if they could be anything else—welcomed this opportunity.

＊＜   ＊＜   ＊＜

Rand shook his sweaty hair out of his eyes and shoved his sleeves up his arms, not hesitating in the forced jog away from the timbering site. Nathan was on his heels, Cadell in front of him—and none of them knew what this summons was about. The Annekteh had never pulled the men off work in the middle of the afternoon before.

None of them knew, but Rand could guess.

Some one of them had struck out at the invaders, and met success.

The state of the meeting hall seemed to affirm his guess. The yard was packed with tired-looking people, dirty from their labors. Most of the boys were absent, out in the hills somewhere; those present looked as confused as everyone else. Well, then, no one had been *mistaken* for deer and shot, which was something Rand had considered trying some time back; the Annekteh had had to leave the boys their bows for hunting, and Rand felt certain he could lay his hands on one . . .

His sister and their mommy sought him out, looking tired and frustrated. The two had been fixing a broken door on the barn this morning, and bore the scrapes to prove it, the kind of scrapes which no doubt held any number of splinters. *Man's work*. Rand put his arm around Lenie's shoulders and tried to keep the hatred off his face, hatred at what these creatures had done to his pretty sister and to their mommy, whose sorrow for Willum chased around her features when she thought no one was looking.

But there was no time for conversation, to see if the women knew anything. The last of them was still arriving when Nekfehr paced out of the barn, his booted heels hitting the ground with the force of his anger. Behind him came another plainsman, and across his shoulders was something—*someone*—rolled in a tarp. The hill folk gave the two wide berth as Nekfehr strode into the midst of them and stopped; the plainsman dropped his burden to the ground and gave the tarp a yank to unroll it.

Phew. Rand's nose wrinkled; Lenie turned her face to his chest. The odor assaulted them right along with the very sight of the dead man—rank vomit and the stench of his fouled pants. His lips were bluish, his face contorted. Rand thought he recognized one of the men who usually walked the hills in patrol.

"It is clear that this man was poisoned," Nekfehr said tightly. "It will be easier on you all if the guilty party steps forward now."

Rand wasn't the only one to startle when Jason spoke. Big of Adam's apple and nose, his arm tightly around the shoulders of his wife and their recent firstborn, he said, "Don't reckon it had to be any of us. There's plenty in the hills this time of year that'll poison them that doesn't know what to look for. Cowslip's nasty, you don't cook it through. Pokeweed's coming on to poison stage."

"My men are new to this area. That does not mean they are stupid."

"We fed them at noon," one of the women said; her name was Ester. She had several young children clinging to her, and Rand knew she was in the handful that stayed at the meeting hall with the young ones. "Along with the children. You don't see any of us took sick."

"Pokeweed poisoning has that look to it," Jason said. "Plenty of that along this bottom."

This time of year, poke was safe enough, and standard fare. But the berries—not out yet—and roots were poison. Rand glared at Nekfehr. *Take one of us, then. Take me, and see it's true.*

"We gathered some this morning, for poke sallet," Ester said. "He was with us. I done saw him pull up a whole plant, and told him to leave it be. Mought be he didn't."

In two steps, Nekfehr reached her. The children scattered as he gripped her arm; she stiffened, but there was hardly even time for anyone to protest before he shoved her away. "You're lying," he said. "He was there, but you didn't see him pulling any plants." He looked around at the other women who spent their time at the meeting hall. "Interesting that you feel you must lie to protect someone, when you don't even know that one of these others did anything." His gaze went back to the woman. "You don't *know*, but you're quite certain."

Rand thought the gathering had been a quiet one, but when the leader moved back to Ester, all noise truly ceased. No scuffling, no coughing, no children whispering complaints. With a theatrical flourish, the leader removed his fancy belt knife, and as the woman shrank away from him, presented it to her, hilt first. Astonished, hesitant, she took it, her wide, worried eyes watching him, trying to see what he wanted of her.

And then he Took her, a gentle touch on her arm. Her face showed no sign of the internal struggle Rand knew was there. It was vacant as the leader gazed down at her, and it stayed vacant as she reached up to him, put her arms around his neck, and kissed him. The knife hung loosely in her grip, just beside the veins of his neck, and the lost opportunity was almost as hard for Rand to bear as what the man forced her to do.

"No!" one of the others shrieked, a sudden, broken

sound. Rand's Aunt Bonnie darted to the leader and stopped short, her hands making small, aborted efforts to break him away from Ester. "It was me, I done it! Leave her be!"

The leader broke away from the kiss, and for once his eyes held some kind of expression, a shine of . . . Rand wasn't sure what. "Good of you to try to help her," he said. "But useless." He looked back at the woman and, without taking her empty gaze from his face, she brought the knife down and put it to her own throat, pushing gently. After a moment, a thin line of blood ran down the blade of the knife, over the knuckle guard, and across her hand.

If we all rushed him at once—Rand thought, couldn't help thinking, couldn't help taking that one step, along with all the other men in the assembly. And then they stopped, of one accord, knowing they'd all simply be Taken at once.

"Leave her be!" Bonnie shrieked again, unable to stand it any more, and threw herself at Nekfehr. He caught her wrist with his free hand, not even taking his eyes from his victim's face. Ester stood there, a husk with no will of its own, blood trickling down her neck.

"Don't worry," he said. "I have no intention of killing her. Damaging her will make the point just as well, and she'll still be able to watch the children." At his words, Ester, with quick efficiency, took the knife from her throat, and reached down to slash it across the back of her own knee. Then she returned the knife to the leader.

He dropped his hold on both women to take it, and suddenly the two were screaming, one in horror and one in pain, as Bonnie threw herself down next to where Ester had fallen and wrapped her arms around her newly crippled friend to keen with grief.

No one else moved. No one else dared. The leader turned to look at them, and his eyes still held that oddity of expression, leftover pain and . . . and something else. Suddenly Rand realized that Nekfehr had felt the woman's pain at the cut of the knife. And just as suddenly, he realized that the being had enjoyed it.

Rand took a step back, away from the atrocity of the man before him. Nekfehr caught his eye, saw his understanding. And smiled. A genuine smile. Cadell's hand landed on Rand's shoulder, but it didn't distract him, or keep him from taking another step back.

What did the Annekteh *really* want from Shadow Hollers?

The sun slid over the top of the westernmost ridge—one of a series of long ridges, each poking up behind the other to Dacey's left as he walked the path home, paralleling the twist of his own home ridge and halfway up the mountain.

Still plenty of light left; plenty of time to get home; just because the ridge had shadowed out the sun didn't mean it was true sunset yet. But Dacey picked up his pace anyway, sending Mage on ahead. "Git to home, son," he said, when Mage wasn't quite sure if he meant the gesture he'd made. "She'll know I'm coming, an' she sees you."

Mage gave him a solemn tail wag, hitched his bad leg up out of the way, and trotted out. And Dacey, intensely aware of the blood on his clothes and the deep red stains of it seeped into the roughness of his hands, made his feet move faster and tried to keep his thoughts from doing the same.

Blood. Blood everywhere.

He startled, looking down at himself.

Not a memory. A possibility.

Seeings. Spirits, just what he needed now.

Blaine's frightened breathing in the darkness.

Memory? Hitting him hard, confusing things? Blaine and her nightmares, those early seeings of hers? He knew that soft gasp, the catch in her throat . . .

With a bound, he took the fallen tree in the path—been there for years, it had, and he never bothered to touch his feet to the trunk on the way over, just a hint of a push off the soft, rotting bark with his fingers—but he landed square, held there by the flash in his mind's eye. *Unfamiliar boots landing on the log, skidding off that crumbling bark—*

Snatched by seeing, he stood frozen. *Blaine, scrambling in some confining darkness . . .*

Never were the seeings easy to unravel. But never had they taken reality and replaced it with some other vision. Someone else's boots going over this log . . . twisting back, he discovered the mark of it. Not moving his feet, not chancing to cover any trail sign in this fading light, he finally found heel marks in the spring-soft trail before him.

There was three of 'em, Dalkin had said.

Ahead of him, Mage gave a sharp bark of warning, an angry sound.

Dacey fit the knife back to his bloodstained hand.

➤←   ➤←   ➤←

Dead.

All three *annektehr*, dead. *Nekfehr* death, caught in a vessel with no place to go, no new vessel on hand, no nearby community of *nekteh* for which to leap, to rejoin.

Of all the deaths . . .

In a colony of beings where death was rare, *nekfehr*-death was the rarest. The harshest. The worst.

Three of them.

But not in vain. Nekfehr knew the fastest way south. He knew that he'd found the last traces of seer's blood there. And he'd learned useful bits of trivia, especially from the last to die. "*What have you done to her?*" Dacey Childers had cried, his voice and face and very posture full of the agony of not knowing. Of guessing . . . and dreading.

Immediately after that, the vessel grew too confident, and consequently died.

Savage, Dacey Childers had been, in his anger. In that way humans could be, creating their own vulnerabilities.

Nekfehr would remember—and with him, every *annektehr* in Shadow Hollers.

➴➴   ➴➴   ➴➴

Barking.

Blaine started awake, jammed her head into a branch, and swore softly, a word that would shock her mommy.

Barking in the yard below her—the hounds gone wild. Dacey? Or the Annekteh again? She peered futilely through the darkness, unable to tell. Though there was light enough to move slowly through the woods, she could not see more than dark, moving masses in front of the cabin. Barking masses.

Dim new light flushed the cabin windows shadowy amber, slowly turning bright as that fancy lamp of Dacey's steadied out. Blaine eased slowly away from the rhododendrons, staying down, trying for a better look. Above the barking she heard a sharp tone, and the dogs hushed—at least, mostly. Dacey. It had to be. Didn't it?

"Blaine?" he called from within the cabin, a clear note of worry in his voice. Then, louder, from out in the open, "Blaine!"

She wouldn't yell. Not while she was this far from him, and with that Annekteh-Taken man who knows where. But she rose up and worked her swift way down the hill with little caution for the steep, uneven ground or the full-budded branches whipping at her.

"Blaine!"

She was close enough then, to gasp out a breathless reply. "Dacey, I'm here!" Close enough, too, to see the change in his posture as he located her; how he straightened before sprinting up the hill, and didn't slow until she'd reached him, flinging herself at him without any thought other than the fact that he was back, and her ordeal was over. For a moment he held her tight, a surprising grip that echoed her own fear and relief. And then something changed, and he stepped away from her, his hands on her arms.

"Blaine—" he said, and stopped, his fingers flexing against her arms. Then, more quietly, "Blaine, what happened?"

"One of *them* was here," she said, gulping down air and emotion at the same time, emotion she hadn't realized was lurking there and couldn't quite identify—like only now was it possible for the true horror to come out, now that Dacey was here. "He came at noon, an' he tore the place apart. I hid in the dairy."

"In the dairy," Dacey repeated, doubt overflowing his voice—although she'd left the door up, so that much should have been obvious.

"Way back, up under the floor. Me an' Blue both, for the longest time. He came down and looked, but—" his hands had fallen to his sides, and she faltered. "You act like you don't believe it."

He didn't say anything right away, not until Blue trotted up and headed for Blaine. Then his voice was sharp. "Blue, no! Stay with me."

"But—" For she'd been reaching out to drop her hand on that heavy-boned head, had wanted the feel of it beneath her fingers for once.

Suddenly she realized what it was about. Dacey believed that the Annekteh had been here, all right. He believed that she'd hidden in the dairy.

He just didn't think she'd gotten away with it.

He thought she was a trap, that she was Taken, that she would—why, that she would Take *Blue*.

She stared dumbly at him, waiting to feel mad—no, waiting to feel *furious*!

Instead she burst into tears and spurned them all—dogs and man—running back into the woods she had come from. The dark blot of evergreen rhododendron was almost easy to find, and she threw herself under it. A whole day of being cold, and frightened, and hiding! A day of waiting for Dacey to come back so she wouldn't be alone, and now he was here, and she was *still* alone! And her family was in danger, her whole community was in danger, and she was stuck here with no way to do anything about it, stuck with someone who wouldn't even let her pet his damn dog!

Blaine sobbed into the crook of her arm, great big wracking sobs.

A wet nose in her ear was the first she noticed Blue had found her—and that Mage, uncharacteristically, quietly sniffed her hair. And then there was Dacey's hand on her shoulder, a gentle hand this time.

"Blaine." His quiet voice was almost obscured by the sobs she tried—unsuccessfully—to tame. "Blaine, I'm sorry."

She coughed, and snuffled loudly, and kept her face buried in her arm. She didn't say anything.

"I run into some of them in town," Dacey said. "That's why I'm late. It had me spooked, Blaine. I'm sorry. Come down to the cabin. Bet you're as hungry as I am, and I know for a fact that ham's still sittin' down in the dairy."

She laughed, though it was a sad thing, and said into her arm, "I'm pure hunger from front to back."

"Let's go, then."

It was better than being alone.

She followed him, slowly, back down the hill. By the time she made it to the cabin, Dacey was banging around in the dairy. Blaine picked the bedding off

the floor—even if Dacey slept on it there, anyway—
and straightened it out, making up the bed and folding his quilts while he continued to create odd noises
below. Finally there was a solid thump of the shelf
coming back to rest against the wall, and then Dacey
appeared, ham in tow, up the dairy ladder.

It was the first she'd seen him in the light. "Dacey,"
she gasped. "There's blood everywhere!"

He looked down at himself. "I run into some of
'em in town," he repeated. "And yours, on the way
back."

"It ain't none of it yours?"

He touched the front of his shirt, as though he was
thinking about it, and set the ham down. "Don't
reckon."

She was nearly speechless—but not quite. "Let me
see! You should tend yourself, Dacey, not fuss around
in some stupid dairy!"

He gestured to the meat. "After we eat. I got some
potatoes saved out that'll go fine with this ham."

She could see right off that there was no use in
arguing, though she couldn't keep the reluctance from
her voice. "I got some greens. But I bet they're
mighty wilted by now."

They were, but they went down well. Blaine kept
eyeing Dacey and the blood he wore, all while they
ate. He sat in the chair, she on the bed, and she stole
enough glances at him between bites to see that his
thoughts were wandering in an almost dazed sort of
way.

"Why'd you change your mind?" she asked suddenly, when there wasn't anything left on her thick
pottery plate worth pushing around.

He came back to the present slowly, and set his
own plate on the floor beside the chair. "About what?"

"About me. Whyn't you let me just stay up there,
in them bushes?"

He looked away, his face undecided about which

expression to settle on. Finally, one side of his mouth quirked slightly. "Nothing noble," he said. "Annekteh-Took don't do dramatic-type things. Iff'n they do, it's an act, and easy to see through. It's why . . . why they try to borrow so much from us. *Anne-nekfehr*," he added, without explaining any further.

Both eyebrows went up about as high as they could go. "You mean you knowed it was me 'cause I threw a *hissy-fit*?"

He nodded.

"Huh! You mought have said it was that you trusted me."

"Not in my nature," he said, somewhat apologetically.

She heaved a sigh—more dramatics—and nodded. "No, I guess it ain't." She got up from the bed and picked up their plates, dumping them in the tin basin of steaming water she'd had heating on the stove. She did a quick but efficient washing up, and when she turned around, Dacey was pulling his blood-stuck shirt from its tuck-in at his belt.

Blaine rolled her eyes and went to him, waving his hands away. "I can do that a lot easier'n you."

He *was* tired, she knew, because he didn't protest, just held his arms up slightly so she could tug the thing off. Mostly the shirt came away clean, peeling away from the smooth, tight skin of his side. And then he winced, and the material grew stubborn. She gave him a dark look, and he said gently, "It ain't much, Blaine. Just soak it off and put some salve on it, and it'll do."

That made sense enough. If it *had* been serious, he'd not have made it through dinner so casually. "Lucky for you I had tea water warming up, or it'd be straight from the spring," she told him. "I'll have to get some anyway, and put this shirt to soak."

"Never mind the shirt," he said. "I've got another. We've got other things to do tonight."

She'd follow up on that one in a minute, she

thought, carefully applying a warm, wet bit of rag to the stuck place. "What happened in town?" she asked. "Were they looking for us?"

"Us and any other of my kin they could find—the ones that can't be Took." His face was grim, and she didn't think it had anything to do with the shirt that was now coming nicely away from his side. "There was three of them, that anyone saw. I got two of them in town. The third—well, most of this blood's his."

"You're right on that. This ain't much." She gently wiped crusted blood away from his skin, and discovered just what he'd said—a long, shallow cut that could use a stitch or two but would get along all right without them. "Spirits be on your side tonight, Dacey. You got three of 'em and they done you no worse than this?"

"Salve's on that shelf behind me," he said, getting his distant look back again, and a little bit of a frown. Finally he said, "Mage warned me of him." And then jumped, his skin twitching, as she applied the salve.

"It's cold," she said.

"So I see." His voice was dry, and a little amused, as though he could tell she'd purposely forgotten to warm it. Chillbumps patterned his skin.

"Wish I had something to wrap that with," she said, pretending not to notice. "Mought as well get that other shirt out, before you catch your death. At least you didn't get none on your jacket."

"Wasn't wearing it." He considered her, still somehow carrying that distanced look on his face. "Truth is, Blaine . . . I killed two men today, caused the death of a third. They weren't bad men. Except for the last, they didn't even see me coming—and that's not the way for a man to go. But they were Took, and I didn't have any choice. Talkin' about it right now . . ." He shook his head. "It's a hard thing." Carefully, he pulled out the trunk that lived under the bed and, without undue searching, found the shirt he was looking for.

She wanted to touch him, to let him know she understood, somehow. But she could see that wasn't what he wanted, not now. So she smeared what was left of the salve in little patterns on the back of her hand, and said, "Why ain't we askin' none of your kin to come and help us? Some of the others from the seers' lines?"

"No." His voice was quiet but did not invite argument.

Blaine argued anyway. "I don't see why not. We need all the help we can get, you've done said as much yourself. You said we ain't prepared and can't handle them by ourselves. Then why not—"

"No," he repeated, and carefully pulled the new shirt on. It *was* new, too, as far as Blaine could tell, made with fine, careful stitches and an eye for detail. A woman's eye. She wondered whose. " 'Twouldn't do."

"And why not? Won't they realize how bad we need—"

Dacey snorted. "Blaine," he said, "don't forget they *are* seer's kin. They more'n know the dangers to both your folk and ours, but—we ain't askin'."

"That don't make sense," Blaine complained. "Seein' as we need the help so bad."

He fastened the bone buttons and said, with finality, "We ain't askin' 'cause they can't do it. The youngest of 'em with the blood as strong as mine was kilt today—and he was my oldest uncle. The rest of 'em can't even make it up here to visit me."

She wiped the back of her hand against her skirt and started to say something, but settled for wrinkling her nose at him in thought.

"You got it," he said. "The seer's line is dyin' out. It's hard to make a go when you're all so close kin. Babies die and there ain't no one your own age to choose from. You're lookin' at the last, Blaine, an' that's me." He shrugged. "Some might say the seers

did the wrong thing by takin' us away. Seems we lost
half our people to further south, where there's a fine
big town and some space between the mountains. But
I've touched those Annekteh." Dacey drew his shoulders back in a motion Blaine suspicioned was meant
to hide the shudder that went through them. "I can
understand the seers needin' to leave that place
forever."

→ 9 ←

The last thing Blaine had expected after this day was to find herself climbing the hill not above his cabin, but opposite it—on her way to a night of listening to the dogs run fox. "Dacey," Blaine said, curling her fingers around Blue's collar so he unwittingly pulled her up the steep incline, "just how far is this spot?"

Which wasn't what she really wanted to know. She *wanted* to know why they were climbing this hill at all. She was tired, he was tired, and here they were *climbing this damn hill*.

Dacey looked down at her and she could see his teeth gleam in a rare grin. "Thought I got you hardened up on that hike from your hollow."

"I thought so too," Blaine moaned to herself, catching enough breath to grumble, "I'd like to see *you* climb this hill in these skirts, Dacey Childers!"

When he answered, she thought his voice was as strained as hers. "It'll be worth it. You won't go on no foxhunts to match this 'un at your place."

"That," she said pointedly, "is because I won't be allowed on no foxhunts at home."

141

"Leastways you won't have to see how poor it is without these dogs." There was a smile in that one, one she could hear.

Blaine shifted her blanket roll with an irritated shove, trying to reclaim her dropped skirts with the same motion. She had a sudden scandalous notion involving scissors, needle, and thread.

"This is it," Dacey announced, peering back over the edge of the slope. He extended a hand and hauled her up, settling her on the flat of what could only be the top of the mountain. There was barely enough light to show the terrain, and Blaine squinted out into the brisk night around them.

"It'll be better when the moon comes out," Dacey promised. "We got off a little late, made for a hard climb. But it's a good night—damp ground, clear air. They'll give us a real race tonight."

As long as the dogs did the racing and not her, Blaine thought, dropping her blanket roll to the ground. The dogs in question instantly trampled it, milling around Dacey with eager whines and little, restrained half jumps. Dumb, she thought yet again. Whimsy turned to give her hand a quick lick, generously including her in the excitement. Blaine waited for her to turn away and vigorously wiped off the slobber.

"All right, all right, go!" Dacey said, and laughed right out loud. Their clawing feet spewed bits of dirt and moss into the air as the dogs sprang out into the trees and across the ridge, not yet giving tongue. Mage sat with a sigh and wiped his paw across his nose—looking, Blaine thought, as vexed as old Bayard when he saw the younger men heading off on a hunt. Dacey's hand dropped to his hound's head. "You'll have your hunt, son."

"Why'd you keep him?" Blaine asked. "You must have knowed he couldn't hunt." And then she winced, wishing she'd managed to say it better than that, knowing that somehow, this dog was his favorite.

But Dacey didn't look at her at all, raising his head to peer into the darkness. "He's worth more'n all the others," he said softly. "He'll earn his keep all right." After a moment he looked her way. " 'Course, I am a little soft-hearted at times." Before she could say anything else, he put his hand up. "Shhh. Listen."

Blaine cocked her head in response and heard, floating up from the hollow, the first barks of a hound on scent. "That's Chase," Dacey said, still listening, a smile in his voice. A higher, clearer voice joined in. "And there's Whimsy." Then two at once, a rough booming yell that underscored a lower warble. "And Maidie and Blue. Blue's just out for fun—he's too heavy a dog to keep up with this for long. He'll quit soon."

"How do you tell who's who?"

Dacey's response was startled. "Does your sister sound like your mother?"

"No, of course not." Blaine scowled. "That's not the same."

"Sure it is. You'll get used to it," he said with assurance.

That's what she was afraid of. "How can I? We're going home soon."

"Blaine . . ." Dacey turned his full attention on her. "You're going home, all right—but that don't mean it's ever going to be the home you remember. The Annekteh are there. Just 'cause we know what's happening don't mean we can trot in and make it all right again. Folks are gonna die, Blaine. Things are gonna change. Things have *already* changed."

Blaine stared at him, a stricken kind of understanding seeping into her. She'd been worrying and fussing, but underneath it all, she'd still refused to see. She had thought Dacey could tell Shadow Hollers how to fix it all. That he and his Annekteh lore *could* fix it all.

"If it was so bad, why'd we leave 'em?" she finally blurted.

Silence from Dacey, but not for long, and when he spoke, it was with resignation. "You know why. Way things went, it was the only thing to do." Resignation, and a sort of weight she could almost see settling on his shoulders. "I went up there after 'em. Wanted to spy 'em out and warn your people. But . . . I hadn't counted on *them* catchin' *me*. And when you got me loose, it probably spooked 'em big. Leavin' was the best thing to do. It gave me a chance to tell my own people. It kept you safe. And I'm hopin' my not bein' there has took some of the pressure off them, so they'll be easier on folks. But—they probably moved in on 'em the day we ran."

Blaine was speechless for a moment—though when the words came, she nearly shrieked them. "And we're on a *foxhunt*?"

"We're safest out here," Dacey said, letting her panic get lost in his easygoing voice. "We don't know for sure only three of them come down the river after us. It weren't smart to stay in the cabin tonight. On the morrow, we'll go back just long enough to pack up some things. So . . ." he said, looking at her so the light from the rising moon silvered his hazel eyes, "enjoy this foxhunt, Blaine. You'll need the memory when things get rough."

He was right. Of course he was right. Blaine found herself savoring the memory, less than a full day old as it was. She'd smiled with Dacey when Blue trotted back to their small fire and threw himself down, pressing his stomach against the cool earth, his tongue lolling far over the side of his mouth. His hoarse panting covered the baying of his packmates, the rhythms of which Blaine had just started to understand. Occasionally, as he cooled, Blue looked her way and gave a hopeful thump of his tail. Finally Dacey absently patted the ground and the dog went to curl up next to him and Mage.

The dogs had run for a few hours, and then their barking changed. Even Blaine could tell they weren't moving anymore. "Are you going to kill the fox?" she'd asked as Dacey sat and listened.

"Not tonight. It's for fun tonight." He patted the horn at his side. "I'll let 'em bark down that hole for a while and then call 'em in."

And that's what they'd done. Sat atop the mountain under the stars, listening to the night music until Dacey lifted the horn and made it moan through the trees.

Just recollecting the sound made her shiver even now, in full daylight—though not in the same way as the eerie howling that had started this whole adventure. It was a call of fellowship, one that had triggered Blue and Mage into howling along, and it made her shiver because . . . it was so *right* somehow. Primal, but *right*.

Blaine forced herself back to the present. She and Dacey had been traveling since early morning, after a surprisingly satisfying, if brief, sleep on the ridge. Burdened with supplies—even Blue carried a little pack, the only dog big enough to do so—they stopped for a full-blown lunch. They had things to eat before they went bad. And now she sat, full, her knife hovering uncertainly over the garment.

For she'd had it. She was full sick of hiking in these skirts, of tangling up in them and having to jerk them high to get any climbing done. She had Dacey's needle, and his thread—she'd been thinking on this for *days*—and she'd determined to divide the full skirts down the middle and sew them up split.

Yet despite that determination, she hesitated, easily imagining Cadell's scandalized cry and seeing Lottie mourn over good clothes ruined.

In sudden clarity, Dacey's recent grim words came

back to her. *She'd never again see the very home she had left.* Perhaps she'd never even again hear those familiar parental cries of objection.

The knife slid from suddenly nerveless fingers, but only long enough to fall into her lap. Then she snatched it up and poked it into the wool, cutting carefully but steadily. When it was done she threaded up the needle and started the awkward process of mending the very clothes she was wearing.

Dacey stretched out longways on the hill—feet downhill, head up—and politely kept his gaze elsewhere while she sewed—big, rough stitches she promised herself she'd refine later—but Blue had no such manners. He wandered into their resting spot and straight over to the bit of high ground Blaine had chosen, intrigued by the unusual arrangement of the material—and of course without respect for the fact she was still wearing it, much as he had no respect for the fact that her braids were still attached to her head. He stuck his nose underneath the panel of wool and blew his cheeks out, tossing his head in the air to flip the cloth around.

"Hsst," Blaine said, and waved a hand at him. "Quit, you old hound."

Wffbt, he did it again, sending air through his nose and lips as he wagged his tail and played with the new toy.

"You're rude," Blaine hissed at him, ignoring Dacey's quiet laugh. Blue left her to go to the amused, friendly sound, and she quickly bent back to her sewing. Uninterrupted, Blaine managed to finish her task without too much more time lost.

She stood and checked her handiwork. "What do you think?" she asked finally, looking upon herself. "Will Mommy faint?"

Dacey swiveled his gaze away from the treetops to cast a critical eye on her split-sewn skirt, looking like he'd known all along what she was up to. He was silent just long enough to start her hands on their way to her hips, and then shook his head. "Don't reckon," he said. "I've seen some fancy ridin' skirts like that, come from the south."

"Woman wearing this in public, on purpose? I'd say that's a great big fib." But his gaze pivoted back to pin her, and she hastily added, " 'Cept there wouldn't be no point. Don't reckon I'm worth the trouble."

Dacey watched the trees—there were some king-lets flittering at one another, far above them—until Blaine had packed the needle away. Then he said, "Think highly on yourself, I've noted."

Blaine backed against a slender poplar, her impulse to snap an answer quickly fading. She thought of her cousins—*by the time you look old enough to marry, Blaine, you'll be an old spinster, an' your only bulges'll be fat!* She thought of her daddy, vexed at her sassy mouth or independent spells. And Lenie, trying so kindly to make Blaine more like herself—more like she *ought to be*. At least Rand understood . . . or tried. And Mommy . . . if she wasn't wondering whether Blaine was quite normal, she seemed too tired to care one way or another.

"I ain't got no sense," she told Dacey, though it was obvious the words were not her own. "And I'm as ugly as homemade sin."

"You ain't," he said in a practical voice. "And what does that have to do with how *you* think on yourself?"

Blaine stuck her chin in the air. It was supposed to be defiant, but even she knew it was only to hide a permanent hurt. "They don't tell Lenie things like that."

"I'll bet Lenie don't pay 'em no mind if they do." He gave her one of those see-right-through-you looks. "It's what you think of yourself that matters, Blaine, not the trouble others give you for being you."

She didn't answer. Even if she *knew* what she

thought of herself, she'd be hard put to stand against what she heard from the others day after day.

"Do you think," Dacey started again, his voice cutting the still air as though he'd never paused, "that Lenie could have made the walk from your home to mine? Would she have come back to that camp to see if I was all right? How 'bout your cousins? Would any of 'em have slid down that hill in the rain to cut me loose?" He looked at her, and he sounded almost angry. "Let 'em talk, Blaine. Let 'em talk."

Ascending to the Sky Mountain Gap hit them both hard, and they rested an extra day at the summit. It was a rugged, wearying climb, and Blaine hated to think about going over the ridge proper. But after that, after their supplies had dwindled and they started foraging along the way again, the going seemed almost easy—back to ridgeline travel that quickly carried her toward home. And Blaine found that she had other things to sustain her, now, things she clung to as she got closer to a home that wouldn't ever be as she remembered. All she had to do was think of the look on Dacey's face when he'd said those words. *Let 'em talk, Blaine.* If he believed in her, maybe one day *she* could, too.

And in the meanwhile they closed in on Shadow Hollers. Except—

"This don't look familiar," she said as they stopped to get their breath at the height of the afternoon a fair week after they'd set out. "I don't remember coming down this big ridge when we were going to your cabin."

"Right you are," Dacey said, pausing with his hand on Mage's head, as ever. He gave her a brief and tired smile. "I'm bringing us around to the west of your area instead of the east, where we left from. Didn't seem real smart to stumble right back in the way they chased us out."

"Are we close, then?"

"Day or so," Dacey shrugged. "But we're not goin' in as soon as we get there."

"How can we help if we just *watch*?" To be so close, and not *do* anything . . .

"We can't help *no*body if we blunder into the Annekteh first thing. We got to take stock of things, Blaine. Got to see what's best for us to do."

Blaine sighed, leaned against a thick oak and rubbed her shoulder where the pack strap had done a good job of making a raw spot over her collarbone. "You got something up your sleeve, Dacey Childers, and I wish you'd tell me what it is."

He raised an eyebrow; it was meant to profess ignorance, even if it fooled neither of them. Blaine said crossly, "You know what I mean. One minute we don't have any defense against 'em and the next we're waitin' so's to best get at 'em. Anyway, you wouldn't have come all the way back here if the best we could do was chuck stones at 'em. I been real good about this, waitin' for you to tell me. But now I'm askin'."

"Don't trust me no more?"

"No. Well, *yes*, but . . . give a body some peace, Dacey!" Blaine thumped her heel into the tree behind her, awkward under his gaze but determined.

"There are reasons, Blaine." He watched her frustration a moment, like he might say something else, but finally ended their respite by shaking his head again—once, regretfully—and following Mage's limp along the mountain.

Reasons. She scowled at his back, and impulsively stuck her tongue out at it. Childish it may have been, but she felt so much better she did it again. She waited until he was just out of sight, and pushed herself away from the oak to follow. Unlike their first journey, she was entirely comfortable following the slight trail scuff of his soft-soled boots in the winter-dampened groundcover of last fall's leaves. If she ever lagged too far, Blue came back to see if she was doing anything interesting—all proud, with his silly half-filled packs—so there was no worry about getting lost. And she liked walking alone as much as walking with Dacey's silent company.

It was, after all, something she'd been doing for years.

The next day Dacey left her to scout ahead, so she *knew* they were close. Although she couldn't identify the individual ridges around her, they had a familiarity, a pattern she had always seen and would always recognize as home. But now she had other hill formations in her mind, as well: the intimidating rise of Sky Mountain, abrupt and clifflike on one side, sloping and more accommodating on the other. The wider valleys and less sharply sloped hills of Dacey's home hills, rambling along in less well-defined ridge formations. And in her mind and dreams, a new awareness of a place where there were no hills, where the ground was flat and grassy.

Blaine waited for what seemed a whole day while Dacey scouted, though the sun above her seemed to think it was still only just past noon. Blue stayed with her, and Dacey had left his coat on the ground; the other dogs periodically returned to it. His pack was there as well, considerably bigger than hers. She poked through both of them, dispiritedly noting that unless she supplemented the midday meal, it would be cornbread and dried meat for their dinner again.

The sleeping lump of Blue caught her eye. If that big dumb hound could occasionally supply them with fresh meat, she ought to be able to do the same. She knew enough to recognize a rabbit run when she saw one, and could at least make a few snares. Blaine rose to her feet and secured the packs in a tree— not good enough to keep them from bear, but enough to discourage the dogs—and she trusted *them* to discourage anything else. She tried to creep away without attracting Blue's attention—free of his packs, he was looking for amusement—and for a while she thought she'd succeeded, but soon enough he lumbered from the trees to fall in beside her, plenty pleased with himself.

"Come on, then," she said ungraciously, as if she had a choice. She walked the ridge in his company, trying to put everything—Annekteh especially—out of her mind, thinking only about rabbits and rabbit terrain, and not about the fact that these hills were no longer quite the sanctuary that they had been. She hadn't hiked long when a slash of sun through the trees caught her eye.

Without thinking she pointed it out to the dog and he thudded happily down the slope, used to directions from Dacey. She followed more carefully, and discovered the cause of the clearing while Blue was eagerly snuffling around in the thick berry briars that had grown up in it. A lightning-struck oak lay scattered, its grave washed in the sunlight; young oak saplings reached up for the patch of sky, sharing the space with intermediate growth like the briars.

Rabbits. No doubt about it. She crossed her arms and contemplated the best spot for her snares.

Blue's yelp startled her, annoying and alarming at the same time. Now where had he got to? More important, what had he got *into*? Blaine circled the briars with some haste, searching out his whine.

There he was, in the thickest of it. "It's a *rabbit* run, Blue," she said. "You're a *dog*. A big *dumb* one, at that." He'd been trailing one of the creatures, no doubt, forging through the thorny labyrinth until he'd hit a tight turn and found himself suddenly jabbed from all directions. From within the thicket he gazed mournfully at her, his eyes rolling white and the tip of his tail wagging with much hope.

It was the tail that did it, the way its white-flagged

tip wiggled at the sight of her despite the way the rest of it was held fast. Her mouth twitched in a smile. "All right," she muttered, already knowing that she would regret it.

Knife in hand and cutting herself free along the way, she carefully moved in on him, shedding blood of her own for her trouble. Twice she had to cut her clothes free of the tough canes, but when she finally reached him, it was the work of moments to get him loose. Blue backed out of the run with her, and only hesitated long enough to rub against her once, shake off, and trot to the head of another run.

"Oh, no you *don't*." She grabbed him and used the phrase she had heard from Dacey. "No good, Blue, *no good*."

He plumped his bottom on the ground, his brow wrinkling in sorrow. With the burn of her own scratches strengthening her resolve, she easily ignored him, putting herself between him and the briars as she pulled a few strands of wool from the ragged seam in her skirt, braided them, and began the construction of a snare with one of the oak saplings around the edge of the briars.

"What're you doing?"

Blaine jumped back from the snare, catching her skirt on a briar and stumbling over her own feet. She ended up on her rump, staring up at the boy who had spoken.

She didn't recognize him. He was of her own height but sturdier, endowed with nondescript hair and features—aside from a pair of ears that stuck out just a mite too far. But his clothes and short bow were of the sort she'd seen all her life, and she was sure he was from around here. She might have even seen him once or twice at gatherings.

"I'm setting a snare," she said finally, not without some indignation. "Which is a lot better than sneaking up behind somebody."

"Sneakin's the only way to move around these hills lately," he drawled, with a great show of being relaxed while he kept his distance. "Say, ain't you one of Cadell Kendricks' girls?"

"What iff'n I am?" Blaine spoke with much airiness, trying to offset the fact that she was sitting on her bottom looking up at him. Getting up didn't seem to be a great idea, considering that she was still snagged. *Wouldn't* that *present an amusing picture.*

Then she thought of the Annekteh, and Dacey's caution that she wouldn't be able to tell who was and who wasn't Taken, and she began to pick at the briars that held her, trying for a casual air, even more casual than the boy.

Not an easy task. He said, as indifferent as she could imagine, "Then you're a piece from home. I'm Trey Mullins. Seen you a couple o' times at the meetin' hall, I reckon, but not many. Suppose you tell me what you're doing in my parts?" And, finally, his posture had stiffened; the request was just a touch on the far side of politeness.

"Ain't none of your business, I don't reckon," Blaine said, panicking inside. *Annekteh*, he had to be.

Both young people froze at the sound of an ominous rumble, looking to each other with accusation and suspicion. A slightly louder rumble made them both look to Blue. The noise reverberated in his chest, and with raised hackles and curled lip, he was nothing Blaine wanted to be on the wrong side of. "Blue!"

Then she thought again, and smiled at Trey. "I really don't have any control over him," she explained, with all the regret she could muster.

Dacey's clear baritone rang down into the sunlight. "*Blue.*"

Blaine sighed, muttering, "But he does," not caring if Trey heard her.

"Blaine?" Dacey questioned her with the single word, giving Blue another stern look as he closed in on them. The dog quieted, although his hackles remained spiked above his shoulders. Mage limped down and sat next to Dacey in his perpetual spot at the man's right, regarding Trey with only a moment's interest.

"I'm setting a snare so we might could have something other'n dried meat for dinner," Blaine said.

"And just look what you caught," Dacey said dryly. "Who is he?"

"Lives a couple hollers away from my folks. I don't know what he's doing here . . . maybe he's Annekteh, Dacey?"

"I am not!" Trey said hotly.

Dacey shook his head, passed his hand over Mage's head. "No, I don't reckon he is."

"How do you know?" Trey and Blaine asked at the same time. They glared at one another.

"Ain't you the one that's missing?" Trey said to her, still sporting a fine hateful face. "What're you doing *here*? Don't you know your folks has give up on you?"

"If they'd only ever listened to me in the first place—" Blaine snapped back, but stopped. That wasn't fair. It was Rand who hadn't listened, and it just pained her so much to think about her folks that striking out was easier than facing up to it. She picked at a briar, freed it from her skirt.

Trey let it pass; he'd honed in on Dacey. "Who the spirits are you? Someone fancies himself an expert on the Annekteh? Don't mean nothin' to me. I'm tellin' you now, I don't aim to let you cause trouble for us."

Dacey eyed him back, and there was something about his look that made Blaine think of Mage when he was about to show Chase or Blue their true place in the dog pack. "Let me put this plain. I'm the only hope you got of freein' yourselves from the Takers. You'd best think about how to help us, not about throwin' threats at us."

Trey waited, arms crossed. "You ain't told me *nothin'*, yet. Who *are* you? You got some stake in this, you better convince me of it."

"I got the same stake as anyone else," Dacey said, and his voice grew hard. Didn't like to be pushed, Blaine thought, surprised at this side of him, and even proud of it. "More so, maybe. No one forced me to come up here and take your part in things, but I come, and you're a fool to walk away from that. I'm from the old seer's line is all you need to know, and where I met up with Blaine don't make no never mind." He looked Trey up and down. "Iff'n you're smart, you'll see we're your best chance to save Shadow Hollers."

Trey snorted. "You take yourself too serious."

"That's my problem. You going to help?"

"How?" Trey asked, suspicion narrowing his eyes.

"Meet me regular and tell me about their doin's—of their habits, or any plans you get wind of. Take a look at your neighbors and make sure they ain't Taken, let me know if they are." Dacey paused, but Trey didn't say anything, just waited. Blaine, riveted to their conversation, forgot that her bottom was growing damp from the ground, ceased worrying at the briars. "Some food'd make it easier to hide up here, if we ain't have'n to traipse around lookin' for it ourselves. Oh—and I need to know if they got pistols."

Trey stared at him a moment, taken aback. "You don't ask for much. How do I know *you're* not—" the thought was occurring to him too late, and he knew it.

Dacey grinned. "Let me touch you."

"No need," Trey said hastily, and then gave Dacey a troubled look. "It don't really matter. I don't trust you, one way or the other."

Dacey gave him a hard look. "And I don't trust you, either. For all I know you'll go runnin' down that mountain and tell the Annekteh of us. You want to make it back home, you'd best convince me you'll work with us."

Trey started; he'd clearly not even considered this possibility. Finally, he said, slow and careful, "I don't reckon I have to trust you just yet. Iff'n you ain't nothing, you'll do no harm out in these woods. Iff'n you're somethin' . . . well, then, maybe you'll be of some help after all. I'll give you that much." And he squared his shoulders some, waiting to see what Dacey would make of it.

Dacey gave him a grin, one that startled Trey. "That's a might better answer than playin' like you'll throw right in with us." *Us*, he'd said. Blaine liked that. "Don't reckon I trust you, either. But it's a start. You go off and see if you can round up some of the things we need. And tell me—they got guards around, or patrols?"

"Some. They don't range as much, since . . . well, they kept tangling with trap lines." Trey's answer was reluctant, his belief in Dacey shallow.

"Do they know everyone? Would they know if someone new showed up?"

"Reckon they would—the Taken, at least. They seem to swap knowin' stuff pretty easy, an' if one of 'em don't know us, another 'un would. The regular men know most of us by sight, I'm thinkin, iff'n you don't count the children." He shifted, twiddling with the knife strap some more, an uneasy expression coming over his face; he glanced quickly at Blaine and then away.

"That's a start." Dacey gave a single nod, his thoughts going inside for a moment. Blaine knew the look, knew he'd be quiet with those thoughts for some time now. But he gave Trey one final glance, his eyes clear in the bright sunshine. "You keep in mind—you go home and tell what you've learnt today, you won't be doing anyone any favors."

"Still think you take yourself kind of serious," Trey said, making a face. "But I'll keep hushed. It ain't worth the trouble I might cause even if you *ain't* no one."

"That means Blaine's folks, too. Don't let on she's alive."

"Dacey, no!" Blaine lifted her head, stricken.

"I'm sorry, Blaine," he said gently. "But you know I'm right. You ain't put yourself in no safe place by throwing in with me. And we can't give them any cause for wondering about us."

"But—" she started. "But—" But he was right, even if he didn't say right out what he meant. *She might yet be dead before this was over.*

"You mean go on lettin' 'em think they've lost two?" Trey said, scowling and unwilling.

"Two?" Blaine said blankly. "What're you talking about, *two*?"

Trey's dismay knocked the scowl right off his face. For an awkward moment he didn't say anything, and when he did speak it was to Dacey. "I'll keep hushed," he repeated.

"Two?" demanded Blaine.

Dacey shook his head at Trey. "You've done stuck your foot in it. You'd better tell her all."

Abashed, Trey spent a long moment staring at the ground. When he did raise his eyes, he looked more through Blaine than at her.

"It was your brother," he said. "They used him as an example, so we wouldn't give 'em no trouble. He's . . . dead."

Dead! Blaine's hands curled into fists, scrunching up the skirt she'd been trying to free. "Rand?" she said faintly.

Trey's forehead wrinkled. "That don't sound right," he said. "It was William or some such . . . he was the only one. That's all it took."

"Willum!" Her voice barely raised . . . but inside,

something screamed. Tears spilled down a face which felt dead and strangely expressionless. "He was only a *baby*," she said, as if it would make Trey change his words.

"I know," Trey said, still not looking at her. "We all know. It's part of what's kept the rest of us in line."

Dacey drew Trey a few steps away from Blaine's grief. "You mean to tell me that's all they've done? They've killed one child, and touched no one else?"

Trey grew abruptly withdrawn, and fiddled with the thigh strap to his knife. He deliberately kept his eyes on Blaine as she finished untangling herself, carefully and thoroughly slicing the offending branches to slivers as she ignored the tears on her face. "No, that ain't *all they've done*. But mostly they leave us be . . . as long as things are goin' the way Nekfehr likes it."

Dacey digested the information, shook his head—this time to himself—and rubbed a hand over the back of his neck, lost in thought. "Blue," he said absently as the big ticked dog sniffed anxiously at Blaine and made a hesitant move in her direction; she ignored them all, dazed, taking in events like she was using somebody else's eyes. At Dacey's voice Blue sat next to Mage, plainly worried; Dacey gave his ears a quick, absent rub.

Blaine carefully folded her knife and climbed to her feet. She barely noticed Trey's attention to her odd skirts, and had little interest in his comment to Dacey as she moved out of the briars. *Willum.* That's all she could think of. *Willum.* Hardly old enough to do more harm than squash a bug and they'd killed him.

With a sudden, nearly physical blow, Blaine's old dream rushed in on her. *The trees built momentum, crashing to the ground, tangling, rolling—rushing down toward the Kendricks homestead.*

Willum was there, his chubby face contorted in fear. "Blaine!" *he shrieked, terror distorting his voice into a high keen.*

"Willum!" she cried, and ran for him, reaching out to scoop him up as each step forward took her further and further away. "No! Willum!"

Deeply startled, she stared at Dacey. *If you've got seein's, you'll learn to sort them out . . .* What other dreams had she had, the ones that seemed too real? Hadn't he been in one? And Rand? She scrambled around her memories, trying to find visions she had once worked hard to forget. She thought . . . she thought—

Trey's voice scattered the tenuous recollection, as he cleared his throat and tried to move past the moment. "I can get you food," he said, and something had changed in his voice, as if being a part of Blaine's grief had tipped his trust their way. "Be hard to bring much without gettin' questions from my ma, but I can get some. And no, they ain't got pistols. They barely take to bows—afeard of 'em, the Takers are, even if they don't say it."

"Hoped as much," Dacey said. "Can't grab hold of someone and Take 'em, stop 'em from killin' you, iff'n you ain't close enough to touch 'em."

"About them other things—well, I'll do my best. Don't know what good it'll do you."

Dacey didn't take the invitation to elaborate. "We'll be here early morning. Will you?"

"Can't get away every day. I got huntin' to do. And they keep track of us, sometimes." But he nodded, and his face showed reluctant agreement.

"You'll have time enough to hunt." Dacey cast a concerned eye on Blaine, touched her arm, seeing if she were ready to go and practically turning her to do so even as he asked one last question. "You got any dogs?"

"Couple o' hounds," Trey said. "Mostly tree." He nodded to the top of the ridge; for the first time Blaine saw a redbone, hanging back as aloof as Mage could be, watching them.

"Plainsfolk won't know the difference. Iff'n you hear 'em askin' about dogs runnin' the hills, you tell 'em yours got loose. Don't want 'em to wonder about mine."

Trey nodded, and moved uneasily, and ducked his head. "I'll come back tomorrow, then, with some food. Just don't do nothin' to change my mind 'bout you, hear?" He gestured to his dog, and headed up to follow the ridge north.

Blaine barely noticed him go.

Blaine spent the afternoon fiddling with the fire and trying to warm her toes, quietly crying, full of unbidden images of Willum. Willum at three, and never the chance to get any older. Willum with his bugs and boasts, all boy, keeping the whole family running to make sure he stayed out of trouble.

She simply couldn't imagine that she would never see him again. That she wouldn't even have the chance to say good-bye, to be with her family when they consigned him to the ground, his young spirit to join the rest of those that lived among these hills.

Dacey foraged through the afternoon, dropping off more wood for her fire, offering a hand on her shoulder, gathering a mess of young nettles to boil up for supper. He settled in at camp when the hounds took off after an early fox, making the hills ring; he gave her what privacy he could, immersing himself in the construction of a lean-to, pausing only when the trail cry faltered. When the hounds worked out the puzzle and took off again—even Blaine could hear it was Whimsy in front, with her clever nose—he smiled to himself and returned to work.

Blaine wiped her eyes then, annoyed and even surprised when they immediately welled up with tears, as if on some mission of their own and not paying any attention to the fact that she'd decided to boil up those nettles. Blue was still off on his halfhearted

chase of the fox, and Mage had long since moved
away from Blaine's awkward patting to pace around
the camp area, lifting his nose to the breeze and licking it to freshen the scent he winded. Pining after
the chase, she figured, wiping her own wet nose.

But Mage found the scent he wanted, and his
hackles rose. His head lifted, his jaw dropped just
enough to let the sound out, a face she'd always
found endearingly human, even in her own family's
hounds. At first she heard no sound, just a prickling
at the nape of her neck. Then his voice lifted in a
clear, rising moan that was at once beautiful and
terrifying.

Blaine froze. She'd heard that sound before, the
one that had haunted her up out of sleep and inspired
her to go check on those strangers again. Dacey, too,
stopped to watch his dog, wearing a grim sort of pride
that Blaine couldn't understand.

Blithely unaware of the scrutiny, Mage repeated
his statement twice, then went to curl up where
Dacey knelt by the lean-to.

"Why'd he do that?" Blaine asked after the quiet
that followed, her voice still thick from all her tears.
Only the faint, distant baying of the other hounds
disturbed the silence. "I heard him before, too.
Before . . . all *this*."

"It's just his way of saying he's scented his prey
and is ready for the hunt." Dacey gave his dog a
speculative look, one that told Blaine he wasn't so sure
as he sounded. He tossed some dried bark fuzz into
the air and watched it drift with the slight breeze.
"More homesteads that way, Blaine?"

"I'm still not just sure where we are," Blaine said.
"But if we're due east of my homeplace, then north
of us is the mouth of the creek and the river, and
where our meetin' hall is." She imitated Dacey's
actions and watched three times as the fluff of bark
floated away from the north. "I guess bein' up here

on this ridge puts us clear, though . . . they ain't gonna get none of our smoke."

"I'm hopin' not."

Of course he'd already taken the vagaries of the wind into account. *Of course.* She closed her mouth tightly and vowed to quit trying to help someone who didn't really need it. "Don't understand why you keep me here. Ought to be a way to get me back home, secret-like. I ain't any help to you."

"You ain't in the way, either," Dacey responded easily. He gave her a wry smile, a touch of self-deprecating humor in his eyes. "Truth be told, iff'n it was safe to take you home, I'd have it that way, but it ain't. And havin' you here . . . keeps me from feelin' alone."

Alone? Dacey? But he was that kind, wasn't he? He *chose* to be alone . . . didn't he?

Then he grinned, just a little bit of tease lurking there. "Besides, you can take right good care of yourself, I've noted. I reckon I'll need your help before it's done."

Blaine stared into the fire and didn't answer him. She longed to be doing anything besides sitting here, thinking. About Willum. About her role in the days to come—dreading it, and at the same time, dreading the thought that she didn't really have one.

The shelter caught her eye, almost done, with the long evening twilight dimming its back corners. Empty back corners. It seemed Dacey hadn't thought about bedding.

That was something she *could* do.

"Goin' for bedding," she announced abruptly, and took his big sheath knife. Circling north of the point, she went in search of hemlocks and some fine, springy branches. The north-facing slope held a grove of them, as was often the case; Blaine set to work, cutting a few selected branches from the younger trees and leaving them scattered around the grove as she went, breathing

deeply of the fresh sap. When she reckoned she ha
enough—which she judged more by the fact that he
fingers were as sticky as she wanted them to get tha
by an accounting of branches—she shoved the knif
and sheath down against the waistband of her skirt an
found a piece of forked deadwood. Dragging it fron
tree to tree, she jammed her boughs against the fork
hurrying as the twilight faded. When she had so man
they spilled off her stick no matter how careful sh
was, she turned back for the campsite.

And hesitated. She'd come further than she'
meant to. And as she paused she caught a sudde
lungful of spilled bowel and bloody meat, startlin
herself with the discovery of a deer carcass jus
outside the grove. Deer carcass, but not with the ski
torn up and eaten along with the rest of it. With tha
turned inside-out look that a bear left to its meal.

Oh, spirits. Hungry spring bear.

A low, coughing growl made her stiffen. Behin
her. Unhappy sounding.

Blaine peered cautiously over her shoulder an
wished she hadn't. The sight of the bear was enougl
to take the strength from her legs. From anybody'
legs. It wasn't a huge bear—downright skinny bear—
but it looked big enough, staring at her from thos
small, cold bear eyes and making an irritated nois
deep in its throat.

"Nice bear," she said, from a dry mouth that only
let half the sounds out. *Stupid*, the same dry-mouthed
voice squeaked inside her head. *Stupid, so close to
a bear claim and not even knowing it*. The bear stood
tall on its hind legs, shifting from one to the other
clacking its jaws at her, working up some foam
nodding in a jerky, spookily human way.

She trembled, afraid to move, afraid not to. Maybe
just one, quivering, uncertain step . . .

Wrong. The bear dropped down and snarled ter
ribly at her, slinging its head, slinging spit.

Blaine shrieked and darted forward, her hemlock forgotten, the noise of the bear's pursuit filling her world. *Tree, tree,* tree!

With the bear's breath warming her heels, Blaine spotted the black-barked spire of a small black cherry and she leapt for it, shinnying up its rough skin. No lower branches, they'd all been broken off by—

Black cherry. What was it that bears liked more than anything, would climb plenty high to get? *Black cherries.* And what had her daddy always told her? *Bear comes around, don't you run. Set up a ruckus, squall at it. Black bear don't care enough to come through that.*

But she'd already run. And she'd already climbed— was *still* climbing, fast as she could.

Oh, spirits . . .

She had to get further up than the bear would go. Young tree, skinny trunk . . . surely she could do that. Surely she could—

"Get away!" she screamed mindlessly at it, digging knees and ankles and arms against the rough bark, blessing her split skirts and not daring to look down. The tree swayed with their weight; she ignored it . . . until it gave an ominous creak, dipping wildly against the slight bend in its trunk. She clutched it convulsively, squeezing her eyes shut, waiting to feel either claws or the sudden crack of the tree.

Nothing. Blaine dared a glance down and discovered the bear had stopped, too, its furry arms wrapped around the tree, for the moment looking as uncertain as she. Until it saw her gaze, taking in the black glitter of its harsh coat, the soft brown of its face—even *that* was skinny—the furious curl of its amazingly mobile lips. Then it cared again, and lurched up at her.

I'm going to die. Either way, I'm going to die. Blaine glared downward, hurling an ineffective curse at the bear's upturned face, kicking at its nose. It

snarled back and swiped at her, snaring the heel
her boot and ripping leather—ripping the boot rig
off her foot. She shrieked, digging her toes into t
bark as she scurried out of reach.

But her skin was torn, her arms were tired, h
grip was loosening. The bear, enraged to see her ju
out of reach with the tree swaying in increasin
alarming circles, snarled at her, coughing hot brea
on her ankle. "Gitgitgit!" she hollered, slipping dov
with the effort. She lifted her head and closed h
eyes and bellowed, "*Dacey!*"

There wasn't even a chance he would hear he

She pressed herself against the crispy black ba
and felt a new chill travel her spine as the cool hand
of Dacey's knife touched her stomach. A chill, an
sudden hope. Blaine hugged the tree trunk with on
arm, easing the knife out of her waistband, moveme
that triggered the bear into another round of fru
trated threats;. Its wild swipe caught her skirts, ri
ping them, sending the tree into violent movemer
they both clutched at it. Perversely, half out of h
mind with fear, she growled back at it. And then sl
slipped again, and there was no more choice—

With a yell for courage, she dropped back an
drove the heavy knife down, into the bear's eye.

The bear stiffened. It jerked and slid and fell aw
from the trunk, landing with a thump and crack th
Blaine felt through her suddenly tenuous grip. Sl
was nearly upside down, torn away from the tree wi
her effort. Only one hand was close enough t
scrabble at the bark; for a moment she thought sl
would come down the tree and land headfirst on tl
bear—unmoving, was it dead?—but she managed
right herself, wrapping each limb tightly around tl
trunk no matter the cost to her skin. She put her fac
against the cool, rough bark and hugged it, hugge
it until she knew she had to climb down or fall dow
no matter what waited below.

Slowly, with respect for her scrapes, she descended the tree.

On the ground she fell to her knees and simply stared at the bear. It was a big, black lump of fur that moved bonelessly under her tentative shove. Dead. Tears of blood oozed down the bear's face; the knife still jutted out of its eye, an insult. Blaine stared, and wiped her nose against her sleeve, suddenly aware of the many tears on her own face. Then she smoothed back the hair that had pulled out of her braids, straightened her homespun shirt, and stood.

"Stupid bear," she muttered, with only the smallest sob. She kicked it. As an afterthought, she jerked the knife out of its eye socket, and kicked it again.

A joyful roar of challenge rang from the hemlocks and Blaine whirled, shoving the knife out in front of her. Blue charged out, hauling Dacey with his braided leash, and pounced on the bear, roughing it mercilessly.

Blaine dropped the knife, sagged against the tree, and covered her face with her hands, moaning. "*Blue.*"

"Down, Blue," Dacey commanded. He dragged the dog off the bear, giving his collar one good shake. "That's enough!" Blue, shaking and whining, barely managed to restrain himself, but Dacey ignored him. "Blaine, you hurt?"

"No," Blaine said, although she frankly wasn't sure. She let herself slide to the ground, and moaned again. That last shock had been the last she could take. "Damn bear. Damn dog."

Dacey relaxed a little, though his eyes searched her, as though he didn't quite believe her. "Spirits, you put a scare on me! I heard that squallin' and shriekin' all the way to the camp. But Blue won't jump trail and we had to track to every doggone tree you cut." He eyed her again, apparently finally convinced that she was indeed whole, for he relaxed some. "You give that bear some insult?"

"Why, I walked right up to it and slapped it,"

Blaine said. "Told it to stay outta my way. Spirits
Dacey! I reckon I got too close to a kill." She nod
ded in the direction of the deer.

He went to take a look, back in short order. "Bea
don't kill nothin' that big, but he's sure enough bee
eatin' on it." He hunkered by the creature, runnin
his hands over it. "Damn skinny thing. Sickly."

"Didn't look so sickly when it was chargin' afte
me," Blaine said sourly.

He grinned at her. "No, I reckon it didn't. Tree
you, did it?"

"Better'n Blue could've," Blaine sighed, pulling u
her torn skirt to look at her shins and the black chip
of bark embedded there.

Dacey rolled the bear's heavy skull around to chec
out the injury done to it and let it flop back to th
ground. "Broke its neck when it fell—though it migh
well have been dead before it hit the ground. Damn
you done good with that knife." He stood and wipe
his hands on his pants, and he was grinning that quie
grin. "Yup, Blaine. You can take right good care o
yourself."

She didn't see what was so amusing; her expres
sion must have said so, though he didn't give it any
respect, and kept right on being amused.

"Give over that knife and I'll gut it. Bear meat'
tough, but it's food."

Blaine tossed the knife to his feet. She stood, settle
her skirts back in place, and shook out her legs, snatch
ing up the damaged boot and jamming it on.

"Where you off to?" he asked, looking up from th
bear.

"I spent all that time cuttin' those hemlocks,"
Blaine said. "I'm not leavin' 'em."

Dacey shook his head. "Take Blue with you."

She thought he was hiding another smile.

→ 10 ←

Dacey gutted and dressed the bear and they dragged it back to camp together. At first of the opinion that it wasn't worth the trouble, Blaine changed her mind late the next morning. She awoke to discover that each move was an adventure in discomfort; the many scrapes on her inner legs and the tender skin inside her elbows were crusty and stiff and Dacey, in anticipation, had cut out the bear's sparse spring fat and rendered it. Before Blaine had a chance to make her first complaint, he handed her a little hickory basket full of grease, then busied himself with the dogs so she could minister to the sores high on her thighs. The crude liniment made her smell gamy, but softened her skin so it didn't crack open with every movement.

With her hurts soothed, Blaine went to the rocks below their camp where they'd found a slow trickling spring. The cold water sent goosebumps running up her arms and down her back, but left her feeling cleaner; it freshened her eyelids, swollen from all her crying the day before. Willum's death still hung over her, making her thoughts thick and full of pain, but when she climbed back up, she was ready to see what Dacey had planned for the day.

He didn't give her a chance to ask. As she entered the camp he looked up from the bear meat he was stripping to dry over the coals—for the dogs, he'd said; bear meat was good eating, but one so stringy as this one, they might as well give mostly to the dogs—and said, "You're willing, I need you to see Trey today."

"Me?"

"I think it'd be good to get to know him—and him, you. It'll be easier to work with him if something sudden comes up. Iff'n you're still looking to help, that is."

"Well . . . 'course I am." Blaine's expression took a turn toward wary—not a thing to do with Dacey, for the dogs had circled around her, closing in with hesitation but clear determination. Whimsy finally butted in close, nudging Blaine's skirt aside so she could sniff and lick a greasy scrape. Blaine pushed her away, not gently. "Quit!"

Dacey made a clicking noise between his teeth, a reminder to the dogs that he was watching. From under the hair that had fallen across his brow, he looked at her, thoughtful. "Just wander over to where we met him yesterday," he suggested. "Listen to what he's got to say. But Blaine—" this time he looked full and clear at her, his bright hazel eyes filled with quiet emphasis. "Don't put yourself out in the open till he shows, and watch him a good bit even then."

"You said he wasn't Annekteh."

"He ain't. Accordin' to him, none o' the folks have been Taken. But there's more than one way to control a body, Blaine. He's much as told us how they've been doin' it."

"Willum," Blaine breathed, a hundred different scenarios of revenge tumbling through her mind.

Dacey nodded and laid another strip of meat on the greenstick drying rack he'd lashed together.

"Don't be doin' anything to get yourself in trouble," Dacey said, as though he had read her vengeance-filled thoughts of a moment before. "Just listen, come back and tell me what he says."

Blaine shrugged. "All right." She rubbed a stray smear of grease into her skin a little more thoroughly. Maybe one of her snares had caught a rabbit. She hoped so, since Dacey seemed to have forgotten about breakfast. With a sigh, she got to her feet.

"And take Blue with you," Dacey said.

Blaine stopped. Blue, rabbits and briars. *No good*, as Dacey would say to his dogs. "He'll just be in the way."

"Not if you tell him to get out of the way," Dacey said without missing a beat.

"He won't listen to me," Blaine said, and winced at the petulance she heard in her own voice.

"I reckon he will, at that. Call him."

"Blue," Blaine said reluctantly. The dog lifted his head from Dacey's blanket and gave her a surprised look. "Here, Blue." His tail thumped. He stood, shook off, and trotted over to her.

"Tell him to sit," Dacey said quietly. Blue cocked an ear at him, but continued to wait, tail gently waving as he stared up into Blaine's face.

"Sit, Blue."

The hound watched her, ever wagging his tail, as though she hadn't spoken at all.

"No, *tell* him," Dacey told her, surprising her with the command in his own voice.

All *right*, then. "*Sit!*" she said. Blue sat with a thump, watched her a moment, and turned his attention to the itch that plagued him. "He did it," she said, not quite believing.

" 'Course he did. He's got a crush on you, remember. Now, you tell him to stick close—*with me*, tell 'im—and he'll stay right with you. Iff'n he goes after somethin', tell him *no good*. That ought to keep you out of trouble."

She gave him a peeved look, on the verge of telling him she didn't need any dog to keep her out of trouble. Then she thought about the bear and simply nodded. "With me, Blue," she said as she took up the hike to the clearing. The dog followed happily, never straying very far from her and readily responding to her call when he did—that is, as long as she *told* him instead of merely suggesting the commands.

They walked along the ridge, a distance that seemed longer now that she had an actual goal and wasn't simply wandering. She even wondered if she'd missed the clearing, and was thinking about turning back when she saw its bright flash. Sunlight, partway down the mountain. Blaine slowed, her hand on Blue's collar—and her blinder in the other. No point in taking chances, if Trey had talked, or brought Annekteh with him; the blinder would hide her. She stopped and stood there, watching for movement, looking for the grey of the pants that Trey had been wearing. After several moments of nothing, she moved closer and did it all over again.

At last, satisfied that if Trey was hiding she wasn't going to be able to find him anyway, she moved down into the clearing and chose a seat behind a soft old tree trunk that lay along the hill. Blue sat on the first command, then lowered himself to the ground. Blaine's hopes of his continued good behavior didn't last long; he was soon shoving her arm with his big cold nose, courting her attention. "Quit," she told him, pushing him off, keeping a hand on him so he'd maybe be under the influence of the blinder, too. "Just because you done listened to me don't give you the right to get familiar."

With a sigh, the hound put his head on his front

paws. They waited—Blaine for some sign of Trey, an
Blue for whatever she might want him to do nex

Despite Blaine's vigil, it was the dog who fir
raised his head and pointed his nose down the hil
He growled and sniffed the air, then thumped his ta
once. "No," Blaine said, quiet but as firm as she
ever been with him, stopping him when he woul
have risen to greet Trey. Now she could hear hir
too, making his way up the hill with slow but stead
steps.

She watched as snatches of him became visib
through the branches and briars, and then as h
reached the clearing and stood there, his medioc
features uncertain as he looked around. It was at th
moment, as it became clear that he was afflicted wit
her own malady of ungainliness, and that his knee
and elbows didn't seem to know in which directio
to point, that she decided he might be all right.
he'd come to a collected and graceful halt, she kne
she wouldn't have been able to stand him.

She waited for another few minutes and shove
her blinder into her pocket, standing up behind th
tree. He noticed her immediately, relief on his face
although his features quickly reverted to their su
picious set. When she was close enough, he said, '
didn't figure you'd come."

"I got just as much stake in this as you," Blain
asserted. "More. I got Willum."

"That's true," Trey admitted, and then they stare
at one another.

"Well?" Blaine said when her patience ran ou
which, truth be told, didn't take an excessive amou
of time. "You got anything worth tellin' us?"

"Plenty," he said in a haughty tone, obviousl
considering whether or not to impart his wisdom. Sh
waited, and he relented. "Let's get out of this clea
ing. It's a fine place to meet, but it's a good plac
to be watched, too."

"I know. I done the watchin'," Blaine reminded him.

Trey gave her a *look*, and probably would have set on her with some sharp retort, but Blue's whine cut through the air instead. He'd decided that they weren't so interesting after all, but he definitely wanted another chance at the rabbits. He looked up at her, face arranged to be its most beseeching—ears down low and pitiful, eyes showing sad white.

"No good, Blue," Blaine said sharply, envisioning a noisy hound rabbit-bawl in the middle of their clandestine meeting. Blue looked away from her, doggy refusal to accept her words even though he still obeyed them, staying by her side as she led the way to the log.

"He does *too* listen," Trey said, dignity lost in the sputter.

"Yeah, he does," Blaine said guiltlessly, settling down on the damp ground behind the fallen tree. "Now, quit wastin' time—said yourself you didn't have much of it."

"That's so." Trey leaned against the log and studied her openly. "Expected to be dealin' with Dacey."

"Do you want I should go back and tell him you don't know nothin'? Maybe he'll come hisself, tomorrow. 'Course, maybe he won't. He don't want to be seen messing around the hills—they already had him once."

"So how are you so sure he's not Taken?" Trey asked, removing his hunting knife from its sheath for the sole purpose of digging little holes in the rotted bark of the tree.

"He's not. I seen what they did to him." She paused at the memory of the fear on Dacey's face, and the way he'd changed when she saw him next . . . the way he always changed, when he thought of that day. It occurred to her for the very first time that they could have simply Taken him to learn what they wanted, and why hadn't they? But no, now weren't the time for such questions, not with Trey watching her face so close. "No, he ain't one of 'em. That's for certain-sure."

He looked at her through the forelock of dull brown hair that had fallen over eyes of an equally indeterminate muddy brown, and offered her nothing.

Blaine thought that if he was in her family, he'd have taken a bath more recently than the obvious several weeks it had been. "Listen here, Trey. Maybe you was expecting Dacey, but I ain't gonna go runnin' to the Annekteh with whatever you tell me and I ain't gonna forget it before I get back to him."

"I can't believe yer runnin' with him at all!" Trey blurted. "Y'ought to be at home, not leavin' your folks to worry an' takin' up with some stranger. It ain't *seemly*."

As if she'd been able to get help when she tried! As if all she'd done hadn't been worth anything, when here she was, back in the thick of things—not hiding out down south, like would have been safe. Blaine jumped to her feet, her bound-together braids hitting her back with the vehemence of her motion. "You don't know nothing, you—you squirrel-brained—you jug-eared—you . . . you coward!" She knew she'd struck home when he lunged to his feet as well, his face red, but she didn't let up, not with the amount of mad riding her shoulders. "Afraid to tell your business to a girl, that's what your problem is! Well, I don't want to hear it, neither—doubtful you got anything worth listenin' to!"

She stalked a few feet up the hill and turned for another salvo. "And you listen to this! There ain't nothin' unseemly about Dacey Childers! He's more of a gentleman than you can ever pretend to be"— *'cause he'll take me for who I am, an' trust me to do what I can do*—"And I ain't *runnin' around* with him like you think!" She gave him another glare for good measure.

"I don't got much to tell you noways," he snapped back. "And I ain't afraid to tell you nothing. There's just no use to it, 'cause you can't pass on what you don't understand."

As Blaine began to draw breath for a reply, Trey gestured at her torn up legs and snorted derisively. "Yesterday when I saw you, you was tangled in briars, and now look at you! Your skirt's all ragged, and your boot's a mess, and your legs are all tore up. It's sure you ain't got a clue how to handle what you're into, and I ain't takin' no chances."

Blaine's pent-up breath whooshed out as she searched for the proper words, words to curse him so bad the flies wouldn't light. Then she realized the truth of it, and drew herself up. "I guess I handled that bear just fine," she said airily. "*I'm* alive, and that's better'n the bear got out of it."

He didn't hesitate for a minute. "You yell it to death, then?"

"I stabbed it in the eye and kilt it." She lifted her chin. "I might be back tomorrow, or I might have more important things to do. Dacey'll come, then, I reckon. You want his help in this, you better be here." She turned her back and stalked up the hill, one sharp "With me, Blue!" drawing the hound to her side. It took most of her willpower, but she managed not to check if Trey was watching her leave.

By the time she got back to camp, she wasn't feeling so self-full. Dacey *had* trusted her, and she hadn't taken care of things as needed. But . . . in some ways, he'd *not* trusted her. And still wasn't telling her everything. Why *hadn't* the Annekteh Taken him?

It didn't help that he greeted her with an amiable smile, and that he was fleshing out the bearskin, or the way he heaved it up so she could admire it. "It'll be a nice pelt when it's tanned," he said. "Won't look near as skinny, then." And he actually winked at her.

Blaine soberly assessed the thing. "It looked a lot bigger when it was comin' for me."

"That's usually the way of it," Dacey agreed, his mouth lingering in a one-cornered grin. He draped the skin back over the fleshing log he'd rigged and worked at it for several minutes before asking, "Did he show?"

Blaine gave a shrug that turned into a reluctant nod. "Didn't have nothing to say, though."

"That so?" Dacey lifted his head just for a moment, but it was long enough to make Blaine look away.

"Yes," she said. "That's so."

"Maybe tomorrow," Dacey said, shifting the skin to work on a new spot, scraping away the bits of flesh and fat left from the skinning. The dogs arranged themselves in a circle around him, their ears cocked high in hope. Even Blaine could smell the fresh pelt, and she was glad that at least its blood no longer hung heavy in the air. Neither her empty stomach nor her sudden mood were prepared to endure the raw smells associated with Dacey's job.

She moved a little further upwind and leaned against the granite wall of rock that formed one edge of the camp. It reminded her of her rock at home. *Home. Willum. Family.* This one, too, sat at the top of a hill. Unlike her own familiar perch, it was backed by an accessible, if not inviting, peak of dirt and trees. It beckoned to her, but she turned her back on it.

"Why didn't they just Take you?" she asked without preamble.

"How's that?" Dacey responded quizzically, one eyebrow arching in amusement.

Blaine felt her face grow warm. *Could have come on to that some better.* "When the Annekteh had you at their camp," she repeated, phrasing her question more carefully, "why didn't they just Take you? Why'd they fool around with that jimson?"

Dacey scraped steadily at the skin, carefully angling

his knife so it wouldn't cut through the pelt. His shoulders suddenly seemed too stiff to do the job right. "I keep forgettin' you saw that."

"You weren't of any mind to pay attention to me."

"No." That stiffened him up even further; he waited long enough that she thought he wasn't going to answer at all. But she knew he was thinking about it by the too-deliberate way he worked, so unlike the casual skill he usually employed. Then he stopped working altogether, and his faraway gaze narrowed. She might as well not have been there, and he might as well have been carved of stone—until he took a sudden, deep breath, and started working again. "I did get one advantage from the seers," he told her, as though those intervening moments hadn't happened. "The Annekteh can't Take me. I should've told you before."

Her mouth dropped open, until she caught herself doing it. *Spirits, yes, you should have told me!*

But no. He'd probably had his reasons. He always seemed to. And then, a buried memory—a word she'd found too jumbled to understand at the time, but had since heard Dacey use . . . *Why can't you be* made *nekfehr?* the Annekteh leader had demanded of Dacey.

The clues had been there. And so was the fact that while Dacey might give her little things to do, he clearly didn't trust her, not clean through.

"I know it now," she said finally. And went to climb up on the rock and look out over the mountains.

➤←   ➤←   ➤←

The timbering went well. Random problems still occurred where they shouldn't, but no more deaths. No more *accidental* trappings or poisonings. Nekfehr found himself impressed with the humans' resourcefulness, their wordless conspiracies. Questioned, Taken, the temporary vessels could only reveal their own minor actions. Yet these people knew each other well enough to make their isolated and insignificant behavior add up to something significant, indeed. *One woman needing to gather poke. Another talking about root foods. And not a one of them mentioning the strange poisonous characteristics of the pokeweed. All of them, managing to look elsewhere when a hungry man tried a new food.*

No planning, no discussion. No witnessing. And yet . . .

But such tricks seemed all they were good for. They knew nothing about their lost magics, about the *suktah*. They had not tended or encouraged new *suktah* growth. Perhaps the Annekteh had been *too* efficient in eradicating seer lore. These humans did not even know where the natural *suktah* groves grew. And surely . . . *surely* the groves had returned, after all this time.

With the *suktah*, the Annekteh could direct their vessels to build *nekfehrta*, the linking structures. And the *nekfehrta*, placed at intervals along the trails between established Annekteh colonies and the new lands they intended to conquer, would create the security and freedom the Annekteh needed to achieve expansion unhindered.

The *suktah* had to be here. Eventually, the Annekteh would find it.

➚➔   ➚➔   ➚➔

Blaine fretted her way through the rest of the day, half resentment, half worry. Resentment—*Dacey didn't trust her, after all she'd been through with him.*

And worry—her family. Surely, she thought, it would be all right to creep on over to her own ridge and at least check on them. She had the blinder. The leaves would be out any day now, making it so much easier to hide on the slopes. And the book, her old seer's book . . . she could get that, too. Even if she did have all the sensible parts memorized. . .

If he don't trust you now, what'll he do iff'n you risk such a thing?

But if he didn't trust her, why should she blindly trust him? Why not do what her heart longed to do?

And still she couldn't bring herself to it, not when she knew he was depending on her even without fully trusting her, and so spent the rest of the day on little nothings—turning the meat on the drying rack, mixing up the last of their corn meal and flour for a midday meal, watching Dacey finish work on the bear hide and carefully roll it up while he cooked its brains to mix with the ashes for tanning—though he said something about getting salt to preserve it until he could make a batch of oak tannic.

And why did he spend his time on some dumb old bearskin? Why wasn't he planning and scouting, and getting ready to make some kind of move?

But she'd learned something from his quiet, and that was to watch, to observe until it might make some sense to her on her own. She finally decided he really *had* been depending on what Trey might have had to say, and couldn't act without it. It didn't make her feel any too good for walking out on the boy. She spent the evening tending to her many scrapes and went to bed while Dacey was still listening to the hounds run trail, Blue panting by her side.

The next morning Blaine rolled off her hemlock bedding before the sun peaked the mountain. Dacey was still asleep on the other side of the shelter, with all five dogs lumped around him. He sprawled on the ground, his legs stuck out from beneath his skewed blanket, his hair tickling over his face in a way that ought to have woken him. Blaine sat against the back of the shelter and drew her knees up to her chin, considering him.

He figured in her dreams these days—only they were not real dreams anymore, just snatches of disjointed moments. *Shouting in her ears, the view of a hillside from way up in the trees, standing in the rain outside a trio of young pines*—nothing that made any sense to her. Except that every time they showed Dacey, his eyes had that harrowed look. The trying-to-survive, not-certain-of-making-it look.

This morning his face was quiet. Blaine nibbled on a rough fingernail and wondered about him. The way he'd reacted to her question about the jimson had made it clear that the memory still pained him, and yet here he was again, facing the Annekteh, the ones who had done that to him.

Maybe she should warn him about her dreams. She had dreamt about hiding in the dairy, hadn't she, and hadn't it happened? She'd had strange dreams about Willum . . . *.Willum.* And even if these new dreams didn't hold anything of any sense, anything but bits and pieces . . . Yes, she should tell him. *Standing in the rain, outside a trio of young pines* . . .

No.

She couldn't.

For Dacey Childers was the one who could help her people, but not if she scared him off—even if he wasn't so easy to scare; he'd proved *that*. But *he* knew the lore; he knew how to deal with the Annekteh. *He* was the one who had traveled all the way up here on the strength of seeings. Her people knew none of these things, and they needed him. And anyway she'd had dreams all her life, dreams that had never meant anything, that no one ever did anything but scoff at. How much worse, if she scared him off for *nothing*.

She closed her eyes, rested her forehead on her knees, and wondered how she'd feel about this moment if Dacey was killed. Then, much as Dacey must have done the previous day after her questions recalled the jimson-fear to his mind, she took a deep breath and put it behind her. It was time to get on with the day.

Dacey had not moved when she returned from splashing her face at the spring below the rocks. *A real gone-from-the-world sleep.* Blaine took the knife from where it lay by the bearskin and found one of the hickory baskets she'd made the day before. There would be no berries for the picking this early in the season, but maybe she could find some old sumac clusters to spice up their drinking water—or maybe some hemlock. Yes, she definitely had a hankering for hemlock tea.

Anything was excuse enough to be gone when Dacey decided it was time to head for the clearing to meet Trey. Blaine paused as she tiptoed past the lean-to, looking again at the relaxed expression on his face. Just like that moment over Lottie's supper the first time they'd met, she realized anew that despite his self-possessed aura, Dacey was far from her father's age. She leaned down to straighten his blanket, carefully so as not to wake him. Then, so he'd know she'd be safe, she hissed at Blue. The sleepy hound got to his feet after only three tries and followed her out on the ridge, his tail wagging in its slow, pleased way.

Blaine made sure it was at least noon before she returned to the camp. She had managed to find some sumac after all, and she held forth the basket as a kind of peace offering when Dacey looked up at her.

He said nothing to her, and she saw no accusation in his gaze—yet there was something there that demanded an explanation. Maybe it was just from

within herself. Either way, Blaine refused to give in.
"He have anything to say today?"

"Plenty," Dacey said, amusement in his voice and
eye. "Most of it about you."

Blaine set herself and the basket down and began
to pick the dried bits of winter-dried leaf out of the
berry clusters. "I got plenty to say about him, too,
if I was the type to do it."

"Oh, he weren't bad-mouthin' you, Blaine," Dacey
said, and Blaine looked up to confirm that she had
actually heard teasing in his voice. "It was mostly
questions he had. Wanted to know if there was really
a bear, for one. And he asked how you'd joined up
with me, and how far we'd walked, and did you slow
me down."

That one earned a snort from Blaine. "Nosy. And
sounds just like my daddy, who probably still don't
believe I been walkin' the hills on my own for years,
even though I bet Rand's spilled it by now."

"He did ask some about Mage, and how he'd got
crippled up," Dacey said.

"Means he's nosy about everyone, not just me,"
Blaine concluded. "How *did* he get crippled up?"

Dacey ducked his head to hide his smile, though
she saw it anyway. Oddly enough, she wasn't piqued
by it. She liked seeing it on him. "He was born that
way," Dacey told her. "With that back hock not
bendin' right. The way I figure it, he has so much
heart, it took some out of the rest of him."

Hmm. Hard to act snappish after a comment like
that. "Didn't Trey have nothin' to say about the
Takers?" she asked, drawing herself out of Blue's way
as he came trotting past her from the woods, sticking his head in Dacey's lap and rubbing his face on
Dacey's legs, groaning in a happy kind of way.

"Some." Dacey slapped the hound's sides resound-
ingly, and then pushed the dog over so he lay with
his legs dangling loosely in the air, tilting his head

backwards. His lips fell away from his face. He looked utterly ridiculous, and Blaine found herself hiding her own smile. "To be fair to the boy, Blaine, he come up with a lot for only two days. I get the feelin' he already knew the answers when I first asked him. Anyway, seems there ain't any of 'em Taken, not besides some of the strangers, and not even all of them."

Blaine looked up suspiciously. "I thought only seers could tell."

"That's true. The rest of us can't, not right off. Not if someone's just come up to you, even if you know 'em. After a few days of watchin', you can tell. Them that's Taken don't do much thinkin' and actin' on their own, so unless the Annekteh are havin' 'em do something special, they mostly act like their heads're up in the clouds."

Well, that made a certain sort of sense.

" 'Sides that, he says they don't stray from the meetin' hall too often. They're used to plains, not hills, and they get lost too easy. The guard patrols take the same paths each time they go out." The words were straightforward; his expression was not.

"They don't sound like they'll be too hard to handle," Blaine observed. "The look on your face don't agree."

"It's that man who leads them," Dacey said, his gaze troubled as he looked over the ridge, the direction in which she'd pointed out the meeting hall. "Nekfehr. Trey had some to say about him, and none of it good. The man's half mad, your people think. There's no tellin' what the Annekteh can take from the mind of a clever madman."

"It don't matter," Blaine said, swallowing her revulsion. "He can't be everywhere. We can outdo the rest of 'em in the woods."

Dacey didn't respond right away; his expression was distant, thoughtful. "It's a mite trickier than that," he said, absently reaching down to smooth the top of Mage's head. "For one thing, they keep the kids in the meetin' hall during the day—the older ones an' a few of the mothers watch 'em while the folks are workin'. Trey said the men are in the hills, timbering, while the women try to keep up the farms."

"Then why isn't *he* timbering?" Blaine asked accusingly.

"So you're askin' questions too," Dacey said, and grinned. She scowled back at him. "Trey and a few of the older boys have been told to see to the hunting. And to look out for sassafras groves, which if they've found, Trey don't know of it. They don't tell each other much, so's one can't be Taken an' give away everything."

With the men in the hills, it might be possible to get to them, make plans with them. And the boys . . . if they were off on their own, hunting, it wouldn't be too hard to talk with them, either. Yet there also had to be some way to ensure the safety of the little ones. All these possibilities . . . and no ideas in her head, no matter how hard she looked. "What do we do next?" she asked finally.

"Next," Dacey said, staring into the trees as his hand stilled on Mage's head, "I need to have a look around."

"What do you mean?" But she was afraid she knew just what he meant. He meant leaving her alone at the camp while he went off and flirted with the Annekteh. Again.

Dacey stirred and looked back at her. "Trey's told me most of what I need to know. But I'm not familiar with your meetin' hall and the lay of the land around it. I don't know how far astray the men are timbering. I got to go have a look."

"That don't sound safe to me."

" 'Course it ain't safe," Dacey told her. "If it was safe, we'd not be having this conversation at all."

→ 11 ←

Dark confusion, dark pain, silent screams—

Dacey stumbled, so taken with the seeing that he lost track of his own feet.

Blaine screaming, Blaine terrified—

He fell, catching himself on his hands, his fingers digging into the rich, cold groundcover. When had a seeing ever hit him so hard?

Blue, roaring to Blaine's rescue, spitted on a sword. The shelter in the background, Blaine kicking it down, struggling between two men . . .

Magic, coming back to these hills. Heritage finding its way home. He flicked a sluggish worm from his fingers and righted himself.

Of course it ain't safe. His own words hung in his ears as he resumed his trek north on the ridge, following Blaine's directions—given her best guess at exactly where they were. He was on the trail of the Annekteh again; last time he'd been here, he'd walked right into them. Of course, he hadn't really been sure they were here, and he hadn't paid close enough attention to Mage's disquiet. This time, he would

watch Mage more carefully. He would watch *himself*
more carefully. And maybe he would figure out those
intense but paltry seeings before it was too late to
avoid the shadows they cast.

Shadow Hollers. Once they had been full of seers.

Dacey gazed out over the hollow to the east of
him, finding the double-chimney trail of smoke that
Blaine had described to him. Two ridges east and
south to the head of the hollow he went, Mage at
his heels and the jays crying overhead. When he
paused, he looked down the hollow that held the
meeting hall. Before him, to his left and right,
stretched the ridges that defined the west and east
sides of the extremely short hollow; they met at the
crooked crotch of ridges where Dacey stood.

He hunkered down behind a young oak and the
sparse cover its typically stubborn, clinging brown
leaves offered, and inspected the area—slowly, his
gaze barely crawling over the cleared flats along the
creek, his wood sense fired high. The base of each
northeast slope showed signs of hasty timbering, and
the contours of the hills there were laid bare to the
rain and sun. Another big tree went down as he
watched, and the cry of its fall made his eyes glint
a little harder. A dust cloud raised from ground that
should have been damp and nurturing new growth,
not dried-out and scarred.

Dacey turned away from the sight. The men were
locals interspersed with dark-clad plainsmen—obvious
even from a distance simply by their lack of exertion.

Inaccessible allies and bored enemies. It was the
lay of the meeting hall that he needed to understand,
the important thing. The hall sat nearly at the mouth
of the hollow, nestled in a protective dip between
two points of the west slope. It was on one of the
biggest flats he'd seen in this region, with the creek
fairly wide and flowing into the Dewey River, the
bright shine of which he could see from here. Half

of the mildly sloping flat was swampy, filled with sycamore and willows and tall dead trees. The higher part
stood cleared for a small fenced pasture that butted
against the hall. Just barely visible to him was the
barn that sat higher up in the little dip; the projecting
point of land rose before him to hide all but one
corner.

A breeze from the north pushed against them, and
Mage lifted his nose, whining deep in his chest. With
the next breath he would have broken into a howl,
and Dacey gently put his hand on the dog's nose, lowering it and cutting off the noise. Mage ducked his
head down and whined: a different, wanting-to-please
noise.

"Good boy," Dacey murmured, running his hand
down one of the long, soft ears and giving it a gentle
tug.

Two men came out of the front door of the hall,
armed with steel that glinted spears of sunlight at
Dacey. They started up the point on the far side of
the hall from Dacey, and headed north, away from
him. He could see their well-trod path scarring the
hillside—evidence that Trey had been right, that the
plainsmen followed the same patrol each time they
went out. There was a similar pair of paths following the ridge south of the hall, and along the opposite ridge, too.

Although the spring buds were finally broken, they
gave only a tint of green to the hills, and didn't
provide Dacey with any cover. Tomorrow might be
a different story, but for now . . . the men would have
to be well out of sight before he moved on. Mage,
unable to understand the delay or Dacey's preoccupation, butted his master with his head and nose.
"Shh," Dacey said. "Anyone'd think you were dumb
ole Blue, carryin' on like that." But his hand traveled to the dog's back and rested there.

He waited until he could no longer see the patrol,

and even then, moved at a stalking slow pace. Slowly, while the sun climbed high enough to push the shadow of the east ridge down the contours of the west, he worked his way to the closest point, and looked down on the hall.

They had made themselves quite at home, he thought, his eyes ranging over the few men playing at swordfighting in the space before the building, moving on to encompass the ruckus at the stables behind the meeting hall, where one of the mules expressed its opinion of the shoeing process. The noises carried clearly uphill, and he could hear the loud hiss of steam as the blacksmith shoved a shoe into the bucket of water next to the forge. The man holding the mule was abusive to both animal and farrier. *Plainsman.*

Keeping a wary eye below—but knowing his own noise wouldn't travel downhill as well as theirs came up—Dacey crossed behind the barn to the other point, checking out the back of the hall. There were no windows in the back wall—sassafras logs, with a sweet cinnamon tint to the old wood—just a few high transoms. If the Annekteh managed to hole up in this hall, it would be difficult to get to them. The building was inviolable from the rear and a frontal approach from the river flat would leave the attackers in the open. The only successful strike against this structure would be a burning campaign from the rear.

If there were hostages, they would die.

So there could be no hostages. And he would have to figure a way to get any confrontation away from this building, or far too many people would be lost in the taking of it.

He would have liked to get a closer look at the east slope, to see how approachable the timbering area was, but that would require several hours of maneuvering, and it was time to leave here—before he pushed his luck too far. With a careful eye to the men who sparred in front of the barn, Dacey headed back up the point.

He was the most vulnerable here, climbing away with his back to the enemy, and his heart hammered harder from the tension than from the work of the climb. Once atop the ridge, he found the patrol path and moved himself well to the other side of the ridge flat from it, for even though he had seen the plainsmen heading the other way, there might certainly be more than one patrol out. When he reached the head of the hollow, he would head west again, back to camp.

But the ridge widened as it reached the head, and this side of it curved gently west, threatening to disorient him. The only way to check his position was to head to the other side and sight in on the seam of the two ridges where he'd started out, and that would mean passing over the patrol path again.

Couldn't be helped. Cautiously, he moved crossways over the ridge, discovered he'd indeed come as far as he should have, and pointed himself west again.

Voices.

Dacey froze, pointing a commanding finger at Mage that stopped the dog in midstep. Indecipherable snatches of conversation, but with an accent that made them instantly identifiable. Close, and getting closer. Dacey slid off the path and down the hill, making good use of the rhododendron that so loved any hint of a north-facing curve. Mage crouched down beside him, lifting his nose to the scent of the newcomers but unconcerned by it. They approached without paying him any mind, not even raising their gaze from the path as they searched for purchase in the slanted ground.

Dacey waited, knife in hand but at the ground, between leaf layers where it would create no tell-tale glint of metal. Only his eyes moved, following them as they drew abreast. *Go on*, he urged them. Only a few more steps, and he was safe . . . .

A few more steps he wouldn't get. One of the men stopped and said something Dacey couldn't catch, then started off-trail. Mage lowered his head, his hackles rising in threat.

Dacey gave an inner groan as the guard, still walking, fumbled at his pants; the man had only left the path to relieve himself. He spotted Dacey before he even came to a stop. Dacey erupted from his camouflage, knife first, barreling through the astonished plainsman's hasty defense. *Just a man. Not even Annekteh*. He buried his knife deep under the man's ribs, jerking it out again to slash across his throat, blinking against the spray of warm blood that washed across his face as they tumbled to the ground together.

A yell of anger warned him of the second man; he turned, still half entangled in the first, scrubbing his eyes clear with his forearm. The man was almost upon him before he realized it, and Dacey scrambled backwards, crablike, clutching stickily at a knife that was no match for the sword sweeping down at him. A quick roll; sharp metal hit the ground and chipped up bits of dirt and leaf that stuck to his face. Another quick roll, downhill, sliding more than turning, nearly out of control—

Dacey clawed himself to a stop as Mage's angry snarl filled his ears. The plainsman's bellow told him the dog had scored, and suddenly all he could think of was that heavy sword cleaving his dog in two; sharp fear fueled his scramble back up the hill. The two were sparring, the man limping and slashing, the dog snapping, leaping in and out of range with an agility that belied his handicap. Then Dacey was no longer thinking at all, as he snatched up the dead man's sword and ran the plainsman through from behind.

The man slowly turned to face Dacey, his disbelieving gaze on the sword point sticking out of his body. He dropped his own sword, touched the bloodied metal that was killing him, and gave Dacey one last look of astonishment. Then his knees gave out and he folded lifelessly.

Dacey turned away, his chest heaving with exertion. *Only men.* Revulsion washed over him; he closed his eyes, closed them tight. Then he stumbled to the knife he'd dropped, wiped it roughly against his leg, and walked away from the slaughter. *Not Annekteh, not this time.* Men, just men, wanting just as much as he to live through this thing.

Dark confusion, dark pain, silent screams . . . Blaine screaming, Blaine terrified . . .

And this was just the start. Dacey's walk turned to a jog to a run, a run that couldn't put the last few minutes behind him no matter how long he kept it up.

Mage followed at his heels.

Blaine lay quietly on top of the high rock. With her eyes closed, she could pretend it was *her* rock. The breeze that blew across her face was the same, and once again she was hidden from the world below, impervious to its problems. Her rock. Above her homestead. Where Sarie and Willum played, and Cadell waited on her with some chore or lecture. Completely lost in the fantasy, she sighed contently, shifting her arm to dislodge a pebble from beneath her shoulder blade.

Twenty feet below her, Blue gave a bellow of warning that nearly stopped Blaine's heart. She jerked over on her stomach and peered over the edge of the granite as the other dogs, lost in the trees, joined in the chorus, more than making up for tardiness with enthusiasm. By the time she spotted them, they were beating their tails against trees and each other with the sincerity of their apology to Dacey.

For the first time, he gave the animals only a perfunctory greeting. His face was set and closed. Hard. He hadn't even noticed her. And . . . were his clothes wet? Pleasant as it was—warm, almost—it sure wasn't warm enough to take a dunking.

Questions. Always he presented her with more questions . . . but with that look on his face, she wasn't about to ask them. As he straightened from the dogs and glanced around the camp to locate her, Blaine called to him, giving him a little wave as he looked up and tried to find her.

He lifted his hand in greeting, and sat down by the warm ashes of the morning's fire.

That was it? After all this waiting? Placing her feet sideways on the extreme slope, Blaine made her way down the hill that butted back up against the rock, getting only halfway down before she called out, "Well? What did you find?"

"What Trey told me I'd find," Dacey said.

Nope, not talkative.

Not that he was ever what she'd actually call talkative.

"I guess that means we can trust him. Some."

Dacey retrieved two partially burnt sticks from the ashes and laid them as the base for the evening fire, then seemed to realize she had spoken. "Some," he repeated. "Tomorrow, Blaine, don't wander off. We'll go talk to Trey together."

"If you like," she said, being clear it was agreement and not acquiescence. A tiny prod, to see what she could get from him.

Nothing.

"Dacey—"

He gave her a sharp look, cut her right off. "No."

Maybe it was her hurt that spoke to him; maybe his own innate sense of fairness. But something made him look away, to say, his voice tight and strained, "I'm too used to doing some things on my own, Blaine."

That was it. Not enough to suit her . . . but it was a request, and she honored it.

He laid the fire and cooked in silence; they ate in silence. Blaine took a short walk south along the ridge with Blue, stretching her legs, giving Dacey some time to work out whatever had grabbed him up so bad. When she returned she found him no less troubled, and for a while she sat away from the fire, with only her thoughts and Chase, who lay on her feet, for company. Dacey sat opposite the fire from her, and she watched him, not caring that he was aware of her scrutiny.

Something had happened while he was scouting, that was for sure, but she might never know what it was.

Blaine sighed and found she was stroking Chase's homely head; she pulled her hand up and put it in her lap with the other, sitting quietly. There was no need for conversation, after all; there was enough of that in the woods already. Since early twilight two horned owls had been booming back and forth at each other, one on the top of her ridge, the other half-way up the hill opposite them. Their cries wavered and echoed against the hills, sometimes lost in the rustle of the rising breeze in the trees. The air had grown damp as well as chill, catching the odor of the ground and holding it close to the earth.

Weather coming.

Blaine checked the sky and found that the stars were mostly hidden behind a layer of clouds. But the moon, almost directly overhead, was at its strongest, and its light pushed through. Blaine slid to her knees to get a better look, leaning back on her ankles in a limber way she took for granted.

She stifled a small cry of delight, for the moon was

circled by a hazy halo of light, shaded faintly by the colors of the rainbow. A glance at Dacey confirmed that he was still deep in his own thoughts, and though she'd have rather shared it with him, she contented herself with watching the haloed moon while the owls quarreled at one another.

Never mind that it all meant rain for the next day.

Blue ambled in from whatever investigating he'd been up to, and settled heavily by her side. Mage appeared from the darkness with him, but circled the camp restlessly, casting the breeze. For once, Dacey seemed to pay him no mind. The hound circled and mumbled, and when he finally stopped, it was to throw his head up and moan his way into a howl.

Dacey looked up from the fire to regard his dog with surprise; Mage's cry hung in the air, shocking the owls to silence. Suddenly Whimsy gave a little yip and added her voice, and then Blue's rough tones joined in. From wherever they sprawled, Dacey's hounds joined the chorus; it echoed around the two humans with an eerie command of the night. Unearthly, mesmerizing . . . gooseflesh raised on Blaine's arms.

The song ended as suddenly as it had begun, and Mage limped back to Dacey.

Blaine nearly lost her balance when Blue shoved his head under her arm to demand petting in the wake of his song, but she was not distracted from the fact that Dacey checked the air with a bit of shaved tinder. Nor was she too busy with the petting to remember that the breeze had also been from the north the last time Mage had called.

Chase, apparently dissatisfied with the conclusion of the last howl, started another, and the others quickly joined him; Blaine had to shove Blue away from her ear. This time the howling was innocent, devoid of the quality which had bemused her moments before . . . almost invigorating.

When she heard a new voice, Blaine glanced, startled, at Dacey. Not only was he grinning, he was imitating the dogs with an accuracy that told her it wasn't the first time. She laughed, and after a moment, tried it herself, following Blue's intonations and surprised at the sudden wild, happy feeling coursing through her. No wonder the dogs sang so often, if it made them feel so free, yet so completely part of each other.

When the chorus ended, the night closed in again, dark and silent. Blaine looked at Dacey, who hesitated on the brink of retreating back into his own silence. But then she couldn't help it; she giggled. How silly, to howl with a bunch of dogs! How . . . remarkable that it was so fun and easy to do.

After a moment, he grinned back at her. The owl on the opposite ridge grew bold and called softly into the darkness, and despite the coming rain, the air seemed clearer.

✦✦   ✦✦   ✦✦

Nekfehr grimaced at the howling, flinging the contents of his bacco spit-cup on the fire with a vehemence borrowed from the *annektehr*'s unwilling, unnamed human vessel. A disadvantage, he realized for the first time, of the Annekteh commonality—hearing that howling from so many ears at once.

The sound had somehow—so quickly—come to represent Shadow Hollers resistance. Come morning the humans would perform their tasks with a secretive, grim determination. He wasn't even sure they understood why.

Nor did the Annekteh. But they knew someone worked against them. More than just the petty sabotage, more than dark looks of defiance. Someone had killed,

had turned plains blade against plainsman, an unmistakable act of rebellion.

It was not to be tolerated.

Only one of the Shadow Hollers men
carried the guilt of it . . . but all of them
would pay.

✦ 12 ✦

"You got somethin' particular in mind, you want me along?" Blaine negotiated the ridge behind Dacey, speaking to his back as they walked the faint trail to the clearing and their meeting with Trey. She wasn't much looking forward to it, although she didn't distrust him. Not exactly. It was more a matter of not knowing him well enough *to* trust him.

Dacey seemed to have made some peace with himself today, but his natural reticence was still at the fore. "Just . . . didn't want you sitting alone today, is all," he said, waiting long enough that she thought he wasn't going to answer at all, and she wasn't at all sure of the one she got.

The rain she had predicted was falling on them, a drizzle that had taken a while to work its way through the trees but now put a faint sheen on the branches and buds around them. Blaine's shoulders were long soaked through and the front of her shirt clung to her slight frame; she plucked it away from her skin in annoyance, wishing it had at least been cool enough to close up her jacket. Mage, his fur spiky wet, stalked stiffly at Dacey's side with complaint in his eyes. Dacey himself seemed resigned.

As they sighted the clearing and headed down to it, Mage hesitated and took a few steps uphill, his eyes on Dacey. "All right," Dacey told him, and the hound moved up to skirt the edge of the woods while they entered the clearing and felt the full force of the rain.

And full force it was, opening up on them with apparent malicious glee. Trey called to them; he was standing out of the rain, in the windbreak of several young pines at the lower edge of the clearing. Memory assailed her—*standing in the rain outside a trio of young pines . . .*

Blaine hesitated, startled, even as Dacey lifted his hand in greeting and moved ahead. She stumbled after him, struggling with her wet and damaged boots on the slick, briar-tangled ground. The rain ran down her face, dripping off her brows and lashes; she could barely see Dacey stepping into the shelter of the pines, and—

Sudden commotion, a sound of surprise and anger, a swirl of motion in between the trees pines—

Blaine squinted through the rain, alarmed, uncertain. "Dacey?"

"Blaine, git—"

A boy's shout cut him off, a shout and a cry of protest and an unmistakable grunt of surprised pain.

"*Dacey!*" She lunged for the trees, would have plunged right into them—if a substantial, unfamiliar figure hadn't stepped out and brought her up short, almost yanking her off her feet. Angrily, she pushed away the tendrils of wet hair plastered to her face and tangled in her lashes, and discovered a grim-faced stranger—a huge dark-haired young man who held her tight, his big hand latched onto her arm.

Blaine twisted away—or tried to. She might as well have been held by stone. The young man only pulled her closer and shoved the wet gleam of his knife at her, a swift and silent warning. She drew in a startled breath, frozen at the sight of it so close to her eyes.

Not so Mage. His bad leg hoisted out of the way, Mage charged down the hill. The big youth gave a shout of warning, jerking Blaine around as he aimed a solid kick at the dog. Yelping, Mage skidded sideways, half-lifted off the ground.

Mage! Blaine didn't think, didn't consider the consequences or the odds . . . she just *did*, while the boy was still off-balance, while she had the chance to yank at him and make it worse, at the same time kicking him behind the knee; the leg went right out from under him. He fell heavily, and she was on him in an instant, jamming one knee in his stomach and the other on his groin.

Not all of Lenie's advice had been useless.

The youth turned greenly white and writhed beneath her, but Blaine rode it out, scrabbling up the knife he dropped and holding it right at his throat, holding tight to the slick-wet, pine-needle-covered hilt.

Mage, half in, half out of the pines, growled steadily. No one else said a word.

She didn't like it. She didn't like it at *all*. She shoved the knife right up against the boy's throat— big as he was, he was still a boy, probably not any older than Blaine herself, and that gave her courage— along with the marked paleness of his face. "Don't you move," she warned him, and then raised her voice. "Dacey?"

The reply came in Trey's voice, equally wary. "Burl?"

Trey.

Traitorous, mold-brained Trey!

Blaine scowled down at the screwed-up face of the boy beneath her; he still fought to control his pain. She hoped he couldn't pee for a week. "You'd better tell 'im you're in trouble," she said, and the rain dripped off her nose and onto his face.

After a moment, working hard to raise his voice with all her weight on his stomach and keeping a wary eye on the knife, he called, "Trey!"

Trey pushed his way out from beneath the heavy boughs and stopped short at the sight of them, his alert expression turning into a scowl. "Burl! I *told* you to watch for her!"

Blaine glared at him. "You traitor—we *trusted* you!" Burl wiggled beneath her, and she hit him. "Keep still!"

"If you don't get off my stomach I'm gonna throw up," he groaned.

"Then throw up!"

"*Me*, the traitor?" Trey said, and his temper was as hot as hers. "After what *he* done? You're lucky I didn't just put an arrow in the both of you." He spat his disgust on the ground.

"What do you mean, *after what he done*? He ain't done nothing to you!" She smacked Burl again to quiet him, and demanded, "Is he all right?"

"Come see," Trey invited, grim malice in his voice.

"And give you all the chance to grab *me*?" she said scornfully. "I ain't stupid." All the same, she wished she had a free hand to wipe the rain out of her eyes, that she didn't feel so precarious on top of Burl now that he wasn't distracted by her savage blow to his tender parts. She pushed the knife against his throat just to remind both him and Trey that she still had the advantage.

Short-lived advantage. Burl had had enough; his scowl matched her own. And then someone within the pines gave a thin cry of angry alarm, followed by a grunt of pain; Blaine started, and Burl moved. Burl moved *fast*. He jerked his head to the side, freeing his throat. He yanked the knife away from her, threw her off his stomach, and jumped up, snatching the knife on his way—and snatching Blaine, too, almost effortlessly lifting her until her feet barely touched the ground. "You little bitch-child," he said. "Why, I ought to—"

"Just set her down, Burl," Trey said. "Bring her in out of the rain. She wanted to see her hero's all right—though it don't mean he'll stay that way."

They stared at one another in hate-filled silence—and then, startling them all, someone groaned, the kind of sound a man made when he didn't have a choice, didn't quite know what he was about. Trey gave the pines a surprised look, and Burl shoved Blaine aside long enough to sheath his knife, then took her arms just above the elbow, holding them close to her sides. She couldn't move them at all; her feet hovered just above the ground. Numbly, she wondered how she'd ever gotten the advantage over this brute in the first place. *Too dumb to know I couldn't.*

Burl shoved her through the pines, never minding what their branches did to her face. Immediately behind the big pine were two others, smaller trees in a triangle that created a mostly dry shelter between them. And within there was Dacey, and a third boy—a scrawny, smug-looking creature who stood over him.

"Dacey!" Blaine strained uselessly against Burl's grip as the third boy gave Dacey's crumpled form a lazy kick, turning him over. Mage, crouching by Dacey, gave a lip-wrinkled snarl but held his place, enough of a warning that the boy backed away a step.

Burl paid Blaine's struggles no mind, turning to speak to Trey through the pines. "Trey . . . we got a problem here."

Blood covered the entire side of Dacey's face. They must have roughed him up some besides, but the blood was all Blaine could see, all she could think about. "What have you done?" she cried. "Why?"

Trey pushed his way into the small area, took in
the scene before him, and swore. "Estus!"

The boy shrugged. "I got careless with this rock,
is all." He was younger than the others and Blaine
had the feeling she'd seen him before, although she
could not place his thin, sharp features. He held out
his hand and tipped it so the bloodied rock that he
held rolled slowly off his palm and thudded into the
needle-covered ground.

Trey swore at Estus again, and turned to Blaine.
"Dacey said he was on our side." His chin stuck out,
defiant, but his eyes looked a little panicked. "He said
he was gonna *help*." He snorted. "Now the Takers are
takin' the menfolk over, one by one, siftin' their
thoughts—lookin' for *him*." He pointed that chin at
Dacey. "I know it was him, 'cause it sure weren't one
of us."

Blaine jerked against Burl's grip, having not the
slightest effect on him, and almost screamed in her
frustration. "What are you *talking* about?"

"The two men he killed, o'course," he said angrily.
"The Takers are blamin' us—your own people, Blaine,
not this outsider you're tryin' to protect."

"You're lyin'!" But her mind went to the look on
Dacey's face when he'd returned to camp the previous afternoon. All wet . . . washed clean. *Of blood?*

Trey instantly sensed her doubt. "I'm not an' you
know it."

He wasn't. "But that don't make *this* right!" she
cried, suddenly fighting tears. She gave another futile
twist; it gained her nothing. But Trey shrugged, and
Burl slowly released her arms, momentarily resting
his hands on her shoulders as a warning. Blaine
threw herself down beside Dacey, where Mage
whined his worry at her. *Fix this*, he seemed to say,
when he'd never so much as bothered to look at her
before.

Trey looked at Estus. "Can't say as we meant to

hurt anyone," he said, and then gave a sudden shrug. "Then again, I can't say as I care that we did, either."

"Dacey was right." Blaine's hands resting on Dacey's shoulders were gentle—her gaze, resting on Trey, was fierce. "You *are* a fool." Mage, following her gaze, lifted his lip and rumbled; Trey took a step back. "We'll lose everything without his help—*everything!*"

"An' what makes you so sure?" Trey snapped back, mindful of the dog. "What do you *know?* Do you know his seer's lore? Or does he hide it from you, like he hid killin' those men?"

"You keep yourself quiet!" Blaine cried, wild to defend him but realizing she had no defense at all. She *didn't* know what Dacey had in mind. He *had* kept the killings from her. "You don't know nothin'! Dacey knows more about the Annekteh than anyone I've ever met! *He's* the one they're afraid of—he's the one they tortured, wantin' the same answers you do!"

"Tortured?" Burl said, looming behind Trey. "Why not just—"

Dacey groaned, pure relief to Blaine. She hissed Burl to silence and gave Dacey a tentative nudge. "Dacey?"

His eyes, one of them washed with blood, flickered open—

Blaine had an instant of warning, no more—the wild look in his eye, full of alarm—and he flung himself to his feet—or almost on his feet, swaying, backed up against one of the pines in pure animal panic. One hand clutched at long needled branches for support, not doing much good.

He thinks they have him. "Dacey," Blaine said, cautiously getting up on one knee. Behind her, the boys had frozen, all their aggressiveness startled away with Dacey's unexpected explosion.

"Stay back!" he gasped, spitting out the blood that had run into his mouth.

"Dacey," she repeated, more gently this time, a

tone of voice she hadn't known was in her. "It's Blaine. You're safe." And glared at Trey, daring him to open his mouth and deny it.

"Blaine," Dacey repeated. One leg gave out; he caught himself, but barely held it. His expression wavered into confusion. "Blaine."

"Blaine," she said firmly. "You're safe."

As abruptly as he accepted her words, he lost the fight to stay on his feet, going down on his knees and elbows, cradling his tender head in his hands. His groan was one of frustration, of trying to understand.

"Be still," she commanded, and he was, relaxing slightly under her hand on his shoulder. She stared accusingly at Trey. "I don't know what happened with those men," she said, "but I know it weren't worth this. Just what were you going to do with us?"

"Give you to the Takers," sneered the thin-faced boy. Blaine gave him a scornful glance and returned her attention to Trey.

"I figured once they had the killer, they'd leave our folk alone." Trey gave another shrug, a gesture she was growing to hate.

"And what made you think they'd pay a bit of attention to you?"

"They'd just have to Take him over for a minute to find the truth," Burl offered. "That's what I was sayin'—"

And once again Blaine cut him off. "Trey, you're such a . . . a . . ." She searched for the words, and took Dacey's again. "*Fool.* If you give him up, you'll hand over our only chance to beat this thing—fer nothin!! He's seer's kin, Trey, they *can't* Take him."

"They—*what*?" Trey stared at her as if he couldn't comprehend her words.

"You heard me," Blaine said grimly. "More'n likely they'll Take *you*. Then you'll see what trouble is!"

"*Spirits*," Burl said, low and troubled.

"He asked you to trust him. To work with him. Now look at what you got—you can't take him to the Annekteh without making trouble for yourself, and there's no telling *how* much sense you knocked out of his head for good." She lifted her chin, looking straight at Trey. "Even if I did have some notion of his plans, I wouldn't tell you. Not now. So you might as well git. Spend some time figuring what you're gonna do now."

Estus snorted. "We're takin' you all back, o'course."

"Shut up, Estus," Trey said shortly. "Ain't you listened to a thing?"

"We're takin' 'em back," Estus repeated, looking hard at Trey and Burl. "They don't gotta Take him, not if they already know him. They'll be grateful to us!"

"I said *shut up*. I ain't so sure no more," Trey said.

"Fine time to be knowing that," Blaine said, contempt heavy in her voice. Trey ignored her and sat next to the larger pine, his face pensive. Blaine figured he had plenty to think about.

Burl sat next to him, eyeing Blaine and Dacey, making her wish his face was more friendly. Blaine couldn't imagine how she'd missed seeing him before this. He must be in one of the westernmost families in Shadow Hollers. Just like the rest of these boys, damn their hides.

Dacey gave a low groan, stirred like he was thinking about sitting up. Estus reached over to give him another kick, but Blaine slapped the offending foot away. "Haven't you done enough?"

"Estus," Trey said, without looking up from his thoughts, "I'm beginnin' to think it was a mistake to ask your help. If you hadn't brained him with that rock, we wouldn't be in such a fix."

"He was goin' for my knife, Trey," Estus protested, moving back from Blaine and Dacey.

Quietly, Dacey said, "What happened?"

Thank goodness. That almost sounded sensible. "You just lie there, Dacey. You'll feel better in a bit."

"I doubt that," he said, as a strange look passed over his face.

Burl straightened in alarm. "Trey, he's gonna—"

"Get him outta here! It's the only dry place—"

But Burl didn't wait for him to finish. He grabbed Dacey under the arms and hauled him out of the pines, and Blaine was still sitting, blinking stupidly, when she heard the sound of retching. Oh, his poor head. Estus could have picked a smaller rock!

"Trey," she said, thinking suddenly of her book, of how well her tea had helped after Dacey's escape from the Annekteh, "you got to let me go find him some white pine bark to put against that head. And . . . sassafras. I need sassafras."

Trey gave her a quick, hard look. "The Takers—"

"Want sassafras groves," Blaine interrupted. "I know. I think . . . Dacey says the sassafras soaks up hill magic, Trey. You find any, you can't tell 'em!"

"Hill magic," Trey said, injecting scorn into the words.

"You never mind whether you believe it or not. Just say you won't tell! And let the others know, too."

"We don't tell 'em nothing," Estus said, butting into the conversation with much bravado. Blaine ignored him.

"Iff'n you need sassafras . . ." Trey started, but trailed off and didn't pick it up again. Blaine would have pressed him on it, but Burl returned, with Dacey draped over him, rain diluting the blood on his face in little runnels.

"Dacey," Blaine said, going to him as Burl eased him down against the bare lower trunk of one of the pines. White pines, she realized suddenly, with their long, soft needles. Then all she needed was sassafras . . . "Dacey, you doin'?"

"Damn, I've been better," he said, wiping a hand

across his face and looking at the red-stained palm. "Trey, I reckon we got some things to straighten out here—"

This time, Blaine recognized the look. So did Burl, for he pulled Dacey up and out of the shelter. Trey watched them go, thoughtful. "I want to talk to you," he said abruptly, standing.

"So talk." Blaine frowned up at him. "You're the one who's making decisions around here, I got *that* clear enough. Don't need my say-so for anything."

"Alone," he said, warning Estus off with a look. Estus, none too happy, backed away to the edge of the pine cover and stared out at the clearing. When Trey was satisfied, he sat on the pine needles next to Blaine. "I ain't figured what to do now," he confessed, his voice low.

"You started it. You finish it."

"But it weren't supposed to go like this! Spirits, I was mad enough, but I wanted to *talk* to him first, find out what happened—gruesome as that killing was, I hoped he had reason. But he ired me, wouldn't have a thing to do with me once he saw Burl and Estus." He stared moodily at Estus' back. "Still . . . if it weren't for that dimwit, we'd be all right. But if what you said about him bein' safe from the Takers is right, and without me hearin' his story . . . well, I just can't take him down to them. Just get myself in a fix, that way."

"What, then? Now there's two more that knows of him an' me, and us without Dacey's brains on this thing—at least not for sure. He could sleep for days. That don't leave us in a real good spot."

"Aw, we can trust . . ." Trey hesitated, met her eyes for only an instant. "We can trust Burl."

Blaine looked at Estus and shuddered. "He's squirrelly. I don't like him."

Trey did not respond. When he looked up at her again, his expression had grown resolute. Decided.

"Listen," he said. "I c'n tell you where to find a right big patch of sassafras, great big tree, bunch of littler ones around it. Takers don't know about it, and I ain't gonna tell 'em. None of us would, less'n we thought we was about to be caught at the lie, or Took. We play 'em like that. You get that sassafras, you think you can help him?"

"All I know's that I can try. And that workin' sassafras has done helped me before. Close your eyes." She reached into her jacket pocket, waiting for him to comply, gesturing impatiently with her chin when he didn't. "Do it, I ain't going anywhere. Won't work if you're looking straight at me all the time."

Reluctantly, he closed his muddy brown eyes. She took up the blinder, wrapped her hand around it, and waited. Not making a sound, not doing anything to locate herself to him. After a moment, he cracked open a wary eye, and his face opened in astonishment to find her gone. Just as fast, it closed down again in a scowl, and he was about to leap to his feet when she let go the blinder.

"See?" she said, grinning at his astonishment.

"You were—you were—"

"I was right here. And I done that with sassafras, but I ain't saying how."

He narrowed his eyes at her, angry at being fooled, angry that she knew something he didn't.

"Seer's lore," she relented, finally. "I learned it from an old book I found."

"Damn," Trey said. "Them Takers are bad enough already . . . what if they could do that? We couldn't even see 'em coming!"

"Don't tell 'em about no sassafras," Blaine said grimly.

Trey looked away from her, giving a sudden shake of his head. "No," he said. "I'll make sure of it." Then he scrubbed his hands through his drying hair. "Maybe I got an idea. But you'll have to go along."

"You tell me, first."

"All right." Trey leaned forward to speak confidentially, his eye on the spot where Estus had left the pine shelter. "Look, Dacey ain't goin' nowhere, leastways not for a day or so, right?"

"I'd say not," Blaine agreed, sighing at a timely round of retching from downhill of them. "Even if I can do something with the sassafras . . . I ain't no seer. I'm just guessin' at what I'm gonna try. He's not goin' to be ready for dancing any time soon."

"Then how's about tellin' Estus we can't move Dacey down to the Takers till he's got his senses back—even Burl can't carry him *that* far—an' leavin' him here to watch y'all? I'll fetch that sassafras for you. I found—no, I ain't sayin'. Takers got too many ears. Just ask you this—you want the bark, like for tea?"

"Estus?" Blaine wailed as quietly as she could. "You said yourself you don't trust him no more!"

"I don't. This Taker thing's been too much for him, I guess—he ain't like he used to be. Squirrelly, like you said. But we need time to think, and as long as he's up here, he can't be ruining things by blabbin' to the Takers' men."

That was true. "But he ain't likely to behave himself, neither. Not without Dacey to watch him."

"Get that Blue dog down here. He'll watch good enough."

She gave him a reluctant nod. "I reckon I'll go along with keeping Estus here, if you give me Dacey's knife back—Estus don't gotta know—and if you check on us tomorrow. I don't think it'll take more'n a day before he can go as far as our camp. Then we're quit of you."

Trey didn't answer right away. Lighter fluffs of dry hair stood out from the darkened skullcap of his head, and he stared at Blaine's wet, scratched legs, perhaps forgetting that it wasn't polite. When he looked up it was to stare pensively at his two compatriots, his mud-colored eyes looking weary. When he found Blaine watching, he shrugged. "I thought I was doin' the right thing."

"Iff'n you all try to follow us to our camp when we've moved on, there'll be plenty of trouble," Blaine said, without acknowledging his meager apology. "I don't care what you tell your squirrelly friend. Since you believe Dacey's killed once, you can just figure he'll do it again."

Trey lost his air of repentance and scowled at her. "I bet your daddy wore his hand out a-spankin' you."

It was a comment Blaine saw fit to ignore. She stood and squeezed the water out of her skirt, smoothing it out the best she could, watching as Burl returned with Dacey again. Her boots—a smaller, thinner soled version of the mid-calf boots Trey and Dacey wore—were soaked through, and she bent to pull them off, and to peel off the worn socks beneath. *Blue, first.* Then she'd see to Dacey, clean up that wound some.

As the second boot dropped to the ground, she looked again at Trey's face, its sharp angles made unattractive with his continued scowl. "You might start us a fire, if you can," she told him, and walked barefoot to the edge of the tree shelter. "And yes, I want the bark, like for tea. I need somethin' to soak it all in, too." How he came up with that, she didn't care.

"Hey," Estus said, startled to find it was her rather than Trey when he turned around. He reached for her arm and she took a step away from him, tossing her head in annoyance, ignoring the fact that Burl had come up behind her.

"You got a fondness for handling other people," she told him. "But you better not try it with me, or you'll be more'n sorry." He was of her own size and maybe a year younger, and she backed her words with enough fire to make him hesitate.

It was nothing more than a brave front as long as Burl's large form stood behind her—but she needn't have worried. "Estus, you've caused enough trouble," Burl growled. "We needed to talk to that man, you fool! Iff'n she goes after you, I'm gonna watch."

Hesitation flickered across Estus' thin features. Instead of dropping his hand he brought it up in an unnecessary gesture to push his limp, shoulder-length hair back from his face. Wet, moldy straw-looking hair, Blaine thought, but refrained from saying so, content with her little victory. She looked at Burl; he nodded slightly and gave her a barely discernible smile, an acknowledgement of sorts.

Blaine stepped out of the shelter and looked out at the clearing. The rain had slackened and was back to a drizzle, coming down lightly enough that it made no sound, but merely muted the noises of the woods.

Blue. They needed *all* the dogs, if for nothing more than warmth, and she'd already decided she wasn't going to leave Dacey alone with Estus. The last she had seen the hounds, they'd been curled up downwind of Dacey's shelter, their noses tucked beneath bony, inadequate tails.

She thought of Dacey's howling, of the yelping he used to call the dogs after a hunt. She'd heard it often enough, and surely it wasn't much harder than howling with the pack. Blaine looked over her shoulder at the young men behind her, and resolved that if she was going to bark into the woods, she'd do it with confidence.

Blaine lifted her voice to the hills, imitating the yodeled yelping that Dacey used. Mage whined and appeared from the shelter, leaving Dacey's side to circle her anxiously, looking into her face, trying to understand her purpose. His gold spots were all but hidden in his wet fur, his white coat gone grey with rain. She patted his broad head—like Blue's, it had a little keel at the back, an odd shape of skull that was becoming familiar to her fingers. She took another breath and tried again, and this time Mage joined her, giving the come-to-ground call in a commanding tone, giving Blaine confidence as well.

She repeated the call twice more, then rubbed behind Mage's ears in thanks. His wet tail thumped twice against her leg before he walked stiffly back to the shelter and Dacey. As he passed Estus he lifted his lip in a silent snarl, and Blaine hid a smile from the boy. Even Mage knew who had made the trouble here.

"What was that all about?" Burl asked her, talking to her back. Estus had gone back to Trey, and was sullenly listening to his firm directives. Blaine felt her shoulders stiffen at Burl's intrusion; she just couldn't help her resentment—even if he *had* offered to watch while she lit into Estus.

"I just called the other dogs," she said without turning around. "We ain't got blankets, an' this rain's put a chill on everything. I got to keep Dacey warm somehow."

"You know," Burl offered, moving up beside her, towering over her, tall and thick-armed and intimidating, "I reckon I don't really know what-all's going on. I thought I understood before we tangled . . . but I swear it's got all mixed up."

Blaine gave him a scornful look—*fine time to come to such,* after *Dacey was down and hurting*—but felt bad at the flush that washed across his face. He'd only been doing his best to protect his family, even Dacey would say that much.

"Anyways," he said, talking over the awkwardness, "I guess if I done had to get knocked down by a girl, I don't feel so bad iff'n it was a girl who kilt a bear."

"Trey told you," Blaine said, of sudden mixed feelings to know Trey had been talking about her. "It was a puny bear. Dacey'll tell you so."

"Still an' all," Burl said. "It was fine done, from what Trey said."

From what Dacey had told him. *Fine done*. She liked that.

The woods emitted an intermittent scurrying noise, one that quickly grew closer. Blaine let her breath out in a gust of relief when she saw the hounds pelting down the hill in a scramble of leg and tail. They swept by her without regard, except for Blue, who stopped to shove his wet nose into her hand. She wiped her hand off on his damp back, making sure he didn't see her smile, and went to the pines to watch as the dogs ran around Dacey and sniffed at him, then collapsed of one accord, all around him like a living blanket. Mage took his place by Dacey's chest and rested his chin there, soulfully eyeing the people that surrounded him.

Blue sat on Blaine's foot with a thump, and she had to wrest it free. He looked up and wagged his tail against her ankle, setting his seal of approval on the scene in front of him. "I'm glad you're happy," she murmured, despite the fact that her sarcasm would be lost on the brute.

Trey approached, Estus in his wake. "I'll be back in a bit with what you wanted," he told Blaine, nodding at Burl to join him. Wanted to talk, no doubt. And then, to Estus, "And I'll be back here tomorrow with food for you all, an' make sure everything's all right," but his eyes flicked to Blaine to catch her nod. Blaine almost felt sorry for him, now that he was caught with an accomplice who couldn't adjust to the changing situation. *Almost*.

She watched as Burl and Trey moved into the mist of the falling evening, quiet on the damp ground. When they were out of sight, she turned to give Estus a wary look.

He looked back at her, a grin twisted across his face. "Don't give me any trouble, now," he said. Blaine lowered her head to glare out from under her eye-lashes. She was beginning to despise this boy.

At her feet, Blue shifted, paying close attention to Estus for the first time. He peered up at the one who opposed his girl and offered a growl, almost conversationally. Blaine grinned back at Estus. "No," she said, "I don't guess we want any trouble."

→ 13 ←

As daylight faded, Blaine ripped out a section of her already abused skirts. She shook rain off the pine boughs for water, and cleaned the drying blood from Dacey's face, soaking the clotted gunk from the wound above his temple and wishing his head was as hard as the white oak heartwood his hair took after. Dacey lay still and pale and unresponsive ... but she felt he was there. Awake. Just unable to face the world.

Trey returned, spoke a few words to Estus, pressed some sassafras bark into Blaine's hand, and muttered something about returning on the morrow. Estus watched him go, then set to gathering wood—sullenly; Trey must have ordered it done. He had a cup on his belt, too, like the older men who liked to share a bottle of sippin's, and he offered her that, just as sullenly. Blaine cleared the pine needles down to the dirt and built a fire with Dacey's matches. The wood started reluctantly and burned resentfully, filling the shelter with eye-stinging smoke but little warmth. Just enough to steep the pine and sassafras bark within the blooded rag. Then she not only washed the wound with the steeping bundle, she gently prodded Dacey into sipping a goodly portion of the tea.

From the look on his face, he was hoping it would stay down. So did she.

Eventually, she'd done all she could. Cold pervaded her bones and even her wool clothes didn't keep her from feeling the damp; she moved over to curl around sweet little Whimsy, and Blue found a place at her back. A tumble of Dacey, dogs, and Blaine—curiously satisfying—they slept, while Estus, dressed warmly and never as wet as they, turned his back to them and sat at the edge of the pines.

Dawn came none too soon for Blaine. She moved outside the pines and peered up at the misty, lightening sky, trying to guess the day's weather. Too soon to tell. She stuck her hands in her armpits, shifted her cold feet in the dew, and waited.

At last, a spark of sunlight glimmered over the eastern ridge. She sighed with pleasure at its warmth, immeasurably thankful that they were on an east-facing slope. Blue came and sat beside her, anxious about some doggy thing he could communicate only by staring intently at her. She shrugged at him—and then heard the loud growl of his empty stomach. And although she laughed, privately her own stomach was asking the same question. She gave his ear a quick rub—no real consolation for either of them.

Behind her, Estus stood and stretched, and Blaine's smile faded; her thin-boned face set into stubbornness. She did not turn around as the boy approached.

"Thinking about going somewhere?" Estus said, giving her a hard stare—it was supposed to be intimidating, she was sure. She didn't acknowledge his question or his presence, but turned her head to contemplate the suddenly crucial forest above the clearing. Blue peered dumbly at Estus, perhaps wondering if this human would provide him a meal.

"Hey," Estus protested sharply. "I'm talking to you."

There was little, Blaine thought happily, that pricked the self-important ego like ignoring it. Another lesson learned from Lenie—although one not willingly taught. Estus, scowling and well-pricked, took her arm, digging his fingers in, and gave her a little shake.

Blaine examined the progress of the leaf growth around them. *Another few days and they'll be leafed out full for sure.*

He'd had enough. Muttering a curse, Estus yanked at her, trying to jerk her off-balance—to jerk her attention his way. Blaine turned on him, yanking back, her facade of remote disinterest shattered. Estus started, suddenly and obviously realizing that she was taller than he, and even had an uphill advantage. The day before, threatened by Dacey, he'd gone for a rock. Now his free hand flashed for his knife.

It never had the chance to get there.

Blue, faster than Blaine ever would have guessed, soundless and precise, clamped his jaws around Estus' arm—not the knife hand, for he had no concept of *knife*, but that arm which held her. Blue simply sat, his lips draped over the limb, his jaws firm; his very weight dragged Estus' hand off Blaine.

Estus made a squeaking noise and tried to free himself, his knife forgotten.

"Blue!" Blaine exclaimed, but could not manage to sound displeased. *You made me do this*, Blue seemed to say to the boy, his eyes sad and reproachful. Blaine crossed her arms in front of her chest, smiling at Estus.

"Blue." The voice was gentle but commanding, and Blue released Estus to trot gracelessly into the pines.

Estus stared at the blueish-red puncture marks on his arm as Blaine pushed past him, ignoring him again, and back into the pines. "How do you feel?"

"I've been a whole lot better," Dacey said. He sat up—slowly, and with care, but he looked like *Dacey* again. *The tea.* Though she'd been hoping and

half-expecting, Blaine stared at the closing cut on his
temple, taken aback by how good it looked. No swelling. No oozing. And his eyes—clear. Thinking. In
charge of himself.

She felt a sudden sharp pain for skills and knowledge these hills had lost along with the seers and their
books. Maybe a seer's book would have told them how
to save Lenie's betrothed . . . .

Maybe not. Surely not even sassafras could do
everything.

The dogs tumbled away from Dacey and mean-
dered off, nosing the ground. "Stick close," Dacey told
them, wincing again at his own voice. "You reckon
you can straighten me out? I seem to disremember
exactly what's happening here."

"I'm not surprised," Blaine snorted. "You took a
lick hard enough to knock the whole of last month
from your head. If it weren't for—" *the sassafras*—
she glanced at Estus, not trusting him enough to say
even that much, "—that headache brew I gave you,
I'll bet you'd still be mumbling nonsense."

That got a reasonably piercing look from him;
Blaine grinned to see it, and added, "Besides, they
lit into us so fast I doubt you ever did know just why."

"Trey," Dacey ventured, gingerly feeling his head.

"Well, that there's the one that hit you." Blaine
nodded at Estus, who glared at them and flexed his
bitten arm, staying right out at the edge of the pines.
"Trey weren't too happy about it."

"Neither am I." Dacey's hazel eyes sharpened on
her, reminding Blaine that he still waited for answers.
"What happened?"

Well, he had reason enough to be short about it.
"Trey said two of the plainsmen done been killed, an'
all our menfolk are being questioned—Taken, he
said—to find out who done it. He figured it had to
be you." She scowled. "He was gonna turn you over
to 'em."

"Then why are we *here*?"

"I had some words with him. Guess he thought better of it."

"I reckon he did, at that."

She couldn't quite decipher the look on his face. Dry amusement, maybe. "He's coming back today— gonna try to straighten things out." Blaine glanced at Estus, who had turned his back on them, then leaned forward to add quietly, "The only reason he left that boy is he don't trust him no more—especially not to keep quiet. Estus thinks he's watchin' us, but really he's up here so he can't cause no more trouble."

"Leastways they didn't hurt you," Dacey said, tipping his head back and closing his eyes—but not before he caught sight of Blaine's wicked grin. He opened them again, one eyebrow raised in question.

"Oh, one of 'em came out for me," she told him. "I wish it hadn't been Burl, though—he turned out decent. Estus would have deserved it, and he wouldn't have been able to get me off, neither." His other eyebrow went up. She made her voice extra airy. "Just something Lenie told me about." Though, as Blaine recalled, Lenie's strategy had been more of the kick-and-run variety. She added, "It turned Burl green."

One side of Dacey's mouth turned up; he shook his head and she was sure of it now—dry amusement. "Lenie done good by you this time."

She was glad to see that smile, quick as it had been, but there was no avoiding the hard words for good. "Dacey," she said, her voice low, "what're we gonna do?"

"Wait for Trey," Dacey said. He shifted, a wary and cautious movement, legs crossed and somewhat akimbo, and rested his head in his hands. "We still need him. And we still gotta make him see that he needs us."

"I can get away," Blaine offered quickly. "That Estus ain't hardly bigger'n me, and that's not saying

much for 'im. I can get past if you want me to." With
or without the blinder.

"I know you could. But there ain't much use in
it right now. We'll wait and see what Trey has to say
for himself."

When Blaine realized that was all the comment she
was going to get, she settled down and folded her legs
beneath her. She tried to follow the disquiet she felt,
to understand it, only to discover how much she hated
to see him like this. It somehow took her mind to
the Annekteh, to Nekfehr and his jimson and how he'd
literally crammed it down Dacey's throat. How that,
too, had seemed to tear something from him, the quiet
command he had of himself.

She found herself suddenly, fiercely glad that the
Annekteh couldn't Take him.

No wonder he got that look on his face, sometimes.
If it had been her with that jimson, Blaine would have
settled in for a nice long stay at Dacey's cabin and
not returned to Shadow Hollers. But Dacey . . . Dacey
was somehow more afraid of *not doing* this than he
was of doing it.

She sighed and settled her chin on her drawn-up
knees. He would be all right, given time. "Dacey,"
she said softly, not wanting to wake him if he'd fallen
asleep again. He opened his eyes. "About what Trey
said . . . about those men . . . I knew something was
wrong the other night, Dacey. I told Trey you didn't
kill them . . . but you did, didn't you?"

He looked away from her. "They weren't Annekteh,"
he said, quietly enough so Blaine had to lean forward
to hear. "I've done killed before, but they . . . *they* were
just doin' a job." He dragged a hand over his face. "It
adds up."

"I know," she said, still quiet. She glanced over to
the sunlit clearing to see if Estus was watching; there
was no sign of him. She touched Dacey's arm. "I'm
sorry."

"Sorry?"

"That it happened. Trey said . . . it was gruesome. I know you wouldn't have chose to do it that way. But we ain't playin' games, Dacey—we knew that. We're facin' more than just killin' those men. We're facin' killin' our own, iff'n they're Took. That's the stakes here."

"Well," Dacey said, after a moment's consideration. "You're right at that." He smiled at her, even if he did look a little distant. After some silence—comfortable enough—between them, he said, "I sure could use some food."

"I reckon that's a good sign. I don't know if Trey'll remember we ain't got nothing to eat, or even when he'll get here," Blaine said. "But I hope it's soon, and I hope he brings a whole pail of biscuits!"

→ 14 ←

But it was late before Trey got there, and he arrived in a rush of effort, throwing himself on the ground to recover from the climb. Estus immediately materialized from where he'd been lurking above the pines, and Blaine moved from the sunshine of the clearing to join them. Blaine stood on one side of Trey's supine body, Estus on the other; the two regarded one another coldly until Trey recovered enough to sit up. "Burl's on his way with a pack," he panted. "Couldn't keep up with me."

"What's the rush?" Blaine asked.

"Gotta talk to Dacey," Trey said. "We gotta decide what we're gonna do . . . the Takers got reinforcements and workers on their way!"

"They *what*?" The voice was Dacey's, and it was startled. He was at the edge of the pine shadow, almost steady, his attention riveted on Trey.

Trey squinted against the sun to examine Dacey's lean form. "So," he said in evident relief, "Estus didn't mash your head too hard after all."

"Not for lack of trying," Dacey said dryly, affording

Estus a brief glance of annoyance, and—like Blaine—
not mentioning the tea. Trey knew, if he'd think about
it; the others didn't need to. Dacey shed his jacket
in the warmth of the sunlight. "Limber up your
tongue, Trey. There's no reason for them to bring in
reinforcements now—they got things under control.
The loss of two men ain't enough to be callin' for
help."

"Point of fact, these ain't the first two they've lost,"
Trey said. "But I think these new ones been on their
way for a time longer than since those men died."
He hesitated, as though he wanted to ask about that,
but met Blaine's gaze and then looked uneasily away.
She knew, then, that he'd given up on demanding
anything from Dacey, was down to asking—and hoping, and glad for the help. "They had us in the
meetin' hall today, called us early. That's why I took
so long gettin' here." Then he paused, stuck at what
he wanted to say, until it finally came out in a rush.
"Those extra men are comin' 'cause they'll be needed
to watch more workers! They're bringin' in a whole
bunch of plainsfolks, just up and *movin'* a whole
village. They ain't plannin' on *goin'* once they get this
wood!"

Dacey's voice was tired as he sat down on his
jacket. One hand rubbed at the bridge of his nose,
the other arm dangled over his knee. "Humans give
'em more than trees, Trey."

"I—" Trey said uncomfortably, "I thought if we give
'em a hard enough time—an' we *have* been, don't you
make no mistake about that—they'd get what they
wanted an' leave."

Dacey's eyes flashed up; suddenly he was full of
energy, full of anger. "You don't know *nothin'*. After
all you seen, you still don't know *nothin*! You think
they don't want us for more than any damn wood?
Even *suktah*? You think they don't want you for what
they can do with you, what they can *feel* through you?

What do you know of Breeder towns and Feeler towns and Feeders, and livin' your whole life under Taker chains? What do you know of what they can *do*—" He faltered then, inner pain flickering across his face, resistance to it and then surrender to it following one on another. His head dropped; she saw his jaw work.

Blaine threw herself down before him, taking up his face between her hands to say most fiercely, "That ain't happenin' *now*, Dacey, none of it's happenin'. It's past you!"

His hands shot up to grab her wrists, a startlingly tight grip, and she couldn't tell if his deep-down groan was from his pains or his memories. "It ain't ever past," he said, barely audible.

Unbidden, Blaine thought of her brief terror in his dairy, thought of her dreams—no, say it, *her seeings*—of Willum's death. No. Maybe it wasn't ever truly past. She touched her forehead to his, and whispered, "But you ain't alone," and let him hold her that way.

After some moments his grip eased, and he pulled away to meet her gaze, just to look at her. She couldn't tell what went on behind those eyes, just met them, honest and wet-lashed. When he let her go and looked back to the boys, somehow he'd made that interlude a private one.

Except for Trey, who looked at Dacey with a strange kind of understanding, and acceptance. "They Took me oncet," he said, his voice as low as theirs had been. "Reckon I don't like to think on it. But all of a sudden I got a better understanding of it."

No one said anything; even Estus was purely at a loss. Blaine sat back on her heels, found Blue at her back, and twisted to put an arm over his sturdy shoulders.

Eventually Dacey gave Trey a nod, and went to rubbing the bridge of his nose. "When are the others supposed to get here?"

Trey answered in a voice not quite steady. "They said eight days."

"Eight days," Dacey repeated. "All right then. That means we got to make our move in less. That's some sooner than I had planned, and I'm gonna need all your cooperation. *All of it.*"

Trey swallowed visibly and looked away. "I ain't gonna cause any more trouble."

Dacey gave him an even stare. "There's only one way to beat the Annekteh, an' that's if you can tell who to stay away from in a fight, when they're jumping from body to body. You can't, but I *can*. That's a fact you'd better make sure everyone understands—especially them with rocks in their hands."

The boys gave what amounted to a communal gulp; not one of them could meet his gaze. But Blaine was staring right at him, thinking, *how?* and wondering why he hadn't told her. *Because you can be Taken, Blaine Kendricks, that's why.* But it didn't seem fair, somehow, that she should have been the one with him all this time—the one to *rescue* him—and still get her information in cautious dribbles, just like anyone else. That he couldn't be Taken. And now, unlike everyone else, somehow Dacey could tell the Taken right on the spot. And he still, she was very aware, hadn't told them just *how* he did it. Not the seer way, not considering he claimed to have no real seer skills, and only the occasional seeings . . .

After a moment, Dacey pushed his hair back—careful, he was, about it—and said, "The only ones free of constant watchin' are the older boys, am I rememberin' right?"

Trey nodded.

"Then I need to see 'em. Make an excuse to have 'em come here together—big cat tracks or some such. I want 'em here tomorrow. Don't tell none of 'em why ahead of time—we can't chance any more problems."

"I can get 'em here," Trey said confidently. He hesitated, then asked, "An' then what?"

"The less anyone knows, the less chance of it gettin' out," Dacey said evenly.

Trey's face reddened and he looked away, but the color faded fast. "I guess I deserved that."

"I was speakin' of the chance that the Annekteh might Take anyone, at any time, if they're still tryin' to clear up the killings," Dacey said, tipping his head against some inner pain. *More tea,* Blaine thought. The bundle ought to be good for a weak third steeping; she'd already gotten more of it down him earlier in the day. Given the way he struggled with himself, without that tea he'd not even be opening his eyes at all. *Damn Estus and his rock.*

"You ought to go lie down," she said. "You'll be in the thick of it soon enough."

"I'm fine, Blaine," Dacey said, tilting his face back to catch the sunlight, closing his eyes. "In a day or two I'll even be fit for killin' Annekteh." The boys made enough sheepish shuffling noises to scare off all the game in the area. Blaine glared at them.

"I ain't gonna cause no more trouble," Estus mumbled before Trey could prompt him. "I don't reckon I understand this so clear any more."

Ignoring him—it was getting easier—Blaine said, "I need to get some goods from our camp, Trey. Don't give me no trouble over *that*, neither."

"You can go," Trey agreed, "but Burl's bringing some stuff. Most anything you'll need, I'd say."

"We had a mess of bear meat drying by our fire, but I suppose the critters have got that now." Blaine tried to recall how they'd left the camp. "But we'll want his pack, and whatever meat's left, so we can feed the dogs . . . ."

"I'll help, iff'n you like," Trey said.

Blaine stared suspiciously at him before deciding the offer was sincere, then shook her head anyway.

"We might need to fall back to it, iff'n they get a-holt of you," she said decisively. "It won't be much to carry." She glanced at Dacey and moved across the clearing, gesturing for Trey to follow. Surprised, he only hesitated a moment, then followed her uphill to the log where she'd first waited for him.

"Listen," she said, pinning him hard with her gaze, "you leave off bothering Dacey about those men."

Trey looked troubled, but nodded. "It's done. We got more important things to handle, now. He's . . . he's right convincin', in what he knows of Takers."

"What he does, he does for good reason. You just trust him on that. I've staked my life on it." She couldn't help a little smile. "Don't mean I always understand what he's up to, that's for sure. But do you think he'd have risked comin' up here again iff'n we didn't *need* him?"

Trey scowled and scratched his nose, glancing back down at Dacey. Finally he said, "It's a good thing he's got you watchin' over him, Blaine Kendricks."

Blaine snorted. "He don't need me, nor anyone else." But she thought of the way he had gripped her arms, held on to her. Taken strength from her.

Burl put an end to the conversation by arriving, huffing and puffing, at the bottom edge of the clearing. It was little wonder that he'd not been able to keep up with his smaller friend; he was burdened with a leather, basket-bottomed pack that Blaine sized up purely by how much food it might hold. Burl grinned up at her as he unshouldered his burden, and she moved downhill with haste. Estus already crowded close.

Burl slapped Estus' hand away from where it fumbled at the rawhide ties, and took over the task. When Blaine got there he was groping around in the small pocket set atop the pack, his broad face impatient. Finally he extracted a palm-sized clay jar, which he extended toward Blaine. "It's my mommy's own salve," he explained as Blaine tentatively accepted the jar. "For him." And he jerked his head in the direction of the pines.

Blaine held the cool clay in her hand and cocked her head at him. He was a little like Blue, she decided—once he accepted you, there was apparently no halfway. "I'm grateful," she said finally, and didn't mention that the tea had already done most of what Dacey needed.

"Now can we eat?" Estus said, peevish.

Although his sharp features probably always appeared hunger-pinched, Blaine empathized with his eagerness to be at the food. She reached for the pack, and Burl tipped it her way.

"What about Dacey?" Trey asked. As one, they looked at him, discovering him asleep with his face still tilted to catch the sun.

Blaine shook her head. "Let him sleep," she said. "He'll be the better for it. Time enough to get food in him when he wakes on his own."

Burl was nodding his agreement. "'Member that time I fell outta the ole apple tree?" he asked Trey. "Food weren't no welcome sight for two days, till my stomach settled."

"Only time I can think of you turnin' it down." Trey grinned, a regular boy again, if just for a moment.

Dacey was some better off than that, Blaine knew—and would be even better once she resteeped that tea. "You all go right on talkin'," she said, turning on the pack and tugging at the ties to the main section. "I can't stand it no more." Estus pitched in beside her and the two of them discovered an oilcloth bundle of cornbread and chicken, sweet molasses cake and a few of last year's grubby carrots. When Blaine lifted the bundle, Estus pulled out the waterskin beneath, and they sat down together, too interested in the food to maintain their animosity.

It was her first meal in . . . well, it *seemed* like days.

Never mind that the chicken was greasy and the cornbread crumbly with age; the water had sat in the skin too long but it was sweet to her throat even so. She quit reaching for more before her stomach wanted to, looking at the ample remainder longingly but knowing Dacey had yet to eat—and that they had at least another day before they would be able to provide for themselves.

Estus blithely reached for more chicken, but a stern look from Blaine brought him up short. "We gotta save some."

He opened his mouth to protest; Burl murmured his name and the younger boy subsided without a word, although his expression said much.

Blaine stood and straightened her ragged skirts with a shake. "Believe I'll get those things from our camp," she announced. "I'm taking Blue, so don't none of you follow, or I'll know it."

"We'll stay right here," Trey said dryly.

She called Blue to her side—he could just as well wear his packs and help her out on the way back—and started across the clearing and up the ridge, stopping only once to peer back and see the boys sitting just as she'd left them. Satisfied, she struck out at a good pace.

She ignored the faint trace of the path she and Dacey had forged from camp to clearing and went straight up the hill, using Blue's back as a brace when the going was steep and wishing she had his four tireless legs. Halfway up she looked back, satisfied that none of the plainsmen could follow the trail.

The roundabout route made the going hard, and when Blaine finally reached the little shelter she was more than ready to throw herself down on the hemlock bedding—an impulse she made no attempt to resist. She rolled over to her back and waited for her breathing to ease and her heart to stop pounding in her ears, her vision filled with the woven shelter above her—a sight her memory somehow turned into a fond and seemingly longstanding thing.

There had been a sort of timelessness to the days of travel with Dacey and his crazy dogs—of learning their voices on trail, of learning to relax with Dacey's company, of realizing that he truly didn't care about her differences, didn't set any impossible, un-Blainelike roles for her to fill. He just demanded that she be the best Blaine she could. And as quiet as he was, he shared himself in a dozen different ways.

As if she truly mattered.

Trey's attack had ended that timelessness and now things were moving again, and at a pace much too quick to suit her.

Blaine sat up and drew her knees to her flat chest, wrapping her arms around them. She stared out at the mountains unwinding before her, where the dull colors of winter had suddenly been replaced with an uneven mottling of green—poplars first, bursting into full leaf and making green points against the dull brown of the other dormant trees. The vibrant pink splashes of the redbuds had faded, but the dogwoods still made splendid puffs of white across the hills.

She wondered if the beauty of the mountains would ever again seem so piercing and bright. It occurred to her that when this ordeal was over, she would be once more chained by her father's rules, her parents' expectations. She'd likely never walk the hills again.

When this was over. The thought repeated itself, then modified. *If this ever ended.* What if they could not defeat the Annekteh? What if the people she had grown up with remained enslaved, Annekteh labor and . . . *toys*? Trey had found a sassafras grove, she was sure of it—what if the Takers got their hands on it? What if Blaine herself could never go back to them, but was forced to the mountains, running the ridges with a pack of dogs and their master, and the faint hope that maybe someday they could help?

Freedom. Of a sort.

But the freedom she longed for would be no freedom at all if the way of life she left behind was
destroyed. If she had to think of Willum's death and
know it went unavenged, unspoken for.

Blaine heaved a great sigh and climbed to her feet
to survey the camp for the first time. She wasn't
surprised to find Dacey's drying racks reduced to twigs
and scattered throughout the site, the meat gone.
There was, however, one big haunch that had yet to
be cut into strips for drying; Dacey had hung it at
the end of a high, slender maple limb, counterweight
to his pack. High enough that he needed to hook the
pack with a stick to pull it within reach.

High enough that even with the stick, she couldn't
quite reach it herself.

Blaine picked up what she could. She refolded the
blankets, and fitted Blue's packs to him. Her own
small pack sat, undisturbed—no food in it, so that
wasn't surprising—in the high crook of a tree. After
she had tugged it down, crammed the contents of it
into Blue's packs, and shoved the blankets into her
own, Blaine stood beneath the meat, unhappily considering her options. She ruefully inspected the barely
healing scrapes from her last exploit in a tree, and
then finally hoisted herself into the maze of maple
limbs. Getting to the level of the meat was easy, but
there she stopped, staring at the mostly horizontal
branch and the rope looped over it.

Can't believe I'm doing this for a bunch of dogs.

But she did. She crept along the branch, wishing
it felt more substantial beneath her. When she could
finally reach the braided rawhide rope, she tugged
the pack up, lowering the meat until Blue took notice
and made a few interested leaps at it. Surely that was
far enough. Blaine quickly backed off the branch and
descended to reassuring solid ground.

She turned from the tree to discover that Blue had

beaten her to the meat, had latched on and pulled it down with his weight. Blaine didn't begrudge him a bite. The more he ate, the less she had to carry, and she had yet to figure out how she was going to carry any of it.

Reluctant to cut the rope, she hauled on it, lifting the pack in little jerks until it hit the tree limb and she had to perform all sorts of antics—running this direction and that with the rope, hoping a different angle and her weight hitting the rope would pull it up and over the top of the branch—before it hit the ground next to the haunch, barely disturbing Blue at his meal. In the end she couldn't manage the knot at the pack and had to cut the rope there. She pulled a few more things from it to add to her smaller pack—what little food was left, mostly—and, grunting and grumbling, jammed it up in the crook where her own pack had stayed safe.

Then she turned to the haunch. She gave it an exploratory nudge, a halfhearted attempt to lift it. Not a chance. Besides, it was greasy, and bordering on rank. Blaine made a face at it. Well, she'd drag it. It was only fit for the dogs, anyway, and knowing the way they ate, they'd probably gulp it down, embedded rocks and sticks and all. Blaine made one last circuit of the camp, found nothing else worth taking, and shouldered the pack, tying a loop in the middle of the rawhide and coiling the rest so she could drag the meat more easily. Even so, it bumped and caught on every little stick or root in its path, and if it wasn't for the thought of hungry dog eyes watching her while she ate her own food, Blaine would have abandoned it a hundred times over.

At least it kept Blue attentively at her side.

No way to hide *this* trail. She used the deer path, walking further along the ridge where the slope down was more acute. There she hesitated, wondering if she'd gone too far. It would never do to try coming up here, but . . . maybe she could slide down without too much trouble. She dropped the rawhide rope and paced the edge of the slope, finally choosing a good, steep but smooth stretch of hill that was devoid of rocky outcrops. Taking up the rope, she made her way off the crest of the ridge, then dug her heels into the ground and allowed herself to slide.

Relief. It would work. Every so often her butt bumped the ground and slowed her down, and even the meat caught on enough roots to keep it in control. Maybe hauling the haunch wouldn't be so bad.

She wasn't counting on Blue. Suddenly the rawhide loop tightened around her hand and jerked her to a stop, throwing her around on her face. She came up spitting dead leaves, her progress slowed but not altogether stopped—and the haunch was directly above her, bearing down on her—*gaining* on her.

Not for long. "No!" she yelped in futile protest, as the temptation of the moving haunch again proved too much for Blue. He charged it, playful and delighted, and grabbed the thigh bone.

Astonished at his strength, Blaine gaped, horrified, as he lifted the meat off the ground. Horrified, because he couldn't possibly be strong *enough*, not to hold his leverage—

She clawed the ground, fighting to stop her progress, to move aside, to—*Blue, no!* Off balance, upended, the hound flipped onto his back and tumbled down the hill with his prize.

Securely tethered, Blaine plunged after him, wildly out of control.

Bump, spin, tumble, her arm jerking near out of its socket, a wild mash of images assaulting her eyes, bump, spin, tumble—*are we stopped*? Blaine couldn't quite tell . . . her limbs had ceased moving but her head wasn't sure. As she propped herself up to brush the hair from her eyes, Blue climbed to his feet next to her. He gave an ear-popping shake and regarded the meat with a puzzled but respectful stare. For an object without teeth or legs, it had somehow gained quite an advantage over him.

"Blue," she groaned. *Dumb, dumb dog*. He only transferred his puzzled gaze to her, his ears cocked into floppy, inquisitive black wings. *Spirits!* Blaine added up her bruises and plucked futilely at the twisted rawhide biting deeply into her hand.

Blue's decision to stumble over and nudge her was not a wise one. Her temper flared; she dealt him a slap that resounded against the opposite hill, and ignored his surprised yelp. The rawhide was unyielding and painful; her hand had turned a funny blueish color. She wasn't even sure she could get a knife between the rawhide and her skin. Did she even still have her knife?

Yes, it was still there. Relief. Carefully, mindful that Dacey had just sharpened it for her the previous day, she sliced at the rawhide until it gave way and spent several pained moments simply massaging the abused hand. Blue, cowed and tentative, crept up to her. *I'm not speaking to you.* "No good," she grumbled at him, struggling out of the pack so she could shift the jumbled contents, pushing him away again and again until one more solid smack gave her peace. Bruised and aching, she tied the pack closed and shouldered it, taking the rawhide in her unmangled hand as she continued her resolute trek back to the new camp.

Blue slunk behind her as she dragged herself to the pines, clearly the worse for wear—her shirt torn, one of the makeshift seams in her skirt unraveling, and a fat lip blooming on her face. When Burl met her to take the meat, he wasn't slow to notice.

"Did you run into another bear?" he teased, not unkindly.

Blaine went haughty on him, not answering in the least. Shrugging, Burl moved out of her way as he hoisted the haunch to his shoulder with an ease that made her all the more vexed. Blue stole into the pines ahead of her and curled up into an abject ball beside Dacey, whiffling a sigh out through his flews. Lowering herself to the ground across from the cold ashes of the fire, Blaine struggled out of the pack, an awkward process better undertaken on foot. *If I could've stood up even another minute . . .*

Burl plunked the meat down outside the pines and untied the rawhide. The hounds jumped to their feet, whining, and casting quick glances from Dacey to the meat.

"All right," he told them, and they charged for the haunch; Chase leapt right over him to get there. Mage, never anything less than dignified, stalked over, lifted an eloquent lip, and claimed his spot. Only Blue stayed where he was, whiffling out another sigh and twitching his tail so it lay over his nose.

Dacey gave him a concerned look. Blaine said, "He got his fill before we left camp—made a lighter load for me." She rotated her shoulder to ease some of the soreness, and noticed Dacey had eaten as well, and that his face was closer to its normal healthy complexion—lightly tanned, a bit darker than her own thin-skinned and freckled countenance. "You look a mite better."

"Guess I was just hungry," he said, still looking at Blue. He laid a hand on the dog's back and gave him a few gentle pats. Blaine divined that he was not in a talking mood, and that suited her just fine. She lay back to regain some of what the hike from the camp had taken out of her.

When she opened her eyes, the pine shadows had stretched up the hill to meet the woods above the clearing. She sat up. *Ow. Ow-ow-ow.* Moving more carefully, she rubbed the bleariness of a late afternoon's sleep from her eyes.

Estus was nowhere in sight, a pleasant surprise. At

the edge of the pines, Trey watched her stiff, fuzzy-brained movements with amusement, and beside him, Burl and Dacey seemed to be discussing trapping; Mage and Blue lay at Dacey's feet, and the other dogs were nowhere to be seen.

"Where's Estus?" Blaine asked, the words barely beating a yawn out of her mouth.

Trey jerked his chin toward the woods. "For all the Takers know, we been out hunting every day. Yesterday Burl and I had to make stories about bad luck. And excuses for Estus—said he'd stayed the night, laying out new traps and double-checking the snares. He's got to have something to show for it."

Blaine massaged her sore arm. "If he doesn't get anything he can always lay it on the big cat Dacey made up for tomorrow. Those plainsmen won't know the difference, they're hill-blind. I heard 'em talking once and they didn't even know for sure that we have deer here."

"You listened in on 'em?" Trey asked, surprised.

"I heard a lot more'n that, too, but it weren't fit for my ears nor your'n." She grinned at him. "Thought you'd learned to quit judgin' me by how I *ought* to be, Trey."

He shook his head, apparently at himself. "Have to keep learnin' it all over, I guess. Might need Estus' rock, to pound it right in there."

Blaine looked at him in disbelief, and discovered he'd gone to grinning. Teasing her, he was, and not in a mean way. In a way that made her feel that she'd earned something. She snorted and lifted her chin, but it was just as much teasing him back as anything.

"Trey, you ready to move on?" Burl asked, turning from his conversation with Dacey. "We need to, we're gonna talk to the others afore curfew."

"Ready enough," Trey said, and picked up the bow he had leaned against a tree.

Burl caught Blaine's attention with a gesture at the

pack he'd brought. "I know you got some of your own stuff now, but keep that. There's more food and blankets at the bottom."

"I thank you," Blaine said, envisioning the luxury of a blanket both above and below for the night's sleep. "Don't seem like you're mad anymore, then, about yesterday?"

"Oh, I got over that quick," Burl said, cheerfully enough. He got to his feet, letting Trey take the lead. "The bigger they are, the harder they fall, and I've had to take that to heart."

Blaine laughed at that, watching as they walked the switchbacks down the hill and into the woods below the clearing. Dacey watched, too, no longer looking as though the ground might fall out from beneath him. When he turned and caught her eye, his look was a searching one, and she couldn't quite interpret it. "You look better," she said. "Wish I could get a fourth steeping from that bark, but there ain't no use to tryin'."

"It's done what's needed," he said, looking down at Blue with a small frown. Blue whiffled a sigh, and refused to meet Blaine's eye when she caught his gaze.

"What's wrong with Blue?" she asked, taking a step for him, reaching out—

But a new, ugly sound intruded upon the clearing, stopping Blaine in mid-step. Mage stood in his usual spot at Dacey's side, staring at her, his upper lip slightly curled. It was, she realized in surprise, more of a comment than a threat, but it was astonishing all the same. "Dacey, what—?"

Dacey softly cleared his throat at the dog. Mage settled down to the ground, laying his chin across Dacey's foot. "Not sure," Dacey said, and he didn't sound happy. Like he'd listened to something that Mage had to say, and it weren't any too good for Blaine. He frowned at Blue again, and lifted his head to look at Blaine more sideways than straight on. Darkly thoughtful.

Blaine frowned. "Iff'n there's something wrong, I sure wish you'd let me in on it."

He matched her expression with one of his own, one a little more narrow-eyed. "I'm thinkin' you ought to know."

Blaine looked helplessly back at him. Suddenly, the one person who had accepted all her odd ways was questioning her, judging her—and she felt it clutch at all the long-pained parts inside her. "Dacey, if I did somethin', just tell me!"

"Blaine, I don't *know* just what's wrong. When you got back, Blue come creepin' into the pines like a whipped pup. That dog's sulking, an' he's doing it big. You're the one was with him—you tell *me*."

"He fell," Blaine said. Her hand still bore signs of the rawhide, too. "Dragged me down with him. Just dumb."

Dacey shook his head. "He don't care none about stuff like that. It's all play, to him."

Uncertain, Blaine said, "I smacked him over it . . . surely that ain't it. He had it coming, the way he almost killed us both."

She'd seen his anger directed at Trey. She'd never felt the force of it herself, and it hit her hard, even though he didn't so much as raise his voice. "Do you think that Blue's got the wits to figure what would happen?"

Blaine blinked back at him. "I—"

"Blaine," Dacey said, and his hazel eyes were dark and serious—uncompromising—"Blue's just a dumb ole hound, but he's a good fellow, and don't want nothin' more than to please who he loves. For some reason he's chose you to dote on. You dislike it that much, I'll see to it he don't bother you no more. You just return him the favor."

Blaine gulped, surprised to feel tears welling.

"But—I didn't know it would bother him so—I didn't mean nothin' . . . "

"Neither did Blue," Dacey said evenly.

"Oh." Blaine found that her voice was very small. She'd gotten used to her father's disapproval, or the way Lottie never stood up for her, creating a dull, chronic ache of disapproval. This was sharp and piercing and made her throat hurt too much to swallow. She went to the dog, uncertain, and knelt by him. "I'm sorry, Blue," she said, and hugged him—all bony legs and floppy ear, a bulk that filled her arms.

His tail stirred and he tilted his head toward her, eyes rolling white in trying to see her face—but he, too, was uncertain.

"Please, Blue?" Blaine laid her cheek on the top of his broad head. His tail thumped the ground, more assertively this time. He rolled over, forcing her aside with his weight, and assumed a totally absurd position on his back, waving his forefeet in her face. She drew back to smile at him.

Dacey set his hand on her shoulder—gentle, and with a little squeeze. "I knew once you understood how it felt you would never let it pass."

She found herself suddenly able to breathe again at that touch, that forgiveness. Better yet, acceptance. And a little surprise. "You mean you—you did that on purpose? You made me feel so bad on purpose?"

"Don't mis-take me, Blaine. I meant every word I said. Blue's give over his heart to you—he did right from the start. That ain't to be took lightly. I know your daddy's taught you a dog has a certain place—but try to do Blue right."

"Daddy don't think a girl's got any place walking the hills, neither," Blaine said soberly, then slid into a sly grin as Dacey took her meaning. He stroked his hand lightly over her hair and turned away, his thoughts leaving his face to move inward.

Annekteh, Blaine knew. It was always Annekteh when he had that face on, that being-alone look. She looked down at Blue and shook the paw he offered from his supine position.

Here was someone who needed her.

→ 15 ←

Annekteh magic . . . in the plains, limited to their natural abilities to Take their vessels, to inflict certain kinds of pain— a skill developed by their craving for *anne-nekfehr*—and to sense other magics flowing nearby. In the mountains, with magic running through the ridges like veins of gold, the Annekteh remembered old skills, worked to develop new ones.

Just now they sensed something amiss. Something with a seer's feel, just as there had been on the day the plainsmen brought in Dacey Childers, the day the Blaine-child had somehow freed him and fled with him from these hills.

If he was back, he'd been more circumspect.

But the Annekteh grew more attuned to the ridges. And when Nekfehr sifted through the input of all the local *annektehr*,

he liked it not. Needed more, if he was
to find any conclusion in the nebulous
taste of seer's magic on the hollow-
twisted breezes.

He had magic and men at his dis-
posal. Perhaps it was time to go looking.

＊＋　　　　＊＋　　　　＊＋

Rain drizzled through the early dawn, obscuring
the landscape with a grey mist that drifted as ran-
domly as a school of fish. First veiling Blaine's entire
field of view, then suddenly lifting to reveal the small
gathering before her, it painted the Shadow Hollers
boys unnaturally clear in the crystal pockets of dry
air. She sat quietly on the log at the top edge of the
clearing and studied the assembly as the boys waited
for Trey and Burl to tell them why they were there.
Some, like Trey and Burl, looked on the edge of
manhood, while some hardly seemed old enough to
be hunting on their own. All were dirty and tired,
and shooting covert glances at Dacey where he stood
next to Blaine.

She counted twenty all told, and thought it was
a mighty poor force to be setting up against the
Annekteh.

"I know you thought you were here after big cat,"
Dacey said. The boys stopped milling about and
stared at him, only then realizing that Burl and Trey,
rather than organizing them for a hunt, were simply
sitting and waiting. "But you're after something much
bigger, somethin' that's already got its claws in you."
He spoke with the quiet, comforting assurance she
was used to hearing from him, and the boys' murmuring reaction quickly silenced. "My name is Dacey,"
he told them. "And I'm your last chance against the
Annekteh. The Takers. And now you already know
enough to get everyone in a pack of trouble, you
choose to go back and tell it. Even so ... if you ain't
up to this, you better go now." The expression he gave

them was neutral and far from accusing. Statement of fact.

But Trey got to his feet and glared at the youngsters assembled before him. "I second that," he said. "Go if you can't take the thought of what we aim to do. But any of you let word of this leak and the rest of us'll—"

Dacey's quiet-throat clearing—the very same noise he used to quell Mage—stopped Trey short, and he settled for giving them all a hard look before sitting again. No one else moved. No one else spoke. Several of them looked to be on the edge of bolting, and some of the others—the youngest ones—were about ready to cry from relief.

Someone had come to help stop the nightmare.

"There's two things we got to do," Dacey told the apprehensive youngsters. "The first is get your families free, out from being hostages. The other is to drive the Annekteh away. In order to do them things, we got to kill every last one of them that's Taken."

Their hope grew, shining through as determination; they nodded, jostled one another, muttered rebellious phrases.

It was Dacey's next words that turned them all back into scared children. "Now think on this. As soon as the *annektehr*—the Takers inside—realize we're killing them, they're gonna start Taking more vessels—ones you won't want to hurt. But you're gonna have to keep right on at them—trying to kill people you know and maybe some you love."

The silence that followed was complete, down to the wind that should have been moving through the trees and the birds that had been quarreling over nesting areas. It was Whimsy who broke the gap, finishing a yawn with a loud and ridiculous squeal.

Dacey gave her the briefest of affectionate smiles, and looked back at his young warriors. "We'll use the bulk of you fightin' in the woods, part of you as runners to the men, and the last of you to take back the meeting hall," he said. "We'll go for the known Taken, first—be easy to start with, you all know who they are. Once they have a chance to spread, to Take others, I've got a way to tell you who to go after. You'll be using bows and slings and whatever throwing rocks you can find—nothing up close—and if you hesitate to aim where I say, you'll be turned on as one of them. I want you to think about what that means."

"But how c'n you *tell*?" The question came as a plea, from one of the youngest children there. The stricken look on his face showed that he, at least, realized he might be ordered to kill one of his own.

"I know," Dacey said, flat statement. "If they ain't *nekfehr*, you won't be pointed to 'em. You got to accept that right now or this won't come off."

Even Burl's face showed the reality of what they faced. Blaine stroked Blue's head, feeling as invisible as if she'd been clutching the blinder. *Dacey, you're scaring them off*, she thought, watching the sniffling, scared bunch.

Dacey seemed to see it, too. His voice gentled down some. "I know I'm a stranger to you. It's the only reason I'm not caught up with the rest of your menfolk. Trust Trey and Burl iff'n you can't bring yourself to trust me. And iff'n you can't do that, trust that I hate the Annekteh as much as anyone. If that ain't enough, you just better figure you only got a short span of days before more o' them get here, and I'm the only one standin' here to tell you how to get free before that happens."

There was no denying that. They had only days before their lives were forever changed, they were children, and here was someone who would—who *could*—tell them what to do. A few of them looked up at him, earnest-faced and somehow uncertain at the same time—*we want to believe in you* expressions— but they didn't know if they dared.

"Any one of you let on that something's up, and the Annekteh'll Take you," Dacey said. "They'll slap you down before you get started—and they may never let you go. You keep that in mind until you hear from Trey or Burl just what you're to be doing, and when." His face took on a different kind of intensity. Hope. Purpose. "An' you keep this in mind—we can do this. They don't know I'm here. They're weak, in thinkin' that they can't be hurt, when they can. *We can do this.*"

He sat down on the log next to Blaine. The boys stirred, and turned to one another, still flashing frowns and uncertainty at Dacey, talking in what started as whispers but rose to chatter punctuated with emphatic exclamations. *They'd do it*, she thought. It wasn't like they had a choice. "What do you think?"

"They'll do," he said absently. "I reckon they got to."

Blaine snorted. "Half of 'em ain't old enough to find the outhouse at night by themselves."

"I know." His voice was quiet.

Not in a talking mood. Blaine left him alone, busied with the task of staring down the few glances coming her way as the boys filed out of the clearing. Glances filled with silent questions about *her*—for although she knew some of these boys, they appeared not to have recognized her. She didn't know whether it was because of their numbed condition or because of some change in herself. Upon inspection she certainly appeared the same.

She couldn't say the same of Dacey. Never mind the jagged healing spot above his temple; she was getting used to that. She looked instead at the darkness under his eyes and the strain around his mouth, high contrast with the grin that came so easily when he sang with the dogs. "They would rather fight, even this dirty, than live under the Annekteh," she said, almost before she knew she intended to speak.

Dacey looked at her in mild surprise, and after a moment, a quiet smile barely stretched the corners of his mouth. Then he looked out at the abandoned clearing and the sunshine that had risen over the top of the opposite ridge to sparkle through the hollow, changing the grey fog into brilliant clouds that gathered densely unto themselves as they drifted upward. "By the time this is over, even if we win, those boys will hate me. I'm askin' them to do things children ought not even think of."

"They've already seen and done things they ought not even think of," Blaine said, petting the velvet of Blue's ear. "You're the one that told me, way back at your cabin, that things was never goin' to be the same. You're the one who knows all about it. How can you doubt what you're doing? I don't."

"Don't you?" Dacey asked, looking at her, that clear-eyed look of his.

Blaine frowned at him. "You might make it easy and just let me say so."

"Ain't my way," Dacey said, but a hint of humor had returned to his face.

She couldn't help it. She stuck her tongue out at him. And then she stuck her chin on the heel of her fist and looked out at the shifting clouds, enjoying the sounds of birds reclaiming the clearing with the boys gone. The past few days had seen an explosion of green, and the trees showed a multitude of hues in their fast-growing leaves. Many times she had watched similar weather and similar views from her rock, and now she could almost pretend . . .

But not quite. She glanced at Dacey to find him lost in his own reverie, comfortably companionable here, on the heels of a declaration of rebellion. And when she looked back upon the cloud that drifted its way up the hill toward them, its first tendrils curling at their feet, she found it had changed. Involuntarily, she sat up straight, gaping at the shadows, the tint of purple that now reached for them. She dug her nails into the rotting wood of the log, searching for something real and solid as the color deepened.

"Dacey," she said unsteadily, unable to tear her eyes away from the miasma that flowed around her calves. "Dacey!" she repeated more insistently, her voice going shrill and terrified. Beside her, buried in dark fog, Blue growled.

The moist fingers shifted up to her thighs and Blaine could stand it no longer—she stood to flee, looking wildly for escape, finding that the rest of the cloud had risen above them and covered everything, leaving only a few dark, looming and unidentifiable shapes. "Dacey!" she shrieked. Beyond reasoning, beyond terror, she dropped to her knees to bury her face in her hands, a thin, insubstantial target buried in purple mist, rocking and keening in fear.

"Blaine." Two strong hands gripped her shoulders, shaking her against the rhythm of her own movement. "*Blaine*." He gave her a single, tooth-rattling shake and she suddenly realized he was *there*, turned to huddle in against him. "It's all right, Blaine. They ain't here. Just a Taker trick."

"Wh-what?" she said, muffled through her hands.

"Look," he said firmly, turning her away and gently but insistently removing her hands from her face.

The clearing shone before her, washed in sunlight and strong shadows. Above, the dissipating mist still shone faintly of purple as the clouds rose to evaporate in the sun.

"I—I thought they were *here*," she said tremulously. "I thought they had us."

"Just tricks, Blaine."

"But—didn't you see it?"

"Not until I looked for it. It weren't nothing more than what a good seer could have done in the days when they were strong. Just trying to scare us."

"Well, damn," Blaine sniffled, "they did a good job."

"That's all right," Dacey said, sliding back to sit on the log again. "Iff'n we hadn't got them some scared, they wouldn't have bothered to do it."

"But they don't know we're here," Blaine said, sitting back on her heels and wiping her face with a sleeve that left her more smudged than she'd been. "Do they?"

"I don't reckon," Dacey said thoughtfully. "They might could suspect I'm back, what with those men dead."

"That's enough," Blaine muttered, still shaky as she rose to her feet. She was beginning to feel ashamed and more than a little bit angry.

"It's all right, Blaine," Dacey repeated quietly, although when she looked at him, his gaze was on the faint path leading toward their old camp. After a moment he fumbled with the buckle that wrapped the leather upper of his boot around his lower calf. The soft leather sagged, spilling out the winter wool lining. He pulled a small pouch from the wool and relaced the boots.

By now Blaine knew enough not to ask, and merely watched with curiosity until Dacey stood, emptied the pouch into his hand, and held it out to her. Within were four completely nondescript dull white objects, each about the size of one of her front teeth. Blaine blinked and stepped closer. They *were* front teeth. Someone's cutting teeth. She wrinkled her nose at him and deliberately stepped back again.

"They're teeth, all right," Dacey said, in complete sympathy with her expression. "And more. They're protection."

"From what?" Blaine asked, skeptical.

"They're Annekteh Took. *Were*," he corrected himself. "Now they're wards, iff'n you know how to use them. Set 'em in a building, it's safety from Annekteh."

"Then why ain't we used 'em before?" Blaine said, not quite a demand. She was just as glad they hadn't.

"They ain't without risks," he said, tilting them around in his hand. "They pretty much make a path that's easy for the Annekteh to follow. Once you use 'em, they know where you are, and that you got magic. 'Course, once they get to you they can't actually get in, but then neither can you get out. I was countin' on these to help us hold the hall if we take it."

"Strikes me this is one of those things you been keepin' from me." She leaned just a little closer, deciding she definitely didn't want to know how they'd been acquired in the first place. "Why tell me now?"

"I want you to take them."

"Oh, no." Blaine's interest evaporated. "They're yours. I don't want nothin' to do with 'em."

"I'll show you how to use 'em," Dacey said, giving her as intent a look as he ever had, "and then you'll take 'em. You got to. Up to now I've been your safety, Blaine, not that you've needed much. I figured I could protect you from being Took, and it weren't worth the risk of using these, shoutin' to 'em that we were here. But I reckon they do know that—or at least think it—or they wouldn't have played with the mist. And things are gonna get confusing soon. You won't be as safe no more. You take these, and if the time comes you need 'em, use 'em. But don't lose 'em, 'cause you'll be the one setting them at the hall."

"Dacey . . ." she protested, and he brought his gaze up from the teeth to look directly at her.

"Blaine," he said, "I know I've said you could take care of yourself. If you couldn't, I wouldn't be giving these to you now. I need to give them to someone I can depend on."

Human teeth. That was bad enough, but to know they'd been Took? Blaine shuddered. *Someone I can depend on*. Slowly, she extended her hand. The little grey objects tumbled into her palm, warm from Dacey's own. She stared at them.

"Now listen close," he said. "I don't want to go through this too many times—I got yet to make it back to the old camp today."

Blaine's gaze had been oddly drawn by the things in her hand, but now it wrenched back to Dacey. "You can't go, not if they know you're around, not when you're still puny from that rock!"

"That's all true enough, but . . . we might need a place to fall back to, Blaine. I want it set to rights, and I want it safe—and if they know we might go there, it won't be safe. It's got to look like no one's ever been there. I don't reckon that's how you left it."

"I'll go, then." They did need his pack, and her bearskin still hung over a branch plain as day. "You know I got restless feet. And *you*—iff'n I could boss you around with any luck, I'd be sending you back to rest while you can."

He rebuckled his boot, considering her words. "It's good sense, I can't argue that." Straightening, he stretched, scrubbed his hand through his hair—one side of it, anyway—and nodded. "Iff'n you're truly—"

But he stopped short, stiffening, off-balance with his stretch and jerking to catch himself. "No," he breathed, and his expression changed so rapidly Blaine had no chance to follow, to figure out what was going on. He made no effort to give her that chance. His face closed up; he straightened. "I reckon I need the chance to stretch my legs, Blaine. I won't be gone but for a while."

"Dacey," she said, all set to protest, lifting her chin to its most stubborn elevation. "I can't stop you, but I ain't stayin' behind."

"You'll be all right," he said, picking out one of the teeth from the group on her palm. "It's got to be done. Now listen up, I'll tell you how this is done."

She gave him a cross look—*it's not* me *I'm worried about*—and bent to the task of learning the wards. Then she'd see about who went and who stayed.

With the wards secured in her pocket, Blaine had watched Dacey take the hill to the old camp. Mage walked along behind him, his nose to the wind and actively searching the air; the other three foxhounds were off on some errand of their own.

It should be me.

But he hadn't wanted it. Had gone in that one strange moment from considering her sensible offer to steadfastly refusing it, to refusing even her company.

Leaving her with this handful of disgusting old teeth.

But he had his reasons, whatever they were; he always had his reasons. And he was right enough not to be free with them, not with the Annekteh around. So Blaine went over the ward procedure in her head three times—it was simple enough, if distasteful—then quit the clearing in search of a willow and, perhaps if she were lucky, sassafras. By the time Dacey returned from his ill-advised hike, he'd probably be in need of more of that tea. Meanwhile, Trey had been thoughtful enough to bring more food, so she had no intention of foraging unless she saw something irresistible.

The sassafras remained elusive, and she moved down toward the creek in search of willow. It was easy found, and she stripped off a few wands for tea before she cut a branch to transform into a willow whistle on the way back.

Blue hovered around her as she brewed the tea, and she let him taste it when he insisted; he gravely lapped it, but only once—and his tongue flew around the inside of his mouth, trying to rid himself of the bitter taste. Blaine laughed and then had to say she was sorry, and he forgave her by cleaning her arm from wrist to elbow with that same big tongue.

For an afternoon that came on the heels of a purple mist and the gathering of miniature warriors, Blaine enjoyed herself almost indecently. Now that she'd accepted Blue's affection, and even allowed herself to return it, she discovered that his companionship was entertaining. She didn't even begrudge cutting off some of the bear meat for him so he wouldn't pester her about the warming bacon and beans.

But when darkness fell, Dacey's portion of the beans sat dried and cracked at the edge of the fire. Alternately worrying and dozing, Blaine sat against one of the little pines, a blanket wrapped around her shoulders and the blue-ticked dog on her feet. A few owls hooted back and forth at one another while the dying fire occasionally shifted, sparking in the darkness. Now and then the trees moved enough to rustle in the breeze. Blaine listened to the soft intrusions, comfortable with them. When Blue gave a soft whine she didn't stir.

And then something made the hairs on the back of her own neck stand up. An instant later, Mage's eerie lament filled the air, swallowing the other night noises with its intensity.

Blue jumped to his feet, his hackles rising, his whine growing into the sort of moan which could only rise to a howl. Blaine grabbed his collar, struggling to keep the blanket around her shoulders as she stood. "*No good*," she said. "We don't want to call no attention to ourselves." Unhappily, Blue subsided, looking up to her for reassurance.

After some moments, when the night noises resumed and Blue gave one of his whiffling sighs, Blaine sat back down. She was halfway to the ground, her ankles crossed, her balance precarious, when Blue gave a sharp bark. She snatched at his collar again; he tore through her grip like a favorite knife through a weak pocket and was in full cry before her bottom hit the ground. Blaine stared stupidly after him, and only belatedly—and futilely—shouted, "Blue! You get back here!"

The rustling noise of his progress up the ridge faded. She was alone.

Blaine closed her eyes—frustrated, searching for patience and fortitude—but they opened again, quick and very wide. She knew that Mage song, that very noise. Not any old hound howl, not talking with the others up on the ridge. Spirits, it was the very one he had sung the morning she found Dacey tied and struggling.

A hound's cry of mourning.

They've got him. The Annekteh have Dacey again.

"Blue!" she cried into the night. *Don't leave me to face this alone!*

Blaine stepped outside the pines, only to discover that the evening mist blanketed out the sky and all but the lowest branches of the trees, leaving her no sign of moonlight. No way to find him. No way to keep herself from blundering into the Annekteh, were they out there. Agonizingly indecisive, she clutched the blanket together at her throat, her fingers tight in the wool fabric. Squinting into the darkness for answers.

Something shuffled in the woods, something close and slow and quiet. But before her frustration could turn to fear, she heard Blue's whine.

"Blue!" Had he really come just because she'd called? Surely not. Surely he was only confused. He came to her, head low and forehead wrinkled, and Blaine gave him a quick hug—making certain sure to get a good grip on his collar.

Moon or no moon, Blue could find Dacey.

His braided leash lay in a coil beside the blankets, and Blaine wasted no time hooking him up. She crushed the already dying fire into coals and bent over to touch her head to his. "I can't find him," she said. "But you can." First a hug, and then she gave his shoulders a little push forward. "Go ahead. Find Dacey."

She didn't imagine he actually understood—but he was free to go where he'd wanted all along, and he knew *that* well enough. He took off with Blaine in tow, unwavering and determined, his course certain and detouring for only the most major of obstacles. Blaine went on four limbs almost as often as he and scaled slopes as fast as she ever had, yanked upward by her hold on the leash, one hand before her to ward off obstacles she couldn't see.

At last, worn out with the effort of dodging branches that were already in her face and of stumbling over invisible tree roots, Blaine dug her heels in. "Blue, wait," she panted. Grudgingly, the dog stopped, just long enough for her to loop the leash in front of his throat as a choke. She held the ends of the loop in both hands and slowed their progress to a fast walk. Not long after that they hit the top of the ridge, and the going was as flat as it ever got.

Blaine caught her wind and eased her grip on Blue. Instead of taking off again, he slowed, lifting his nose to the breeze, jerking in tiny whiffs of air between thin whines.

A ghostly white shape lurched out of the mist at them. Blaine gasped, but her instant of terror quickly turned to relief. *Mage.* The dog came directly to her, whining, his head and tail low. The dog who had hardly ever even glanced her way . . . wanting direction from her. "With me, Mage," she said softly, and he fell immediately to her side, leading her, looking back to see that she followed.

She wasn't at all sure she wanted to see what he'd show her.

They had not far to go. Three other spirit-white

shapes appeared in the darkness, two of them milling uncertainly by the third, and coming to greet her—touching her hands with their cold noses, whining, beating her legs with their tails, moving on to do the same with Mage and Blue. Two of them came. The third waited.

Blaine reached out her hand to touch each hound, offering a rare caress. Whimsy's cold nose pressed firmly into her hand as the little bitch crept closer, while Chase winced away, whining, as she came upon the terrible swelling around his eye and half his face. "Dacey," she murmured, feeling sick.

She moved to greet Maidie and stumbled over the edge of her bearskin. *That's why they're here*, she realized. Waiting on the bearskin, something of Dacey's, for his return. She reached for Maidie—

And stilled, startled by the cool feel of the sour old dog. Gently, Blaine shook Maidie, then snatched her hand away as lifeless bones moved beneath her touch. With a cry of dismay, she threw her arms around the nearest hound, hugging tight, staving off tears and a suddenly overwhelming fear for Dacey. *They kilt his Maidie!*

But Dacey, at least, was surely still alive. They needed what only he could tell them.

Blaine took a deep breath and pulled away from the dog, surprised to find that she had been hugging Mage, and that Blue stood anxiously beside her, waiting for the chance to push between them and claim his spot back. She drew him in, gave Mage a thankful pat, and gathered the dogs around her to wait out the long night.

When morning came—or close enough to make out the dim outlines of the woods—Blaine dragged the golden-specked form of Maidie from the crumpled bearskin and built her a cairn. The four remaining dogs made anxious circles around the abandoned camp until Blaine took the free end of the leash and captured Chase with it. Mage subsided with a word, having apparently taken her authority to heart— although as the sun rose, he could not contain a howl.

Blaine made a careful search of the area around the bearskin, finding nothing of Dacey—no clues, no struggle, and a trail so broad, made by so many feet, that she didn't dare follow it. So she folded the drying pelt, and reluctantly unleashed the dogs so she could tie the skin and haul it back with her. Bereft of their master and their confidence, the dogs followed her meekly back to the clearing. She arrived at the pines just as Trey and Burl came up the hill from the hollow.

Trey stopped Burl with a touch and they both stared up at Blaine. "What's going on?" Trey asked, taking in the pelt and the four subdued dogs, turning it into suspicion. "Why have you got Mage?"

"Because they got Dacey," Blaine answered wearily, unable to spare Trey the blunt answer. She rushed on with the rest of it, circumventing his questions— she only wanted to get this over with. "He went back to our first camp—he wanted to clean it up so we'd have a safe place if things went bad. He was still going dizzy sometimes, he shouldn'ta gone—" her voice broke, but forced her way past it. "He got to the camp, he musta. . . . I found this," she finished, dropping the skin, "and the dogs. The old bitch is dead."

Trey dropped to a knee to take a quick but firm look at Chase's face, dismissing the dog with a quickness that told Blaine all was well. "He shouldn't have gone," he muttered, standing to face her, anger blooming on his face, maybe a little fear. "He risked *every-thing*—he lost it! Why'n spirits didn't you *stop* him?"

"Did it seem to you like I could boss him around?" She glared at him, stiff in her anger, the dogs swirling around her like windblown leaves. Finally Blue nudged her hand and she turned to stalk into the pines.

Damp cold ashes greeted her from the fire circle. Resolutely—as if by following normal procedures, she could claw her way out of Annekteh trouble—Blaine knelt and began arranging tinder.

"I got biscuits," Burl's voice came almost timidly from behind the curtain of pine. "Mought still be warm, iff'n you eat quick."

Blaine sat back from her task. "I could use a warm biscuit," she said, suddenly exhausted. Something to fill her stomach and take her mind off what was happening.

Dacey, in the hands of Annekteh again. *It ain't right*. He'd come up here to help, and been caught. He'd come back, and been betrayed. And now they had him again. It wasn't even his fight! Not truly.

She took the warm, honey-soaked biscuit Burl offered and looked up at him, finding Trey just behind him. "It's *our* fight."

Taken aback by the suddenness of it, they both used a moment to follow her thinking. Then Trey shook his head. "Blaine . . ."

"*No*. Listen. It's true, Dacey's the only one who can tell the Taken right quick." Not that she knew how. "But we've still got something we didn't have before." She dug the grotesque wards out of her pocket, showed them to the boys. "We won't have to worry about the meeting hall once we get it, and they won't be able to Take whoever we can get in there. All we got to do is time it so the timber men are warned we're making trouble, and get free of their guards before the Annekteh start Taking 'em as fighters against us. There won't be many Annekteh-Took to kill, not if we do it fast—you know who they are, right? Start with 'em! And you know those plainsmen don't know a thing about hill fighting—they ain't even allowed a short bow."

"And just how do you know so much all of a sudden?" Trey demanded.

"I been with Dacey for weeks," Blaine said, standing up to stare him straight in the eye. "And I'm the only one here who got two good looks at their camp before they moved in on us. I heard 'em talking and I know they're plain thick when it comes to mountain woods. They're fighters, not hunters. Well, we'll *hunt* 'em!"

"Maybe we *can* do it," Burl said slowly.

"An' maybe we can't," Trey countered.

"What have we got to lose?" Blaine plunked her fists on her hips and challenged him with a lift of her chin. "It's only a few days now till those others show up. More Annekteh, more guards. What chance do we have then? And if it don't work . . . we won't be no worse off."

Still there was hesitation on Trey's face, though Burl turned to him, nudging his shoulder, nodding. "She's right about that, Trey. Even if we can't do it . . . better to have *tried* than to give up now."

Trey looked . . . frightened. That was it—frightened. Not, she thought, of the fight—but of the responsibility of making the decision. "Trey, we don't have to tell the other boys that Dacey's gone," she said. "You know 'em best—you split 'em up and assign groups. You know the pattern of the guards, too. *We can do it, Trey.*"

We have to believe we can, if we're gonna even try.

"Yeah," Trey mumbled. "Maybe. I'll think about it. But you *gotta* be certain about holding that hall, Blaine, 'cause without Dacey aimin' us . . . well, we sure ain't gonna be able to hurt our own unless we *know* they're Taken."

"I can make the hall safe," Blaine asserted, pretending she was as confident as she let on.

"All right then." Trey scrunched pine needles beneath his heel and walked away, leaving Burl holding the rest of the biscuits out to Blaine.

"Iff'n we hear anything about Dacey . . ." he said.

"Thanks," Blaine said, taking the bundle. If she heard anything about Dacey, she had every intention of trying to get him free. But she didn't say it, not right away. She knew they'd both argue against it, that they couldn't risk losing any of the three of them, not if they wanted this fight to go on.

Blaine watched the boys make their way down the hill; too soon, she was alone. Blue nudged her hand, his eyes on the biscuits, wagging his tail so hopefully that his bottom wiggled and danced against the ground where he sat. She turned to him, suddenly very glad for his presence. It was going to get lonely enough up here as it was.

Does anyone know you're here in Shadow Hollers? What happened to our Brethren in the south? Will there be others of you coming?

He'd been tired and light-headed, knowing Blaine was right and at the same time unable to risk her—unable to risk that his seeings held truth. *Blue, roaring to Blaine's rescue, spitted on a sword. The shelter in the background, Blaine kicking it down, struggling between two men . . .*

Truth, indeed. He'd known to watch for them. *Should have told her the seeing. Should have stayed* away.

But the camp needed securing. From the camp the Annekteh could find the clearing. In the clearing they could find Blaine and Dacey. It had seemed like too great a hazard, when the Annekteh were roused to the point of throwing around magic in the mist.

To someone who couldn't think straight.

Drugged. Dry mouth, empty stomach, full bladder. Throbbing head. *Don't talk, don't talk.* Say nothing. It was the only way to make sure none of his words would be betrayal.

Would you like something to eat? Would you like us to loosen those ropes? Implied promises. The smell of dusty straw in his nostrils, the scratch of it against his cheek. The questions, over and over again.

Does anyone know you're here in Shadow Hollers? What happened to our Brethren in the south? Will there be others of you coming?

Pain, then; plenty of it. Annekteh pain, scorching along his nerves until he had no control over his body. Annekteh fear—drugs and plains magic. Until he couldn't take it any more and live, and so found a seer's wall to hide behind. A wall he knew he might never make his way back through, where he felt nothing—but could still dimly perceive Annekteh fury at the old seer's trick. Where he could barely hear the pronouncement about his life—cold, cold words. *He can still be of use. A warning. But first we clip his wings.*

They propped him up against worn stall boards, limp and unresisting. They pulled his eyes open, and through the veil of the seer's wall, he saw gloved hands bearing a dipper of water, magicked water that splashed into his open eyes. And then he saw nothing at all.

Blaine spent a long day alone and worried, and expecting to stay that way. But just before nightfall, Trey returned, Burl at his side and the redbone hound at his heels. Blaine, caught by surprise near the tiny trickle of a creek not too far away, heard them call and came running, her hair wet from a feeble washing. Unbraided, it fell below her bottom, swirling wetly around her arms and snagging in the pines as she ran to see why they'd come back. It couldn't be good . . . .

From the looks on their faces, it wasn't.

"What's wrong?" Impatiently, she flipped a length of hair back over her shoulder. "What're y'all doin' back so soon?"

"Dacey," Trey said grimly.

Her heart—her hope—fell so hard that she felt it hit in her tightened throat, her suddenly heavy stomach. "He . . . he ain't dead, is he?"

Trey shook his head, exchanged a knowing look with Burl. "He'd be better off that way, from what I seen."

She looked from one to the other of them and finally burst out with, *"What?"*

"They got him all right," Burl said. As usual, he'd taken the opportunity to bring her food; he handed her a sack that she accepted without even thinking. "They been at him all last night, from the looks of it. They've got him blind somehow, though there ain't a mark on him—leastways, not near his eyes."

"Blind," Blaine repeated in a whisper. Struggling to remain calm, she asked, "How'd you find him?"

"Didn't have to," Trey told her. "Right before suppertime, they had us at the hall—all the boys that wasn't out hunting, all the men over from the timbering. They marched him right out in front of us like some kinda prize. Wanted us to know they had 'im."

Burl added, "And they wanted answers."

So Dacey wasn't giving them none. Blaine found that she was twisting her hair, and forced herself to quit. "And?" she said.

"I purely thought Estus was going to give us up, from jitters if nothin' else," Trey said, but from the relief in his voice, she knew Estus hadn't. "Lucky that the timber men made enough protest to draw attention away. The leader said he'd give us the night to think about it. Seems to want to do it without Takin' us all—like he thinks that means he's broke us. He says iff'n he learns who all's in with Dacey, no harm'll come to 'em—nor Dacey. He just wants it out in the open."

"You believe that?" Blaine asked, incredulous.

Burl said, *"We* don't."

"We can't take no chances either way," Trey said. "Iff'n no one comes to the leader before then, he's gonna kill Dacey tomorrow. An' he's gonna have all the women and children gathered there to watch." He paused and put extra emphasis on his next words. *"In the hall."*

Understanding dawned. "Then we wouldn't have to worry about any of 'em being left unwarded," she said. "We're . . . we're gonna do it"—she didn't have to say what *it* was, not for any of them—"*tomorrow morning.*"

"We surely are," Trey said. "Estus is makin' the rounds now, tellin' the boys. We're gonna stick right to plan, and not tell no men till it's happenin'. This is bungled up enough as it is."

Blaine's wet hair felt suddenly cold against her shoulders; she wrapped her arms around herself. Something was yet unsaid, else Burl wouldn't be hovering with such an anxious look on his face. Else— Burl wouldn't be here at all, not just to tell her this news. She tossed her head, a small gesture that was only false assertiveness, and lifted her chin, taking the conversation her own way. "I'm goin' after him," she said. "You all gonna help, or not?"

She half expected them to protest, but Trey only gave a grave nod. "We got to," he said. "Ain't no way we'll get to him tomorrow, in all the fuss. They'll kill him first thing, iff'n they can. And it don't matter if we do get him out—all the families will show up at the meetin' hall tomorrow like they've been told. Everything else is set—the boys know what to do. If something was to happen—well, so long as one of us can use those wards . . . Besides," he added, his voice surprisingly casual, "I said it oncet—I been in Taker hands once myself. I just can't leave him that way, not without *tryin'* to do somethin'."

Burl said, "Me'n Trey are out coonhunting. Thing is, we got some coon from Estus before we come. So we need to find somethin' else to do with ourselves."

"You just wait for me to braid up this hair, and I'll show you somethin' to keep plenty busy!"

But Blaine's fingers were too riled up, like the rest of her, to braid hair without a lot of fumbling and dropped sections. She was taken flatly by surprise when Trey stepped in. He muttered something about braiding his little sister's hair, and quickly finished the job for her, even binding them together in the back like she often did.

They moved out with surprisingly little fuss and bother, heading over the ridges to the meeting hall, and getting there just as final darkness came over the mountains. Now Blaine stole a glance at Trey as they eased themselves to the ground above the meeting hall barn. He wasn't picking at her any more, challenging her every word like he'd done when they'd met. *Only days ago, now.* Part of her didn't believe it; part of her was more grateful than she would have anticipated. He just, she decided, had other things on his mind.

Far, far back up the ridge, Blue sounded an indignant bark; he and the redbone waited tied and unhappy. Mage lurked somewhere close by, unobtrusive and omnipresent. Below them, the barn waited—a blot of darkness under a waning moon and an increasingly cloudy sky. There were no streaks of light peeking from around the shuttered loft and closed doors, nor was there light coming from the meeting hall.

"Don't they even have a night watch?" Blaine asked, in quiet disbelief.

"I reckon they do," Trey said. "Reckon he's just not pointin' hisself out with a light."

"It was what we were hopin' you could help us with," Burl told her. "We'll check it out on our way in, but we need you to watch for us while we're gettin' him out. Someone could come up on us."

"But—what'll I do iff'n he does?"

Trey dismissed the question with an impatient shake of his head. "It don't matter. Any noise you make'll warn us—tell 'im you've come to talk to the leader about Dacey, for all o' that. He won't see you well enough to know you ain't been around before. We'll get you out of it before it comes to that."

She wondered if he was as confident as he sounded. And she thought it was all easy for *him* to say—she'd rather be fetching Dacey and let Trey do the watching. But on the hill above the enemy camp wasn't a good time to argue about it, so she said nothing, discretion newly acquired. Instead she stared at the barn, a building in which she'd often played.

It was built into the side of the hill, and the lower level had a main door that faced the hall, while the side against the hill had a loft door. It was possible to walk into either one of them. The loft held hay and grain, and the lower level had four stalls and a big fat aisle. Dacey, the boys thought, was in one of the stalls. In two of the others were plains mules, creatures they would take great care not to alarm.

Without discussion, they crept down the hill to the loft door, tucked into the darkest shadow the night offered. They moved slowly, step by step, steadying one another at the awkward places, Trey at the lead and Burl coming down behind Blaine.

Just outside the door they put their heads together, and Trey, in a murmur so low there was barely any sound at all, said, "We go in slow. But there might be one of 'em in there—the first any of us makes a big noise, we all got to go for it. Once we're below, Blaine, take the main door."

She nodded, and moved in against the barn, out of the way and as out of sight as she was ever going to get. And she waited, thinking she'd never realized that a body could open a door so slow, while Trey and Burl inched open one of the small double doors of the loft. Then again, she'd never thought anyone could open that door without making the biggest kind of squeak, either. One after another, they slipped into the loft, making no more noise than the sound of Burl's shirt brushing against wood.

Once inside it got harder. There was a narrow walk space between the piled hay and the outside wall, but there was also enough hay scattered under their feet to make the going excruciatingly slow. Opening the door had been an instant's work compared to moving so carefully, transferring her weight so slowly, while her muscles trembled with fear and burned from the unusual effort. *Spirits, it'll be morning before we reach him. . . .*

At the edge of the loft Trey paused, the only one able to see below—if indeed he could make out anything in the darkness. Blaine heard nothing but the rustle of one of the mules as it spread its legs to make water.

Under the cover of that noisy stream, Trey moved out, ignoring the ladder and swinging down to hang for a moment before lightly dropping to the floor; Blaine did not need Burl's prodding to do the same, and even though she was less graceful than Trey, her light weight made no more noise. She felt more than heard Burl join them, and by then their cover was gone, except for the slight shuffling of the mule.

While Trey and Burl silently checked the other stalls for Dacey, she backed up against the mule stall, close to the main door, and waited, every nerve trying to jump right out of her body.

The mule behind her remained restless, nosing its hay and shuffling in the straw; if the boys made any noise she couldn't hear them. She was aware when the mule came up behind her, and half expected it to nudge or lip at her—curiosity she could do without. She'd move closer to the door, then, maybe peer outside—

Two strong hands clamped down on her arms and Blaine gave a muffled shriek, too startled to do anything else but stiffen in fear.

"Well, well, missy," said a voice in her ear, his breath on her neck making her skin crawl, "wandering around in the dark, are you?"

Men make water, too, said a sarcastic inner voice.

Out loud, Blaine stammered, "I—I—come to see the leader. 'Bout that man."

"Did you now? And you thought our boss might be sleeping out here in the barn?" The man tightened his grip on one arm so hard it felt near pinched in two, and used the other to close and latch the stall door after he came around it. The mule snorted.

"No, I—I—" *I'm babbling* "—I done got scairt, is all. Changed my mind." *Trey, where are you?*

"Too late for that now." He shoved her toward the door. "You won't have any say about it once he touches you."

Blaine didn't like the way he said it; she didn't like his flatlander accent in her ear and his flatlander hands on her arm.

She bit him.

He jerked his fingers out of her mouth with a curse, never loosening his other hand despite her struggles. She cried out as he reeled her in and she felt more than saw him draw back his hand—but the blow didn't come. His grip convulsed around her arm; his whole body stiffened. When he fell, he took her down with him, dragging her to the dirty floor. Then his bowels voided, and she realized that those tightly clinging fingers belonged to a dead man, that he was *dead*, and he was *never going to let her go*. . . . Blaine slid away into panic, scrabbling for purchase on the slick plank flooring while animal fear noises grew inside her throat and forced their way out of her mouth.

The boys were tugging on her then, as a strong broad hand clamped over her mouth and Burl's anxious and angry voice hissed, "Then *cut* it off, Trey, I don't care!" In her ear, soothing words—"We done got him, Blaine, it's all right now, c'mon"—and then she was free, and heaving great hysterical breaths, but finally returning to herself. Burl patted her arm, suddenly awkward, and moved back from her.

Trey's voice came from near the door. "No one's movin'," he said. "It warn't all that much noise, anyway." He came back to them and from the sound of it, wiped something on the dead man's clothes. His knife, Blaine thought dully. He was the one who had killed the man. She ought to say thank you.

"Did you find Dacey?" she whispered instead. "I done did my job—I found the guard."

Burl snorted from near one of the back stalls, while Trey whispered a curse. To Blaine, he said, "We found him. We can't rouse him none, though. He wasn't himself this afternoon, neither, but I was hoping . . ."

"Let me see," Blaine said, not waiting for his response before she tripped to her feet, making an overwide detour around where she imagined the dead man was, and aiming for where she'd heard Burl. "Is he in here?"

"Right by the door," Burl told her, his voice low. She crouched down and felt around with her hands until she found Dacey. She thought that at one point he'd probably been propped against the wall, but he'd fallen over. She found his hands in front of him, but though she brushed the cleanly cut ends of the rope that had bound him, his fingers remained tightly entwined. She took those hands, tried to unclench the fingers and couldn't, shook him to discover he was tense and almost stiff.

"Get a mule," she said quietly.

"We can't take a—"

"Yes, we can! We got to get him away from here! They done something horrible to him, we got to get him away, get him out of it—"

"Maybe he'll never get out from under it at all," Trey muttered, but she heard him lift a halter from the nail by the stall and open the door. The mule snorted distrustfully at him. "Don't give me no fuss, mule," he muttered, flat dire threat in his voice.

The mule must have believed him. There was

silence, aside from the little snicking noises of the halter buckles; Blaine ran her hand up and down Dacey's arm, trying to warm some life into his limbs. The quiet hollow clopping of hard oval mule feet in need of a trim came down the aisle and stopped beside her.

"Here we go, then," Burl said, bending down beside her to snag Dacey's arm and leg, shift his grip a few experimental times, and then heave Dacey up without so much as a grunt—except on the mule's part.

"He ain't goin' to stay," Trey said. "And we got to get out of here—we done fooled around long enough."

"Put Blaine up behind him," Burl suggested.

"I don't know how to ride no mule!" Alarm laced the protest in her voice, but Burl paid it no mind; his hands nearly met around her waist as he lifted her up and plopped her on the mule behind Dacey. Dacey's hair tickled her forehead and his back warmed her as she clutched frantically for the mule's sparse mane, her arms tight around Dacey's ribs.

"Don't worry," Burl said. "We'll stay right here on either side."

Trey pushed the main door open, letting in the fresh smell of the damp night, the sound of gentle rain against the ground. Compared to the pitch dark of the barn, the overcast night seemed almost bright. "Nothing there," he whispered. "Let's go!"

Blaine squeaked as the mule moved forward and she lurched backward; the mule snorted testily but moved on out of the barn, and she quickly learned the rhythm of its walk. Dacey was so close she had to turn her head aside, resting it on the broadness of his shoulders and trusting that the boys would not lead them under some low branch.

Blue's sporadic, frustrated bark led them to the top of the hill and far down the ridge, a slow process—full of grunts and *"Get him!"* when Dacey tipped too far one way or the other, while Blaine's fingers cramped so tightly in the wiry mane that she lost the feeling of them. The trees protected them from most of the slow rain, pattering in the leaves and only occasionally down her neck. She figured that the odd procession must have nearly reached Blue and the redbone when the mule gave an unexpected pitch, a snort of effort, and scrambled up one last projection— leaving Blaine behind. She slid right off its rump, with one loud, indignant cry of protest that ended in a grunt when Dacey landed on top of her.

"You all right?" Burl asked as he separated them, sitting Dacey up against a tree and standing Blaine on her feet. She staggered a moment, thoroughly disoriented in the dark. At her side, Mage appeared, whining anxiously.

"She's fine," Trey said abruptly, turning the mule around, tying the rope up behind its ears, and giving it a hard smack on the butt. The animal kicked out at him and ran down the hill. "We've come far enough. Ain't no way to take him as far as the clearing, and it'll just mean a longer walk for Blaine come mornin', iff'n we do."

"You mean . . . you mean you figure I'm gonna stay out here in this rain all night?" Blaine sputtered, building up a good head of indignation.

"It's not that far a walk," Burl said quickly. "I'll fetch your pack. You head on home, Trey. I'll be along shortly."

"Don't get lost," Trey muttered, but added, in the silence that followed, "I'm obliged to you, Burl. Reckon I'm plumb tuckered."

Burl's response was offhand, but startled Blaine— and made her instantly forgive any shortness of temper Trey might have shown this night. "That man done run you some today. You'd think he coulda found some others of us to run word around and gather us all up."

Trey shrugged, visible only in silhouette. He moved a few steps away, stopped again. "Meet us by that biggie sycamore below the hall, Blaine. Just after first light. Things'll probably hop fast when they find that guard."

"Our luck, they'll start Takin' people right away, lookin' for answers," Burl said, as if he was just now realizing it.

"Oh, I'm bettin' they will," Trey said dryly. "We'll just have to get there first."

Blaine's voice was hard. "I'll be ready."

They left her alone then, getting wetter as the rain fell hard enough to come through the leaves. She fumbled to close the buttons of her coat—she'd lost one tonight, somewhere—and went to Blue. The dog's entire bottom wagged with his tail, and instead of his usual deep-chested noise he gave her anxious whines. When she loosed him from the tree, he ran straight for Dacey, snuffling and nosing him, and finally giving one sharp, frustrated bark.

"It's all right, Blue," Blaine said, even though she didn't think it was. Blue flung himself to the ground and rested his chin on his forefeet, mournful, as Blaine knelt by Dacey, wishing it were light enough to see his face well. During the ride he'd loosened up, but it only meant that he was more like an old rag doll than a plank of wood. She found neither reassuring.

She moved up until her knees bumped him, and—hesitantly—touched his shoulder.

His eyes flew open. They stared at her, black in the darkness, and there was no change on his face, no recognition in his expression.

Nothing.

"Dacey?" Blaine asked, tentative and thinking of the jimson. Had they broken his mind with it? Or simply used some other vile, unimaginable magic? She trapped Dacey's cold and lifeless hand between both her own, warming it. "Dacey," she said, and squeezed the hand. "C'mon, Dacey, it's me, Blaine. Look at me. *Look* at me!" Her voice rose and cracked, and momentarily gave out.

It had no effect on Dacey.

She couldn't look at his dull stare any longer; she looked at Mage instead. The hound pawed his master, and not gently. In his throat, frustrated canine words gargled out as modulated whines. Blue responded, until both of them were whining in Blaine's ear, enough to drive her to distraction. Mage was always the ringleader, always setting off the whole dumb pack—always setting off . . .

"Howl, Mage!" Blaine urged, startling the dog into silence. *Damn.* "C'mon—he'll hear it if he hears anything!"

The dog stared at her, his ears low, cocked back in his resentment of her interference. Blaine rolled her eyes, beyond exasperation. "Ow-wow-wo-ow," she tried, not finding it easy to hit the right tones without the dogs guiding her. "C'mon, Mage," she muttered, tightening her grip on Dacey's hand. "C'mon."

"Oowh," Blue offered, the quietest of monotone howls.

"Yes, Blue!" She repeated the sound just as he'd done it, only louder, and he talked back to her. Mage had had enough. He burst into full and glorious howl, and Blue sat up to sing with him; Blaine joined them, never taking her eyes off Dacey.

After a moment, Dacey blinked.

He blinked; his vacant expression turned to a frown. Blaine stopped howling, suddenly feeling silly, and the dogs faded uncertainly into silence. "Dacey?"

He shook, shudders that came deep from within and trembled through his frame—wave after wave of them, while she held his hand and ached with the need to help, to make them stop. And eventually they did, fading into shivers that might just as well have been from the rain. His free hand reached slowly for his eyes, stopping a mere whisper away before falling to the ground again. It fumbled at the leaves and pebbles there, and slowly became sure enough of the earth to leave it be. What she could see of his face in the darkness showed her his confusion—absolute, unmitigated by anything he'd heard or touched.

"It's me," Blaine said softly, convinced they'd somehow fooled with his mind. "It's all right, now, I've done found you and you're safe."

He shook his head, more like a dog with water in its ear than a man saying *no*. Then he closed his eyes, and took a deep breath; Blaine held her own. Waiting. Hoping.

"How long has it been?" he asked, his eyes still closed, another shudder running through him.

"Just a day," she said, trying to keep her voice level. "Me an' Burl an' Trey just stole you back from 'em. Are . . ." she hesitated, not knowing if she should ask, not able to stop herself. "Are you back to yourself, Dacey?"

"As near as I can tell," he muttered, and seemed to be taking inventory. "Just . . . trying to put it all together."

"What did they . . . I mean, *how* did they—"

He gave a low laugh. It sounded on the edge of a sob. "*They* didn't," he said. "That is, they done plenty . . . but it was me who had the last say. Old seer's trick—I'd heard of it from my granmamaw. Didn't ever think I had it in me." He covered his vacant eyes with his hand, squeezing hard on Blaine's at the same time. "*Spirits*," he whispered. "I didn't ever think I'd *need* to have it in me."

"I was so afraid I wouldn't get you back . . . Dacey, I didn't know *what* to do."

He laughed again, sounding the same as the last one. "So you started a howl. Right clever of you. Takes another seer, usually. There ain't no comin' back from that place on your own." He squeezed her hand again, a clear *thank you*, and then withdrew his own. "You were right. Oughtn't to have gone back to that camp, not feelin' like I did."

"You had a seein', didn't you," she said, letting the accusation into her voice. "Right then, when we were talkin' about it. You were gonna let me go, and then suddenly you wouldn't."

He nodded. "I had a seein'," he admitted. "You and Blue . . ." He didn't finish, and clearly didn't intend to. "Just goes to show you there's more to bein' a good seer than gettin' a seein' now and then. It's what you do with 'em."

"We can use *any* kind of seer tomorrow," Blaine said. "We . . . we're makin' our try, Dacey. Takin' the hollers back. Come morning."

He needed a moment to think about that. "Is Trey keeping them boys in line?"

She nodded.

"Blaine?" he asked, his face and voice filled with an uncertainty that was foreign to her.

Nodding. Stupid. "Trey's done fine," she said quietly, and without thinking, brushed sorrowful and uninvited fingertips across his brow and lashes.

He took her hand away from his face and gripped it hard, and Blaine realized that he again drew strength from her instead of the other way around. Hatred flared in her. *Annekteh*, she thought, making it into a curse. "We're going to drive them out," she said, and that hatred found its way into her voice.

It was Blue, naturally, who lightened the mood. The big dog came up behind Blaine and stuck his cold nose down her neck, eliciting her undignified squeal.

"You sit on the wrong thing?" Dacey asked, wry humor in his voice.

"Just Blue an' his cold ole nose," Blaine told him. She looked at the hound—he panted amiably in her face—and thought of his sour companion. "Dacey," she said, "about Maidie—"

"I figured she was hurt pretty bad," Dacey interrupted, his voice flat. "She . . . she was a good ole dog. Too old to be taking on men."

"I don't think she suffered none," Blaine said, stroking Blue's absurdly long ear. "She was gone by the time we reached the bearskin, and Blue drug me there right quick, soon as we heard Mage howl. Nearly kilt me, he did," she added, a complaint made to keep up her end of that disaffection. She realized she was petting the dog and quit.

Dacey seemed to be struggling, still trying to gather his thoughts. "Tell me about tomorrow."

"They were going to kill you in front of the women and children. We don't know what they'll do now, but everyone'll gather up like they're supposed to, and we can ward 'em all if we take the hall. I . . . I told Trey and Burl about the wards—I had to, it was the only way to convince them we still had to make a try at it—" She hesitated, but Dacey only nodded.

"It's all right," he said. "You done good to keep 'em thinking about an attack at all."

"They got the boys divvied up, give 'em their roles. I'm s'posed to meet 'em at the bottom between the river and the hall tomorrow morning."

"Where are we now?"

"Not so far from there," Blaine said, her own question in her voice as she heard the intent in his inquiry. "You ain't plannin'—"

"I can set the wards, Blaine, an' it'll free you up to do something else—talk to the women, most likely—they're gonna be some scared, not knowin' what's happening and all."

"But Dacey . . ." Blaine protested. "It won't be safe gettin' to the hall, an' you ain't gonna be able to do any duckin'."

For a moment, he said nothing; he was quiet when

he did speak. "You can leave me here, and there ain't a thing I can do about it. But iff'n those flatlanders manage to follow the trail you made gettin' here, I'll be waitin' for 'em, pretty as you please. Or you can move me to a safer place, an' if *you* don't duck right, no one'll know where I am—including me. That'd suit the Annekteh just fine."

Blaine didn't answer with anything more than her sigh. "Then you ought to get some sleep," she said. "Burl'll be coming back with the pack, and I'll rig a shelter from the tarp. Be some food, too, I reckon—beans an' bacon, mostly."

"A stomach as empty as mine ain't apt to be picky." For the moment he was Dacey as she knew him best—laconic, seeming like he knew his world better than anybody.

"How'd they do it?" she asked then, unable to contain a horrified curiosity. "Does it hurt?"

Dacey turned his head away. "No," he said, "it don't hurt. It's their magic. They wanted answers, and didn't get none. I reckon they thought it was a way to hobble me."

"Maybe it won't last," Blaine offered hopefully. "Plains magic ain't too strong hereabouts."

He said nothing.

"I won't have you givin' up, Dacey Childers," Blaine said, suddenly fierce. "We're gonna lick those Annekteh tomorrow, an' everything will be just fine. Includin' you."

"Yes, ma'am," Dacey said, but she was glad to hear a little fire beneath his teasing meekness. *Still Dacey, despite it all.*

→ **17** ←

Blaine huddled close to Dacey as they tried to stay under the greased tarp and out of the gentle but steady rain, but she felt like she might as well be alone. He slept soundly, exhausted, while her mind bounded from thought to thought like the hounds on a scent. Fear, mostly. Different kinds of fears—of death, of being Taken, of watching others Taken . . . of killing them. That she wasn't planned to play that role in the rebellion didn't keep her from fearing it.

And in the end, she feared what would happen *after* the fight. What would happen to her life. One way or the other.

She shifted to curl up more tightly over her knees. They had found the thick angled remains of a fallen poplar and used the space between the stump and the tilted trunk for their shelter, and now Dacey sat against the trunk, holding the canvas closed against the rain with his body. The small shelter stayed stuffy and too humidly warm; risking the rain, Blaine pulled up an edge of the canvas and stuck her nose out for the fresh, damp air. She was thankful for the rain even if it *didn't* stop by morning, for she could easily imagine the boys moving around the hills at will while the heavier men slipped and slid around the slopes.

A big, cold drop rolled off the tarp and splashed onto her nose, and she pulled her face back inside.

Beside her, Dacey stirred, gave a slight start.

"Didn't mean to wake you," she said.

"It's all right." He tugged at his jacket, pulling the front open in the warmth they had created. "It's just I . . . keep expecting to see things when I open my eyes. Foolishness."

She didn't say anything, still too lost in her own mind to come up with any words that seemed right.

"Blaine?"

"Just been thinking," Blaine said. " 'Bout what you said oncet. That things would never be the same. Seems to me that there's some changes would do me good . . . but *those're* the ones I'll never see. I found the Annekteh when I was lookin' for those changes . . . climbin' around the hills, runnin' away from bein' skinny and from endin' up like my mommy. Now I don't reckon any of that's got me anywhere—no matter how tomorrow turns out, I'll end up the same way. Married off, tied to a big family, everyone sayin' I'm not quite right. We're lucky, we'll free Shadow Hollers tomorrow . . . but not me."

"You *have* been thinkin' some," Dacey responded in surprise—then in silence. "Surely it ain't all like that," he said after a while. "Surely there's some good to look for. Livin's hard work no matter how you come at it."

"I know," Blaine said quietly. "But it's easier to take when you got a choice how you're going to go about it."

"Don't you?" Dacey asked. "Really?"

"I don't follow you."

"You can take care of yourself, by yourself—if you really want to—and I think you know it."

She frowned at him, knowing he couldn't see it. "Maybe I do know that. Now. But that don't mean I'm strong enough to make the choice."

"There's that," he admitted. "It ain't a small thing. Tell you, though—climbin' around the hills may not get you anywhere in the long run, but I sure am pleased you were at it when they had me the first time."

Blue—his timing impeccable—stuck his damp and doggy-smelling head in the shelter, shoving his nose beneath a spot of tarp Blaine was sure she had weighted down. "Sometimes," she said, trying to push him back out again, "sometimes I got doubts about that. I surely never reckoned on *him* when I got you free."

But Dacey just laughed.

"It's a long piece till mornin'," Blaine said, trying to sound cross. "Get some sleep."

Blaine flew. She must *be flying; she was way up in the air, looking down at the hill beside the meeting hall. Branches obscured her vision, scratched her face, became frustrating obstacles. She needed to see, to help the boys below her.*

Young and determined, they fought a desperate battle against the plainsmen—who seemed to be rallying. Those plainsmen filled her vision; somehow she couldn't force herself to focus on the boys. No, the plainsmen only, first this one and then that, just regular men. Or not quite regular—they were warriors, blooded men. Against boys.

She despaired, and her chest ached fiercely with tears she seemed unable to shed. No, I don't want to look at them, she cried as loudly as she could, if only inside her head. But she couldn't stop herself—and then suddenly she didn't want to stop herself. Suddenly she needed to see.

For a purple finger of mist came up and touched

one of them, and just that fast, he was surrounded by a hazy aura of purple. Not purple, exactly—no, the dark, bruised blackish color of the clouds she'd seen so long ago.

One after another, faces flashed before her, a dizzying array of enemies. All touched by the Annekteh magic. Taken.

Wait, that was no enemy! That was Jason! *Jason,* wreathed in bruised purple. And that *man*—she knew him, too! Suddenly familiar faces mixed freely with the ones she didn't know, tainted visages that forced their way to her mind even when she tried to close her eyes.

Her world jostled. Rocked.

They'd seen her, flying above them. And they had the magic to fly up and get her.

They were coming up to get her.

→ 18 ←

Gone! Dacey Childers, gone!
The guard, dead.

Of all Nekfehr knew—along with the fact that his nameless vessel secretly cheered the prisoner's escape—foremost was that Dacey Childers—blinded, locked behind a wall of his own making—had not made it out of this barn on his own.

One of the mules was missing; there would be tracks, tracks even he could follow. Nekfehr recalled the howling, on a ridge not far from here.

Meanwhile, the women and children were already scheduled to arrive, and shortly. Let them stay here, and wait. When Nekfehr returned with Dacey Childers, they would watch him die. And then they would feel the depth of cold, relentless Annekteh wrath, until Dacey Childers' accomplices came forth.

There were reinforcements on the

way—plains people long accustomed to Annekteh demands, long broken. It didn't really matter how many of the rebellious mountain folk survived to welcome them.

＊＊   ＊＊   ＊＊

When Blaine threw the tarp away from her head, she found a dull grey world, a predawn coated with fog and drifting patches of mist. The dogs were curled up together in one damp pile beneath the fallen tree, although Mage had somehow insinuated himself into the shelter and was pillowing Dacey's head. Dacey's bruised face was worn; the Annekteh had left new marks, but not many. *Only inside.*

His closed eyes looked utterly normal.

She hated to wake him, but . . . traveling along the brushy bottom with a sightless man was going to take longer than the quick trip she'd been planning.

Dacey roused instantly at her soft touch on his shoulder; he sat, blinking hard.

"All right?" she asked.

"I reckon," he said, and then stretched just like it was any other morning in their lives.

"I'll be right back, an' then we got to get gone," Blaine told him, climbing to her feet and searching for the closest discreet bush—she didn't care if he *couldn't* see. She gave him time to attend to his own needs, too.

When she returned he had the canvas folded and tucked into the pack she'd brought with her. He was making to sling it over his shoulders, and she quickly put a hand on it. "No," she said. "I'll take it. You lose your balance with this thing and you're gonna fall twice as hard. Leastways *I* can see what I'm tripping over, so I won't have no excuse when I fall. Which I'll do," she added under her breath.

Dacey hesitated only a moment before releasing the pack. "You can shed it once we reach the river," he said. "It'll be easy to find there."

Blaine pushed her arms through the straps and shrugged to settle the burden. It wasn't that heavy, but it had been made for Dacey, and it hung down to bump against her bottom. She sighed. No complaints about it, not today—she couldn't have him insisting to carry it.

Gingerly, she took Dacey's hand. "Ready?"

"You take me into anything on purpose and I'll see you regret it," he warned her lightly, then surprised her with a slight squeeze of his hand. "Go ahead."

Blaine did do her best to caution him of the sudden drops and the rocks in his way, and in fact when one of them fell it was her, watching so hard for him that she forgot to place her own feet with care. The ridge quickly dropped away, narrowing into a point only a few feet wide that dropped further down and merged into the wide river bottom. The trees shrunk in size and number, and soon Blaine was leading them through a winding maze of low-crowned sumac with only an occasional willow or sycamore.

At one of the bigger sycamores she stopped and secured the pack, wedging it firmly into the low crotch of the tree. She passed a sleeve across her forehead to wipe away sweat that would never dry in this humid morning air, then turned to Dacey.

"It's not far, now," she told him. It came out like a warning rather than a reassurance. "We ought to run into those boys any time."

"Take it slow, then," he said. "I want you to see 'em first. I want you to see *anyone* before they see us. Step by step, Blaine. We got the time."

She wasn't sure they did. She took the advice to heart anyway, and their progress slowed. Twice Dacey had to stop to take a stern voice to Mage, who couldn't seem to help growling. Chase and Whimsy stayed at the pack—or, at least if they left it to roam, they had accepted it as *home*. Blue had simply refused to stay—or rather, he had waited until Blaine and

Dacey had gone some distance, and then showed up at their heels, his ears low but his face determined—and the leash chewed through. Mage's mood infected him and he walked along on his toes, his hackles slightly raised, as he looked for something at which to growl.

The sun's token appearance had faded behind the clouds before Blaine tightened her grip on Dacey's hand, bringing him to a stop. The barely audible sounds of the meeting hall drifted to ear as the women and children gathered there, and Blaine crouched, tugging Dacey down with her.

"We're behind the biggest sycamore you'll ever see," she said, putting his hand on it so he could appreciate the girth of the tree. "Three others are supposed to meet us here. I hope they don't take too long about it."

"I was about to say the same of you," said a relieved voice from behind the curve of the tree.

"Blaine," Dacey said reproachfully.

"Twenty-seven men can link hands around this tree," Blaine said, unperturbed, "and I can't see through it to know when someone's on the other side. Besides, it's Burl." Burl and two others, all of whom came quietly around the circumference of the sycamore to join them.

"Dacey," Burl said, both a welcome and a question.

"He wouldn't stay," Blaine said. "I guess . . . I don't blame him none."

Burl gave Dacey an even look. His doubt showed clearly, even before the one-shouldered shrug he gave Blaine. But Dacey was there, and there was little to say about it now. Instead he briefed Blaine. "They been strange about the dead guard, Blaine," he said, ignoring Dacey's start—Blaine had deliberately left out the details of his rescue. "They ain't made no big fuss about it, ain't even questioned the women—just lettin' 'em gather, like they were told yesterday. The leader has took off by himself, up the hill. Ain't never seen that happen before."

"Up the hill?" Dacey said. "The same hill you drug me up last night?"

Blaine's throat went dry. Big ole mule feet making tracks, and she'd wanted to leave him there, alone.

Burl cleared his throat. "I take your meanin', Dacey. Guess I'm right glad to see you, at that." He looked off at the hill a moment. "Estus has took his crew to warn the men what we're up to, and Trey ought to start a fuss up the hill any minute. Most of the plainsmen are chewin' their tongues outside the hall, but they'll get a move on right quick, if things go as we reckon they will."

It was about to happen. It hit her suddenly, deep inside. She leaned back against the dry, flaky bark of the sycamore, releasing Dacey so he couldn't feel the sudden clamminess of her hands. Blue whined.

"You've faced 'em before, Blaine," Dacey said, knowing her too well.

"Not when I knew what I was doing," Blaine said ruefully.

"Just pretend they're bears," Burl offered—and then, checking to see that his friends weren't looking, held out his hand so she could see it shaking.

"So Trey's got the boys on the attack," Dacey said, oblivious to the unspoken byplay.

"Yep. The plan was to catch the two guards on patrol and make sure one of 'em got away." Burl moved out from behind the tree, exposing himself in order to get a good look at the meeting hall. Close behind him, Blaine discovered for herself that between this tree and the building there was only clear pasture; at the moment it held three mules and a pony. Not much cover to her mind, but no one even looked their way.

A single lone man lurched down the hill and into

the hall yard. Even from this distance Blaine could see the blood streaming down his arm.

It had started.

They're doing it. The boys are really doing it. Unexpected pride overwhelmed the fear for a moment.

A very short moment.

The other two boys—Burl's companions, Blaine didn't even know their names—joined them in the open, flattening themselves on the ground to watch the sudden swarm of activity. The tension Blaine felt showed in every line of their bodies, and no one said a word as the plainsmen and Annekteh-Took quickly armed and gathered themselves. Behind the tree, Dacey remained, crouched by Mage and stroking the softly snarling animal. When the noise from the Annekteh mobilization died down, he stood. "How did they leave it?"

"Only two on guard," Burl said shortly. He returned to the cover of the tree—and Blaine with him—to string up his short, powerful hunting bow. "One of 'em's hurt—betcha he's got one of Trey's arrows sticking out of that arm." He tested the string with satisfaction, easing it back to a resting position with no apparent effort.

"They shut the hall doors," reported one of the boys. "Everyone's inside, an' the men ain't paying no attention to anything but that tore-up arm."

"We can take 'em out from the pasture fence," the other youngster said. "Burl can shoot that far easy, an' I can likely make it—so I'll aim for the hurt one. Iff'n I miss, you can get 'im with your second shot— you think, Burl?"

"Yeah," Burl said slowly, looking back around the tree to confirm his team's assessment. Both the younger boys, their faces pale and their fingers clenched too tightly around their bows, eased out toward the pasture. "But there ain't no use in taking chances, so you wait till they're both down before you go ahead, Blaine." He looked back at Blaine, who quit twisting her fingers and stuck her hands behind her back so she wouldn't start again.

"No," Dacey said. "That hall's got to be warded quick. Unless those men got bows at the ready now, we'll go to the pasture behind you, an' Blaine'll take me up to the hall as soon as you start in."

"You can't defend yourselves," Burl protested.

"They'll be too busy with you to care. The hall's got to be warded or none of this is any good."

"C'mon, then," Burl said abruptly, following the curve of the tree behind the smaller boys. Blaine took Dacey's hand, walking him around the tree and then guiding him down to his stomach and elbows in emulation of Burl. They moved along so closely together she could guide Dacey with their touching elbows; occasionally she stopped to shove aside a rock or stick directly in his path. Mage trotted ahead, taking Blue with him.

Slow. They were so slow. She was so certain they'd be caught.

Blaine nearly dizzied herself, watching the ground before Dacey and the hall and the boys in front of her all at the same time. By the time she reached the boys at pasture fence, Burl had already risen to a bold stance, his hand still in position behind the bow as his arrow buried itself in his target—the uninjured plainsman.

The man had just enough time for an amazed look down at the arrow in his chest before he toppled. That was all Blaine cared to see, and she pulled Dacey up, placing both his hands on the top of the split-rail fence as she negotiated it herself. Another glance at the enemy showed that the smaller boys' arrows had fallen short—and that the man's attention had riveted on the two closest intruders.

Blaine and Dacey.

"*C'mon*, Dacey," she muttered, fairly dancing in

place. But a moment's panic was enough for her to realize the plainsman didn't have a bow and Burl would certainly have him down before he could reach either her or Dacey, so she waited until Dacey had his footing and grabbed his hand, pulling him as fast as she dared toward the hall.

She wanted to run, to sprint her fastest as they crossed that exposed pasture, but Dacey stumbled and she kept herself slow. She looked back to see Burl and his two boys coming over the fence after them; her steps got out of synch with Dacey's and their hands tore apart. Dacey skidded back like a horse under a rough curb bit, his expression wary, touched by wild fear. Gut-level fear . . . alone in his darkness. Blaine instantly reversed course, plowing through Mage to snatch up Dacey's hand again.

"Almost there," she said breathlessly, and he followed her after only the merest hesitation.

They reached the rough log walls of the building just before the first of the boys, and Blaine put both Dacey's hands on the wall. "Stay put," she panted, and ran to the corner of hall to peer around the edge.

Two bodies sprawled near the door; there was no one else in sight. *Burl done good.* Back to Dacey she went and they both ran around the corner and to the thick, center-set door of the hall. Thinking *hurryhurryhurry* and nothing else, Blaine yanked the latch free and pulled the door open.

Mage erupted with a savage sound.

"Get down!" Dacey shouted, just as savagely, pushing Blaine to the ground. Most of the air grunted out of her lungs as he flung himself on top of her— *shielding her*—and all she could see was dust and big padded warrior boots. Burl's wordless yell sounded above the horrible snarls of the dogs. The boots pivoted before her nose, both dogs fell on her head, and a much heavier weight pushed Dacey into her back until the rest of her breath squeezed out and couldn't find room to return.

Dacey's sharp command was the first thing she sorted out, although it didn't make much sense. "Don't touch 'em!" he said firmly as he shoved the dogs away from her head and commanded them to stay. Blaine opened her eyes to a limited view of the dusty earth as Dacey shifted on top of her and finally hoisted up his hands and knees, supporting himself on either side of her ribs. Blaine took the hint and quickly pulled herself out from under him, flipping around to get a good look at where she'd been.

To her astonishment, both Burl and the unexpected guard were draped over Dacey; his back bowed up against the weight of them. Once he no longer felt her beneath him, he tilted to one side and dumped the bodies to the ground. "Don't touch them," he admonished—her? The boys?—again.

"But—Burl!" the youngest said, and something about the way he said it made Blaine look again at Burl, realize how still he was.

How dead he was.

"What happened?" she blurted, crawling to them, unable to keep from reaching out to Burl—although she stopped herself before she actually touched him. "What happened?"

"*Nekfehr*," he said. "I don't know if he's dead. So don't touch until I'm sure."

"*Nekfehr*," Blaine said blankly, and then realized what he was saying. Taken. The guard had been Taken. The guard had touched Burl. And Burl had almost landed on—she shuddered—*me*.

"Blaine, bring me Mage." Dacey's voice brooked no hesitation.

"He's safe," Blaine said, reaching for Mage's collar and to draw the dog over to Dacey.

His hand met hers on the collar, tightened briefly over it. Under his hand, Mage snuffled at Burl in a

disinterested way; Dacey felt Burl's arm, followed it
to his chest, let his hand rest there. "He's dead. It's
safe."

"The guard behind the door," the smaller boy said,
looking—and sounding—far too young to be part of
this. "Burl saw you go down and he come right into
it all, and him with just his knife."

"If Burl hadn't died he'd have been Taken," Dacey
said quietly. "Which do you boys think he'd've chose?"

Neither of them answered. They didn't have to.

"All right," Dacey said. "Burl done himself proud.
Now we got to carry on. We got three bodies that
need to be drug off and Burl to put careful in the
barn."

He climbed to his feet, moving slow—like he still,
somehow, carried Burl's weight. After a moment, the
oldest boy wiped his nose with the back of his hand
and exchanged a newly determined glance with his
partner. Together, wordlessly, they began moving the
bodies.

"The wards?" Dacey asked.

Blaine barely heard him. Still on her hands and
knees, she stared at Burl; he'd had so much strength
in him that she hadn't considered he'd be the first
of them to go. *There's no sense to it*, she realized.
Just chance. Any one of them could be next.

"Blaine?" It was a tentative voice, one that should
have been familiar—if it hadn't been so changed. She
looked up into the pale and haggard face of her sister
Lenie. "Blaine, is that . . . how can it be you?"

"Lenie!" Blaine lunged to her feet and grabbed her
sister in a hug. After a startled moment, Lenie hugged
her back, but there was no strength or conviction to
her embrace. Blaine hardly noticed; she caught sight
of her mother and tore away from Lenie to rush into
the hall. "Mommy!" she cried, and would have thrown
herself at the woman, had she not seen the strange
wariness in those eyes. "It's *me*, Mommy, it really is!"

The woman who stared back at her was hardly the mother she'd left. That woman had been tired but striving anyway. This one was lank-haired, skinnier than her wayward daughter—doing as she did because someone else held her to it, and not because she had any drive of her own. Blaine saw no hope in those empty eyes, and she stopped short of the hug she'd been aiming, her hand trembling as it reached for the side of her mother's face.

"Blaine," Dacey said sharply from the doorway.

Hastily, Blaine dug into her pocket for the wards, settling for a quick touch on her uncomprehending mother's arm. "You watch," she said. "I really am here. And them Annekteh are gonna rue it." She turned, quick, jaw set—

And left her family. Again.

"Here," she said to Dacey, taking his hand and turning it palm up so she could empty the leather pouch into it. In return he held out his other hand, offering her the hunting knife and hand both.

"Do it," he said.

Blaine just gave him a startled look. Dacey had told her about this, about how the wards needed to be immersed before they were placed, an act which bound them and made them seek out one another. Immersed in anything but water—which left nothing when it evaporated. Preferably in blood, the living substance of which lent strength to the wards.

He had told her about it, prepared her to handle it herself. But he now obviously intended for her to cut him, and she had never even considered such a thing.

"Blaine, I don't aim to lose any fingers trying it myself. Now do it, before more Annekteh get here!"

Galvanized, Blaine snatched the blade and pressed it across her arm, cutting deeply enough that the blood welled freely, running into her palm and spatting through her closed fingers onto the ground. She upended her cupped hand on Dacey's own, which was still waiting to feel the knife. "I couldn't do that to you," she said, her voice as pale as her face. She took his other hand and tipped the teeth into the little pool of blood.

His expression went from surprise to understanding to frowning regret, but he said nothing. Finding the tiny grey lumps with his finger, he stirred them around to make sure each was completely covered with her blood. "Take me around the building."

She did so without hesitation, still dripping blood. Moving quickly but without fumbling, Dacey felt out the end joints of the logs and deliberately pushed the wards, one at each corner, back into the dovetailing. Blaine winced. She'd been planning to put them on the ground, and she suddenly realized how easy it would have been to scuff them aside—even a strong wind might have done it. Their nerve-wracking run across the field together had not been for nothing, that was certain. If only he wasn't . . .

No, that wasn't even worth thinking. Even blind, he was the best chance they had.

"Southeast," Dacey muttered over the last ward, naming it as he had named the others. Blaine led him back to the doorway, and put his hand on the doorjamb in a quick, silent explanation of their position. From the crowded room within, Lenie watched her, standing right up front. Lottie was nowhere to be seen. Blaine wanted to find the words to tell her sister things would be all right, but she just stared, her throat on the edge of speech and no words to fill it.

Unaware of her distress, Dacey stepped away from her, just inside the doorway—but when Mage tried to follow, he gently but firmly pushed the dog back out. "Listen," he said to Blaine—that voice that meant he knew her inner struggle, that he needed her to hear him anyway—"Take those boys and follow the path behind the hall. When you get there," and she had no need to ask where *there* was, "hang back. Watch. See who's touched by who, and let Trey know. Them that's fightin' won't have the concentration to do it, Blaine—you got to keep track, the best you can."

Blaine's mouth was open, her mind blank. She didn't want to go. She didn't want to leave her family, or Dacey—or the safety of this hall. But he was right, and she knew it. The boys needed all the help they could get, even if it *was* just her.

Dacey dropped his hand to Mage's head. "Take Mage," he said, more words with intensity behind them.

Blaine forged right over it. "Dacey, not Mage! He's your—"

"Take him!" Dacey repeated sharply, hesitating, his head held at an angle that let her know he was thinking about all those behind him, choosing his words. "And *watch* him—watch him close." With that he took possession of her still dripping hand and closed his own fist over it, holding it in the air above her head.

"Seek," he commanded in a perfectly ordinary tone of voice which in no way prepared Blaine for the sizzle of energy that raced around the outside of the log hall, flaring at each concealed tooth and ending at her own fist with a soundless blast that knocked her back and almost knocked her down.

"Dacey," she pleaded, staggering to regain her balance. But it was done; Blue and Mage were outside the warded building, and although there was no longer any sign of the energy, she knew its protection could be broken only from the inside.

Dacey shook his head at her, his face resolute. "Go," he said.

Blaine stared for a scant moment longer—one last look at her mother, who had joined Lenie, still almost lost in the group crowded behind, but not against, Dacey. At last she saw the realization in Lottie's eyes, the slow recognition that her girl still lived. At that, Blaine turned away.

"Blue, Mage," she commanded, "with me!"

Careful to stay away from the open but warded doorway, Dacey leaned gratefully against the wall—solid, supportive, and easily pictured in his mind. Outside, Blaine's footfalls grew faint, merged with the two boys', and faded.

It should have been *her* in this building—safe, away from Annekteh, and convincing her family that she was still alive. It should have been him out there—not weak from Annekteh drugs, not blind. Not still reeling from his time behind the seer's wall.

But he'd done this to himself, as he always did. Pushing into places he hadn't been asked, rescuing a people who didn't even know he existed. All for the sake of some seeings, and the fear of facing the feelings he'd had when his stubborn ignorance meant his mother's death.

No. For more than that. For the sake of Blaine and her family, for all the others who didn't deserve life under the Annekteh. He'd done it to himself, but with reason. With purpose.

He just wished he hadn't also done it to Blaine.

The air turned close and stuffy despite the open door. The hall was crowded, no doubt about it— sheer humanity could not hide from Annekteh-dulled eyes. And except for the breathing, they were silent, incredibly silent for a group that included children.

He knew what they were looking at. Him. The blind outsider who had worked magic in front of their hall.

"We're safe from the Annekteh now," he said, and that, at least, he could announce without question. No one would breach those wards, Annekteh or not. But unliving objects—like arrows—surely could. Unfortunately, in order to close the hall door, some-one would have to break the wards. One of those details lost in the panic of the moment . . . Better simply to block the thing. Then someone might see out more easily, as well.

No one seemed to have moved; he found it unnerved him to address a crowd of silent, unseen strangers. But he kept confidence in his voice. "If any one of us leaves, those wards will have to be reset." It was a process that might take only a single word, if the teeth had not dried completely, or pre-cious moments, if they had. "That includes reachin' out for that door. Is there ary a table in here?"

Silence followed his question, long silence. He drew a deep breath. "I know you don't have a full understandin' of what's happenin'. But . . . I need your help."

Finally, he heard a rustle, and then a quiet, hesi-tant voice. "There's tables."

"We got to block this doorway. Annekteh can't get in but arrows an' such can."

"Table on end will do it," offered another voice, one that took on a little confidence. *Always helps to give 'em something to do.*

"They're heavy," protested yet another voice.

The first came right back, firmer now. "There's enough of us here for it."

After that, speech died down to grunts of effort and mutters of direction; Dacey stepped aside, moving down the wall, and listened as they dragged the table to the doorway. "Here," he said. "I'll tip it on up."

Strange how he encountered no one on the way, brushed no arms, felt no swish of skirt. Their retreat had been quick and unanimous. He found the end of the heavy plank table and saw right away why they'd been hesitant; it was huge, with thick, heavy boards. He ran his hands over the age-polished wood, learning the shape of the thing, and searching for the right handholds. Not at all sure he could actually do it, he dipped his knees and lifted, straining against the weight. It moved most grudgingly— until, abruptly, it lightened, raising almost easily under his hands. Someone—or more than one—had come to some sort of decision about him, and pitched in. His smile was more inward than outward as the table rocked into place, but it marked a definite victory.

"It covers near the whole doorway," someone declared, and there was no dissent. Dacey ran his hands around the edge of the table and found only a small gap between it and the door frame. He nodded to himself.

"And what now?" said the first voice that had spoken to him. "Now we just sit and wait, wondering what's happening in our hills?" The woman stepped close, close enough to touch, for Dacey to feel her breath on his face as she peered at him . . . challenged him. "Dacey Childers, is that you? The Childers that traded for food? Has my Blaine been with you all this while?"

"Yes'm," Dacey allowed. "She's been a good hand, Missus Kendricks."

"And you didn't see fit to bring her back to me?"

"What I saw fit," Dacey said gently, "and what I could do . . . those were different things. If I'd've brought her back, it would've put her in the trouble you all were already in. As it is, she's done helpin' get rid of 'em."

A dozen voices echoed his words, a wash of hope running through the building. Disbelief clamored on the heels of that hope, until at last they saw he would not try to speak above them and grew silent again.

"It ain't won yet—though we got a good start, getting you in here and warded off, safe from Takers. But we've got a chance. Our only chance, before more of 'em get here."

"How?" Lottie said. "What kind of chance can any of us have, against a Taker?"

"I been working with your boys, your hunters. They can do it." *They better.*

"Our *children*?" That was another woman, her voice rising above the gasps of the others.

"They're men after today. Best you remember when they come back home."

"What if they don't come back?" Lottie's voice was hard, accusing . . . telling him plain she couldn't afford to lose another.

He didn't answer right away, looking for some way to soften the words and finally opting for his characteristically direct manner. "Reckon some of 'em won't. Blaine told me that you—and they—would have it that way before settling in to the Annekteh. Was she wrong?"

The question drew another moment of silence. Then, someone's voice, strong and clear, said, "No. She weren't wrong. We all feel that way."

"We've done talked about it," another agreed, and then there was a general murmur of consensus; it grew into louder conversation, and the whine of a child wanting food, and a general rustle of activity.

Dacey was glad for the reprieve. Facing these women was almost more difficult than standing up to the Annekteh, and that . . . *that* didn't bear recollection.

As if his thoughts would give him a choice. *Out-numbered. Set upon so sudden, so completely, by the plainsmen searching for the owner of the hound with the wild howl.* He warned off the dogs, too late to save Chase from a heavy, flat-bladed sword blow to the face. *Mage, ever obedient—crouching at a distance while Dacey rocked from the blows of the plainsmen, one on top of another—rending the air with his angry snarls.* Maidie, ever independent, charging in to take Dacey's part.

His distraction at her broken body was the last thing he remembered before he awoke in Annekteh hands.

He pushed aside such memories with desperation, remembered Blaine's touch on his eyelids instead, and her horrified wonder. *Did it hurt?* No, not at the time.

But it did now.

Stripped of everything but the habit of his confidence, he stood in the darkness of a transom-lit hall and waited with a large group of people who weren't sure they trusted him, and were almost sure they blamed him. He missed Mage's pressure against his leg, and the head that was just the right height to receive his habitual caress. He hoped the dog was doing Blaine some good.

Both hounds fell into place at her heels, and Blaine joined the boys at the head of the path into the woods. They led her upward, and her feet followed, bypassing the fear in her heart. *Up the hill*, Burl had said. Trey had started the fuss, had chosen the spot— killing one of the Annekteh-Taken warriors on patrol, the boys told her, and thus instantly rousing them all—it wasn't far, just below the ridge south of the meeting hall.

Just a few panting, never-ending, too-short minutes.

They heard the fighting before they saw it. Below them, the hill had a gentle slope, and rhododendrons thickly blanketed the area. There was plenty of cover for boys—but not for men. Trey stood uphill of the conflict, directing his young warriors. Blaine's companions ran ahead to him, exchanged a few quick words, and peeled off, taking position on the upper side of the struggle.

It must have been a perfect attack for the boys, Blaine thought, trying to decipher what she saw, feeling strangely removed from the fighting even though she was completely out in the open. The plan had been to concentrate the first fighting on the known Taken—those men who now sprawled between the bushes, dead or dying.

But the Annekteh had Taken more plainsmen, Blaine was sure. And those linked by the Annekteh fought with incredible teamwork, worrying and working the boys with frightening precision, seeking to trap them within range of the long blades. One of Burl's teammates narrowly scrambled away from a blow that would have cut him in two. They needed help.

They needed help.

Blaine tried to get Trey's attention, but he was in the thick of it; he loosed an arrow even as he scrambled out of blade's reach. Scooting beneath a rhododendron to safety—or as safe as he was apt to get, for the moment—he emerged and finally sighted Blaine.

"Get out of here!" he hollered, waving her off in a broad and violent gesture.

She shook her head at him, and sprinted through the fighting, throwing herself up into the waiting arms of the tree that towered over the battle. "I'll watch for you!" she hollered to him as she reached for the next branch, well out of the way of the men below her.

As Blue and Mage curled up at the base of her tree, Trey flung her a nod and nocked another arrow to his bow, burying it in the man who was still trying to reach him through the bush.

This wasn't going to be hard at all! She could spot all the warriors from here, or nearly all of them; she wasn't even settled before she'd waved two boys away from trouble. If she could keep them away from the Annekteh, no one would have to face killing kin or friend—no one would be Taken. And that's what the warriors were trying to do, now, she was sure of it; they'd started herding boys into Taking distance—or trying to.

But the men were dying and the boys had no casualties, taking every advantage of size and their nimble young limbs and slowly gaining the advantage. Finally the men gathered their wits and grouped together, shielding themselves, behind a bush near Blaine's tree—she could see them all from above, note who had lost his helmet, spot who was balding.

None of them so much as glanced up at her; they were busy enough protecting themselves—although against arrows, they had little defense. Several of them had shields, but not enough—and not of a size to protect them from arrows. The fight had become a slaughter—but a slaughter with no regrets.

It all changed in an instant.

The timberers, buoyed with their freedom, came charging off the ridge and straight into the huddled warriors. Snatching bladed weapons from the dead, betting their lives that they could kill their enemies without being touched by them, the men plowed through the battleground before they even realized that victory of a sort had already been achieved. Frantically, Blaine tried to shout them off, tried to keep track of who touched whom, but it was impossible.

The fight, nearly won, was suddenly just as close to lost.

"Fan out!" Trey bellowed, motioning his boys back and away. "Don't touch anyone!" Ducking, weaving, sliding to safety—the boys were in constant flight, with no chance to pick out targets of their own. Blaine felt herself slipping into panic—she had no idea who was Taken and who was not.

Suddenly, as though she was seeing from her eyes and her head at the same time, she remembered flying. *A dream, that had been a* dream. But she found her gaze lingering on a plainsmen she clearly remembered as bearing a bruised purple aura.

Hadn't she dreamt about Willum? Hadn't she dreamt about Dacey, worn and haggard and standing blankly—*blindly*—in the woods? And had she been *flying* in her dream, or just high in a tree, higher than she was now?

And hadn't Dacey called her dreams seeings, and said the magic was coming back to the hills?

The plainsman crept up on one of the boys—and his weapon pointed back behind him. Not an attack. The stalk of Annekteh looking to *Take*, clearly marked in her memory.

"Trey!" she hollered, waving her arms, pointing at the man. "Trey!"

But all Trey's attention was wrapped up in escaping the plainsman who recognized him as the boys' leader. There was no doubt what was on that one's mind, and a simple touch had nothing to do with it.

Or maybe not *all* his attention. For when Blaine rearranged herself in the tree to bring him back into sight, Trey carried an extra bow and quiver. He came straight at her tree, losing ground with the effort but determined enough that when he ran beneath her and flung the stolen weapons upward, she was ready to receive them. She hooked her ankle through the crotch of a small branch and flung her arm out to its very limit, snatching at the bow and intertwined quiver strap.

A few arrows spilled out as the quiver skewed around in her grip, but Blaine hauled in her catch and pressed her body back against the tree. Those few seconds had taught her the fear of exposure—and driven home how much Trey had risked to respond to her. Anxiously, she searched for him, and finally spotted him slithering along on his stomach at some speed while the foiled warrior fought to disentangle his scabbard from a gnarled old rhododendron branch.

Reassured, Blaine looked at the weapon still clenched tightly in her hand. The bow grip was slick with fresh blood, making her wonder which of the dead—*which of their own*—had dropped it. She pulled her shirt from her skirtband and carefully cleaned the grip. Without contemplating the evolving sequence of her actions, she pulled an arrow from the quiver and nocked it.

Then she looked below.

The boys were still running, their expressions nothing but fear. The men around them were parents, brothers and uncles, and some of them were Annekteh. But without someone to point out who was enemy and who was still kin, not a boy could bring himself to attack.

But Blaine knew.

She spotted the plainsman from a moment before and raised the bow. She could come nowhere near a full draw on the short bow, but she pulled until her arm trembled, and released. He was close, and it took him in the lower back—astonishing success.

She looked out on the battle with new eyes, eyes with a dream memory imprinted like double vision, flickering visions that made her blink, made her eyes water. Then suddenly it seemed to settle, and make sense. Men and boys mixed in intricate, familiar patterns, and Jason abruptly drew her focus. She knew him as a young man who hunted with her daddy, and saw him as *nekfehr*, lying in wait for one of the youthful fighters.

Blaine raised the bow and shifted so there was room to pull back at this new angle, then carefully sighted to the center of Jason's chest. She wondered if his pretty wife had had their baby yet, and she let the bowstring roll off her fingertips. The arrow wavered, but hit its target—

With barely enough force to cause a shallow wound. Jason bellowed in surprise rather than pain, searching for his attacker—

And then another arrow thunked home, a solid and fatal attack that had certainly not come from Blaine. Confused, she twisted around to discover three boys just outside the melee. Estus was lowering his bow, and he found her in the tree, gave her a little nod.

The runners, Blaine realized. The ones who had been chosen for size and stealth to reach the timberers. The men must have outrun them on the way back, and now they wisely held back at the edge of danger—until Estus realized what Blaine was doing. He couldn't have known *how*—but he had followed up on her attack anyway.

For that, she almost forgave him the blow to Dacey's head.

Now he spoke quickly to the boys with him and they separated to cover three points of a triangle, moving quietly across the hill until they were in position to see Blaine and take her direction—and act on it.

Blaine took advantage of them immediately. The other boys were tiring, and their game of slither and dodge would not last much longer. She found a man she didn't know, closing on a panicking youngster. *Him*, she thought, remembering clearly. But there was no response when she pointed.

When she looked, she found Estus spreading his
hands in perplexity, frustration on his face. *He can't
tell*!

Of course he couldn't. He was at the edge of the
action, she was in the middle of a tree, pointing down
into a roiling rhododendron patch. As quickly as she
could, Blaine notched another arrow and sighted on
her target—missing him completely, but marking him
for two swift arrows from beyond the battleground.
Without hesitation she found another dream-marked
man, sighted, and guided Estus' arrow to his heart.
When the third man went down, the boys in the
melee began to comprehend; they never thought to
question how she knew, and there was no doubt on
her face to make them wonder.

For them Blaine could point, and between the
pointing and her badly aimed arrows, the enemy fell.
In moments the boys and timberers regained their
confidence, and the Shadow Hollers men turned
savagely on the invaders.

And on their own. At Blaine's gesture, one youth
took grim aim on his uncle—only to be shoved
aside by a friend who had no blood ties to stain
his hands.

She was crying, Blaine realized suddenly. Tears
splashed on her wrist, and even the dream vision
wavered. But she never hesitated. And as she took
aim at another of her neighbors, she realized the
Annekteh had caught on to her. *They were coming
up to get her*.

Just like the dream. *The dream that had ended* . . .
now.

Blue stood at the base of the tree, his hackles
raised, his intent clear. But Mage gave a particularly
vicious snarl and drove him away. One of the *nekfehr* reached the tree, stretching for the lower
branches, making the trunk tremble under Blaine's
white-knuckled grip. A second joined him, stopping

in the lower branches, waiting. Blaine froze, entirely unable to move. *The dream ended—*

You can take care of yourself, Dacey said in her head. Her own inner voice chimed in, annoyed at her surrender to fear. *You outclimbed a bear, Blaine Kendricks. Now get going!*

Blaine climbed. Skinny Blaine reached up for the next branches, thin arms hauling her relentlessly upward. Angular Blaine—covered with nothing more than stringy muscles and not an ounce of pleasingly curvy fat—shinnied up a spot bare of handholds and found herself swaying in slender branches. How much further before the tree broke and dumped her? The quiver banged against her back and she dropped it on the head of the man closest to her, spewing arrows into the bushes below. The bow had fallen unnoticed moments before, and had hung up just above the ground—the same ground where tiny chicken-sized people ran around.

Way down there.

Blaine gripped the slimming tree trunk tightly as it swayed in ever increasing arcs, caused more by the *nekfehr* than herself. She dared not stop climbing. She closed her eyes and stole height, hand over hand. Better to die in the fall than be Taken. Burl had already made that choice, and she could make it, too.

Then the tree shuddered. Blaine peered down over her shoulder, astonished to find the closest man toppling backwards out of the tree. As he twisted and fell, breaking branches all the way down, a tiny Trey figure below gave a salute of his bow and darted back out of sight.

Blaine rested her forehead against the tree. Selfishly, she wanted to stay right there, safe in her perch—or, as safe as she was likely to get. She no longer had the bow and arrows to guide the boys. She didn't know how else she could help.

A child's death shriek cut right through her; her

eyes sprung open. She could join the fight, that's what she could do. Go down and grab another bow—for even if she couldn't guide the others as well from the ground, *she* would know what she was aiming at— Taken or not.

The renewed trembling of her tree nearly changed her mind again—*the second man*—and she got ready for another chase . . . but he was descending, not coming after her.

Descending? Blaine blinked and took a better look. The Taken—hill folk and plainsmen alike—were gathering up to defend each other's backs. Weary little boys and their fathers dotted the trampled, body-strewn hillside, warily eyeing those three remaining warriors—and the few local men with them. *Taken.*

Anxiously, Blaine searched the faces on both sides, and discovered her father and Rand not only standing, but standing apart from the *nekfehr*. Rand's arm seemed to be bleeding, but that was all. The only sign of hurt on either of them. She found herself ambushed with a wash of emotion—*they're alive, they're safe*—and hid her face against her arm, blinking away tears. She made them quick ones, though, smearing them away as she felt for the branches beneath her feet. Time to come down.

The two groups stared at one another, prickling hostility. Slowly, Trey brought his bow up, arrow ready. A ripple of movement spread around the clearing, boys and men following his lead. Ready to cut the *nekfehr* down in cold blood.

The silent standoff lasted only an instant.

The *annektehr* ran—leaving their vessels, returning to the Annekteh whole so far away. The effect was barely noticeable, a strange wavering of the air like heat from a rock; Blaine fancied she saw a tinge of purple. The small circle of former *nekfehr* separated into confused hill men and three panicked warriors, abandoned by the Annekteh—and reacting with instant, unthinking hostility, turning on the dazed hill men standing with them. For that they died, pierced by a dozen different arrows.

The Shadow Hollers warriors stood another long moment in silence, until one triumphant whoop filled the air, followed by a dozen others. Blaine dropped out of the tree; Blue instantly accosted her. "All right, all right," she told him absently, trying to spot her father and brother from this new angle. She found Cadell easily enough; it was his practical voice that cut through the noise.

"It's too early for that," he said. "There may be more of 'em hidin' in the woods. They ain't all *here*, that's for sure. We know some of 'em are dead by the timber, but we got to get an accountin' of 'em *all*." His calm words stopped the back-slapping cold, and exchanged it for apprehension. No, they weren't done yet.

"They might could try for the meetin' hall," Wade agreed. "Do a search between here and there. And we need to get some of the women up here, to tend the wounded."

"Cadell." It was one of the five, the once-Taken, who still held themselves apart from the others; Blaine didn't know any of them by name, though she'd seen them all at dances and meetings. "It seems to me you might best keep us separate, and under watch. I feel myself again, but I ain't takin' no chances."

Cadell nodded thoughtfully and turned to Rand. "See to it," he said. Then, when Blaine thought that he had looked right past her and not recognized her, his gaze came to rest squarely on her. His voice was quiet but clear as he said, "Blaine. Estus said you was here . . . You done good, Blaine. Hang here until we make sure it's finished."

Blaine gave a single nod. *You done good, Blaine.*

How long had she waited to hear those words? She
wanted to run up and hug him.

She didn't.

She stayed with Blue and Mage, while Trey teamed
up with Cadell to direct the mixed force in a sweep
pattern of the hill. If there were *annektehr* still out
there, she wanted to be no part of delaying their
demise.

When the last of the searchers faded away, there
was awkward quiet beneath the ash. The five men
clustered together under Rand's watchful eye, but his
attention was clearly torn, his gaze flicking often to
Blaine. Leaving Blue behind, Blaine went to join him.

Rand gave her a small smile and shake of his
head—but no invitation to tuck under his arm like
she'd expected. "I told Daddy you were all right. I
just knew you'd gone on with that Dacey feller."

"I didn't have any say at the time," Blaine told him,
feeling rebuffed.

"I don't see how you done it. How'd you get this
planned? How'd you tell who was Took just now?"

Blaine shrugged. "It's an awful long tale, Rand.
Maybe some day I'll get around to telling it all."
Rand took a good look at the fatigue on her face
and held out the arm that was not bleeding, a
belated invitation. Relieved, grateful, she moved to
accept it.

Mage slunk between them, snarling. Blaine stopped
short at the sight of him; the dog's ears were laid flat
back, his lips wrinkled up in the ugliest face she'd
seen him make.

"Mage?" she said hesitantly, wondering if the dog
had somehow been Taken. Mage crept closer to Rand,
his low-slung posture accenting his lurching gait, his
snarling loud and constant.

"Blaine, call him off," Rand said uneasily, slowly
dropping his arm. The five men beyond him moved
apprehensively, shifting away from the dog.

"Mage, no!" Blaine said with as much authority as she could muster. "Sit, Mage!"

The dog ignored her, continuing to stalk Rand—although he wasn't, Blaine suddenly noticed, getting any closer to her brother, just circling.

Circling Rand.

"Dacey?"

The voice was hesitant, and Dacey felt that if he made the wrong move it would whisper back into the gathering. It reminded him of Blaine somehow, and he took a chance.

"Lenie?" he asked.

"Yes," she said, relief evident. "Won't you tell me what's happening? Are you . . . all right?"

"Not many here are that, I'd say." Dacey looked straight at the direction of her voice. "The boys have organized and hope to free the men. They're going to fight the Annekteh. We . . . we just have to wait and see how it turns out."

"But there's no seer. All the older folks said we couldn't do nothing without no seer."

"You can't do but what you try to do," Dacey told her. When she didn't respond, he added, "In the Annekteh Ridge, the folks were spread out, and never got a chance to use the wards like we done. We got all the children, and you women, safe. It'll make the difference."

"And Blaine's been with you this whole while?" Her voice said she wasn't sure if that was admirable or scandalous.

Dacey nodded. "I'm real sorry you all thought she was kilt. It was safest for her that way." He blinked then, and hard. His obsidian vision seemed to have greyed. Distracted, he said, "She's done good, Lenie. She's held things together at times when we would have lost all chance otherwise."

Suddenly she was there, directly in front of him,

blurred and dim, a blonde-headed face of worry. Dacey took a startled step back and pressed the heels of his palms into his eyes.

"Dacey?" she said, sounding a little wary.

Cautiously, he took his hands away. She was indistinct, but she was there. Her hair was drawn tightly back, her dress wasn't clean, and her face was smudged. She was a beautiful sight.

"We're winning," he said under his breath. Winning, and weakening the Annekteh magic.

She just looked at him, obviously teetering on the edge of trust.

"Look," he said holding his hand up and following its motion with his eyes. "The Annekteh magicked my eyes, but the spell's fading." He blinked, trying to erase the grey veils that still dimmed his sight. "They've done lost strength. Some of 'em's gone."

"Some of 'em?" she repeated. "I thought it was all one, that just spread."

"More than one, all connected." Dacey's attention was on the blocked doorway and the silvery nimbus beyond the table. He hadn't actually seen the ward when he was practicing with Blaine, and distracted, he added, "Lenie, girl, I can't explain it now. You just take my word for it—them boys have got the upper hand."

Confused, Lenie nodded. "I don't know about you, Dacey Childers," she said. "Don't know how much to trust you. Don't know how much of this is your fault. But . . . I guess you're doin' what you can to get us out of it." She took the hand of the little girl who had been by her side—Sarie, if Dacey recalled rightly—and led her away.

Dacey looked at her straight back a moment, suddenly able to imagine Blaine sparring with this young woman, and the struggle between them—so different, yet with the same kind of fire. He shook his head and put the thought behind him, leaning up against the smooth old wood table to peer out the door, squinting through the silver glow to focus on the hill opposite the hall.

His eyes narrowed at what they saw there. Shades of shifting purple centered on the side of the hill, pulsating, oozing—and fading. The leaves, a sickening shade of green overlayed with violet, brightened into fresh spring colors.

He turned and laid his back up against the wall. He'd never seen such things before, but he knew instantly what it was, and that knowledge didn't come easy. The talents of his blood, wakened by the tampering of the Annekteh.

Seer's eyes. Seer's responsibilities.

And no one to teach him. No one of the old blood left to show him the ways—and a spirits-damned time to learn, on the hills against the Annekteh. The wavering patterns of light over the mountain should have meant something to him, he was sure; it could have been anything from magic in process to mere indications of Annekteh presence. There were shades other than purple adorning the mountain as well, and for those he had no name.

Dacey suddenly realized the women were all watching him again, staring at his odd behavior. For the moment he couldn't respond to them; he was caught up in *seeing*. Seeing the frightened and apprehensive faces around him, some of them brighter than they ought to be, given the transom light. The great stone fireplace at the end of the hall, which somehow radiated its sturdy construction; the minute detail of the black smoke stains tracing their way up the wooden logs at the sides of the fireplace, which he shouldn't have been able to see at all from here.

His restored sight meant he should be up on the hill with the others. His new sight meant he *had* to be there. He could make sure all the *annektehr* had been driven away, and that none were hidden amongst the men, playing possum till it was too late to stop the spread again.

To go out was to break the wards, and if he hesitated long enough for them to dry he would have to go through the complete procedure to reset them. He had to go *now*.

Dacey turned back to the table and placed his hands against it, using all his strength to move it just enough so he could slide sideways through the space he'd made.

The silvery light flickered out. Immediately, he turned, holding up his fist—unwashed, it might yet have some trace of Blaine's blood. "Seek," he muttered. For an instant there was nothing; he waited, tense at the sluggish response. Silver light sizzled and blinked, evanescent and uncertain—and snapped abruptly into place, strong against his touch.

"You're not leaving!" Lenie protested through the narrow opening by the table; her words drew a tumble of objections behind her. They might not completely trust him, but they wanted him here.

He ignored the objections. "I reset the wards, but nary one of you go through or they're broke for good. Have you got that?"

"Yes," she said, taken aback.

"And should any men come back, you stay where you are. Don't come out for none but me or Blaine. Do y'hear?" He stared fiercely at her until she nodded, and he hoped he'd frightened her enough that she would ensure their compliance.

He turned away from her and ran from the hall. The path up the point was distinct, pounded out by Annekteh patrols, and all the steep places were marked with great gouges of dirt stepholds. Dacey, unarmed and unmindful of it, barely slowed to take them. He was seized with a sense of urgency, and he felt Mage's anger course into his thoughts and become his own. He didn't take the time to question such feelings, but pushed on. Pushed hard.

There was trouble on the hillside, and Blaine was in the thick of it.

⇥ 20 ⇤

All is not lost. The Blaine-child was within reach—and with the Blaine-child, they could break Dacey Childers' spirit. Surprising enough he had any spirit left at all. But it was he who still drove this fight, who charged for this very spot at top speed, new seer's magic whirling around him. *That* was a mystery for another time. For now, they had enough— the memories of the *annektehr* lost in the south, lost to Dacey Childers' fierce fears for the Blaine-child.

And almost within reach, the Blaine-child herself.

They would present Dacey Childers with a decision that would kill him as surely as any Annekteh blade.

In moments all will be regained. Shadow Hollers and Dacey Childers will be ours.

⇥⇤   ⇥⇤   ⇥⇤

"Mage, *stay!*" Blaine said desperately, her hands clenched with fear for the dog. "Oh, please *stay.*"

Slowly, reluctantly, he stopped, trembling in every limb with the effort of obedience.

"He's all right, I think," she said, relaxing a fraction. "So much has happened—he's just upset. He doesn't know you. He's Dacey's dog."

Rand looked at the ever-growling Mage and shuddered. "I hope that's it, sissy," he said. "I hate to think your friend's dog has been Took, Blaine, but I'll kill it if it gets any closer." His injured arm made a bow useless, but he hefted the short sword he'd scavenged.

Blaine tugged Dacey's knife from her skirtband and pulled the sheath off. "I reckon I'll help you, if it comes to that," she said sadly, wondering what she would tell Dacey; she walked over to her brother, carefully watching the dog and not watching Rand at all.

Mage *stayed*, sinking to the ground and trembling all over; his snarl built and his eyes fairly snapped with fury. Blaine hesitated, staring at him, at a loss. She hefted the knife, trying to imagine using it, wondering what force it would take to drive the heavy blade into the dog, and in the next moment knowing she could never hurt this loyal creature, Taken or not. How ever had the boys been able to kill men they knew, on this battlefield?

A new sound cut through her hesitation, one that had been grumbling in the background, unnoted. It crescendoed into a bellow of rage—

And it came from Blue. He bounded from the tree where Blaine had left him and zeroed straight in at her and Rand, his face filled with such savage intent that Blaine's mouth dropped open in astonishment. In the corner of her eye, Rand's sword moved up and ready. "Don't!" she said sharply, reaching to stay his hand.

"*No!* Blaine, no!"

The yell rang across the hill and Blaine froze. *Dacey. How . . . ?* As confused as she and running up against Mage, Blue stumbled to a clumsy stop.

"Blaine, *no!*" Dacey repeated, coming into sight at a reckless run, looking at her—*looking* at her—and at Rand. She turned to exchange a baffled glance with Rand.

The eyes he turned on her belonged to someone else. Some*thing* else.

"Rand!" she cried, refusing to believe. *Unable* to believe. Rand, *nekfehr*. Taken.

He beheld her with reproach. "*Seer's blood.*"

"*No,*" Blaine said, her voice quivering. *No, this can't be Rand. No, I ain't got no seer's blood.* She gave Dacey a wild look—entreaty, denial—but Dacey didn't tell her what she wanted to hear; he was snatching up a bow from beneath the tree, capturing arrows from the bushes—the very weapons she had dropped. The *annektehr* in Rand paid him no attention, and focused only on Blaine.

"Yes. Your brother knows of your dreams, Blaine Kendricks," Rand said. "So do we. We saw you, there in the tree. And we're not through here—so you must die. Or become one of us, if your blood runs too thin."

"Rand, no," she whimpered, edging back, trying to gain ground without triggering the *annektehr* into action. Behind her, Mage snarled, a wave of sound that rode the swells of his breath.

Watch Mage.

Dacey's advice rang through her ears—too late. Mage had known Annekteh scent all along, had howled for Annekteh quarry. Had tried to warn her before it was too late. And Dacey had done his best to tell her so without placing the unique dog in danger.

Having at last stumbled on to it, Blaine turned to dart away and also stumbled over her own feet, falling hard on Blue.

The dog scrambled to get out from under her. Her hand locked on his collar and he dragged her, gaining precious distance before he stopped, obeying the tug of her weight. Stricken, Blaine blinked up at her brother—*not her brother*—tightening her grip on the knife she had almost dropped.

She had seen the boys fight their own. Now it was her turn.

He moved for her—but glanced up and froze.

Dacey stood well within range, an arrow aimed directly at Rand, no doubts on his face. His chest heaved from his run up the hill, but his aim did not waver.

He wouldn't miss.

"Dacey . . ." she said. *Don't kill my brother, Dacey, please*. But another inner voice, one she couldn't bear to hear, pled for something else. *Don't let him live like this*.

"That's right, Dacey," Rand smiled, but not any smile that Blaine was used to seeing on that face. And his voice seemed twisted, with a sudden strange, flat accent. The *annektehr* within Rand. "He's her brother. You kill him, and she'll hate you forever."

"You've lost," Dacey said evenly. "Might as well leave that boy be."

"Have we?" Rand sneered, another expression Blaine had never seen on her brother's face. "You know nothing. You've no magic in you. And you won't kill me, or you would have done it by now."

"I *had* no magic." Dacey raised an eyebrow. "You done changed that yourself, trying to spell my eyes. Go home, *annektehr*. Take *all* the *annektehr* with you. This is over, and you'll never get another chance." He pulled the bowstring back another inch. At this distance the arrow would half go through its target.

"You won't," said the *annektehr*, taking a step toward Blaine. "She'll be lost to you."

Blaine tightened her fingers around the knife and looked at Dacey, desperately trying to read him. "Dacey . . ." she repeated, and this time she didn't know what she was asking for.

Rand—only *nekfehr* now—grinned, and took another step. "You won't," he said again. "And once I touch her, you'll never win. You can't kill her."

"That's the truth," Dacey said mildly, as Rand bent, reaching for the bare skin above Blaine's boot, below her too-short skirt.

Blaine closed her eyes. *Rand,* she thought, overwhelmed by memories of how close they'd been, of the understanding he'd always given her. *If only you'd listened to me.* There was little chance of both of them coming through this—there was little chance of *either* of them coming through this—but he was one of the few *annektehr* left in the hills. Maybe the only one. And if Dacey wasn't going to . . .

Rand, I'm sorry. She turned on her hip and plunged the knife upward, ready to spring away out of reach. Hoping to.

"Blaine, no!" Dacey snapped, a sound as taut as the bowstring he released, as sharp as the thunk of the arrow hitting its target. Blaine froze, and waited for the body to fall. To fall on *her.*

Nothing. No smothering weight, no cry of pain. Cautiously, Blaine cracked her eyes.

Arm still flung up before his face, Rand stood as frozen as she, his eyes wide with terror—*human* eyes, *human* terror. An arrow quivered in the tree beside him. Blaine looked at Dacey, and found reassurance in his satisfied smile, the relaxed way he lowered his bow. The *annektehr* had run.

Blaine jerked the knife back behind herself and dropped it. If she had her way, Rand would never realize how close she had come to killing him.

Or at least to trying.

"Rand?" she asked, unable to help the hesitation

in her voice. She looked at Dacey again, saw his nod, and rolled to her knees to reach out to her brother. At the pressure of her hand he lifted his head; another split-second of indecision and he hauled her into his arms for a crushing hug.

"I thought I was kilt," he said, and she felt his head lift from her shoulder to look up at Dacey. She snuggled happily into him, hearing the pureness of proper mountain speech in his voice again.

"So did the *nekteh*," Dacey said, joining them as Mage stood up, shook off, and trotted over to him.

Blaine twisted around to look at him, her expression incredulous. "What iff'n it hadn't left him, Dacey?" *What if I'd been Taken, too?*

He shook his head. "You gotta play it as it happens, Blaine," Dacey said. "The decisions for the *what ifs* don't gotta be made, and I don't reckon you'll ever hear an answer to that particular question."

He bent down to pick up the knife she'd dropped and handed it out to her. Blaine didn't move to take it. "It's yours, Dacey."

"No." He shook his head once, decisively. "Take it. You know how to use it."

She'd killed a bear with this knife. She'd almost killed her brother. There was respect in his eyes for that, an expression that made Blaine feel sick and proud at the same time.

She took the knife.

Mage hovered at Dacey's side, no sign of hound wrath on his face. Mage, who came from a seer-bred line of dogs, and who had done his best to protect her. And Blue, who had charged in to help his endangered packmate with no thought for his own safety. Now he came up to nudge her hand, looking a little long-eared and embarrassed at his part in a sequence of events that made no sense to him.

Blaine rubbed his floppy ears, but her attention stayed on Dacey; he stood alert, and looking down

the hill as though he could see through the rhododendrons to something else.

Something that put that intent, worried look on his
face.

Beside her, Rand straightened, tense, also watching Dacey. He murmured, "The Taker . . . when it had
me . . . it knew there were others left—I felt it. That's
why it was so cocky, so easy to scare off."

Blaine suddenly realized the one person she had
not seen in this fight; she stiffened. "Nekfehr."

"Yes," said Dacey.

They left Rand with his voluntary prisoners and
ran for the meeting hall. It was a scrambling race,
along the curving side of the hill, over the slight rise
of the point, and then down, down behind the barn.
Blue bounded along beside Blaine as she fought to
lift her tired feet above snagging roots and deadwood,
sliding in the deep humus and snatching at the
blessed support of the trees around her. Even so, she
pulled ahead of Dacey.

They descended between the two points and into
the little bowl that held the hall and barn, where the
confusing babble of activity there overcame the noise
of their own movement. Blaine stopped herself up
against a tree, lying against it; Dacey came up behind
her and used the same tree to steady himself, his arm
reaching over her head. Breathing hard, they listened
to the sounds, tried to decipher them. It sounded like
the women had broken the warding, and were out
with the men in the yard.

Or was it a little more strident than that?

The ear-piercing scream of a child broke through
their questions. Dacey pushed off the tree and ran
break-neck down the hill, leaving Blaine in a struggle
to catch up.

Though she wasn't entirely sure she wanted to.

They came down behind the barn—in Blaine's case,

smack up against it, as it stopped her out-of-control descent. Dacey had his back to it, trying to slow his breathing, his eyes closed as he listened and assessed what they could hear—though it wasn't as clear, here on the same level and behind the barn, as it had been uphill.

Angry men's voices, snatches of phrases, a clear threat. Blaine caught Dacey's glance; his face was grim. No, this definitely wasn't over. Not yet.

Dacey smeared the sweat off his forehead with his sleeve and straightened, leading the way to the downhill edge of the barn. They crept around it, not heeding too much to the noise they made; there was enough of that in the yard to cover their steps.

When they could see the yard, Blaine crouched down low. Dacey came up behind her, his hand on her shoulder; both stayed against the rough old wood of the barn slats. Dacey breathed a curse in her ear as the situation became apparent.

The women were out of the hall, all right. They mingled freely with about half the men from the fighting, and they held hastily snatched implements of war—the pitchforks, shovels and mattocks from the barn. The men had knives and bows, but precious few arrows. The children were hiding, clinging, no longer crying, crowding against one parent or the other.

They all faced off against three men. Nekfehr and two others.

"*Annektehr*," Dacey murmured to Blaine. "All three. The last of 'em, I believe."

Annektehr, and they had a little girl.

Her name was Rossie; Blaine had watched over her a time or two. She was Willum's age, a feisty little girl who was not good at taking orders—orders like *stay in the hall*. Though one of the men had a good grip on her, she was obviously not Taken, not with the genuine terror on her face, the high red blotches from tears. She wasn't moving—not even a squirm, not with the big knife up against her chest like it was.

Dacey walked past Blaine and right out into the yard, to the side of the standoff. "If you kill her, you're going to die."

Nekfehr tipped his head, a salute of sorts. "We have no intention of dying. If we can't come to terms, we'll simply Take this child." He gestured at Rossie, in the grip of his man, and bestowed upon her a look of false affection. "It's amazing how many of you she'll be able to touch before anyone can bring themselves to kill her."

Dacey shook his head. "I can kill her before she reaches any one of them."

Someone gasped; a mother's cry of dismay. Dacey had left the bow behind; Blaine had his knife. But as he moved between the little girl and the crowd, it was clear enough to Blaine that he would simply intercept her before she could reach any of them.

"Then they'll likely kill *you*," the leader said.

"Not until after you've done died a dozen times over," Dacey said. "Seems a fair enough trade, to me."

"Dacey, no," Blaine breathed. But no one heard her; no one even knew she huddled beside the barn. They were frozen—afraid, now, to do anything that might tip this confrontation the wrong way.

As though it were no big thing, Dacey looked Rossie in the eye, got her attention. Then he stepped toward her, reaching his hand out in invitation.

"I think not," Nekfehr said. "You've done enough."

His attack was snake quick. He lunged forward, apparently unarmed, but Blaine saw the tuft of *something* in his hand, all but hidden from view. She ran from the safety of the barn, crying a warning—but by then Dacey was already in motion. He leapt aside and into the attack, bringing the side of his hand down hard against the man's inner elbow. And though it made no sense to Blaine, Dacey didn't hesitate, folding the arm around his hand, and shoving Nekfehr's own hand back at him. It slammed into the man's own chest.

And to Blaine's astonishment, Nekfehr crumpled. To *everyone's* astonishment, including the men who had backed him, somehow Dacey's touch held death—or impending death, for the man still quivered at his feet. For an instant, they were frozen with surprise, and in that instant, a warrior cry filled the air. High-pitched, a woman's challenge. Lottie Kendricks charged out of the crowd, her pitchfork held high. She buried it in the chest of the man who held Rossie, then yanked the child away.

Dead silence, while the remaining *nekteh* backed away from them and the entire assembly stared at Lottie, wondering if she'd been quick enough. She lifted her chin and said, her voice fierce, "They took my Willum. They wasn't having this 'un, too."

In an unspoken threat, Dacey moved between Lottie and the final *annektehr*, his stare hard, his warning unmistakable. The man hesitated. Then his eyes rolled back in his head and he collapsed in an untidy, quivering heap.

Beside him, Nekfehr gave a little jerk; Blaine eased up to Dacey's side, looking down at the Annekteh leader with trepidation. To her surprise, Dacey's face held nothing but compassion. "It's over, Nekfehr," he said, crouching by the man, his voice reassuring; he picked something off the man's chest and dropped it in the dust, grinding it to pieces with his toe.

"Not Nekfehr," the man gasped. "Shauntan. My name—" he stiffened, his jaws clenching, and somehow spoke anyway, "—is Shauntan. And—I thank you." He jerked again, and Blaine looked away.

When she looked back, he was dead.

Pandemonium. Rossie ran to her mother, was swept up and kissed frantically all over her tear-stained face. Boys and men who'd been watching out of sight on

the hill came rushing down to their families, turn
ing the yard into a tumult of whooped greeting
embraces and tears. Blaine found her own famil
everyone but Rand, and they somehow managed
hug each other all at once. Sarie, who needed som
moments to realize that this person truly was he
older sister, took to squealing Blaine's name over an
over again, until Blaine hitched the girl up on he
hip and held her there, enduring the stranglehol
around her neck.

Thus encumbered, she turned back to Dacey, wh
had been standing alone over the three once-Take
but who was now becoming the focus of the yar
Slowly, silence fell again, as they regarded the uncoor
inated shuddering of that which had once bee
human—the remaining *nekfehr*, the vessel—and whic
now seemed like an empty shell.

"They get like this when they've been Took lon
enough," Dacey said. "Be a mercy to kill him." An
he turned and walked away, through the path tha
opened for him.

Blaine slid Sarie off her hip and followed him
the barn, where he turned back to watch the gath
ering and the indistinct, solemn action that took plac
in the center of it. *Mercy*.

"Dacey," she said, "what happened? How'd Ne
fehr die? Looked like it was purely from your touch

Dacey glanced at her, startled. " 'Course it wasn'
He had a dart. Same kind o' dart that kilt my uncl
Didn't expect me to know of it, I'd say."

"Oh," she said, still a little numb from it all. Th
men who were crouching over the leader's bod
obviously hadn't found the dart yet, not from the loo
they were giving Dacey; she remembered that he ha
crushed something. The crowd broke up, leaving th
bodies in its wake as people started to put things
rights. There were tables to be straightened, wounc
to be tended, stomachs to be fed. Blaine frowned

little. "They act like they've done forgot there's a whole 'nother crew of them Annekteh headed this way."

"I don't reckon," Dacey said. "They can't win a fight here when we're ready for 'em, which we are. And they know there's seer's blood here now. They'll turn back."

"But what about the people they already have?" Blaine asked. "They're still there, aren't they? Up north?"

"That's another fight, Blaine," Dacey said gently. He was hardly imposing, leaning up against the barn as though it was the only thing that held him up, his face still pale and marred from Annekteh—and Estus'—ill-treatment . . . but there was something about him that drew her gaze to him. Blaine tipped her head up to meet his eyes. They were still hazel, still clear and kind, but she understood once more that he had gained more than the simple sight he'd once had.

He would be leaving soon, she suddenly realized. It simply wasn't like him to drag out his part in this victory. Despite her respect for his natural reserve, she just couldn't *not* do it. She stepped forward and wrapped her arms—skinny as they were—around the breadth of his shoulders. She could feel the weariness there, but when she drew away his face also held the same playfulness she'd seen when they sang with the dogs.

She didn't guess she'd ever really understand him.

"Go to your folks," he said. "Me'n Mage'll walk the hills a bit, I reckon."

→ 21 ←

Blaine arranged tender spring flowers on the tiny mounded grave that held Willum. The fine carpets of short, early flowers were almost gone—spring warmed fast in these parts—but he had enjoyed picking them, so she'd made a special effort to find a few stragglers.

She sat back on her heels and stared at the grave, the newest in the small family cemetery up behind the barn. Lenie had come up with her, but hung back by Granpapaw's headstone.

Blaine had found her sister changed, a quieter person, someone whose comments were sincere even if not always what Blaine wanted to hear. Under the Annekteh, she had been driven hard, saddled with Cadell's chores as well as her own and Blaine's. Now that she was free of them, Lenie returned to watching after her appearance, but she presented a more somber image while she was at it. Blaine understood that in the mixing of the people of the hollows, Lenie had found someone to interest her, and the attention was being returned.

Respect for the dead demanded decent time before a wedding, but Blaine expected it would soon be her own turn to find someone.

Strange. She had helped to free her kin and neighbors. Now she felt like she had traded their freedom for hers. She was already back to the old life she had always fought against. Daddy hadn't thought to forbid her the hills—yet—but it had been only a bare week since her return. Several times she'd been out in the hills with Dacey, as he walked the ridges and searched for signs of Annekteh interlopers with his seer's eyes.

But he was due to leave after the dance party tonight, and surely then it would occur to her father that Blaine should not be allowed in the hills. Not if she was to devote herself to finding a good husband.

Well, Cadell couldn't be expected to look after her forever. Blaine understood that. She also knew that the taste of freedom she'd had would make it harder than ever to settle down.

Thoughts of leaving had filled her mind for days. If she was going to do it, she should do it now, so it would be merely one more shock on top of all the others.

South. Maybe she could go south, to the place where Dacey's glass window had come from. She had seen enough of Dacey to appreciate his loner's lifestyle, and to respect it, but surely he wouldn't mind if she tagged along on his way home, on her way to other places. Surely he'd come to enjoy her company, too.

"Poor Mommy," Lenie said, drawing Blaine from her thoughts with surprise. Since when had Lenie noticed any of what their mother went through? While Blaine's way might have been to run to the woods, Lenie had simply ignored what she saw and set her sights on something of her own.

"Poor Mommy?" Blaine repeated.

Lenie gave her an accusing look. "First to lose y[...]
then Willum—oh, that was horrible, Blaine. They t[...]
Charlane Prater, and she held Willum whilst one [...]
the soldiers—"

"I don't want to hear it!" Blaine turned away fr[...]
the grave to shout Lenie into silence.

"*We* had to *live* it!" Lenie shouted back, th[...]
looked away. When she looked back, the anger w[...]
gone from her face. "Poor Charlane was worse [...]
than Mommy, though we all told her we knew s[...]
had no say in what happened." Lenie's shrug w[...]
matter-of-fact. "You missed a lot, Blaine."

I went through my own trials. "Don't think y[...]
can figure what all I've done, either."

As though Lenie had heard her sister's though[...]
she shrugged again. "I guess you'll be part of legen[...]
now, just like the stories of Anneka Ridge. I do[...]
mean to say you run out on us, nothin' like that. [...]
just you weren't here to see what happened [...]
Willum, nor to see Mommy and Daddy when th[...]
thought you was gone as well. They told us you[...]
been kilt, you know. Havin' you back has done [...]
much for Mommy as bein' freed of *them*."

Blaine stared at her sister, wondering suspiciou[...]
where this was leading. It certainly wasn't anythi[...]
like the self-centered talk she was used to heari[...]
from Lenie, but she still felt resentment creeping [...]
Lenie didn't seem to understand that Blaine had be[...]
just as scared, just as driven, as anyone here [...]
Shadow Hollers. She didn't have any idea what it w[...]
like to hide, trapped and terrified, in a dairy. S[...]
didn't know what it was like to stare over the hi[...]
and yet see nothing, all her very self caught up [...]
anguished worry about her family.

Then she heard a quiet echo of Dacey's voice, o[...]
telling her in his simple way not to worry what anyo[...]
else thought. His assurance that she was special.

instead of firing off the riled-up words on her tongue, she let the older girl talk.

"You still don't see," Lenie said, having realized she was to get no response from Blaine. "I know you better'n you think—no, don't look at me that way. You've changed some, but so have I—and deep down we still got parts that are the same. And I know you're gonna go. You ain't about to settle yourself down here and start looking for someone to work you and order you around. You think I am? But it don't bother me, Blaine, 'cause instead of fightin' it with claws out, I got other ways to get a man to look at things my way. If you'd realize that, you'd quit facin' everything with all that fire in your eye. Things are what they are, and havin' a man to look after you ain't the worst thing that could happen to you."

"Mommy used to have fire in her eye, too," Blaine said bitterly.

"Well, she don't no more, an' that's why I got my own ways of dealing with a man. It's not too late for me, or even for you. But you get all snorty about it and run off to find where things suit you, you're gonna take every last bit of fight out of Mommy. I hope you think about that real hard before you go."

Blaine thought about it. She turned her reflections inward, to images of her mother. First, the tired, resigned soul who simply wanted to keep her family healthy and fed, then a younger version, earlier memories, when that face had smiled more often, had fewer lines in it and less grey in the brown hair that was so much like Blaine's.

But the strongest image of all was that shocking first encounter in the meeting hall, when neither mother nor daughter had quite recognized one another. Blaine now saw that change as a hopelessness worlds different from Lottie's normal worn-out visage.

In the week since the Freed Day, some of th
hopelessness had disappeared, and enough of Lotti
spark—tenuous as it was—had returned to direct t
strict cleaning of their neglected house, to take pri
in what she'd done at the meeting hall—even to ta
pride in Blaine.

Should Blaine leave, what then?

Blaine looked up at her sister, who was satisfi
with what she had wrought.

"I got peas to hoe," Lenie said simply, and l
Blaine alone with the graves. Alone to think abo
what she would or wouldn't do.

Blaine twisted around to stare at Lenie's retrea
ing back—hips a-sway—as she walked down the hi
and settled back to her heels with a sigh. Never ha
she thought there was so much intent behind Leni
ways.

Her sister was right, of course. Or at least, she ha
chosen a way that was right for herself. Blai
doubted she could mend her own looks enough
turn a man's head, and she was sure she wouldn't l
able to sweeten her attitude to the flirt and begui
that Lenie so ably employed. No. Quiet rebellio
sometimes not-so-quiet rebellion. Those were h
tools.

A cold wet smear on the back of her neck startl
her—she jerked around, her bottom sliding off h
heels onto the damp ground.

Blue. How could she have been so deep in thoug
that she hadn't heard the lumbering hound? Sh
patted the ground beside her and Blue pushed
to sit tightly against her. He had missed her, he l
her understand. Well, she had missed him too. It w
comforting to know there was anything out there th
cared as much as Blue.

"Your sister's got some turnin's in her head
wouldn't have guessed," Dacey said. He was up t
hill a-ways, and coming down on quiet feet.

And how long had he been there? Blaine gave him a hard stare, and it was enough.

"I was going down to your house," Dacey said. "Blue brought me here instead. I didn't want to interrupt."

"So you listened?"

Dacey said nothing, only watched her with the intense eyes that would now always be just a little bit different. But then, Blaine had always thought there was a difference, even before the Annekteh unwittingly wakened his seer's sight. Eventually she dropped her own gaze, regretful of her words. She knew his decisions always had reasons. This time it meant giving Lenie her say.

"I guess she hid it well from me, too," Blaine said. "I never figured she saw what I saw in Mommy." She looked back up at him, scowling. "But her way'll never be mine."

"No," Dacey agreed, "you just got too much o' that fire. Don't believe there's any puttin' it out." She scowled harder, but he just grinned at her.

"Well," she finally muttered, and pushed off on Blue to climb to her feet, "I guess I won't never be able to change that. Not till I'm all wore out and got a big family."

"Family's important, Blaine."

Blaine looked down at the soft, scuffed toes of her boots and wouldn't admit that he was right.

Dacey sat down on the ground outside the grave area and looked at Blue. "He'll miss you. I guess he thinks *you're* family, now."

"I never did understand why he picked me, anyway. You know better'n most that I ain't much for a petted-on hound. Especially," she added with fierceness that did not reach her eyes as she looked down at the dog, "one that drools and blows its cheeks out all the time."

"I know. Dumb ole Blue. He tried to save you from

the Annekteh, you know. Too dumb to know he couldn't."

She narrowed her eyes down at him, but he gave her only the shrug of his shoulders under his worn shirt. Those shoulders held a strength beyond the muscles in them, and it showed in the ease of their carriage, in the quiet authority she had always admired in him. She said, "He was trying to help Mage—Rand was about to knock his head off."

"No," Dacey said. "Blue may be dumb, but he can read another dog. The threat was to you, and it was you he was protectin'."

Blaine looked back down at Blue, astonishment making way for affection. "I didn't know he'd do that."

"You protect what you love," Dacey said.

Blaine gave her foot a slight stomp. "Damn!" she muttered.

He raised an eyebrow.

"All right, I can't go! I can't leave her now. Or any of 'em. Not when they need me." Her voice lowered until it was just loud enough to be heard. "But I *want* to go."

"I know."

A quick look told her that he did know, that he really understood. She burst out, "I feel—I feel like a bird, one that's just learned to fly and then broke a wing."

"You'll fly when it's right," he said, and then looked away a moment. He was close to her all of a sudden; she wasn't sure how that had happened. He reached out and touched her hair, running a light hand down to her long braid, picking it up and placing it down again like he'd found a better spot for it. "When it's right," he said again, and she wondered who he was trying to convince; as clear as his gaze met hers, she wasn't sure it was her. He looked away. "I got to go. I've done what I came for, and I don't belong here."

"What if they come back?"

"You know where I am. By then, I'm thinkin', you might have some of your own seers here." He held out his other hand, opened it to reveal dozens of tiny flowers. Spring flowers, the like of which Blaine had searched so hard for—not any she'd seen before. The dark green-stemmed plants bore clusters of yellow blooms, thick as the seed in a milkweed and just as soft. She took them from him and smelled of them, inhaling a fresh odor—the hills after a cleansing rain, or the air on a crisp snowy day.

"I ain't never seen these before."

"Or me. But you'll find 'em aplenty amongst the rhododendrons on the hill beyond the hall."

"The fight ground?"

"The very same. There's magic in these hills, and there always has been. It's just been slumbering of late."

"But . . . flowers?"

"The Annekteh worked their magic on me, and look what happened. And they slung it out all over that hill. To my way of thinking, these here flowers popped up to spit right back in the eye of Annekteh magic. Keep watch, Blaine, and you might could find more signs of change here. Might even be some more magic of your own."

"I don't have no seers in my family line," Blaine said, more than a touch of obstinance showing through. She knew better. Knew things were changing.

"Not yet. Not full-blooded ones. But you've learned this much—there ain't no way to deny the kind of seein's you got."

Blaine snorted. "Magic weren't meant for the likes of me."

"Nor for me," Dacey rejoined quietly, looking at her with a touch of amusement, tucked in somewhere between his angular cheekbones and his eyes.

"But you're different," Blaine protested instantly.
"You—you're . . . *different!*"

"You'd be surprised." He nodded at the grave. "I
brought the flowers for Willum. Seems only fittin' that
the first signs of the magic go to him, first killed in
the battle that woke it. And I wanted to say good-
bye. I'll be leavin' tonight, and I won't be obvious
about it. Just make a scene if I was, and I wouldn't
care for that."

"I know," Blaine said, carefully setting the flow-
ers by Willum's headstone. When she straightened,
Blue was gone, following Dacey up the hill behind
Mage. Blaine watched long enough to see Chase and
Whimsy shoot in from the side, knock Dacey about
with their tails, and bound off again.

"Good-bye," she whispered.

The hall was set up for a celebration, with the
refreshing yellow flowers in abundant display. They
hung in bunches from the corners of the rafters, they
came in sprigs tucked behind girls' ears and in the
men's buttonholes. The room seemed lighter for them,
certainly lighter than the candle and coal-oil lamplight
Blaine remembered—even as bright as the south-
made fancy lamp that Dacey owned.

She leaned against the wall between two of the
massive tables lining the dance area, her breath
coming quick. Although it was well into the evening,
the musicians still played the quick dances. Soon
they'd switch to the slower, more precise figures, the
ones meant for older dancers and courting youth.
Blaine knew those well enough, but had no intention of being dragged into them, not yet.

Soon enough, her parents would host her quilt
party, and all of the women and older girls would
supply a storm of man-talk while they quilted, in one
afternoon, the quilt that Blaine's mother had been
piecing for her since Lenie's first engagement.

Until then, she was undeclared and determined to make the best of the time.

Which meant, as the music strings started up again, rushing back out onto the floor for another whirling dance. She and the other girls were passed from boy to boy, many of whom gave her a wink or smile of recognition—companionable recognition, the kind she was comfortable with. They still thought of her as the girl in the tree who'd pointed out the Taken.

She danced with nearly all of them this evening, even Estus, whose damp and dirty looks had undergone a thorough washing for the celebration. She missed Burl, who would have been a fun if less than graceful partner, and there were plenty of others absent, if not remarked upon. Not tonight. In a day or two, they'd meet for a Remembrance of all the lost ones, Willum included; for now, they celebrated their freedom. Blaine was glad to see her parents, at the other end of the room, joining in on the fast steps of the dance. She had passed Lenie and her new beau some time before. She had even seen her cousins—whose remarks, for once, had been nothing but amiable. She could not help a glow of satisfaction at that.

The music tumbled to a stop and Blaine found herself opposite Trey, who panted as hard as she. She flapped her skirts—regular, whole skirts—up and down to fan her sweaty legs and Trey laughed.

"Let's go outside," he said. "It's cooler." The next dance started, slow and traditional. Blaine followed him out into the hall yard.

"Looks like you're even quicker'n me to shy away from the courtin' dances," she teased as he led her to the well. Trey shrugged, pulling up the rope and dragging out the bucket. He unhooked the dipper from the well frame, scooping up cool water and offering it to Blaine.

An out-and-out courtesy. At first taken aback,

Blaine accepted water and drank her fill. She returned the dipper to Trey with a quizzical look, and watched while he got his own drink.

"Where's Dacey?" he said, wiping his dripping chin.

"Gone," Blaine said sadly. "He told me he'd dodge good-byes. One thing about him, he means what he says."

"Snuck out in the middle of a dance, I'll bet."

"You'd win it," she sighed. She had watched him go, deliberately looking away when he glanced at her.

"I'll miss him, too," Trey said.

She nodded, and they lapsed into silence that didn't trouble Blaine, but that Trey seemed to find increasingly awkward. So she watched him, as the light from the hall played off his face—an unsettled, still growing into itself face—and occasionally sparked off his eyes. She knew it wasn't kind, but she watched him until he broke into an actual fidget. "Uh, Blaine . . . "

"What?"

He hesitated again. "Spirits," he said, sounding almost desperate, "we always been straight enough with one another. I know Lenie's committed to my cousin Nathan, and we both know what that means to you."

Blaine made a noise her parents would have called her on.

"Yeah, I know. I saw enough in the mountain to know you're some wilder than the girls hereabouts—wilder than most the men'll stand for, anyway. You done tickled Dacey that way."

"I did?" Blaine said, then regretted it as Trey's discomposure seemed to deepen. "Sorry," she murmured, looking down at the well just for something other than him to rest her eyes on.

"I . . . I just wanted to say . . . well, *I'd* stand for it. I seen the good it brought to these hills, and I'll never forget it. I just wanted you to know."

"Why, *Trey*," Blaine said, startled into looking straight

at him again—and then could come up with nothing else. *When had he . . . she'd had no idea . . .* Although, thinking back, she could see that at some time he had quit fighting her and begun to work with her. Quit bossing her and begun to listen.

She looked away from him again and up into the dark shape of the mountain that loomed behind the barn. The new waxing moon had not yet made an appearance, but the night was clear. The stars made enough light to show her the darkened undulations of the hills, the scoops and swags that led her eye to the site of the battle. For a moment she was back in that fight, reliving the fears, the uncertainties, and even the joys.

At last she turned her eyes back to Trey, who still waited for a response—*any* response, just to stop the agony of the waiting. With a start of guilt, she smiled at him, a shy expression. "I ain't reflected much about it, yet," she told him. "But I like your words."

He let out his breath in a relieved sigh—she supposed he had worried she might laugh, or scorn him—but it was a good offer. Most likely the best she would get. Someone who already knew the quirks of her ways and who didn't resent them. She would run circles around herself to keep a family tended right, but she would still have the woods and her wandering ways.

If she ever found the time for them.

"Yes," she said, and nodded. "I'll think on that." She knew she should be pleased. He understood her. Respected her, even her strangeness. But . . . her contrary stomach had turned heavy and hard.

"You want to go back in?" He nodded toward the doorway, where a lull in the music and the considerable laughter in its place indicated that someone spun a tale.

"No," Blaine said. "I guess I'll just listen to it all for a while. I enjoy a good dancing, but somehow . . .

tonight I feel on the outside looking in. I never was slaved, like they were."

"But you—"

"I know. I done my part. But I warn't *here*."

He didn't understand, she could see, but he wasn't fighting it. He leaned against the well alongside her and listened to the snatch of voices drifting out of the hall.

She'd done her part, all right. Not that either parent quite believed her stories—especially not her father, who, though as proud as he'd ever been, had told her not to have fancy thoughts of herself, that she'd likely mostly been in Dacey's way.

Rand's instant defense had gratified her. There was the bearskin, he'd argued, and even Cadell couldn't deny that Blaine had been in the ash, directing the fighters below. Anyone else would've sent arrows that hit their mark—Rand had said that with a smile— and at last Cadell had to concede that the stories he was hearing could be true.

But he still didn't seem to want Blaine to put much stock in herself over it. Like he couldn't stand for her to think about it, so he wouldn't have to think about it himself.

Some of those stories referred to Dacey's killing touch, but not one of them identified Rand as the last to be Taken. Rand had not mentioned it, and Blaine, with a chance to pay him back for kept secrets, did not see fit to bring it up.

But now she was home. All she had left of those weeks were the stories, and no one would ever quite know or believe all of it. Blaine sighed into the darkness. It was a clear night, damp and warm—good for a hunt. Her ears perked for the sounds of familiar hound song, disregarding the fact that those voices were behind her and lost forever.

Even now her ears imagined the start of a chorus, using memory in place of reality. *Stupid.*

"What's that?" Trey asked suddenly.

Too clear to be a memory, that was certain sure!

Blaine straightened and took a step away from the well, toward the hill behind the barn where the song had started. It was Dacey she heard, briefly, before Mage joined in and the two younger dogs warmed up. A farewell song.

An unwanted tear shimmered her vision. It was her very own good-bye. No one else could separate those voices, nor know just who started the singing. She listened, entranced, while Trey stood behind her and respectfully kept his silence.

A much closer moan hit her ears, starting as a rough, low growl and rising to a clear, wavering note. Its euphony with the chorus on the hill first stirred her, then startled her. She took her gaze away from the mountain and looked at the barn, certain the longing howl came not from the hills, but from that dark building.

Forgetting Trey, she ran to it.

Tied just inside the barn was a mournful, confused ticked creature. Its ears hung low, and it subsided into a confused whine as Blaine entered. It strained at a braided rawhide leash, its front feet pattering up and down in excitement, its tail tip wagging uncertainly as it sought to understand why the pack sang from the top of the hill, so far from this place and growing farther.

"Blue," Blaine breathed. "Blue, how could he leave you?" She slid to her knees and hugged his forlorn face, slapped his solid chest in appreciation. She pretended not to see when he slyly reached for her braid.

Sudden realization ended her caresses; she stared at the mountain—blocked by the back of the barn as it was—the tears coming down her face fast and happy. *He* couldn't *leave Blue! He* wouldn't!

Trey, too, understood the hound's message, and he took a step back, giving her room for her dreams.

"He's coming back," Blaine whispered into Blue's jowly face.

He gave her a lick upside the cheek and wiped away her tears.

Author's Note

About dialects . . . .

Authors often struggle with the best way to handle dialect. In this case I found I really couldn't write the book without reflecting the unique speech patterns of the particular Appalachian region around which I framed this book. Once that sort of decision is made, it's a matter of how much to play with the spelling, how much to try to convey with the rhythm of the words . . . how much to just plain make up because it's *fiction*, after all.

I tried to compromise. I hope the end result is something that adds to your experience of the book.

➤←   ➤←   ➤←

Doranna Durgin spent her childhood filling notebooks first with stories and art, and then with novels. After obtaining a degree in wildlife illustration and environmental education, she spent a number of years deep in the Appalachian Mountains, with which she fell in love. When she emerged, it was as a writer who found herself irrevocably tied to the natural world and its creatures.

Doranna, who won the Compton Crook Award with first novel *Dun Lady's Jess*, lives in upstate New York with two irrepressible Cardigan Welsh Corgis (Kacey & Jean-Luc Picardigan). You can contact her at:

dmd@doranna.net

or

PO Box 26207
Rochester, NY 14626
(SASE please)
or visit http://www.doranna.net/
Join the Book-Facing Legion at:
http://www.doranna.net/legion.html